IMMORTAL DIVORCE COURT

VOLUME 1

My Ex-Wife Said Go to Hell

KIRK ZUROSKY

Daddy Issues
PUBLISHING

Published by Daddy Issues Publishing
www.immortaldivorcecourt.com

Edited and Designed by Girl Friday Productions
www.girlfridayproductions.com
Editorial: Alexander Rigby, Clete Smith,
Elisabeth Rinaldi, Laura Whittemore
Cover illustration: Carly Milligan
Design: Paul Barrett

ISBN (Hardcover): 978-1-7346252-0-2
ISBN (Paperback): 978-1-7346252-1-9
e-ISBN: 978-1-7346252-2-6

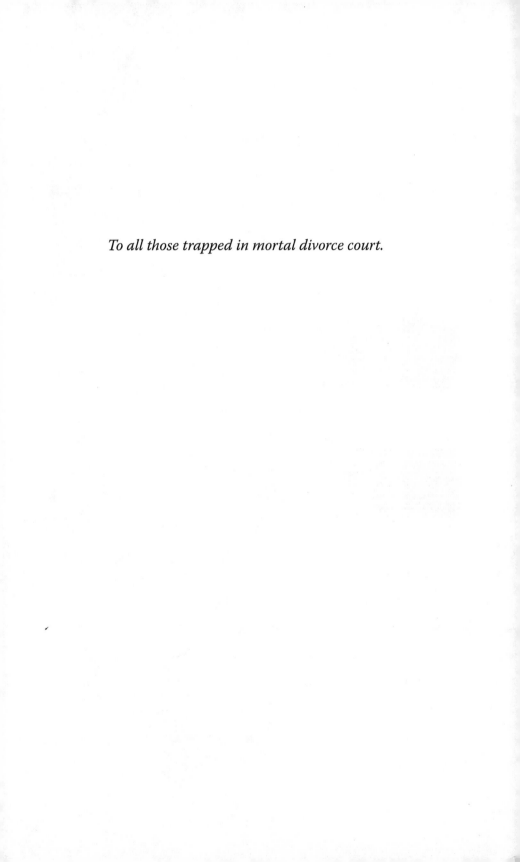

To all those trapped in mortal divorce court.

CHAPTER 1

Everyone thinks their ex-wife is a bloodsucker, but one of mine really is a vampire. Actually, it's not that weird because I am a vampire too. My name is Sirius Sinister, and this is my love story. Though it is probably more accurate to call it my divorce story because of my all too frequent appearances in Immortal Divorce Court.

Immortal creatures are reality not mythology. Vampires are but one of the many immortal races that inhabit the earth. We were here before mortals figured out that whole opposable thumb thing. Mortals walk among us, not the other way around. Immortals bleed and can die, and do not age once they hit twenty-five or thirty. Thus, we don't get older, theoretically just wiser, and if you didn't know any better (and most of you don't), you would think we are ordinary humans. But we aren't. We have remarkable regenerative abilities, and can take an astounding amount of physical punishment and survive—except the brutal financial beatings ordered by the head magistrates of Immortal Divorce Court . . . Well, that brings even the toughest immortal man to his knees. The only reason said immortal man is actually on his knees is that he is looking for dropped gold so he can buy something to eat.

I was born to vampire parents on Sa Dragonera, a small island off the coast of Spain near Majorca, in the year 1425. My parents made their living as most vampires did in those days, as hired mercenaries and assassins. Most vampires have toned but not overly muscular frames, incredible hearing, vision, and dexterity along with acrobatic skills, and the ability to move quite soundlessly. We are also about five times as strong as mortals, which, combined with all the above, made us quite popular as hired killers. You see, the only mortals that know about immortals are the royals, the power brokers, the oligarchs—the very top of the mortal echelon. Forget about the one-percenters, we deal with those that have *all* the cents.

My father, Ernesto, and my mother, Maria, named me Sirio Sinestra, which I changed to the more deadly sounding Sirius Sinister. So, into this world of assassins and contract murders I was born, learning from my parents the tricks of our family trade. By 1450, I had reached my physical maturity and was as deadly as I was handsome. The sweat would glisten on my tanned skin as I flung back my shoulder-length black hair and worked my muscles during my training. Thanks to my parents, I could kill you by sword, poison, arrow, staff, dagger, mace, and my favorite method—by hand.

One day, Father and I went down into a cavern, where he revealed to me his collection of Lazarus stones holding blood from all his special kills. The stoppered stones looked like they were made from marble, but as Father held one out to me, I could see that cloudy white-and-black patterns moved all over it like a series of small storms.

"Why do you put the blood of the kills in the Lazarus stones?" I asked.

"I was asked to," my father said.

"Fair enough," I replied. "Do all assassins do the Lazarus-stone thing?"

"No, only if you are a Specter of Death like me," he said.

"A what?"

He laughed. "Most of the time, my kills are paid for with gold from the world's most wealthy and powerful mortals. Those kills do not get put in the Lazarus stones. When you are acting as a Specter of Death, you are getting your orders straight from the Grim Reaper himself, and those are the only kills that get put in the stones."

"The Grim Reaper is a real person!" I exclaimed. "I get it now, because that is one person, uh, thing, that I would not want to say no to!"

"You are correct there—and of course I do not," he replied. "And, thing, person, or something else, there is no doubt the Grim Reaper is as real as you and me. I have seen the Grim with my own eyes—well, probably too many times, to tell you the truth."

"Once would be enough for me," I said. "Well, I am off to more training with Mother. Have fun playing with your Lazarus stones."

By 1460, I had learned all my parents could teach me, and it was time to leave Sa Dragonera and see the world. Leaving Sa Dragonera was the only way I could take the final steps in my training and hopefully reach my full potential. Of course, the world has a way of teaching you the humility and maturity that your parents could not, and I was about to be taken to school.

First, however, let me dispel some myths about vampires. We do not have pale skin from avoiding the sun. Sunlight is a detriment to us only in that we prefer to kill our marks at night to take advantage of the cover of darkness. Holy water and crucifixes are mortal constructs, though some of us get baptized for appearances or to get closer to a kill. We have been gifted with the wonderful ability to eat our meat raw without any consequences. As you can imagine, the ability to kill and eat your meals without calling attention to yourself by starting a fire is pretty valuable to an assassin tracking his, or her, mark.

We can drink blood for sustenance, which has inspired a whole misguided mythos about vampires among the mortals. Our incisors are oversized and good for eating raw meat or killing an intended target in close-quarter fighting. Yes, I have been trained to go for the jugular. Immortals can and do have sex with mortals, though most immortals stay within the immortal realm to find a more permanent life mate. But if I were to bite you during a wild sexual encounter or during an assassination, I would not turn you into one of us. You would actually have to ingest copious quantities of our blood in comparison to your body mass to be turned into a vampire. Which leads me to

Garlic, and no, I didn't capitalize it because I am in fear of it—that is simply her name. (Though it's true that vampires are not fond of garlic because it plays havoc with our keen sense of smell and ability to bed nubile wenches.)

But I am not referring to the onion's stinky cousin. I am referring to Garlic, the even more stinky vampire Maltese that came into my life in the year 1596. I was at The Theatre in Shoreditch, London, watching Shakespeare's *A Midsummer Night's Dream*. I was a brash young vampire and had prime seats, and had drunk some whiskey with my mates, along with way, way too much wine. As bad luck would have it, the fairy Cobweb, servant to Titania, was played by a real faerie. He forgot his line in act 3, scene 1. All he had to say was his name—Cobweb. He froze for a moment, got red in the face, and said, "Fobschleb." And of all the people in the audience, this young drunk vampire laughed the loudest.

"What an utter buffoon," I announced to a silent auditorium when all the laughter had died down, starting a fresh torrent of laughter. This encouraged me to comment even more audibly on the fairy Cobweb's deficiencies as an actor. Bad idea. After the show that faerie caught up with me in a dark alley to show me his displeasure.

You might think faeries are all magic dust, wings, and glittery goodness. But let me tell you something—you never ever want to piss off a faerie. Sure, they might look human, but the strongest of them can turn their bodies into stone, and their fingernails into diamonds, among other adaptive physical abilities. If you catch a faerie by surprise, however, they are only able to turn their bodies into something a whole lot softer. I hear the faeries that are terrible at turning their bodies into a harder substance can only manage stiff parchment paper on their best day. But this guy, well, he was like fighting a cannonball covered with daggers. Yeah. He beat my drunken ass to within an inch of my immortal life and dumped my nearly lifeless body in a nearby barn.

As fate would have it, the runt of a Maltese lion dog litter had been either purposely abandoned or accidentally left in the barn. A Maltese is a small, fluffy dog favored by aristocrats because the dogs are small enough to fit in the sleeves of their ornate dresses, gowns, and robes. They were quite valuable, and this runt probably got overlooked. So it instinctively turned to the only food source it could find—the blood seeping from the many gashes on my body. For two and a half weeks, I slowly healed, and the runt kept feeding from the blood coming from my wounds. Finally, I awoke to the sensation of a dog sitting on my chest and licking my blistered lips.

"Get off, you," I gasped, and forced open my blood-encrusted eyelids. A blast of garlic assaulted my nostrils, and I looked up to see that the owners of the barn had hung several cloves to prevent their cows from being menaced by vampires. "You smell even worse than the garlic," I said to the tiny white dog with soulful black eyes just sitting on my chest like she owned me. "Actually nothing smells worse than garlic. So that is now your name—Garlic." Garlic yelped, clearing out the rest of the fog in my brain, and hopped off my chest.

I struggled to my feet and noticed lots and lots of dead rats. I looked at the runt Maltese—way too small and all too dirty to try and sell for a drink—and did not think anything of it at the time, assuming the rats had been poisoned. I was simply too exhausted to notice their necks had all been snapped. I set off stumbling through London, still in a daze, and realized Garlic was nipping at my heels. I cut down a side alley and broke into a jog, trying to lose her. Suddenly, two flea-bitten and rather hungry mongrels came out of a scrap heap and went right for Garlic's throat. Or shall I say, they *attempted* to go for Garlic's throat. With a savage growl belying her six-pound size, Garlic ripped one mongrel's throat out and chewed the tail off the other before it ran for its life. She stood back from her kill, giving appropriate deference to me, the alpha dog.

"No, Garlic, that is quite all right," I said. "You can go ahead and feed on that mutt. I don't care much for dog tartar." Garlic began furiously feeding on her conquest, finishing her meal by lapping up the blood of her vanquished victim, which turned her white fur a lovely shade of crimson.

"Oh, that was a jolly good show, Garlic, way better than that god-awful play." I briefly considered adding "death by Maltese" to my assassin repertoire, but no real man, immortal or not, would be caught dead or undead with a fluffy, little white dog prancing along in his possession, even if that dog was a killer vampire Maltese.

"Aye, Garlic, too bad you were not some kind of massive wolfhound or a breed more suitable to my manliness," I said. "Come along now, we'll find someplace safe to leave you where you won't rid all of London proper of its collection of mortal mutts."

As it turned out, I could never ever rid myself of the stink of Garlic. I left her on a farm owned by Harvis, a werewolf friend of mine, figuring the whole canine thing would work out. But I was awoken the next day in my London inn by Garlic licking my face. I returned her to the farm again. Harvis, my werewolf friend, knowing all things dog, gave me the bad news.

"Sirio," he said, raising a craggy eyebrow. "The little bitch has imprinted on you."

"What in the hell are you talking about?" I took down my fine breeches, and took out my immortal splendor. "Is it contagious?"

Harvis howled, literally. "You foppish vampire, return your breeches' boa constrictor to its lair. You do not have mange of the manhood. You are her Pack leader. She will never leave you. You are stuck with that little bitch forever. And, trust me, that is a good thing!"

What wasn't a good thing was entering my room back at the inn to find an unwanted guest.

"Sirio Sinestra?"

Before I could answer, Garlic sprang into action, clamping her pint-sized but razor-sharp teeth on the arm of the faerie I knew only as Fobschleb. He had been caught off guard by my courageous canine, and had only enough time to turn his arm into wood. Unfazed by the growling vampire Maltese attached to his arm and sending a steady flow of sawdust to the floor, the faerie beckoned me forward.

"Have you come back to finish the job?" I said, whipping my travel cloak to the floor. "I have not had a lick of alcohol, so this time you better be prepared to meet your maker." Truth be known, I knew I was not ready to fight this faerie again, but at least Garlic would be there to protect me from the rats and other assorted vermin—human, immortal, and otherwise—that would soon be searching my corpse for valuables.

Fobschleb looked confused. "What do you mean 'this time'?"

"Don't play coy with me," I sneered. "If you were just as good of an actor on stage at The Theatre as you are now, I wouldn't have laughed my drunken ass off. You faeries certainly do hold a grudge, now don't you?"

A flicker of recognition crossed Fobschleb's face. "I see now," he said. "You have had a run-in with my twin brother, Pansy."

"Pansy?" I snorted. Ah, the humor of the cosmos. My ass had been kicked by a faerie named Pansy. "What's your name? Daffodil?"

The faerie shook his head. "No, that is my cousin. Do you know him too? My name is Buttercup."

"Of course it is," I muttered. "Tell me, Buttercup, why are you in my room?"

Buttercup stared down at Garlic who was still gnawing faithfully on his arm, and shook his head at the growing pile of sawdust on the floor. "Can you call off your little bitch? Then, I will tell you."

"To me, Garlic," I said. Garlic dropped to the ground and proceeded to piss on Buttercup's shoes before coming over to sit on my boots.

"Sorry 'bout that," I said, trying unsuccessfully to conceal a smirk.

Buttercup shook the pee off his shoes, reached into his pocket, and pulled out a rolled-up sheaf of papers embossed with an iridescent wax seal. "It is I who should be sorry," he said. "Sirio Sinestra, by the power vested in me by the Immortal Divorce Court, you are hereby *served*."

A rainbow I would come to know all too well shot from the wax seal and struck my money pouch, magically lightening it by ten gold coins. "My gold!" I exclaimed. "What in the hell just happened to my gold?"

"You have to pay the service fee," Buttercup stated.

"But I have no idea what I just got served with," I said, clamping my hands over my pouch to prevent any further magical drain of my resources. "Wait a minute. You said Immortal Divorce Court, didn't you? Ha! This is a complete mistake because I have never even been married!"

Buttercup merely nodded knowingly as if he'd heard all this before. "Immortal Divorce Court does not make mistakes. I suggest you take a look at the name on the petition and see if it jogs your memory."

I opened the papers and pored over them. I could read very well, yet most of the words on the pages could have very well been in another language. These papers had obviously been drafted by a lawyer. How many wherefores, heretos, thereafters, and parties to the first, second, and third parts did you really need to have in one bloody sentence?

I did, however, recognize the name of the deceitful vampire harlot known as Bloodsucker Number One.

I sat down slowly on a chair and hung my head between my legs. Garlic, quite concerned, took this as an opportunity to lick my face. I held up the papers. "I don't understand what all this lawyer bullturd means," I said. "And, what is with all of the really, really fine print? I can spy the crumbs on a field mouse's whiskers at two hundred paces, yet somehow I can't see this crap? What does she want?"

Buttercup took the papers from me and scanned them expertly. "Oh, the usual," he said. "She cannot support herself and needs alimony."

"All my money—what?"

"Alimony, alimony," Buttercup repeated. "You are right in that alimony tends to be all your money, and preferably gold for the ones that dig the gold." He continued reading. "Oh, congratulations are in order."

I looked at the grinning faerie quizzically. "Why?" My anger was headed from simmer to full boil.

"She is also suing you for child support. It seems you two have a child together."

I flew into a full vampire rage, splintering every piece of furniture in the room into so much kindling. "Child?" I sputtered. "We never were married, and we certainly never had a child together!"

Buttercup looked down at the papers once again and shrugged. "Well, these papers say you do have a child together. Little Martin."

"Martin? That was the name of the fellow she was having carnal relations with behind my back. But he was a mortal, and that was over a hundred years ago. He should be dust by now. This is an outrage! I will get my just revenge on her."

Buttercup handed the papers back to me and sidestepped another yellow stream of urinary vengeance from Garlic. "I suggest you dispense with exacting revenge, and get what you truly need—a good lawyer. And I mean a really good lawyer, since she has retained one of the best as her counsel." He opened the lodging room door. "Immortal Divorce Court is not to be trifled with, young vampire," he said. And with that, he was gone into the night.

CHAPTER 2

I sat on the bed, staring at the papers I could not decipher, wondering how this had happened, and pondering, frankly, what in the hell I should do. In the hundred odd years since I had last seen Bloodsucker Number One, my assassin business had taken off. After I left Spain, the royals of England had taken to me, and I to them. I had eliminated enough of their little problems that theater tickets, expensive wine, a veritable cornucopia of immortal and mortal wenches in my bed, and a manor house in Barcelona were all a part of my lifestyle.

I had the world at my fingertips, and I refused to let the visit from Buttercup threaten that world. If only my father, his sometime liege the Grim Reaper, or another Specter of Death would have a not-so-pleasant run-in with Bloodsucker Number One. Getting served to go to Immortal Divorce Court by Buttercup the faerie was forcing me to remember the time, more than a century before, when I had first met that manipulative, cold-hearted vampire bitch. A time from which I thought I had buried all memories.

When I left Sa Dragonera in 1460, I was not some vampire rube brand-new to the nuances of the world. Sa Dragonera is only about one and a half miles square, and our family domicile is built rather invisibly and ingeniously into the very bedrock of the island. Because of its small size, Sa Dragonera is ignored by mortals, and immortals know it is the province of the Sinestra clan. We did not stay on Sa Dragonera, isolated from the world's populace of immortals and mortals. As part of my training, I had traveled with my parents all over the world. Immortals did not then, and do not now, travel by mortal means.

We are able to traverse great distances, using bits of crystals that are part of one massive crystal. I asked my father just where this massive crystal is, and who guards it, or controls it. But he just said that would all be part of my schooling. When we traveled by crystal, he was the one in possession of it, so I had no earthly idea how it really worked. I hated the sickening lurch as my body was pulled through some sort of cosmic wormhole. At the time, I promised myself I would one day actually open my eyes when I jumped through the nothingness. It was just so much magic to me, as was much of the world.

My parents were old-fashioned, in that fighting was our life and our culture. They knew nothing of wine, only blood. They cared nothing for music, only the clang of steel on steel. Clothes to them were functional, as was procreation, and I was their only issue. To them an education was having me learn elite fighting techniques from the very best mortal and immortal combatants. And, with no offense to Garlic, they kept a rather tight leash on me. Thus, I was rather ill-equipped to deal with one of most beguiling and enticing creatures a young male traveler could encounter—the friendly, flirting farm girl.

I arrived on the outskirts of Barcelona, having had to use a transportation crystal on my own for the first time. Before I left Sa Dragonera, my father had looked rather stressed as he told me the key to using a crystal was focus. The only focus I had was when I was fighting, eating, sleeping, shitting, or masturbating. He had me focus on a place that I had been to numerous times before.

"Focus on the Angry Cock," he said, all irritated with me, which, to my knuckle-dragging self, made it even funnier. Father frowned, clearly not sharing my amusement.

The Angry Cock was an inn we had frequented numerous times, but that did not make it any less humorous. I found myself doing my best to stifle a grin and avoid a slap across the back of the head from my father. I stared deeply at the ruby-red crystal he had given me, trying to clear my mind of all things cock, and thinking of only the Angry Cock. I guess that explained why I ended up with my crotch on the back of the neck of the Angry Cock's burly chef, my arms clutching his meaty head to avoid falling off my epicurean equine. I slipped soundlessly out the back door of the Cock without being seen by anyone else, and it was clear that the chef, after blessing himself a few thousand times, would say nothing.

My parents had instructed me to head into Barcelona and seek out the services of Hedley Edrick, an English demon living in Barcelona who ran the College of Immortals, a sort of finishing school for young, impressionable immortals. Hedley would teach me how to read and write a host of world languages, and I would learn about advanced mathematics, science, engineering, economics, and world cultures and traditions, giving me the tools to succeed in the medieval world. But I had the typical mind and maturity of most young men. I thought I knew everything. Book learning just sounded way too boring for me. I did not need school because, of course, I had the world in the palm of my strong vampire hand. School would merely delay my imminent and utter greatness.

So, I originally set out in the opposite direction, but had made it only a mere one hundred paces before parental guilt grabbed me by the neck and sent me back in the direction of Barcelona. "Drat," I muttered to myself. I vowed to just go to the school and pay my respects to Hedley Edrick, look him in the eyes, and tell him man-to-man that I did not need his services.

I soon encountered the aforementioned farm girl struggling with a stubborn donkey that refused to pull his cartload of vegetables any farther down the road. I could not take my eyes off her bountiful breasts straining at the confines of her bodice. The snug farm dress she wore emphasized curves that I yearned to touch. She turned toward me and smiled, tossing her long dark hair off her lovely round face. "Kind sir," she called, with a hand on one shapely hip. "Can you help me with my ass?"

I cleared my throat. "Yes, I can," I said. I came up to the stubborn donkey, and he moved toward me, let me take his reins to lead him, and immediately started walking for home. Now that impressed the farm girl.

Her name was Carolina, and she fell in by my side, looping her arm through my free arm as we walked. The smell of her perfume was intoxicating, and I felt lightheaded and giddy, reveling in every accidental bump of skin on skin or hip on hip as we walked. Once, my hand slipped off the reins as we talked and laughed, and as I went to quickly grab them to prevent the ass from stopping, I realized that he was walking just fine of his own volition, and in actuality I was the one being led.

Carolina had just been sold by her parents to an old woman who owned the farm we were apparently heading to. Carolina's job was to take care of the farm while the old crone was in Barcelona. I just wanted to take care of Carolina, and by the look in her eyes, I thought she felt the same way. So of course I volunteered to help her with her chores. I was not used to wielding a hoe instead of a spear, or a scythe instead of a sword, and soon I was sweating heavily and removed my shirt. I caught Carolina stealing a glance at abs she could bounce a gold coin off, and focused on my tasks with renewed vigor. By the time we were done, the sun was nearly setting, and I could feel hunger growing within me. I needed some real meat, and soon. Luckily, Carolina excused herself and went into the farmhouse to begin her kitchen duties, leaving me to lug some heavy sacks of grain into the barn. "That will take you a while," she said. I merely smiled and had the sacks stacked and loaded before her pretty feet had taken two steps into the farmhouse.

I slipped out of the barn into the forest, and found a tasty doe to replenish my strength. Now that was some delightful venison. I quickly backtracked in the direction of the farm, coming upon a bubbling stream, which led me to a placid pond. The moon was starting to rise, and through a stand of trees, I could see the candlelight in the farmhouse windows and the warm glow of the hearth. Feeling much in need of a bath, I stripped naked and splashed into the cool, refreshing water. I swam for a few moments, pausing now and again to listen to the approaching sounds of night. I dunked my head under the surface, ridding myself of any trace of my meal. When I broke the surface, my keen senses told me I was no longer alone. I could smell the sweat on the back of Carolina's neck, and could imagine what it tasted like between her breasts.

"Catch me," she called out. Carolina rushed out of the bushes, grabbed my clothes, and ran in the direction of the farm. I watched her pert behind disappear into the darkness and pondered my choices. I was rather inexperienced with the female gender. My first instinct, despite my utter nakedness, was to leap out of the water, catch her in about two seconds, take her in my arms, and, and . . . and well, that's why I found myself still alone and naked in the cold pond water.

"What are you, an imbecile?" I announced to the night. An owl hooted back to me in a derisive tone. Hoo, hoo—yes, it said. I tracked Carolina to the barn. "Carolina," I whispered loudly from outside the barn door. "Where are you?" I could hear her bare feet treading up the ladder to the loft.

"Find me," she said.

The scent of her excitement was almost overpowering as I entered the barn and was greeted with the sight of her tunic fluttering to the ground from the loft. I climbed the ladder, and there, stretched out on a blanket amidst the hay, was my Carolina. The moonlight shone through the gable onto her naked body, her curves glowing, and her womanhood shrouded in mystery. "I thought you would never find me," she said.

"No danger of that, sweet Carolina," I said. I lay down next to her, feeling a different kind of hunger, one that I had never acted on before—desire. Our lips met, and our bodies intertwined, and soon we were covered in a fine golden dust from the hay. She took me into her, yet all my vampire strengths and abilities, training, exercise, and discipline had woefully not prepared me for pleasuring a woman. But Carolina was a willing and able teacher, although I must admit, for my first time I was a quick study. As the moon climbed high into the night sky, my lessons progressed, and Carolina's every deep breath and small moan was an ample reward for her eager student. Her fingernails raked my back as she fairly threshed the hay with her ecstasy, clutching me close as our rhythmic movements reached one final mind-blowing crescendo.

There was a certain comfort in having Carolina curled up on my chest, and in hearing the soft lullaby of her sweet breath. I do not remember falling asleep, only that it was a deep sleep unlike any I had ever experienced. The last passing dream-inducing thought in my pleasure-addled brain was pondering why I had not done that amazing act before, and when, hopefully, I could do it again. I could not wait for what the morning would bring.

Dawn arrived, and Carolina got out of the hayloft, leaving me with my morning wood and nothing but her promises of returning to the farm in a few days to take care of it. "Wait for me," she said. "I have to do an errand in Segovia for my witch of an owner. I will make it worth it for you . . ."

I didn't doubt it, and passed the next few days sharpening my blades and hunting. I cursed myself for not going with her, but I had agreed to take care of her ass, and not the fun ass or in the fun way either. I came back from hunting on the third day, and barely dodged a pitchfork thrown by a rather nasty, old crone.

"What are you doing on my property?" she screamed.

"Oh, you must be the witch of an owner," I said, noticing how she had another pitchfork ready in her hand. "And, by witch of an owner, I thought Carolina was saying that because you are cranky, ill-tempered, hideous, and just plain not nice. But, no, you are an actual witch."

She hurled the pitchfork, which split into three different pitchforks as she did, and she gasped in surprise when I dodged them all. "I hate vampires," she said. "I mean, if you can actually catch them, their hearts are so tasty, but you all move so fast you are not worth the effort. Did you kill my Carolina?"

"Who?"

"You are going to have to learn to lie better than that," the witch said. "I can smell her stench on you."

"That's surprising," I said. "You stink so bad yourself that I find it hard to believe you can smell anything at all. Bathe this century?"

This time the witch's pitchfork split into five pitchforks, which I dodged. She shrieked in anger, and all the contents of the barn, including the bewildered ass, were flying through the air at me. It was a good thing I was still on the high of getting laid, because the cantankerous crone did not even come close to harming me.

"I can do this all day," I said.

"So can I," the witch replied. "But the difference is that I am experienced enough to know not to waste my time and energy on someone as insignificant as you. Even immortals don't have infinite power."

I made a show of kissing my biceps. "I am sorry, witch—I couldn't hear you as I was kissing my infinitely powerful muscles," I said. "Next time, maybe I will stick a pitchfork in your big ass, or maybe set your rotting corpse on fire. What do you think of that?" I taunted her.

The witch almost looked reflective. "Good or evil, boy, we must all learn the harsh lessons of this unforgiving world," she said. "Mark my words, the world is going to hand you your comeuppance for being so pompous. Good riddance to you, because I have a lonely faerie to fool and seduce. And, as for you, vampire, well, you are just a fool."

"Seduce? Maybe if the faerie is blind as a bat," I retorted as the old woman just disappeared. It did not occur to me that she could perhaps alter her appearance at will. I shrugged. Ugly inside, ugly outside—at least *that* I knew. Or so I thought, because as I was about to find out some women were exceedingly good at faking . . . well, everything.

I headed to Segovia, intent on having Carolina keep her promise of more sex. But two days into my journey, I heard the rush of a river and jogged out of the forest onto a small plain. Blood was spattered all over the water's grassy banks. I dropped to my knees, my nose telling me it was Carolina's blood. I didn't have to be a trained assassin to know that there was too much blood for her to have survived the attack.

I searched for her body, but I did not find it. All that was left of her was her blood. I didn't work for the Grim Reaper, so I took a Lazarus stone from my assassin's kit and filled it with her blood that had pooled, still wet and glistening, on a frond. Nobody forgets their first time, and I would not forget Carolina, but I had much to learn in the ways of man and woman. I looped the Lazarus stone through a leather cord and placed it around my neck. Wearing it also made me feel connected to my parents, my heritage, and my future as a master assassin.

I set out again for Segovia to toast Carolina with some wine before I returned to Barcelona to learn from Hedley Edrick. I was a mile outside the city when I rounded a corner of the road and saw a young female vampire facing off against a band of wet-behind-the-ears ruf-fians. She was thin and pale with long, straight black hair, with just a hint of crazy in her gray eyes. Though she did not have the frame of a trained killer, she certainly did not need my help in this fight against these posers. But when the young thugs saw me with blood on my hands and a sharp sword on my hip, they did the smart thing and ran. I nodded at the girl, patting my sword to tell her that I would have run from me, too, if I were those boys. I shrugged and went to walk right by her, but then saw she had been protecting a small cart loaded with wine barrels.

"Well, lady, since I saved your wine," I said, "you can save me a trip into Segovia by giving me some of it in reward."

"I could have handled that myself, and you know it," the woman that would forever be known to me as Bloodsucker Number One replied. "Oh, wait—you are an assassin, aren't you?"

"Indeed," I said, mock bowing. "Trained by Master Assassin Ernesto Sinestra himself. So, does that get me some wine?"

"Why, yes, it does," Bloodsucker Number One said. "He is a legend."

I took a big gulp from the goblet she handed to me and silently toasted Carolina. I wrinkled my nose as the wine had a strange, almost flowery scent to it. "What kind of wine is this?" I asked.

"Lotus wine," she replied. "Good, right? If you are not sure you like it, just take another drink—it might need to open up."

I gulped some more, and this time I did not notice the flowery taste. "Yeah, that was better. Well, it was nice to make your acquain-tance, but I am heading back to Barcelona."

"You can finish your goblet, and then go," she said. "I can't let you take it with you—it's a family heirloom."

We made small talk as she refilled my goblet, and I downed it hap-pily. "Thanks again. I am taking my leave now," I said.

"I think you should come with me to Segovia," Bloodsucker Number One suggested.

"I think I should go with you to Segovia," I agreed.

I found myself staying in Segovia, my days spent doing errands for Bloodsucker Number One. Every time I went to leave Segovia for Barcelona, she wished me good luck and handed me a canteen of lotus wine, but at the end of the day, I always ended back up in Segovia!

Eventually, I stopped trying to leave Bloodsucker Number One, and Segovia. She was well connected to the court of Isabella, the sister of King Henry IV of Castile, and had quarters at Isabella's castle in Segovia. At that time in the 1460s, there was lots of turmoil in Spain as the royal mortals were fighting for control of the country. Bloodsucker Number One found out that Henry had betrothed her favorite Isabella to a Spanish nobleman, and flew into a rage. Shoes flew, doors were slammed, and a multitude of unladylike curse words were uttered. Henry needed the money and peace the union would bring. Isabella, the good Catholic, was properly aghast and needed prayer. Bloodsucker Number One needed Isabella. So, I killed the nobleman.

When I returned to Segovia to Isabella's castle with my mission complete, Bloodsucker Number One was waiting for me in her chambers. There was a single candle burning. She asked if I had completed my assignment, and I nodded. She screeched in excitement and danced around the room. I just wanted gold for my kill.

She had the castle servants prepare a meal in celebration, and I was now ready to discuss my fee for the assassination. I asked her to pay me in gold coins as was customary. Instead, she poured more wine. She made toast after toast—one to my skill as an assassin, another to the nobleman's dead body, and the third to immortal life. I staggered to my feet, and then fell headlong onto the floor. I could not move and, through the haze, felt Bloodsucker Number One pull down my breeches. She climbed on top of me and gave me my payment.

That was not the last time I killed for Bloodsucker Number One. My life became filled with lotus wine and death. It seemed anytime I was around her, a goblet of lotus wine was in my hand. One night before I had drunk all my wine, I grabbed her and tried to kiss her. But she stopped me, saying that vampire females did not like to kiss—there were just too many teeth involved. So most nights I just passed out in what had become our chambers. The only conjugal relations that occurred happened after I killed for her. Bloodsucker Number One paid for the killings in the oldest way known to mortal or immortal women. Looking back, I would much rather have had the gold. The emptiness and loss of my identity to the lotus wine and Bloodsucker Number One were growing unbearable, but try as I might, I could not leave her and Segovia.

Bloodsucker Number One's goal was to make Isabella the queen of Spain, so she brokered a marriage between Isabella and Ferdinand II of Aragon. Isabella and Ferdinand had a minor problem—they were second cousins. Thus, they could not marry without a special dispensation from the pope. Paul II was the pope in 1469, and he was more concerned with collecting jewels, being violated by page boys, and wearing the proper amount of rouge to grant their request. Bloodsucker Number One weighed the balance of killing Paul II with the power vacuum it would cause and decided against it. So she found another way. I accompanied her to visit Cardinal Rodrigo Borgia of Valencia. Her many sources told her he was in possession of a valuable secret.

Bloodsucker Number One also had a secret—a secret weapon by the name of Vannozza dei Cattanei—and Borgia was instantly smitten with her. So smitten was Borgia with the beautiful and willing Vannozza that he gladly revealed his secret to us. Turned out Pius II, Paul's predecessor, was not dead but a zombie being held captive by Paul II's guards in the catacombs of a church in Rome. I took out the guards in a very unholy manner, and Bloodsucker Number One escorted out Zombie Pope Pius II. He was literally coming apart at the seams in his happiness at being freed and happily gave us a papal dispensation for Isabella and Ferdinand to marry. He gladly signed any and all documents that Bloodsucker Number One put in front of him, pressing so hard that he dislocated a few of his fingers, thanking us all the while for his newfound freedom. Mission accomplished.

"What are we going to do with the Zombie Pope?" I asked Bloodsucker Number One, who was too busy packing the documents the pope had signed for safe transport back to Segovia to even bother answering me.

"Where will you go?" I asked the Zombie Pope, who was busy flicking his now useless signing hand to and fro, creating a veritable snowstorm of skin flakes that fluttered all around us.

"Home," he mumbled.

"Where is home?" I asked. "Do you need us to take you there?"

"That is not going to happen," Bloodsucker Number One interrupted. "This mission is about me and what I need. Excuse me, that was so rude. I mean this mission is now accomplished thanks to the Zombie Pope, but we have to leave in an inconsiderate manner not because we want to, but because our queen demands we return to Segovia without any undue waste of time."

"But what are we going to do—just leave him here?" I said. "I think that is wrong since he helped us."

Bloodsucker Number One sneered—or maybe that was just her face, I could never really tell—and handed me a wooden canteen filled with lotus wine. "You are not here to think, just to kill," she said. "Here, drink this." And I did. She walked off, leaving me with the canteen of lotus wine that by now was quite familiar to me. I turned to look back at the Zombie Pope, who seemed to be looking at me like I was the man who was undead and needed to be pitied.

"Home," he mumbled again. "Home is Corsignano. It is not far."

"But what will you do there?" I asked. "Everyone knows you to be dead, not undead."

The Zombie Pope pondered this for a minute and shrugged, stirring up some more choice skin flakes. "I used to be a writer," he said. "I wrote something once called the *Tale of Two Lovers*." He thought again for a moment, letting me drink the lotus wine while I waited for him to speak. "That is not you two, and yet you are the one calling me a zombie, hmm. Because right now, you are more undead than I," he said, and with that last papal proclamation, he shuffled off.

I passed those years in a lotus wine–induced fog, indeed feeling more and more like a zombie assassin and fighting in the various conflicts that led to Isabella and Ferdinand taking control of Spain. As the royal couple gained more control, so did Bloodsucker Number One. Since women other than the queen had no real power in 1400s Spain, in my position as the special advisor to the royal guard, I signed all sorts of documents, which my brain was far too foggy to try and read, for Bloodsucker Number One's personal plots and subterfuge. Yeah, that was a bad idea.

One day there was a big hubbub in the castle as some guy named Columbus had shown up to get an audience with Isabella and Ferdinand. There was much revelry and celebrating, for Columbus would find a new route to India, which would mean greater riches for Spain. Bloodsucker Number One wanted her piece of the action. She had herself appointed as a special liaison to Columbus's team, claiming to have special knowledge of the route to India. Since all the conflicts had stopped, and assassinations were few and far between, I saw little of Bloodsucker Number One. The trade winds were blowing, and thus, I was of no use to her anymore. The dealer of death was out of favor in a court focused on the profits of free trade. All of Bloodsucker Number One's time was spent with Columbus and his people, and I was not invited to the meetings and the parties. I took to sleeping in the castle barn's hayloft, and I awoke one morning to feel something I had not felt in years and years. I was myself again. I realized I had not drunk any lotus wine for weeks, and its effects were mercifully out of my system. I also realized Bloodsucker Number One had been using me, and I set out for her chambers to confront her.

Oddly, a guard was posted outside her door, and as I approached, he stepped in front of me gingerly, for my reputation as a death dealer was well known. "No one passes," he said.

"I am not just anyone," I replied. "I kind of live here."

"Not anymore," he said. "My orders are no one passes."

I knew the man in front of me was a good man. His name was Don Indigo, and he had a wife and children and was a loyal soldier. Truly, I did not want to kill Don Indigo, but I had business with Bloodsucker Number One. "How is your family, soldier?"

"Good," Don Indigo replied. He reached up and unconsciously rubbed a thin scar that ran all the way down the bridge of his nose. He had fought many battles in the name of the queen. He was no stranger to pain, but I could kill him in ways he couldn't even fathom, and he knew it. "My family is well."

"Are you looking forward to seeing them tonight?" I queried of this weathered soldier who just knew I was going to kill him, and there was nothing he could do to stop me. Except run.

"Yes," he replied, his jaw tightening.

"Your boy, the youngest, he resembles you. Has your heart, no?"

Tears welled in Don Indigo's eyes. "Yes, he does," was his reply.

I reached into my pouch and pulled out a fistful of gold coins. I rationalized it was more than his soldier's salary for ten years, but I saw something in Don Indigo's eyes that marked him for greater things.

"The boy needs his father alive more than this door needs to be guarded, eh, Don Indigo?" I said, dumping the coins back into the pouch, giving him the whole pouch instead. "Take this gold and leave Segovia forever."

"I will," he said. "But I will not be able to repay you for your kindness and honor if I live a thousand years!"

I snickered at his choice of words, as there was nary a fat chance that he would see even two more decades on this fair earth. I watched him walk away, sincerely wishing this Don Indigo, whom I just inherently liked, all the best in life. I did not have such sentiments for Bloodsucker Number One. I picked the lock on the door and eased into her chambers. There were navigation charts spread across the table, and from the bedroom I heard a great wailing and thrashing. Then I saw a tunic, characteristic of the kind that Columbus's commanders wore, lying on the ground next to one of Bloodsucker Number One's robes. I burst into the bedchamber to see Bloodsucker Number One bent over and completely naked, screaming in passion as Columbus's navigator, Martin, repeatedly steered his rudder into her poop deck.

"What are you doing here?" she screeched.

"Leaving, don't stop on my account," I said. "Martin, if you have chosen your route to India as well as you have chosen your bedmate, Columbus is surely doomed. Good day."

I found my old pack abandoned in the entryway portico and left Segovia. Halfway toward Barcelona, I stopped for a rest, and rummaging in the pack found the Lazarus stone containing Carolina's blood, which I placed around my neck. I had no memory of how it got from my neck to the pack in the first place, but I could only guess that it involved Bloodsucker Number One. Carolina was a pleasant memory, so I was just thankful that the unpleasant memory known as Bloodsucker Number One hadn't maliciously thrown it into the Eresma River that ran near the royal castle in Segovia.

I could not hope to figure out what that narcissistic nag's true motivations had been, but I didn't have to because, for the first time since meeting that horrible harridan, I was truly myself again. And I felt even more myself when I reached deeper in the pack and found a bunch of empty Lazarus stones. It was only a matter of time until they would be filled with the blood of my kills, for it was my destiny to return to my true calling as the cold-blooded assassin my parents raised. I vowed to never work for anyone again, and that included the Grim Reaper. And, I happily said goodbye, for what I thought was forever, to Bloodsucker Number One and to all the memories of being a lotus wine–addled patsy of the bitch of bitches.

CHAPTER 3

Garlic barked in my face, bringing me back to my quandary of Bloodsucker Number One suing me for alimony and child support. Buttercup said I needed a good lawyer, but was that really necessary, I wondered. Couldn't I just explain to the judge that Bloodsucker Number One and I were never married and certainly never had a child together? It was surely a misunderstanding. I had never gone to see Hedley Edrick, and now wished I had done so. I couldn't even understand what these papers causing me so much drama really meant. Surely, Hedley Edrick had a course at his College of Immortals on interpreting bombastic barrister blather?

I glared at Garlic and began packing up. Garlic bounced around happily sensing we were going on a trip. We were—back to Harvis's farm. But from there I would travel alone by transportation crystal to the only place I could think of to find an immortal divorce lawyer—Immortal Divorce Court, which, as expected, is located just outside of the Gates of Hell. Garlic was going to have to stay with Harvis because Maltese, even vampire ones, were not going to be allowed in court. Truthfully, I was not sure of how leaving her was going to work, since she was so attached to me. And if I was honest with myself, as I looked down at her scouting out the trail in front of us like a miniature dire wolf, I was beginning to grow used to her company. But if I disappeared out of her sight and traveled by transportation crystal, she would be unable to scent me and, thus, would hopefully stay with Harvis.

As I walked back to Harvis's farm, the sun dipped low on the horizon, and the road grew deserted, as most travelers did not deem it safe to travel alone or without sufficient weapon-toting numbers in the dark and predatory countryside. Thieves, highwaymen, and other shady characters lurked outside the city limits of London to prey on the weak, stupid, and simply unprepared. I was none of those and shook my head in irritation as I sensed lying in ambush in a copse of trees just ahead four thieves that, by the smell of them, hadn't had a bath in months. Not that their hygiene choices were so surprising, but they stunk so bad that even a keen-nosed mortal may have smelled them at a hundred paces. And judging by the fact that these morons chose to lie in wait upwind, they were undoubtedly rank amateurs. Garlic had sensed them at the same time and did not utter a sound, looking to me as her Pack leader for what to do. Not even the barest hint of a growl escaped her little fanged snout. She was a rather quick study and seemed to grow smarter by the day.

The one thing the ruffians did do was pick a good ambush spot, for to my right was a swamp I knew to be filled with snakes, hidden quicksand holes, and reputedly, one nasty, old bogeyman. To the left, up from the copse of trees where the thieves lay, the ground quickly rose toward a cliff trail that would add unnecessary length to my journey. I could have used a transportation crystal then and there, but I did not want to leave Garlic, vampire Maltese or not, by herself in this predicament. So we would navigate the swamp and dodge the Bogeyman.

As we slid off the trail, my keen ears and Garlic's picked up the sound of children giggling as a late-running caravan made its way down the road toward certain ambush. I waited for the expected sound of heavy hooves striking the ground and metal striking metal that would announce the presence of the hired soldiers that would surely be leading the caravan and repel the ambush, clearing the way for Garlic and me or allowing us to sneak along with it, avoiding conflict. After all, no one traveled at night unless they were heavily armed, or incredibly desperate. Yet only the sound of children's dulcet voices graced my ears.

"What in heaven's name is that?" I exclaimed under my breath as a single covered wagon came around the bend. Garlic huffed quietly, echoing my sentiment. Steering the wagon was a beautiful young girl, perhaps twelve or thirteen, and seated next to her on the bench were two even younger ragamuffins squawking up a storm. The wagon top was adorned with flowers, and various plants stuck out the back. I could not see if there were any adults in the wagon, but as they passed our hiding spot, the look of fear in the young girl's face was clear. They were fleeing someone, or something. But in moments they would be attacked and killed or suffer an even worse fate at the hands of the thieves. "Come on, pup," I said to Garlic. We slinked soundlessly through the growth at the side of the road, one black blur and one small white blur easily matching pace with the wagon.

As the wagon neared the copse of trees, I saw a previously invisible well-hidden rope dastardly stretched across the road, designed to entangle and incapacitate a normal-sized driver, but for the children in the wagon seat, it would surely be fatal. Losing the element of surprise, I swung up onto the wagon, then leaped onto the horses, hearing the scared screams of the children behind me. I briefly whispered in the ears of the two horses, bringing them to a halt with the rope hovering a mere foot or two in front of them.

"Ruin our fun this night, will you, boy?" a cold, deep voice called out. "Now that was a really bad idea." I could see the four men clearly in the dark and could smell the confidence that their numbers gave them.

My fangs glinted in the moonlight as I grinned. I knew a little something about bad ideas. I turned to the children, and saw Garlic sitting between them. "Stay where you are," I commanded. "You will be safe. She will protect you." The children looked at the little white dog and wailed loudly. "Now, now," I said, turning to the children as the men approached the wagon with their swords drawn. "I have an important lesson for you to learn, my little ones. It is not the size of the dog in the fight, but rather—" I leaped into the air, somersaulting into the midst of the thieves. My sword flicked soundlessly as it nicked jugulars, ending the lives of the men who dropped with nary a whimper. I sheathed my sword, and turned back to the wagon intent on completing my lecture. "But rather, it is the size of the fight in the—"

A shadow crashed into me from behind, knocking me to the ground and my breath out of me in the process. I smelled the unmistakable odor of brine and musty death, and rolled over to face the unspeakable horror that was the Bogeyman. Mossy hair hung in unkempt hanks from a misshapen head perched on a body as old, thick, and gnarled as a swamp oak. It stomped its clawed feet and tilted back its head and shouted its rage into the night. The children's fear was palpable, and fear to this forsaken creature was like an easy kill for twenty bags of gold to a vampire assassin—absolutely irresistible.

Then it came for me with the cold deliberation of the murky bog, single-minded in its intent to choke the very life out of me. I dodged its first lunge but not the second, moving a shade too slowly to avoid a crushing blow to my ribs that knocked me once more to the ground. It stood over me victorious, ready to deal the death blow it so craved. It reared both hands high in the air, but before it could bring them down on me and finish the blow, I saw a white shape out of the corner of my eye, and an instant later heard an earsplitting bark pierce the air. I could not believe my eyes for I could see the sound waves travel in the night, or perhaps feel them, and in an instant they enveloped the Bogeyman, and he exploded into a million fragments of peat raining down into the swamp and onto the road. I shook my head, and looked at Garlic in disbelief. "Well," I said, gathering her in one arm and rising to my feet, "that was a neat little trick." I saw one of the Bogeyman's fingers inching across the road toward the swamp and crushed it into dust with the heel of my boot.

The children, too stunned to speak, were visibly shaking. I climbed onto the wagon, and Garlic settled by my feet. I cleared my throat. "I stand corrected. It is not the size of the dog in the fight," I said, "rather the size of the bark of the dog in the fight." I took the reins and whispered to the horses, and we set out for Harvis's farm. For a few short furlongs all was quiet, then the youngest buried his head—at least I think it was a he—into my side and blubbered snot and tears all over my finest travel cloak. "Hey, now," I said. "Please stop with the tears! My name is Sirio, and I will take you to safety." My words did nothing to stop the tears, and after escaping the Bogeyman's wrath, I was now in danger of being permanently boogered by this snot-nosed kid.

The young girl who had been driving this motley crew on the road to disaster finally spoke. Her voice was soft and lilting and sounded rather like a song. "Can you tell us something?" she asked. Her little sister was pressed into her side, not crying just listening. Her eyes were vacant and empty, and I realized that the little urchin was blind and had not witnessed any of the terror that had left her little brother a blubbery mess.

"Sure," I replied. "What do you want to know?" I expected her to ask me where I was from, who my parents were, and all of that assorted mortal gobbledygook.

Her eyes were green and bright, the color of fresh growth in the spring. "Can you tell us if the monster is gone?"

When the girl used the word *monster*, my heart sank, and I felt a strange empathy for this group. Monsters come in all shapes and sizes. The little boy had stopped snuffling, and was looking for me to answer, his lip still quivering. The truth of the matter was that the Bogeyman was like any other immortal and would eventually regenerate itself. Garlic's bark had caused such damage that it might literally take years for the creature to reassemble itself. Or not, I really did not know.

"Yes, it is," I lied, avoiding another volley of tears and snot.

"Forever?"

I paused. I had not seen *that* coming. "You saw what Garlic did to it. It is gone." For a while, at least, I hoped.

For seemingly the first time in her entire life, the oldest girl looked like the weight of the world had been lifted from her tiny shoulders. "My family has been hunted by that monster for centuries," she said. "We were cursed by a witch who was rejected by one of my ancestors. When he married another, she cursed our family to have the Bogeyman hunt us until the last ones were dead. It got my older brother a fortnight ago. And without you and the dog, we would have been surely doomed."

My brow furrowed. Bogeymen did not obey witches or anything else for that matter. They were attracted to fear, and this family must have been able to project their emotions in ways most mortals could not. Over the centuries, the Bogeyman legend had taken on a life of its own with this family, and as each generation dreaded it more and more, the stronger the fear got. "You are fine now," I said, hoping I was right. "What are your names?"

The oldest smiled at me. "My name is Veela," she said. "This little sweetie is Marmitte." She motioned to the girl still hugging her side. "And that is Jova next to you."

I estimated Marmitte was about ten years old and that Jova looked to be about seven or eight. Jova had big gray eyes that had the look of wisdom despite his youth. When he fixed his gaze upon me in greeting, he reminded me of a great horned owl because his dark hair was streaked with tufts of red. "Hello, mate," Jova said, a finger stuck firmly in his nose. "Can I pet the puppy?"

"Her name is Garlic," I said. "And, yes, you may."

The children descended upon Garlic and petted her, and to her credit Garlic ignored the booger fingers on her fur and took a place curled up in the back of the wagon. "Sirio," Jova said. "I love Garlic."

I laughed and grabbed the reins, urging the horses forward. "So do I, Jova. So do I."

Veela and I made small talk until the little ones fell asleep in the back of the wagon, and then Veela, exhausted by her ordeal, joined them. As the sun rose in the sky, I pulled up to Harvis's farm. I spotted Harvis digging fence posts and pulled up beside him.

He stuck the shovel into the ground and eyed the wagon. "Nice wheels, Sirio," he said. "The flowers are a nice touch. And by the smell of them, you have brought me some company." He walked over and put his big hands on the side of the wagon and peered in at the sleeping children. "Nice litter you got there."

I sniffed the air. "You should talk," I said. "Clearly, you have been laying too much manure lately because it sure smells like we are knee-deep in the stuff." Just then, a stocky farmhand who looked to be as old as the dirt he was carrying hove into view. And like a cloud of carrion, the stench got worse. Perhaps it was manure he was carrying. But I soon realized that was not the case. "Who is Stinky there?"

Harvis laughed. "Who? Old Man Tyler over there? Best worker I have had in at least a century."

I sniffed the air again. "And that is probably the last time he had himself a bath of any sort. How old is that fellow?"

Harvis shrugged. "He is Molly's distant, distant cousin. And his mother was a gnome. He is not really that old. He just looks that way. And when he started working here and had to go into town all the time, the mortals started calling him Old Man Tyler, and it just stuck." He saw the look of glee on my face when he told me old short and stinky was related to Molly. Molly and I had always clashed for some reason. Okay, for a sisterly reason, but that was *not* my fault. "Do me a favor, don't mention that little fact, eh?"

"Sure thing, but in a remarkable bit of coincidence, I need you to do me a favor," I said. "I am going to Immortal Divorce Court, and I need you to watch Garlic."

Harvis spat and ruffled the fur around Garlic's neck. She nipped at his fingers playfully. "You can try and leave her with me, but you know she will try to follow you."

"If I travel by crystal, she won't be able to scent me," I said.

He raised one furry eyebrow. "That is what you think," he said. "Trust me, she will find a way. Why are you going there anyway? You have never been married, have you?"

I laughed. "I didn't think I had, but apparently I am mistaken."

"Must have been a good night."

"Not exactly," I grimaced. "And I need another favor."

Harvis began backing away from the wagon, sensing where the conversation was headed. "Oh no," he said. "The dog is okay, the mortal whelps are not. I just got rid of my last litter."

"Who cannot stay here, Harvis Finnegan?" I turned to see Harvis's mate, Molly, with her hands on her hips. She was nearly as tall as Harvis, but instead of his muscle and girth, had long shapely legs and arms that literally made the werewolf by the wagon whistle. Or perhaps Harvis was exhaling a little too hard, knowing what was about to happen next. No female werewolf could resist a litter, mortal or immortal.

Molly walked over to the wagon, and her angry eyes softened into limpid pools as she saw the sleeping children slowly stirring awake in the morning sun. "Oh, they are so beautiful," she cooed. "They must stay with us, Harvis."

"But, Molly," Harvis protested.

"But, nothing, Harvis Finnegan," she snapped. "We can't very well leave them with the likes of him."

"Hey, Molly," I said. "I said I was sorry. I didn't know she was your little sister."

A low growl emanated from Molly's throat, and Harvis did what any fierce werewolf would do and slowly backed away. I was saved from her wrath by Jova waking up crying, causing Molly to scoop him up in her arms. "It's okay, honey," she said, her voice sweet and soft. "Are you hungry? I have breakfast." Marmitte and Veela were awakened by their brother's cry.

Veela looked at Harvis and Molly, trying to assess if they were a threat to her and her siblings, or not. "They are friends," I said. "Good people."

"Good people, indeed," Veela agreed.

"I am hungry," Marmitte announced. "And I have to pee."

Molly took her by the hand, and they all followed her into the farmhouse. I looked up to see Harvis shaking his head in disbelief.

"Well, that worked out great," I said. "Thanks for watching Garlic. Now, how about that breakfast?"

I survived breakfast, avoiding Molly's wrath for the most part because the children's needs came before her dislike for me, aside from the bowl of stew that she "accidentally" dropped in my lap. Garlic pounced quickly and put the stew out of its misery to the children's amusement. Harvis merely snickered, knowing it was not in his best interest to get involved in this little spat. "She'll be okay," he said. "She forgets her own full moon days." It did not matter to Molly that it was her sister that was the aggressor in our little tryst, and who was I to refuse the wiles of a willing, wild-in-the-sheets werewolf? I did not know what Harvis meant by full moon days, and assumed he meant taking her in the ass. Molly's sister and I had coupled on the darkest of nights with but a sliver of moonlight shining down upon us, and little sis was more about putting me into her crescent rather than her full moon, which was quite all right by me!

The children took to Molly naturally, and for the first time I could see Veela was relaxed and comfortable. I told Harvis all about the Bogeyman, and he assured me what I already knew—no bogeyman was a match for a full-grown male werewolf. Harvis was almost seven feet tall and well muscled in his mortal form. But when he was suitably enraged, he was a sight to behold, seemingly growing bigger, hairier, and more deadly. I had only seen this happen once, and it didn't end well for the poor chap that Harvis had thought grabbed Molly's ass. As it turned out Harvis had imbibed a few dozen ales and assaulted the wrong man, who I understand they buried with his hand still shoved up his own ass. It was just bad luck to tangle with a werewolf. But all this was a distant memory to Harvis, because he instead made a joke that Garlic and her powerful bark would be around to protect him, except from Molly.

Harvis and I stood off to the side, watching the children play with Molly. Garlic raced around the barnyard nipping happily at Jova's heels, causing him to shriek with utter joy. "How long are you going to let them stay here?" I asked. "Surely, they have some relatives somewhere that will claim them."

Harvis shrugged, looking at the joy in Molly's face. "They will stay as long as she wants, thanks to you," he answered, playfully punching my shoulder. "If this keeps up, I know that look in her eye. She will want another litter. And I am going to name the runt after you!"

"Well, it is high time I get this nonsense over with and go to the Immortal Divorce Court," I said, cinching up my pack. It seemed like a good time to make my exit as Garlic was so preoccupied with the children. I slipped out of her sight and into the barn. Harvis followed me.

"I think that little puppy of yours is going to find a way to follow you even if she has to travel halfway across the earth to do so," he said.

I laughed and, reaching into my pocket, picked out a handful of crystals. "Exploding barks are one thing. Willing yourself across the world is quite another," I replied. "Give my regards to Molly." I picked out a crystal and dropped the rest back in my pocket, not noticing that I had dropped one on the barn floor. There was a strange pulling sensation as I focused on my destination, and then Harvis and the barn disappeared. The last thing I heard before the barn disappeared and the coastline of Greece appeared was the forlorn howl of a heartbroken Maltese.

Immortal Divorce Court is in a nondescript village located on the Peloponnese peninsula in southern Greece. I had a three-hour trek on a dusty road leading deeper into the peninsula. I stopped for a quick lunch off the road, finding a rock outcropping overlooking the Gulf of Corinth which was well hidden by a thick stand of trees. After a moment of peace to collect my thoughts, I was on my way again. About a dozen times, I thought I saw Garlic out of the corner of my eye, but it was only the reflection of the sun off gleaming bits of quartz in the rocks. I could see the IDC village up ahead, an ominous dark cloud behind it seemingly a permanent part of the landscape. I knew the cloud masked the Gates of Hell and the screams of the lost souls it contained. I walked up to the gates of the village and was confronted with a gap-toothed faerie guardsman posted to keep out the riffraff and the mortals.

"Your papers," he said, yawning in his boredom.

I handed over the papers. He read them and laughed excitedly. "She must really hate you to have hired Feminera the Wicked."

"Excuse me," I said. "Who is Feminera the Wicked?" He kept laughing, ignoring my plight. I bared my fangs and drew my sword and was instantly surrounded by ten of his ilk. I sighed and sheathed my blade. "Can I have my papers back?"

He threw them to me. "Who's your counselor?"

I shrugged. "I have come here to find one."

"Good luck with that."

The faeries jostled each other and winked. This was not going to go well, I thought.

The faerie smiled at his cohorts. "Fine, go into the center of town, where you will find the courthouse. To the left of the courthouse is an inn. Go to the bar, and you will find plenty of attorneys there. Hold on one second. Sirio Sinestra, by the power vested in me by the Immortal Divorce Court, you are hereby *referred*."

The same rainbow that had come from Buttercup's seal shot from the guard's sword and struck my money pouch, magically lightening it by ten gold coins. "Whoa, whoa, I have been served already, so why are you people taking my gold?" I exclaimed.

The faerie could barely contain his glee. "That was not a service fee, my friend. That was a referral fee for telling you where you can find your attorney—nonrefundable of course, assuming you can even find one to take your case. You asked, the IDC provided, you paid the ten gold coins, so now you may pass."

As I walked through the gates of the village, my nose was assaulted with the unmistakable scent of brimstone, and I knew I was right outside the Gates of Hell. I was joined by other immortal men plodding forlornly along as they held their soon-to-be-empty gold pouches close. Behind the courthouse, I could hear the wails of demons and see the flames flickering from deep below. A nearby inn had a sign that read "The Golden Rule," with a picture of the scales of justice weighing gold equally on both sides. "He who has the gold makes the rules," read the inscription. Lawyers. Maybe I really was in Hell after all.

I pulled the heavy oaken door open and entered the inn, feeling one hundred eyes upon me, each judging me instantly as prey, threat, foe, or potential client. I stood my ground, baring my fangs slightly, and let the door slam shut behind me. The inn's many tables seemed to be mostly filled with litigants and their lawyers doing business over tankards of frothy brew and flagons of wine. Smoke filled the air with the stench of tobacco and clove, combining nicely with the unmistakable twin odors of desperation and despair as I shouldered my way toward the bar at the other end of the room.

I was no creature's prey and boldly met the gaze of immortals of all kinds who dared to stare at me as I passed, including some creatures that I couldn't even identify. If only, once again, I had gone to Barcelona to see Hedley Edrick, I might know just what in the Hell, or more accurately what just outside of Hell, I was looking at. On a plaque behind the bar was a sign that read "Make sure the screwing you get is worth the screwing you get." I swallowed the lump in my throat and hoped I was going to find my attorney here. If I didn't, I was surely screwed.

Tending the bar was a satyr well up in years, limping from customer to customer on hooves that were chipped and dirty. His thick spectacles were perched precariously on his long nose, and he kept wiping his hands on a tunic on his humanoid half that had been stained by drinks for the better part of eternity. His lower goat half was mangy, gray, and thinning, and his spindly legs were atrophied from his time tending bar. This guy had been long sent out to pasture. "What will you have?" he bleated in my general direction, his eyes not truly focusing on anything.

"Your finest wine, good sir," I replied.

He either coughed or laughed. I could not tell which. "We have no fine wine here for the likes of you, vampire." I'd had enough of insults this day, and before I knew it, my hand was around his throat. The patrons of the bar ignored what was happening in front of them, except for the one werewolf who took the barkeep's predicament as an opportunity to come behind the bar to top off his beer, and he merely nodded at us. "No," the barkeep uttered as my hand began squeezing his throat even harder. "You do not understand."

"Understand what?"

He motioned to my hand, and I loosened my grip. "Tell me what, then, you ignorant goat."

The satyr rubbed his throat gingerly. "The finest wines have been reserved for the attorneys by rule of the Immortal Divorce Court. Only they may partake of this world's finest beverages. I can, however, offer you a nice one-year-old port newly in the cask."

"No, thanks," I replied. "That does not seem fair at all. Why do the attorneys get the good stuff?"

"I don't know," he said. "But shortly after Feminera the Wicked was admitted to practice before the Immortal Divorce Court, the Head Magistrate deemed it so."

"Feminera the Wicked?"

The satyr shuddered. "Yes, she is the worst, most diabolical, most evil, most overwhelmingly unpleasant divorce attorney known to immortal man. A true nightmare to face in court, and she has gotten so utterly bloodthirsty that no magistrate wants to rule against her, and no attorney wants to oppose her. Now, who is representing your ex?"

"That would be Feminera the Wicked," I said. The room instantly went silent, and one little elf shrieked and collapsed in a heap on the floor. The collective group of immortals raised their drinks to me in a showing of fraternity and outright pity. "To the vampire," one yelled out. "May he leave this place with a single gold coin in his pocket and his manhood safe in his breeches."

"To the vampire," the room cheered in unison, downing their drinks and returning to their business. The little elf was revived with a splash of grog and propped back up by his tablemates. Embarrassed, he pulled his hat low over his little pointy ears and focused only on the drink in front of him. I turned to see the satyr pouring me a drink from an ornate cask into a fine crystal goblet edged with gold.

"There is one exception to the Head Magistrate's rule," he said. "Those that are unrepresented and facing Feminera the Wicked get our best vintage—on the house."

I sat down at the bar and took a sip of the wine, enjoying its incredible body and character. "This is good stuff indeed. What do you call it?"

"Hope and a Prayer," the satyr replied.

I laughed. "Well, I have never been much of the praying type, so I will focus on the hope part." I took another swig of the wine and lifted my glass. "To hope, may it always spring eternal."

"Here goes hope," I said to the satyr, who looked at me strangely. I turned to the crowd and yelled, "Is there any attorney, barrister, lawyer, or counselor that will represent me against Feminera the Wicked?" A brief silence from the din was my only response, and the room grew noisy once more. "Okay, then," I said, turning back to the bar. "Satyr, do you have a name?"

"I am called Cabernet," he said. "But you can call me Cab."

"Okay, Cab," I said. "I need your help. Surely there is someone that will go up against Feminera the Wicked."

"Well," Cab said. "You could try . . ." He shook his head violently as if he were trying to shake the idea out of his brain.

"What is it, Cab, tell me, before you shake that goat brain of yours right out of your head. Who can help me?"

Cab sat down, poured himself a drink, and took a huge gulp. "Ah, cabernet always gets me focused," he said. "There is only one attorney with the legal knowledge, the brashness, and the sheer tenacity to go against Feminera the Wicked and win. And that is Maximillian Justice."

"That is fantastic," I said. "Where do I find Justice?"

Cab sighed. "No one knows. We haven't seen him ever since he lost the Big One."

"Every attorney loses cases," I said. "Where is his office? I need to go there."

"You don't understand, vampire. He lost the Big One."

"What do you mean the Big One?"

The satyr came around from the bar and took a seat next to me. He took an even bigger gulp of his drink and stared at the heavens, bleating unintelligibly under his breath. "Maximillian Justice was the best attorney ever seen in Immortal Divorce Court. He is a demon many thousands of years old, and he was blessed with incomparable wit and legal prowess. He was equally feared and revered by magistrate, litigant, and his fellow members of the bar. His practice was successful, and his accolades were many. Until one day, when there was a knock on his door that would forever change the very fabric of the world and Underworld. For storming into his office in a rush of fire and brimstone was Hades, the Dark Lord himself, with divorce papers from Persephone in one hand, and the charred remains of the faerie who served him in the other."

I laughed. "That is kind of funny. How could Persephone divorce him? She has nowhere to go since she is trapped in Hell for six months of the year anyway. No one could mess that up, could they?"

Cab looked at me with a sheepish—nay, goatish—grin on his face. "Oh," I said. "The Big One. Justice messed up Hades's divorce, didn't he? But how did that happen?"

Cab took another sip of his drink. "Well, as it turns out, it was not entirely Justice's fault, since all Persephone really wanted was more time in the mortal world. Hades refused to give in since the Lord of Darkness is not one for compromise. It was his way, or the highway to Hell, or both, if you were his wife. He made Justice file a motion to keep her in the Underworld for the entire year. You know that expression, 'Hell hath no fury like a woman scorned'? Well, it is even worse when she has to live there. Persephone was so mad that she went for blood and hired a new young attorney, Feminera."

"Feminera the Wicked?"

Cab nodded. "She was just Feminera back then, hadn't quite earned the Wicked yet."

"So what happened?"

"Feminera and Persephone schemed to destroy all copies of the prenuptial agreement between Hades and Persephone. Using guile, deceit, and bribery, they destroyed all copies in the Immortal Divorce Court's files. Persephone threw Hades's copy in the River Lethe, and then came to pay Maximillian Justice a little visit. He opened his door to find Persephone, clothes torn asunder, hysterical as can be, and from her beautiful red lips, she told the story of how his client, the Lord of Darkness, was going to torture her for eternity."

I gasped. "He wouldn't?"

Cab snorted. "You have a lot to learn about women. Of course not, it was all a ruse. For unbeknownst to Justice, sneaking in the back door of his office was Feminera, who took the last copy of the prenuptial agreement and burned it in Justice's own hearth."

"Oh, that is wicked," I said.

"And so she then was named," Cab said. "For the next day, the Head Magistrate had no choice but to classify Hell as marital property and award half of it to Persephone for eternity. Which, if you are here next month, isn't really all that bad, what with all the unicorns and rainbows and—"

"What happened to Justice?" I thought the satyr must be way too into the wine—unicorns and rainbows in Hell? Right.

"Oh, he was ruined," Cab said. "Feminera's reputation grew, and Justice now had made a very powerful enemy in the Lord of Darkness. Not to mention not being able to collect on his legal fees, what with the whole fear of instant incineration and eternal damnation, which even for a demon like Justice would be very unpleasant."

"That is a great story and all," I said, "but, how does that help me against Feminera? How can I find Justice and at least ask for his help?"

Cab shrugged. "No one knows."

There was a great flash of light, and a clap of thunder silenced the bar. I turned to my right to find sitting on the barstool next to me a grinning demon dressed impeccably in fine golden robes. His pointy teeth glinted as if made from gold, as did the small horns that adorned the top of his head like a crown. "Sirio Sinestra, I am Maximillian Justice, and I will take your case against Feminera."

I gasped in amazement, "You will? Against Feminera the Wicked?"

"Wicked my fork-tailed ass. But unethical? Well, now that is a certainty." He smiled again and lit a clove cigarette with his index finger. "And I will do it for free. I hate that bitch."

CHAPTER 4

The next day I ventured to a rather plain-looking stone building that served as Justice's office, where he would prepare me for the next day's hearing. I knocked, and a comely servant opened the small wooden door and led me into an atrium that stretched as high as the eye could see. It looked like you could fit a mountain in there, but how was that possible, since the building I entered was rather modest from the outside?

There was nothing modest about the plush carpets and ornate tapestries adorning the walls, the furniture of antiquity, and statues that were clearly older than me, or even the gold sconces that glowed as bright as day, lighting a path for the servant to lead me deeper and deeper into Justice's abode. She came to a huge marble door that opened smoothly, and motioned me forward. I stepped into a cavernous chamber, seemingly hewn from a single large piece of gold. I heard the demon call to me from behind a wall of dusty books, which quickly turned into a maze of mustiness as I wandered to and fro trying to get to his voice. How big was this private office I wondered, traveling down aisle after aisle of what I assumed were legal books. "Over here, this way," Justice called. "Come on now, we don't have all day. I know you aren't stopping to do a little pleasure reading. Will you come on! Good Lord, for a vampire tracker, you are unbearably slow."

I finally rounded the last corner and found Justice sitting at a dust-covered desk. The massive wooden legs were carved intricately in the likeness of dragon feet, complete with very lifelike claws. The whole desk looked as if it could walk on those scaled, reptilian legs, and I mused that perhaps it really could. It was littered with countless quills of all shapes and sizes, and spilled ink pots by the dozen. Parchment in varying states of use, disuse, and downright abuse papered the floor, the desk, and a large leather chair in front of it that he motioned me to sit on. Justice then ignored me and peered through golden spectacles at some legal tomes in front of him and kept muttering to himself. I thought I heard the distant sound of harp music, so faint that it tickled my ears as I strained to hear it. I brushed at my ears, but the sound remained.

I picked up a huge double handful of papers to gain some sitting room, and nearly jumped out of my skin as two caterpillars the size of hunting beagles slid from the chair and curled up at my feet. "What in the hell are those?" I cried to an oblivious Justice. The caterpillars, one black as coal, the other white as snow, stuck out their cute little pink tongues and began licking my legs, happily cooing like little bug doves. They were actually quite beautiful creatures to behold after the shock of first seeing them wore off. The black one, on closer examination, had thousands of gold sparkles reflecting off its skin, and the white one had an equal amount of what looked to be diamonds reflecting the light from its skin in a beautiful rainbow pattern on the floor in front of the chair.

"Oh," Justice exclaimed. "I was wondering where those bookworms had gotten to. And, oddly, they appear to like you. I find that rather ironic because I don't believe you have read one single book that wasn't assassin related in your entire life, now have you?"

I chose not to answer my volunteer counselor of law, and instead brushed away several centuries of dust from the chair and carefully sat down, ready to tell Justice about my problems. But Justice just went back to perusing his tomes, and the bookworms seized the opportunity to crawl into my lap and curl up for some quality snuggling time. The black one migrated up my arm and began licking my neck, and the white one was successfully nosing its way under my tunic, where its little eager tongue found my bare stomach, causing me to break out into giggles, which only encouraged the little worm even more. "Justice," I said. "Will you please call off your bookworms?"

Justice rolled his eyes and crumpled up some loose paper. He dropped it to the floor, and the worms crawled off me and began snacking on the paper. "Don't complain," he grumbled. "They tried to cocoon my last client!"

Finally, I could tell my new attorney about my problems, and eyeing the bookworms warily, I told Justice everything. When I finished he waved a dismissive hand. "This vampire, why is she going after you? Her case is weak, and her theory is improbable, unreasonable, and inconceivable. Am I missing one of my favorite '-bles'? No, I don't think so. And you aren't all that wealthy. So what is it?"

In all the time I had been served and journeyed to this deity-forsaken place, I had never considered why Bloodsucker Number One was going after me for gold. "I don't really know," I said.

Justice laughed and gnashed his teeth so hard sparks flew. "Vampire, I was not asking your opinion. My question was rhetorical."

"Rhet-what?"

My demon counselor shook his head sadly. "When this is all over, do yourself a favor. Get an education. Pick up a book. Actually read said book. Eternity is a mighty long time to have a vocabulary limited to words solely related to fucking, killing, and drinking alcohol."

I glared at him as my anger rose at his insult. "I meant to go to Hedley Edrick, but it just didn't seem important since my assassin business was doing so well, all right? I am no idiot, Justice!"

Justice's eyes literally shot fire as he sat up in his chair and pointed a flaming finger at my chest. "That's debatable. Listen to me, vampire, I am doing you a favor here. You show your fangs in court tomorrow like that, and I cannot do a thing for you. The Head Magistrate will find you in contempt, and your bloodsucker and Feminera will walk out with your balls. Got it?"

I knew he was right, and nodded. "Apologies."

Justice straightened his robe with both hands. "Now," he said. "Let me tell you a little something about females. Cross them, no pun intended, and they will go for blood. And with a female vampire like her, it is a thousand times worse. And from the look of all the cases she has filed in Immortal Divorce Court, she is pretty darn good at it."

"Wait a minute," I said. "She could not have filed any of those cases, because she said she had never been married."

"Uh, yeah," Justice said, rolling his eyes. "I sure wish I had a gold coin, or two, for every time I have heard that refrain from the men getting taken to court by your bloodsucker. Try maybe one hundred times over her years—that is one ancient, evil bloodsucker you chose to consort with, my friend."

"I didn't know that."

Justice nodded in mock concern. "They never do. But when you walked out on her, it was only a matter of time before she was going to track you down and make your life, well, a living Hell."

"But, she was the one being deceitful and having carnal relations!" I exclaimed.

He laughed. "Oh, that doesn't matter. She has been preying on people for centuries. It is what she does, and it is what she is, and what she knows how to do best. Some women are whores, but your bloodsucker chooses to fuck them in a different way. The Immortal Divorce Court way."

"I cannot believe I am in this mess," I said. "I still rue the day that I met Bloodsucker Number One. I cannot believe this is really happening!"

Justice shrugged, "Oh, but it is," he said. "Tomorrow after the bloodsucker testifies, you have to rein in your emotions, your anger, and your hatred, and tell the truth. Short of contempt of court, you should be walking out of there free of that bitch forever. Two vampires cannot beget an ordinary mortal. That goes against the law of Mother Nature."

"Thank you for listening," I said. "But, I have a question for you."

"It is why we are called counselors," he replied. "What is your question?"

"Why did you come back?"

Justice smiled, fire smoldering in his eyes. He gnashed his teeth so hard sparks flew from them and lit a candle next to him aflame. "Oh, that is easy," he said. "Redemption."

The next day I met Justice outside of the Immortal Divorce Court courthouse. We walked up the marble steps to the main entrance, and I glared at the smirking faerie deputy guarding the entrance. A table filled with an assortment of maces, swords, daggers, and other weaponry was manned by another deputy. The courthouse was ensorcelled so any weapon brought through the doors instantly burst into flame and melted. I could see a few charred spots by the entrance that marked signs of litigants who forgot or imprudently disregarded the power of the law. Those litigants that tried to appear via crystal directly into their courtroom were instead directed straight to Hell. This fact amused me since Justice had told me he had divorce proceedings that had lasted one thousand years, so how would the litigants know the difference in venue?

Then the apparently perma-smirking deputy laid eyes on Justice and nearly dropped his spear. "You," he sputtered. "You are back." Hades's incineration of the faerie process server was legendary among the faeries, and Justice was still the attorney of record for the Lord of Darkness and, thus, was afforded all proper fear and reverence.

Justice smiled at the faerie. "I am indeed," he said. "Better warn your brethren, I hear Persephone is filing some motions tomorrow. Hope that it is not your day to serve process, my friend."

The faerie crumpled to the ground in a clatter of soiled armor, and Justice nimbly stepped over his inert frame. I followed suit, and found myself standing before the doors of the courtroom. The doors were each hewn from a single piece of obsidian and stretched nearly twenty feet high from the stark white marble floor to the ornate gold-tiled ceiling, which was embossed with the scales of justice on each tile. I sure hoped my Justice was going to prevail this day. But a second, more studied look at the courtroom doors caused me to gasp. A myriad of visibly angry faces moved on the doors, each mouthing silent words that fell upon nary a mortal or immortal ear. The faces changed constantly, and it was then I noticed a few of the faces were seemingly happy. Apparently, some of the litigants in this courtroom actually did come out smiling. Who knew? The doors swung open of their own volition, and I followed Justice, but the last face I saw before I entered the courtroom absolutely destroyed any last vestige of nerves I had—for smiling back at me was the absolutely orgiastic face of Bloodsucker Number One. She was holding the gold coins of her past suckers, fools, rubes, and so on, and I imagined in this case that would be . . . me.

Justice motioned for me to take a seat next to him at one of the counsel tables. The room was empty save for us, and a lone faerie deputy jumped like he had seen his worst nightmare at the very sight of

Justice and hurriedly left through a back door. Immediately, the court personnel filed in, all staring and pointing at Justice. I realized I was lucky that he was the only attorney that would take my case against Bloodsucker Number One and Feminera. He ignored the clerks and deputies' collective whispers that grew steadily from a small din to an all-out roar. Finally, Justice removed the golden spectacles from his face and dropped them on his papers. His command of the courtroom was unparalleled as he made slow, deliberate eye contact with each and every person in the room. "Good morning, good court personnel of Immortal Divorce Court," he said. "It is my great pleasure to see you all again. Let's cross our fingers and hope for no godly immolation today. I represent this guy—gratis if you can believe that, because I know I can't."

Instantly, a gaggle of salutations and pleasantries were exchanged between Justice and the staff. I guessed they were happy that the Lord of the Underworld was not Justice's client today. I noted the clerks were all elves, and even with my keen senses, I could barely make out the speed at which their nimble fingers filed paperwork and readied the Head Magistrate's bench for the hearing. The counsel table next to us was conspicuously empty. Where were Bloodsucker Number One and her counselor? Justice must have read my thoughts. "She has two minutes," he said. "Feminera is all about a big entrance, and I am not talking about her anus. And besides, they put in a request to use the disabled litigants' entrance."

"Disabled? What could that mean?"

"You know, disabled—hurt, ailing, not whole, injured." Justice smirked at me. "It means one in their party is unable to climb the courthouse steps due to some sort of malady, injury, or illness."

My nerves were short as it was without my own attorney thinking I was a complete idiot. "I know what the word *disabled* means, but what does it mean for the case?" I said. Justice shrugged and did not answer.

The doors of the courtroom slowly opened, causing the clerks and deputies to try to look even busier to avoid eye contact with Feminera the Wicked. In she strode, an unfortunate mix of leprechaun and satyr, her hooves clomping loudly on the floor. Justice had told me that leprechauns typically made excellent divorce attorneys—what with their aptitude for finding pots of gold. A shock of red curly hair framed Feminera's scowling face and draped down over pink silk robes that ended barely past her bulging hind end. Her legs were not those of a goat but of a leprechaun, but coated with so much red fur that I thought she was wearing some sort of crimson tights. I saw then she did not have hooves after all, but wore high wooden platform shoes to elevate her diminutive stature. Her beady green eyes bored into my skull as she glared first at me then at Justice, who gave her no reaction but acknowledged her presence with a dismissive wave of his hand.

"Feminera," Justice finally said when she had finished clomping to her counsel table, his even tone not conveying the hatred he had for the redheaded nightmare beside him.

"So good to have you back," Feminera answered with a well-executed sneer. "It is going to be a pleasure to take your heart again."

"Dear, dear Feminera," he said. "I did not have a heart to begin with, so only your shriveled, dark, lonely one is at issue here." He looked at her bare left hand. "Still alone I see."

She made a face at him and dropped her papers on the table. I started to chuckle, but then heard the strangest squeaking sound as the courthouse doors opened once again. Someone needed to oil those doors, I thought. Then I saw what was causing the squeaking sound and felt my blood begin to boil. Into the courtroom came Bloodsucker Number One. Her gaudy patterned robe was nearly as short as Feminera's, but her sneer was far superior, for when she made eye contact with me it was as if she was smelling the most odoriferous flatulence ever emitted from a mortal or immortal body. Trailing behind her was a toothless, balding, and nearly dead Martin the Navigator, easily over 120 mortal years old, being pushed by one of Bloodsucker Number One's lackeys in some sort of wheeled wooden chair, which was the origin of the squeaking. He was draped in a simple white tunic, with bare, bony arms and legs jutting out in all directions, making him look like a skeleton.

"Well, that explains the disabled thing," Justice remarked. "It is always funny when the mortals think they are part of our long-living club. That guy is more worm food than top of the food chain, though."

There were bandages covering his neck, hands, and legs, and I realized that Bloodsucker Number One must have been injecting him over the last century with some of her blood to extend his life. He was now a mere shell of a man, but in his dead eyes was a spark that gave evidence of his guile. A conniving intelligence still resided in a body that was hanging onto life by the slimmest of margins and, thus, cheating Death's precipice. As he reached Feminera's table, Martin made several groans and moans and one audible passing of wind. Turning his head with great effort, his blurry gaze roved around the courtroom until his bloodshot orbs found me. "Daddy," he said with a toothless smile and a wink before dramatically falling into a deep and sonorous sleep.

The faerie deputy snapped to attention and played a long series of notes on a brass horn, holding the last one for dramatic effect. "All rise—hear ye, hear ye," he boomed. "May this honorable Immortal Divorce Court come to order."

I rose to my feet and looked at Justice, who was impassive as always. I glanced at Bloodsucker Number One's table and saw Martin come out of his stupor. "Order?" he mumbled loudly to no one in particular. "Cheese, please, and some fine Genoa salami."

The deputy ignored him and continued his introduction. "Please remain standing, for I present to you the Great Decider, the Breaker of the Bold, so bow down now and fear for your gold, for here is the greatest head magistrate of this time and any other . . . Gulth Scorn." The deputy blew on his horn once again, and with a great swishing of robes and flashes of gold, in strode Gulth Scorn, Head Magistrate of Immortal Divorce Court. He looked ancient even for a demon, his stony countenance striated with wrinkles and veins. But his eyes were as clear and black as a moonless night and concealed all evidence of emotion in their shadowy depths.

"Here again, are you," he said, regarding Bloodsucker Number One with the barest hint of disdain.

He continued to scan the courtroom, paying me little attention. His eyes went to Justice, then Feminera, and then back to Justice again. "I knew you would come back eventually, Mr. Justice," he said. He looked over at Feminera and Bloodsucker Number One again. "I just wish it wasn't today. Well, at least you are not here on that business between the Lord of the Underworld and his former beloved. I do not have on my fireproof robes today."

"No, Your Honor," Feminera said. "We have just a simple alimony and child custody matter to resolve."

The Head Magistrate looked at the clearly mortal Martin—happily drooling in his chair—and the two vampire litigants. "Feminera," he threatened. "You had better not be wasting my time with that thing in yonder chair. That is a nearly dead mortal over there if my nose does not deceive me."

"Of course not, Your Honor, and yes it—I mean he—is a mortal," she replied.

He shook his head. "Call your first witness," he snarled.

Bloodsucker Number One took the stand and smiled at the Head Magistrate, who ignored her. The deputy brought over a crystal globe that contained a raging fire within it. "Place your hand on the perjury globe," he said. "Do you swear to tell the truth, the whole truth, and nothing but the truth, or risk incineration in the tenth level of Hell?"

I looked at Justice quizzically. Justice leaned over to me and whispered, "The perjury globe didn't apply with Hades, of course, but rest assured, you don't want to go to the tenth level of Hell. Ninth? Not so bad. Tenth . . . unbearable even for the likes of me."

Bloodsucker Number One made a big production of placing her hand on the perjury globe. Not even the barest vestige of fear in her bearing, since she probably had a vacation villa in the tenth level of Hell. "I will," she said, smirking at me.

"You may proceed," the Head Magistrate said.

Feminera did not waste any time at all with her questions and went right to the heart of the matter.

"Is Martin the son of you and Sirio Sinestra?"

Bloodsucker Number One looked over at Martin, who smiled back at her lovingly, which caused him to go into a major coughing-and-farting fit with the effort. "Yes," she said. "Yes, he certainly is our little guy."

"And you and Sirio Sinestra were married?"

Bloodsucker Number One curled her lip into an even thinner quivering bit of flesh. "Yes, we were," she said, dabbing at her eye to catch a crocodile tear. "That is, until he left me!"

I could not believe what I was hearing. "This is an outrage," I hissed in Justice's ear. "An absolute outrage!" The Head Magistrate looked down from his bench disapprovingly, and Justice kicked my shin under the table, which took me by surprise but did cause me to shut my mouth. Of course I left her, I thought, I left her with Martin's swollen member inside her rear end. How could she be saying these lies? Sure she was female, and evil, and manipulative, and deceitful, but I really wondered . . . Where was she going with this?

"No more questions," said Feminera.

"Your witness, Mr. Justice," said the Head Magistrate.

Justice looked a little alarmed. I could tell that he knew something was not right, and clearly my counselor did not even know what Feminera had planned.

"You are a vampire, correct?" he said to Bloodsucker Number One. "Yes."

"My client, Sirio Sinestra, he is a vampire, too, correct?"

"Yes."

Justice got up and stood in front of Martin the Navigator. "And this wretched creature, that you claim is your son together, is without question a mortal, correct?"

"Yes, he is," Bloodsucker Number One agreed. "A mortal, but a sweet boy . . ."

Justice was getting into his rhythm. "You would agree that it is impossible for two vampires to beget a mortal child?"

"Yes, I would agree that is absolutely correct."

"You would concede that Martin is not the fruit of your union and could not *ever* be the fruit of any union between you and Sirio Sinestra?"

Bloodsucker Number One smiled at him. "I would concede that."

Justice looked down his nose at her. "And it is also true that you and Mr. Sinestra never had a wedding ceremony in a church, mosque, or any other designated holy place built to celebrate and make official the sacrament of marriage?"

"Yes, that is true," she said.

Justice leaned forward. "You and Mr. Sinestra never appeared in front of an emperor, king, queen, major or minor demon, or any other various sundry member of mortal or immortal royalty empowered to declare you married, did you?"

Bloodsucker Number One sat back and thought for a moment. She grinned nervously, baring her teeth. "No," she agreed. "None of those."

I could not believe she would drag me here for this utter ridiculousness. Justice was doing an amazing job. There was no way this could end poorly for me. I could not wait to get back to the bar for a celebratory drink with my fabulous attorney.

"I have no more questions for this witness," Justice said. Nothing appeared to be bothering him. My attorney was in complete control of this poor excuse for a trial. Nothing could go wrong now, I thought.

"Feminera," the Head Magistrate queried. "Do you have more questions?"

"No, Your Honor," Feminera replied.

"All right, I have heard enough," the Head Magistrate said. "Feminera, I am going to see you in my chambers after this hearing. I cannot believe you have wasted my valuable time with this drivel on my last week on the bench. And the mortal is stinking up my courtroom to the high heaven that he is trying to go to this very minute. I may have to suspend your law license for this preposterousness."

"But, Your Honor," she protested. "I have more witnesses. If I may have some latitude, all will be clear in but a moment."

An eerie chill descended upon me, and it felt like the air was heavy as I struggled to breathe. The Head Magistrate peered down at Feminera. "Get to it," he commanded. "And make it quick."

Feminera glanced back at the courtroom doors, but they did not open for her witness. She wiped a bit of sweat from her brow and made a big show of shuffling the papers at her table. The courtroom was deathly quiet, except for the increasingly labored breathing of Martin, who appeared to be now quite comatose. A string of drool ran from his quivering bottom lip to the arm of his chair, but no one at his table appeared to notice or care.

"Feminera?" The Head Magistrate tapped a thin finger on his bench. With his long, sharp fingernails, it really looked like he had talons. But that was probably my overactive imagination at work.

Justice stood up. "Your Honor, we move for a dismissal of this sham of a proceeding."

"As you should," the Head Magistrate said, reaching for his gavel to do just that.

There was a great commotion outside the courtroom, audible through the thick courtroom doors. What or who could be causing all the noise?

Feminera exhaled, looking quite relieved. "Ah, my witness has arrived," she said. "We call His Excellency, Pope Pius II," she said. "The Zombie Pope!" I burst out. "What is he doing here?"

The deputy shushed me with a glare and pointed to his sword. Faerie glare aside, I was about to find out why the Zombie Pope was there. The courtroom doors opened, and in shuffled Pope Pius II, the Zombie Pope. His papal robes were surprisingly clean despite the flakes of skin that fluttered off his arms like a squall of snowflakes as he flung invisible holy water at the assorted adoring masses that only he saw in the courtroom. Old habits die hard, apparently, even when you are half dead. After a short eternity, Pope Pius II reached the counsel tables and thrust both his arms in the air, sending a blizzard of skin flakes in every direction. Zombie-strength skin moisturizer had not been invented yet. "Bless you," he said. "Bless all of you."

Justice stood with an exasperated sigh. "Your Honor," he said. "We object to the witness testifying. Case law is replete about the inherent unreliability of zombie testimony."

Feminera had stood when Justice did and waited patiently for the Head Magistrate to look in her direction. "Your Honor, Pope Emeritus Pius II is no ordinary zombie. He is a pope even in his death, or half death as it is, and thus, he is fully competent to testify about his papal actions. It does not matter if he is a zombie or not. His papal status supersedes that."

Justice shook his head in the negative. "That argument is flawed," he said. "The law is clear in that a zombie brain is just as addled as one who has imbibed too much wine. Pope or no pope, Pius II is still a zombie with a zombie brain and, thus, should not be allowed to testify."

The Head Magistrate thought for a moment. "I will allow the pope emeritus to testify," he said. "But his testimony shall be limited only to any official papal actions he has performed as a pope, and I, as the trier of fact, shall give his testimony its proper weight, considering, though he is a pope, he is also a zombie."

After Pope Pius II was sworn in, he took his seat at the witness stand, and Feminera approached him.

"How many days has it been since your last confession?" he asked, sending the deputies and clerks into a silent tizzy.

"Now that is funny," Justice whispered to me. "The answer is forever."

"I am not here for a confession," Feminera said.

"Then why are you here in the confessional?" Pius II looked generally perplexed.

"Pope Pius, I am here to ask you some questions," Feminera continued.

"You don't have one of those meaning-of-life questions, do you?" Pius II said, causing the clerks to bury their heads deeper into their desks, and even the Head Magistrate cracked a smile. "Because that is something," he said, pointing skyward, "only a higher power can answer."

"I am here to ask you about something you did as pope," she said.

"Why didn't you say so in the first place?" Pius II said. "Go on, get to it, I have a lot to do today."

"In 1469, you were being held captive by Pope Paul II in Rome, yes?" Pius II nodded. "That is true."

Feminera pointed first at her table then at me. "And these two vampires seated at each counsel table are the ones that freed you?"

Pius peered at each counsel table. "Not the demon, but the other gentleman, yes. And right, the lady sitting next to the dead body. They were a lovely couple. I was very happy to marry them."

"Marry us?" I said. "You did no such thing. We freed you from Pope Paul II was all we did!"

Justice glared at me as the Head Magistrate and the entire courtroom all looked at me. "Sorry," I said. "Carry on."

Feminera rolled her eyes. "So, you say you married them?"

"Yes, I did. Right outside the church where I was held captive," Pius II said. "Gave them a papal dispensation for Isabella and Ferdinand, and right after that the nice vampire lady gave me a papal certificate of her marriage to the vampire over there, and I signed that too."

As Pius II spoke, Feminera had retreated to her table, picked up a document, and shown it to Justice. His eyes nearly bulged out of his head, and steam was definitely coming out of his ears. "What is it?" I hissed at him.

"You *are* married to her, you idiot," Justice retorted.

What? How could that be possible?

Feminera handed the document to the Head Magistrate, who nodded and handed it back to her. "Is this the papal certificate of marriage you did for them?" she asked.

Pius II took the certificate from her and looked it over. "Yes, yes, it is," he said.

Feminera handed the certificate to the clerk. "Your Honor, we move the certificate of marriage into evidence."

"Objections?" the Head Magistrate asked, looking at Justice.

Justice stood. "Your Honor, this certificate was issued when Pope Pius II was a zombie. He had no idea what he was signing. She got the certificate by guile, subterfuge, and deceit."

The Head Magistrate looked back at Justice. "He sounded pretty clear as to what he just testified about. One hundred plus years later, his zombie brain still knows he married them. The only one that doesn't seem to be aware he is married is your client, and he *is* married to her. Look, his signature is right there plain as day. As to guile, subterfuge, and deceit, all your client had to do was read the documents he carried with him all the way back to Spain from Rome. I find they were married, and thus, the divorce papers she filed this morning are valid, and I find her grounds for divorce for abandonment to be valid and will reserve my ruling on her just compensation until later on in the hearing. Now, let's get on with this travesty and get to child custody. "

The Zombie Pope left the stand and exited the courtroom, flinging holy water all the way. I could have used a few prayers. Married to Bloodsucker Number One? And now I was divorced. This place was utter madness. I had protested to Justice that I never signed it, but he waved at me to be quiet as Feminera stood to call her next witness.

"We call Sirio Sinestra to the stand," Feminera said.

After placing my hand on the perjury globe and swearing to tell the truth, I looked out into the courtroom. Justice seemed a million miles away, but not so Feminera. She clomped up to the witness stand and could barely contain her mirth as she juggled some documents. She had handed Justice identical copies of the same documents. He read with lightning speed, and all color drained from his face. He dropped what she had handed him to the table and sat back in his seat, clearly defeated. What was Feminera holding?

"You are Sirio Sinestra," she said.

"Yes," I answered. "Of course I am. You know who I am. Why are you asking me that?"

The Head Magistrate looked down from the bench. "Just answer her questions," he admonished me.

Feminera handed me a piece of parchment. Justice sat with his head in his hands, waiting for the inevitable. "Do you recognize what I am showing you?"

"It's a piece of parchment."

Feminera grimaced. "Can you read the top line of this document, and tell the court what it is?"

"I will do my best," I said. "Wherefore, the party to the first part and the party to the second part, hereinafter, forevermore, hereby avow, swear, promise, and elucidate . . ." I paused to catch my breath. Who could read this stuff without passing out from lack of air?

Feminera looked to the Head Magistrate. "Your Honor, the witness is being unresponsive."

The Head Magistrate's black eyes bored into my own, the fierceness of his gaze threatening to burst out the back of my skull with the intensity. "Mr. Sinestra," he said, "if you do not answer her questions, I will find you in contempt."

Feminera smiled. "Again, Mr. Sinestra, what is this document I am showing you?"

"Hey, I am doing the best I can up here," I said. "In the midst of this legal gibberish, I see my name, that bitch's name, and a whole bunch of seven-syllable words, so this is going to take a while."

Feminera turned to the Head Magistrate. "Will Your Honor take judicial notice that this is an approved certificate of adoption from the Immortal Divorce Court files?"

The Head Magistrate reviewed it quickly. "The Court takes such notice," he replied. "Speed reader here, really limited reader over there."

Feminera looked me in the eye. "And will the court take notice that this certificate of adoption proclaims the adoptive parents of Martin the Navigator are my client and this man here on the stand, Sirio Sinestra."

The Head Magistrate nodded. "It is so noted."

I looked up at him, and felt my face grow warm as my anger grew. "That is not true!" I exclaimed. "I never signed an adoption certificate."

Feminera thrust the certificate in my face. "Apparently you did, Mr. Sinestra."

"I think not," I said. "That dead bit of rubbish over there and that trollop are liars, thieves, and ingrates." I snatched the paper out of her hand and ripped it into pieces, tossing them in the air and taking pleasure in how they slowly fluttered to the floor. "Rubbish, I tell you."

The Head Magistrate whirled around in his seat. "I am warning you, Mr. Sinestra," he said. "This is a court of law, and you will maintain your decorum."

"He has destroyed evidence, Your Honor," Feminera wailed. "Hold him in contempt."

Justice leaped from his seat. "Your Honor, the witness apologizes. Another copy is easily fetched from the court files. I will have a word with my client. And quite obviously, we question the authenticity of the signature. Perhaps a break is in order?"

While Justice was talking, the Head Magistrate had his head down and was slowly shaking it back and forth. I saw him take a deep breath. Surely he was going to throw out this ridiculous case, and those fake documents.

"Listen to me, Justice," he commanded. "Your client has one more chance. The next wrong statement or action will be his last in this courtroom. Understood?"

"Yes, sir," Justice replied.

I sat silently picking at my fingernails until I realized Justice, the Head Magistrate, and the entire courtroom were looking at me. "Oh, right," I said. "Yes, sir."

"Court is adjourned for fifteen minutes," the Head Magistrate said.

"All rise," the deputy boomed. With a sidelong glance at me, the Head Magistrate left the courtroom. I walked back to Justice at the counsel table, and we left the courtroom in silence.

"Get in here," Justice screamed, pulling me down a side hallway and into a room reserved for litigants and their attorneys. "Are you absolutely mad?"

"I was a little miffed in there, but I am starting to feel better, thank you," I replied.

"You need to get a firm grip on yourself, or you will find yourself in contempt, and the Head Magistrate will leave you without a single gold coin to your name," Justice snapped.

"This is sheer lunacy," I said.

"Are you sure you never signed those documents?"

Then it hit me with twice the force of the Bogeyman, and I dropped into a chair. "Um, actually I think I did."

"You what?"

"Back when I was in the royal court of Isabella, that devious bloodsucker had me sign all sorts of documents as part of my royal duties," I said, dropping my head into my hands. "Well, I can always deny it is my signature, because, I mean, I didn't read anything I signed because no one does that! That is kind of the same thing, right, Justice?"

"You just remembered it is your signature, so trust me, the perjury globe will know you are lying, and then you will be frying!" Justice exclaimed. "That explains why nothing happened just now. You were not lying. You really had no idea that you signed those papers. But now you are doomed."

"What is our plan?"

Justice shook his head. "I am afraid you are just going to have to tell the truth and throw yourself on the mercy of the court." A bell tolled deeply from some hidden recess, signaling it was time to return to the courtroom.

"If you are a religious man," Justice said, "I would suggest you start praying."

When we entered the courtroom, I saw a vaguely familiar woman sitting next to Bloodsucker Number One. Who was she? I wondered, racking my brain for the answer. Feminera stood as court came back in session. "Your Honor," she said, "if I may call a witness out of order, I think we can shorten this hearing and satisfy our burden of proving Sirio Sinestra signed these documents."

Justice expertly suppressed his smirk. "No objection."

"We call Jane Dough," Feminera said.

Justice leaned over. "Who is this?"

I scratched my head. "I think she was one of Isabella's attendants. But I never knew she was an immortal."

Justice peered at her. "She is definitely an immortal, though for the life of me, I am not sure which kind. Odd. But that is probably not a big concern. Now, as to what she actually says, that is something else entirely."

After Dough was sworn in, Feminera asked her, "What is your lineage?"

Jane Dough was a frail-looking creature with wispy blonde hair, and a frame so thin it looked like a stiff breeze would break her in two. "My father and mother both died when I was very young, so I never got a chance to really know them, my family, or my true lineage."

"How sad," I whispered to Justice. "What a poor helpless creature!"

"Women are never poor and helpless," he hissed back.

"How did you come to be in the court of Queen Isabella?" Feminera queried Miss Dough.

"To further my education," Dough said. "I posed as a servant to get source information for my doctoral thesis on mortal humanity at Oxford. I was tired of dressing as a boy—most of whom were a dumb lot—so with my professor's permission, I traveled to Spain for an independent study. And I realized, what better place was there to learn about mortal humanity than in the royal courts? I mean, you could just watch play after play about royals, because they are always the ones making such a muck of their lives. I thought it would be the best experience to just observe everything."

"Everything?" asked Feminera.

"To be honest things were kind of boring with Isabella, so I focused on finding a man. That is until the two vampires showed up," she said. "Sirio over there was a nice fellow, but there are rocks with more common sense."

I sat up in my chair. "Did she say rocks?" Justice shushed me as Dough kept talking. I had more common sense than a rock!

"And, well, your client gives females a bad name be they immortal or human. So manipulative! He signed anything she gave him. He was like a dog. Until the day—" She stopped. "Even a dog knows if it has been tripped over or kicked. He was kicked, but good."

"But did he sign the marriage certificate and adoption papers?"

Jane Dough looked up at me and shook her head sadly. "Yes, yes, he did. I saw him sign them with nary a care in the world. He never even gave them a second glance."

"No more questions, Your Honor," said Feminera.

The Head Magistrate looked over at Justice, who was deep in thought as to how to get me out of this mess. I thought I could see a fire starting on top of his head. What could Justice do? I *had* signed those papers. "Questions, Mr. Justice?" the Head Magistrate asked.

"Miss Dough," Justice said, peering at her over his spectacles. He stood and walked over in front of Bloodsucker Number One. He pointed at her and turned back to the witness stand. "You said she was manipulative?"

Jane Dough nodded. "I did, indeed."

Justice looked at Bloodsucker Number One, who remained impassive. I was amazed at how much in control she was of her emotions, but then I remembered, she was certainly no stranger to this accursed venue. I also remembered she had no emotions, or heart, or any sense of decency, but I digress. Justice turned back to Miss Dough. "When these two vampires came back from Rome, was the marriage certificate in her possession?"

"Yes, it was," Jane Dough answered. "But the weird thing was she never said anything to anybody about it. And, well, your client, he was clueless as usual." I shook my head at her insult and gave her my best nasty look of death. I looked over at Bloodsucker Number One, who did a poor job of containing her smirk. Why didn't *she* get admonished?

Justice had paused at that answer. "So, she did not act married to my client?"

"No."

"And there was no ceremony of any kind?"

"No."

Justice turned and walked back to our table. "What did she do with the marriage certificate, then?"

Dough thought for a moment. "She kept it with the rest of her secret papers. I guess now we know why."

Feminera shot to her feet. "Objection, move to strike the witness's last answer. Nonresponsive."

The Head Magistrate nodded to the clerk. "Strike her last sentence from the record."

Justice rolled his eyes. "You testified that my client signed the adoption papers of Martin the Navigator, correct?"

"Yes, I did," Dough answered.

Justice got up and again walked over to stand directly in front of Bloodsucker Number One and Martin. He peered at Martin for a second, and the unmistakable hint of a smile crossed Justice's face. I tried to look at Martin, but my view was blocked by Feminera and Bloodsucker Number One. Was Martin even breathing over there?

Justice pointed first at Martin, then at Bloodsucker Number One. "Did my client sign the adoption papers before or after this man and this vampire began having carnal relations?"

Feminera popped up from her seat, an angry redheaded cyclone spitting words and fury. "Objection, objection," she screamed. "Irrelevant! Immaterial! Inconsequential! This witness *cannot* know that!"

For the first time all afternoon, the Head Magistrate appeared to be enjoying himself. "Overruled," he said. He turned to Jane Dough. "You can answer the question, if you know."

"I do know the answer," Miss Dough said. "They absolutely were sleeping together *before* Mr. Sinestra signed the certificate of adoption."

Justice looked at Bloodsucker Number One. "So, she was effectively having relations with her son before he became her son?"

"Objection," Feminera howled.

"I withdraw the question, Your Honor," Justice said with a wink back to me. "Your Honor, I have no more questions for Miss Dough, but I would like to be heard on the validity of the adoption and the marriage."

The Head Magistrate nodded his head. "Miss Dough, you may step down from the witness stand if there are no more questions," he said, looking at Feminera, who shook her head. "May I ask, Miss Dough, what you are doing now?" he continued.

Dough blushed. "Nothing, sir. I have gone as far as immortal education can take me. My doctoral degree in mortal humanities was complete fifty years ago. I am searching for the next path."

The Head Magistrate beckoned his clerk. "As a result of your immortal lineage," he said, "you are eligible for law school. Have you ever considered that? I would be more than happy to sponsor you."

"I could not afford the fee," she replied.

The Head Magistrate pursed his lips in thought, and then his face brightened up as much as it could, all dour things considered. "I will order witness fees payable to you by Feminera's client over there, which will give you the entrance fees," he said. "And you can work as a clerk for me for the rest of it."

Bloodsucker Number One hit Feminera on the arm, clearly outraged that she had to pay something in Immortal Divorce Court. Did the Head Magistrate not know that she was the victim here? Feminera glared her into silence, reading that now was certainly not the time to press her luck and ruin the sort of happy mood of the Head Magistrate. "Don't even think of not paying it," she said to Bloodsucker Number One, probably a bit louder than she intended. "I am telling you, that would be your undoing."

Jane Dough was now a fine shade of crimson. "Your Honor," she said, bowing low. "Your generous offer is a dream come true. I will not disappoint you."

"Go with my clerk. He will get the process started," said the Head Magistrate. He then turned to address the courtroom. "I know legal talent when I see it. That girl is as sharp as a deputy's sword and can probably make one hell of a point with said sharpness. I may have just found my replacement, huh? All right then, Justice, the argument is yours."

Justice stood and spread his arms wide. "Your Honor," he said, "a clearer case of fraud has never been presented in this courtroom. The marriage was a sham. A plot done in secret so that the woman over there could bring this claim against my client years later for no other purpose than to reap an ill-gotten gain."

"Hold on, Justice," said the Head Magistrate. "I have already ruled the marriage was legitimate. And these two people are already divorced as of this morning. Your client's time for contesting the marriage ended when they got divorced. The burden was on him to bring a fraud claim when they were actually married. And with the testimony from the Zombie Pope earlier, all he had to do was read the certificate.

A certificate that he carried himself from Rome all the way back to Spain. He had over a hundred years to figure it out, for goodness' sake!"

"But, Your Honor!" Justice protested.

"But nothing," the Head Magistrate growled. "I will hear you on the adoption in a moment. Clerk, bring me Mr. Sinestra's personal inventory."

I was stunned at the turn of events. "What is happening?" I said to Justice. "What is my personal inventory?"

Justice shook his head sadly. "You are about to become a good bit poorer, my friend."

The clerk handed the Head Magistrate a piece of parchment. "Well, this will be easy," the Head Magistrate said. "Mr. Sinestra, there is the matter of my fee. Ten gold coins for that." That same accursed rainbow shot from his gavel and struck my money pouch.

"What is this?" I cried, jumping to my feet. "You can't take my gold."

The Head Magistrate banged his gavel, and gold chains shot from the floor next to me, encircled my arms and legs, and pulled me back into my chair. "Thank you for taking your seat, Mr. Sinestra. I am just getting started. I grant eternal possession of your house in Barcelona to her, Mr. Sinestra. That means forever, Mr. Sinestra." He peered at the paper for a moment. "Oh," he said. "Who knew? A vampire that saves. Hmm. I also grant her the three hundred gold coins you had buried in the well in that house. Nothing is secret from Immortal Divorce Court, Mr. Sinestra. Tut-tut."

I watched in absolute horror as a rainbow formed over Bloodsucker Number One and rained down a shower of gold. My gold! She shrieked in delight as the coins cascaded on the table, rolled off her clutching hands, and pelted the inert Martin in the face. I struggled against the chains that bound me, but they were clearly a match for any immortal. I stopped struggling as Bloodsucker Number One's golden shower ended, yet I was the one that just got pissed on, and that just made me pissed off! I vowed that I would have my revenge, but this nightmare was not quite over.

"Mr. Justice," the Head Magistrate said. "I will hear you on the adoption issue."

Justice rose to his feet and kicked a gold coin out of his path. He exhaled slowly and was instantly composed. I wish I could have said the same about myself, but my anger was seething to a nearly uncontrollable breaking point. Contempt be damned, I thought.

"Your Honor," Justice said, "*fraud* is the word of the day." He shuffled through my gold to stand in front of Martin and Bloodsucker Number One. "They were having relations before my client signed the adoption certificate. It was a scam, a fraud, a devious plan to take money from my client."

Feminera rose slowly. "Your Honor," she said, "you can adopt anyone you want. There are no constraints on age, gender, race, or carnal relations. Sinestra could have actually read the adoption certificate he signed and contested it. He did not. Or he could have hired legal counsel way back when to contest it. He did not. And clearly Martin is in need of support."

The Head Magistrate nodded. "You know that she is correct, Justice. This adoption is valid."

"What?" I screamed. "How is *that* bloody possible?"

The Head Magistrate turned his steely gaze at me and raised his gavel. "I have had enough of you, Mr. Sinestra."

"Wait, Your Honor," Justice cried. "My client does not have to support Martin for he is dead!"

Bloodsucker Number One collapsed in a well-practiced fit of hysterics. "My son, my son," she wailed, throwing herself on Martin's lifeless corpse. "Oh, my poor son, you were taken too soon!"

"Oh, please!" I yelled. "Will someone shut that woman up?"

In the commotion, the clerk had scuttled over to Martin and nodded to the Head Magistrate, confirming that Martin the Navigator had indeed dearly departed the courtroom. "I am going to shut you up, Mr. Sinestra," the Head Magistrate screamed. "I find you in arrears!"

"I am a rear?" I exclaimed. "Well, you, Your Honor, are a gigantic ass!"

I only understood what transpired next after I saw Harvis again, and he filled me in on the details. After I left Harvis's farm via crystal, Garlic had howled once in her frustration, but then apparently scented me. She did not leave the farm but scoured the premises with her nose to the ground, looking for what, Harvis did not know. A few days later Harvis was doing some work in the barn, and Garlic snuffled in, her nose leading her to the crystal that I had dropped. She gulped it down and disappeared. "Curses," Harvis had exclaimed. "That cannot be good."

There was an audible pop in the courtroom as the Head Magistrate's gavel struck the bench, and I found myself gagged. Garlic leaped up on Justice's table and gnawed the gag off me. The deputies descended to try and catch her and received some lacerations for their troubles. The Head Magistrate struck his gavel again, and tiny chains came up from the floor, threatening to entrap the Maltese, but a few well-aimed barks disintegrated the chains, and she was in no danger. She bounded to and fro and could not figure out how to free me without injuring me. The court guard entered the courtroom, and Garlic's bark was of no use against their riot shields, which merely absorbed the bark's energy with no consequences. Garlic found herself backed into the corner and leaped to the Head Magistrate's bench.

"Garlic, stand down," I called.

Head Magistrate Gulth Scorn whirled to look at the vampire Maltese that had dared take up residence on his desk, then his dark, soulless eyes found me. "Mr. Sinestra, I find both you and your dog in contempt. I sentence you both to fifty years."

Garlic snarled at him and squatted on his desk. "No!" I screamed. "Garlic, no."

Garlic proceeded to let the Head Magistrate know what she thought of his order. He grimaced at the steaming Maltese excrement on his desk. We had just enraged the Great Decider, and the Breaker of the Bold was now going to break us! "Make it one hundred years," Scorn said. "Case dismissed. Now get these ingrates out of my sight!"

CHAPTER 5

The doors of my jail cell clanged shut, and the blindfold that covered my eyes and the chains that bound me instantly disappeared. I could see the faint shadows of the faerie jailers walking away as my eyes adjusted to my dark and dank surroundings. The faeries were still talking and laughing about what Garlic had done on the Head Magistrate's bench. I was apparently a minor celebrity of sorts in this wretched place.

I was in a holding cell in the back of the IDC courthouse. One very small window let in the tiniest bit of sound and light, and my ears could pick up the faint bark of dogs, which signaled the kennel where Garlic had been taken. The walls of my cell were many feet thick, and the door was reinforced with steel and demon magic, escape proof even for the most powerful immortal being. A wooden bucket was my toilet, and it came complete with the petrified remnants of the previous occupant. Justice said he would try to get me moved somewhere tropical and pleasant to serve out my sentence. "Do you good to get out of this part of the world," he had said. He had encouraged me to serve my time and then go see Hedley Edrick. "Get a serious education," Justice said. I, however, was encouraged by the pleasant thought of educating my fists and fangs on Bloodsucker Number One, the Head Magistrate, and yes, even Justice.

There was a great commotion in the courtyard outside my cell. I couldn't see what the ruckus was about no matter what angle I peered from. Then an explosion rocked the courthouse, causing a slight tremor to vibrate through the thick walls. A second explosion soon followed, but this one was closer. Then a third blast caused dust particles to drift down from the ceiling and the very floor to visibly shake and shimmy. I huddled in the corner opposite the wall that faced the courtyard. It sounded like all Hell was breaking loose, and since it was only a short distance away, that was a distinct possibility.

Right before my cell wall exploded into dust, I heard a familiar bark and then, bounding through the hail of dust and stones, came Garlic right into my arms. She licked my face and yelped happily. "Good girl," I said, standing with Garlic still in my arms. "I missed you too!" And the truth is, I really had. We stepped out into the welcoming sunlight and right into the custody of an entire legion of well-armed deputies, spears at the ready.

"Sirio Sinestra," the chief deputy said, pointing his spear at my throat, which elicited a growl from both me and Garlic, "you are hereby under arrest."

"For what?" I said calmly.

"Escaping your jail cell," he replied.

I looked at him in disbelief. "Escape? Now how is that bloody possible? From what cell? My cell has no walls. What did you want me to do, sit in the dust and wait for you?"

"Silence," he commanded sternly.

I motioned to the jail cell. "This place is unsafe, what with those poor excuses for walls. How is a prisoner supposed to feel safe? Place ought to be condemned. I demand to see—" Before I could utter Justice's name, I found myself bound and gagged once again. They had the sense to leave Garlic with me as we made our way to the Head Magistrate's courtroom.

Justice was waiting for me with a mixture of amusement and trepidation on his face. He held a hand out to pet Garlic and took it back quickly when she snarled. "Okay, then," he said. "A fine mess you've got yourself into."

"Mmff," I said through my gag, and shrugged my shoulders. I looked at the bench and saw the Head Magistrate was already seated. He stared first at me, then at Garlic, disapprovingly.

He waved his hand, and my gag and chains disappeared, and I took a seat next to Justice. Garlic sat happily at my feet, her eyes trained on the Head Magistrate. She showed just enough of her teeth that it looked like she was smiling. The Head Magistrate was not amused.

He cleared his throat. "Sirio Sinestra, you are charged with the unprecedented destruction of the courthouse jail and escape from same."

"Your Honor." Justice stood. "If I may."

The Head Magistrate sighed. "Justice, you have just about used up all the good will that you have with the court."

Justice nodded. "I am aware of that, Your Honor. But Mr. Sinestra is innocent. He had no control over this dog destroying the jail. She is no ordinary dog, as you yourself have seen. She is a vampire and entirely sentient."

"Hold it right there, Justice," said the Head Magistrate. "You would have this Immortal Divorce Court believe that Mr. Sinestra did not train this dog to help him escape?"

"Correct, Your Honor."

"And that she is a vampire Maltese?"

"Yes, Your Honor," Justice replied. Garlic had grown bored with the proceedings and lay down at my feet for a nap. I nudged her with my foot, and her eyes flicked open. She turned her head away from the Head Magistrate, winked at me, then tucked her head under her body. Yep, I was going to take the fall for this, all right, I thought.

"All right, Mr. Justice," the Head Magistrate said. "Assuming I buy your argument, how do we prove her sentience? Do we put her on trial? Or do we just execute her?" Garlic's eyes flickered open at the word *execute*, and I saw her body slowly sliding into position to escape if need be.

"Simple, Your Honor," Justice said. "We do not have to even get to that point. As the only known vampire Maltese in existence, Garlic qualifies as an endangered species and cannot by law be harmed in any fashion."

"Very clever," said the Head Magistrate.

"Thank you, sir," Justice said. "I thought as much." Garlic was now visibly relaxed and rolled over onto her back and scratched it against the floor. Milking it, that one was, I thought.

"So, I can't kill the mutt, and your client is innocent of all charges. Is that what you want me to rule?" said the Head Magistrate.

"Yes, sir."

"Frankly I would like to execute the whole lot of you, that blasted vampire Maltese especially," the Head Magistrate said. "Clearly, Justice, you win on the endangered species argument. But I saw the look in her eyes before she did her business on my bench. She meant to do it. Of course, I can't prove that. So, I am going to do the next best thing—for me. Sinestra, as the closest thing to an owner that canine calamity has, is responsible for the destruction of this courthouse. So, the two of them will be serving the remainder of his sentence in the tenth level of Hell. Together."

I gulped, remembering Justice's words about that particular place. If it was bad for a demon, how could a vampire survive? He turned to me and smiled. "Well, I did say I would get you somewhere tropical."

Garlic and I stayed in yet another holding cell for a few days while the Head Magistrate worked out my transfer to Hell. To his credit, Justice seemed to be working overly hard to delay the transfer for some reason. What was the big deal? Like it mattered if I went there now or next week. I ended up staying the weekend in the holding cell with Garlic. The faeries brought us both some fairly tasty wine, a local Greek vintage with delicious minerality, and they seemed to be treating us with a good deal more respect. Or was it pity?

Justice came by to bid us adieu. "I bought you as much time as I could," he said. "You are just going to have to figure this one out on your own."

I did not know whether I should thank him for the extra few days of life before I faced certain incineration. I tried to ask him how to survive the tenth level of Hell, but he brushed me off. "Don't worry about it," he said, and winked at me. "You will be fine. I'll see you in about a hundred years. Stay out of trouble."

Trouble? It was going to be very hard to get into trouble as a pile of ash. The faerie guard came in full riot gear, complete with masks over their faces. I reached down and scooped up Garlic for what would be a very short walk. The guards chained my feet and hands together to eliminate any possibility of escape. I hoped there would be an opportunity for Garlic to save herself, but she just lay in my arms passive and limp as could be.

The guards marched us out of the courthouse and onto the streets, which were completely deserted. It seemed court was not in session while they attended to the matter of repairs. If the Head Magistrate had not given all my gold to Bloodsucker Number One, what remained surely would have been forfeit for the repair bill. We went out the back gate of the village, and there before me lay the Gates of Hell. The pungent odor of sulfur assaulted my nostrils, and Garlic burrowed even deeper into my arms. I saw the guards adjusting their masks and realized their garb was for this literally accursed place and not for me. I could sense they were uneasy, and clearly those who accompanied me had drawn the short straws of guard detail. The gates had been built with rows and rows of disembodied skulls all stacked one upon another, and they screamed a welcoming chorus of doom and despair as the gates slowly creaked open.

Clouds of sulfur and brimstone billowed at us, and without our vampire constitutions, Garlic and I would have been bent over in a choking heap. As it was, it was all I could do to keep walking. Garlic let out an audible whine and was clearly second-guessing her loyalty to me. The gates clanged shut behind us, and thankfully the clouds of sulfur passed, and the wailing of the lost souls stopped. Before me lay a desolate landscape, pockmarked with pools of fire and adorned with piles of rotting carrion. A path wide enough to walk single file along a spit of granite led us deeper into Hell. The leader of the guards motioned for me to lead the way. I took my place in front of the line and began my descent.

Suddenly, a strange humanoid creature whose very innards adorned his skin like living, breathing tattoos, jumped out from behind a boulder, barring our way. He screamed unintelligibly and shook his arms but made no move to attack. Garlic did not move in my arms, and the guards stood stoically behind me, leaving me to deal with this loathsome creature. He seemed quite perturbed that he got no reaction from us.

"I am the Bogeyman," he yelled. "I have come to take your souls."

I shrugged. "You are most assuredly *not* the Bogeyman," I said. "My dog powdered him into bits last week."

The creature was now definitely confused. He stood on his toes, and spread his arms wide. "I am a vampire," he said. "I will suck the blood from your body and crush your soul."

I sighed. "I say, good chap," I said, "I do not know what you are, but you are most assuredly not a vampire."

"How do you know?" The creature looked as befuddled as was possible with a brain where his face should be.

"Because I *am* an actual vampire," I replied. "My parents are vampires. And their parents are vampires. And you, sir, are no vampire."

"Well, I could be one."

I sighed again. "No, you could not, and you are not one," I said, growing more irritated with the heat and the imbecile in front of me. "Get your story straight. Yes, we drink blood, and love an exceedingly rare steak, but we do not and cannot crush a soul. Good heavens, what did they do, put your ass where your brain should be?"

The creature peered through an eyeball located where his armpit should have been, and saw the Immortal Divorce Court guards for apparently the first time. "Oh, the IDC," he said. "My mistake. Carry on." He waved what looked to be an arm. "You may pass. Sorry about that. You never even saw me, all right?" He hurried behind the boulder and disappeared.

With every step, the air grew hotter and hotter, and with no breeze to speak of, sweat dripped off my brow and evaporated with a small hiss when it struck the parched earth. Garlic's head was now firmly tucked into my armpit. Justice had told me this area where we now walked was called Limbo, and I could see yet another gate in front of me that marked the entrance to the first level of Hell. The gate was an amorphous blob of black tar, and every once in a while I could see a disembodied limb jut out in a failed attempt at escape. The guards stopped a good fifty paces before the gate and saluted me. They removed my chains and stood behind me as I turned to face the gate, which did not open so much as create a passageway through the black tar. I took a deep breath, knowing it was my last that would not stink of sulfur, and walked onward to the gate and passed through. Welcome to Hell.

For an instant, in a landscape dotted with flaming pools of acid and rivers of black sludge, I saw nothing but the distorted faces of countless tortured souls and heard nothing but the painful wails that emanated from their parched lips as they tried to escape the pursuit of demons brandishing all manner of fiendish weapons. Then, everything just changed, and I mean changed! Gone were the demons and the tortured souls. Gone too were the flaming pools of acid and the rivers of black sludge. I stood now on a grassy hill high above the lushest, greenest valley I had ever seen. A rainbow painted the blue sky with a myriad of vibrant colors, and down in the valley I could see what looked to be unicorns cavorting in a meadow. In the distance at the very end of the valley, I could barely make out the spires of a great castle made of sparkly stones that reflected back to my shocked eyes all the colors of the rainbow above.

Had I just been incinerated, and was this actually Heaven, if such a fair place existed? Garlic popped her head up and yelped happily. She did not care where we were as long as the fire and stink of the dead was gone. I set her down, and I pinched my arm, reassured to feel my skin. Garlic reassured herself by peeing on a bush.

I made my way down a path and into the valley. As I drew nearer to the meadow, the unicorns scented my maleness and retreated to a far corner, eying me with suspicion. It was like I was toxic to them. Their leader pawed the ground with her front hoof, and the others fell in behind her. I was pretty far removed from virginal and pristine at this point in my life. Did unicorns stampede? I was betting those hooves could do some serious damage. Not needing to take a chance on that happening, I gave them an even wider berth.

We walked by fields bursting with vegetables and gardens of flowers that painted a rainbow on the warm earth. Then, out of a nearby farmhouse came a servant girl dressed in a simple work dress and sunbonnet. Tresses of greenish-black hair fell over her deliciously bare shoulders. Her dress reached just past her knees, and she walked barefoot into the flower garden. Ignoring me, she flitted like a butterfly among the flowers, caressing them gently. The flowers fairly strained at their roots to feel her touch, and as she sang softly to them, her voice clear and enchanting, I strangely felt the same way.

"Excuse me, miss," I called. "Can you tell me where I am?"

She turned and walked toward me. Her eyes were as blue as the sky above and her lips as red as the reddest rose in her garden. She was, I decided, absolutely the most beautiful gardener I had ever seen. Let me correct that. She was absolutely the most beautiful woman I had ever seen—a true goddess. If I were a werewolf, I would have howled. But it was more than just her looks that made me feel attracted to her. From the soft fullness of her face to the rise of her bountiful breasts to the mesmerizing curve of her hips, she exuded a pure, raw fertility that was making my head spin. Garlic sat down next to me and wagged her tail happily. She clearly sensed no danger from this girl.

"You are in Hell," she said sweetly. Her eyes took in Garlic, who was now wagging her tail quite uncontrollably. The gorgeous gardener dropped to her knees and held out her hand to Garlic. "Who is a cute puppy?" she said, causing Garlic to drop on her back and offer up her belly. The girl's voice was so warm and inviting, and the perfume that I could now smell on her was so intoxicating that for a second I considered doing the very same thing.

"But this can't be Hell," I said. "Just a second ago, I saw the real Hell, and then it just changed to this."

The gardener rose to her feet and fixed her eyes upon me, sending chills down my spine. "It is very much Hell," she said. "It is just under new management right now."

I clapped my hand to my head, silently praising Justice for his guile. "Oh, that is right," I exclaimed. "Persephone got Hell half-time in her divorce settlement with the Dark Lord! This amazing place is her doing! I bet that incredible castle over there is hers. Well, Hell has never looked better," I said. "I could stay here forever, you know. By the way, what is your name?"

"You can call me Honey, I am Persephone's gardener," she replied. "And you are very much an immortal, are you not?"

"Sirio Sinestra at your service." I did a little mock bow. "How did you know that?"

She smiled, and for a moment it seemed the sun was shining just a little bit brighter. "Well, first off, all the damned mortal souls are now in Limbo, so you can only be an immortal." She thought for a moment. "Wait a second," she said. "Now, the only immortals I ever see in here come from Immortal Divorce Court to serve a sentence. Are you some kind of deadbeat, cheat, or child molester?"

A cool wind blew as her face now failed to hide her impending wrath. "I am nothing remotely like that," I said. I noticed an ominous black cloud forming above me, and heard a distant peal of thunder. I spoke quickly before a lightning strike accomplished what the tenth level of Hell had not yet managed to.

"Garlic, my dog, well, she is not just any ordinary animal," I sputtered. "Truth is I am not really sure what she is capable of, what she understands, and so on. She is a vampire Maltese. And she did her business on the Head Magistrate's bench, and for that he sentenced us both to one hundred years for contempt of court."

The black cloud literally vanished into the air as the girl burst out laughing. I was very much relieved, but not so much that I could not help but stare like a complete blithering idiot at the jiggling this caused. "Oh, that pompous fool," she cried. "That is superb. Well done, Garlic." Garlic was so excited by this attention that she put her paws on Honey's leg, stuck her nose beneath Honey's dress, and began licking her knee frantically. I swallowed and sighed, deeply jealous of my dog.

"Have you been to Immortal Divorce Court?" I asked when I recovered.

"Yes," Honey said, and frowned.

"Oh, right," I continued. "Did you have to testify at the trial of Persephone and Hades since you work for her?"

The moment was broken by a sharp yapping sound, and out of the farmhouse came running a three-headed Chihuahua. It was pure white and had pink bows adorning its three barking heads and little pink kerchiefs tied around each little neck. Garlic did not snarl or bark, but merely stood her ground as the other dog approached. "Russi is friendly," Honey said. And indeed, the two dogs rubbed noses and set off to chase each other around the garden.

"Are you hungry?" Honey asked.

"Actually," I said, "I am quite famished. It's been one hell of a day." As soon as those words were out of my mouth, we both burst out laughing, and her hand grazed my own for a second, causing my hunger to grow a little more. For her. I didn't remotely care anymore why she had been in Immortal Divorce Court. I followed her into the farmhouse, which was furnished very simply with homemade wooden furniture and benches. Fresh cut flowers were in vases all over the farmhouse, and it smelled like spring. I could see a simple bedroom with just a small bed. Honey lived a very Spartan life in comparison to the utter opulence I imagined that no doubt adorned the magnificent castle across the valley where the Queen of the Underworld resided.

Honey served me a magnificent lunch of nuts, cheese, fresh bread, and a special treat—blood oranges. But these were no ordinary blood oranges, for instead of juice, these contained real blood, which invigorated me and made me feel like myself again. I helped Honey clear the table and found myself standing ever so close to her by the washbasin.

Honey turned and fixed those incredible blue eyes upon me. She reached out a finger and traced a line from the hollow of my throat down to my heart and rested her hand on my chest. I shivered at her touch. "I am one with nature, and I can feel so much with just the touch of my hand," she said. I felt a lot with the touch of her hand too. I didn't care what kind of hot nature elf Honey was, because I just wanted to be one with her!

"What do you feel from me?" I stammered.

"Your heart is full of such an amazing capacity to love and be loved. You are a very special creature. That is a gift."

"What is your gift?" I said to her.

Honey moved her hand from my chest to around my neck and drew my lips to hers. She whispered softly right before we kissed. "I make things grow." Indeed, my heart and my loins were filled with unquenchable desire for her as she led me to the bedroom. She dropped her dress to the floor, and my eyes took in every incomparable curve of her naked body.

Honey undressed me slowly and gently, and I was momentarily dizzy from her intoxicating scent. Her lips found mine again, and I marveled at their softness as her hand found my hardness. She pulled me onto the bed and lay back, and the vampire in me pounced on her, my lips and tongue covering her breasts and stomach in kisses. I continued downward and found her to be aptly named, for her womanhood tasted as sweet as the sweetest honey.

"I want you inside of me, Sirio," she commanded.

Not one to disappoint a lady, I entered her, and we both gasped at the feeling. Time seemed to stop as I brought her to pleasure again and again, and we rolled on the bed from position to position until finally Honey mounted me. She was a sight to behold, and I nearly finished just then. But I wanted to please her, had to please her, needed to please her, and as she rocked back and forth, I could feel the hot wetness of her pleasure and knew I was succeeding. From far off I felt my own pleasure beginning to build, and it kept building and building until I let loose inside her with my whole body racked with the pleasure of this epic experience. I was shaking uncontrollably, and she leaned forward, and curled up on my chest, holding me close until finally I could breathe again.

"You have such raw emotion in your soul," Honey exclaimed. "You give so much of yourself. We must do that again."

Before I could stall, protest, or excuse myself to go outside to relieve myself and gain the relatively short time even a vampire needs between sessions of intercourse, I saw I was ready to do it again. And we did. Again and again and again, and yet again. Best contempt sentence ever, I mused.

Finally, we lay intertwined in the bed, a soft sheen of perspiration covering us both. Honey was a very satisfied girl, but she was not one to linger, and her practical gardener side soon took over. After a few moments, she rose from the bed and shrugged into her dress. "Get dressed, Sirio," she said. "I need you to help me in the gardens."

And so I passed my contempt sentence, working the gardens of Hell, supervised by Honey, while Garlic and Russi ran about, rolling in the sweet, green grass. Honey was a stern taskmaster when it came to the gardens, but the truth was, I threw myself into the work with a passion. It was good work, honest work, and it felt good to use my muscles as I weeded, hoed, baled, and harvested for Honey. Whatever she wanted me to do I did, and I was especially happy about all the hoeing. For Honey worked me hard in the fields and equally hard in her bedroom. There was no routine, no calendar she followed. It did not matter if it was light or dark, rainy or sunny, whether we were in the fields or in the farmhouse. She just came up to me and took me by the hand and led me to the bedroom. I was hers to command.

I do not know if months passed or years, but I do know I was happy. What man would not be happy with good honest work by day and fantastic pleasure by night? But one night Honey took me by the hand, and by then accustomed to our routine, I boldly reached to undo her dress, and she stopped me. "We need to talk," she said. "I have not been completely honest with you."

I could not imagine what she could say that would be so bad. She was probably falling in love with me. "What is it?" I asked.

Honey looked quite distressed. "Look," she said. "I was going to tell you. Really I was. It's just you gave me so much, fulfilled needs in me like I have never had fulfilled. You just give so much of yourself."

I was flattered but could tell from the look in her eyes that I was not going to like what she had to say. "What is it, Honey?" I said, putting a hand to her cheek.

"Blast you," she said. "My name is not Honey."

"I don't understand," I said. "I don't care what your name is. What does your name have to do with anything?"

She shook her head. "My name is Persephone."

"Oh," I said. "Wow, yeah, you are right, and that really does complicate things." I had been fornicating with a *real* goddess.

"More than you know," she said. "In two days, my ex-husband, Hades, gets back control of the Underworld. He has been locked up in that castle over yonder for the last six months."

I gulped. "He wouldn't happen to be able to see what goes on here?"

She nodded, "He sure can. And he is still just as jealous when I am involved as he was when we were married."

"He is going to kill me," I said.

She shook her head. "Simply killing you won't be good enough for him."

"Why is that?" I exclaimed.

She smiled coyly. "Because, sweet Sirio, for the last six months he has been imprisoned in a castle in a land that he controls and has watched you satisfy me in ways he never could—hour after hour, day after day, and month after month. Probably drove him pretty much insane. Well, I mean more insane, because Hades is positively bonkers, you know!" She put a hand to my cheek. "You were the best revenge sex ever."

"What am I going to do?" I asked. How could I avoid the wrath of the Lord of the Underworld?

"We are both going to have to leave," she said. "I am going to spend my usual six months with my mother. Your sentence is almost up. Time passes differently here than on earth, so I think you may only have a few years left of that contempt nonsense of Scorn's."

"How do we get out of here?"

She smiled at my anxiousness. "He cannot kill you if you are not in his domain," she said. "It's in our agreement. There is a doorway back to Earth you and Garlic can take, but the catch is it just randomly opens up to a location. Could be Paris, could be London, you follow?"

"Could be in a volcano, or an avalanche, or above a canyon, or in the middle of an ocean . . ."

She held my hand and looked me in the eyes, and I melted for her all over again. "It is better than the alternative," she said. "It gives you two a chance. And besides, Garlic would not like Russi when he gets his balls back. He is one angry and large three-headed hellhound."

The next day we walked out into the garden with Garlic nipping playfully at our heels. Persephone reached for my hand, and instead of being angry with her for lying to me, I took it. We had made love the previous night, of course, deeply, passionately, and oh, so completely, both giving of ourselves knowing it would be for the last time. Afterward, I thought I saw this incomparable goddess dab a tear from her eye.

We stopped before a stone archway that I had never noticed before, and Garlic immediately sensed something was amiss and barked at it anxiously. When I awoke that morning to Persephone sleeping on my chest, I had remembered that she and Bloodsucker Number One had something in common—Feminera. And according to Justice, Persephone had been quite an actress in the little performance that had successfully wrested half of Hell from Hades. Of course, that was not necessarily a bad thing, I mused. I looked around at the pristine gardens I would never see again and gazed deep into blue eyes I would never forget. So, if the stone archway was a gateway to the real tenth level of Hell or certain earthly death, even for a vampire, I certainly was going out in style.

Persephone smiled that dazzling smile of hers. "Goodbye, Sirio," she said. "I will never forget you or that amazing heart of yours."

I smiled back and nodded. "The feeling is mutual, my goddess."

Our lips met one last tantalizingly tortuous time, and then I scooped up Garlic, and without looking back at Persephone, I stepped through the archway.

CHAPTER 6

Complete and utter darkness, a great rush of air, and momentary weightlessness before the Earth's pull took hold and brought me back home. I splashed into warm water up to my knees and sank into sand so soft that it cushioned my fall. Garlic yelped and leaped from my arms onto a beach whose white sand fairly glowed in the light of the full moon beaming high above. She raced back and forth along the beach, playing tag with the rush of the surf. I inhaled the clean ocean air whose delicious salty smell brought me back to my days on Sa Dragonera. But judging by the warm water and palm trees, I was indeed somewhere tropical. I laughed out loud not sure if I owed my destination to Justice and not really caring where I was.

I walked onto the shore and joined Garlic, taking off my boots and emptying them of seawater. The sand felt cool on my feet, and I dug my toes deeper, feeling the solidness of the earth. With my vampire vision, my eyes quickly adjusted to the moonlight, and I could see just as well as in daylight. I detected a sea turtle far down the beach, and Garlic and I raced to kill our dinner.

After a delightful meal, Garlic and I found a small stream whose water tasted fresh and clean. If this was an island in the middle of uncharted territory, I knew I was lucky to find water and food to sustain us. Since Immortal Divorce Court had taken all my traveling crystals, we could be here for a very long time. I tossed the remnants of our dinner into the waves, and Garlic barked at the silver minnows that quickly scavenged our meal. I kept the turtle's shell to use as a bowl, and we bedded down in a lean-to of palm fronds and bamboo. The next day we would try to see just where we had landed, and if any human inhabitants were around. Since I was not sure if my contempt sentence had expired, I could not risk calling any attention to myself.

I awoke with the sunrise, and Garlic and I quickly set out north into the tropical jungle bordering the shore. Quickly, I found what looked to be an established path. A few minutes later, I came across a discarded ceramic bowl. Clearly, this land had been already besmirched by man. Moving quickly and cautiously we startled numerous rabbits and deer, but they were not our prey just yet. Soon, we came out on another shoreline and saw facing us a good-sized island that dwarfed our new home. In the distance, I could see the outline of a small sloop hugging the shore of the island, confirming we were not alone. I took the rest of the day to explore my little island, which was no more than three miles wide and fifteen miles long. I built a small shelter and fashioned a bed made from an old sailcloth I found discarded along the shore. The stream we had found earlier led to a freshwater spring just a short walk away.

Men had visited this island and would again. I began fashioning a small skiff from a hollowed out log but did not attend to this task with great diligence. I was not in any hurry to leave my island for the civilization that inhabited the island to the north.

One day in my explorations, I found a decapitated humanoid skeleton sitting up against a tree. His skull rested in his bony hands, and his sword was leaned neatly against the tree. He had not been dead long, but the elements and denizens of the island had combined to pick his bones clean. All that remained of him were his clothes, which were made out of the finest silks, and they had weathered the elements quite well. I looked down at my own ragged garments but could not bring myself to strip his corpse. His sword was an entirely different story, of course.

I spent my days practicing my father's art and worked all the rust off my father's teaching and the dead man's blade in no time. Garlic spent her days thinning the island's population of rabbits. The skiff had been seaworthy for a few weeks now, but I was not ready to leave the island. The deer were aplenty, the water was fresh, and aside from the occasional ship passing in the distance, there was no sign of man. I did not care if I ever saw another man again.

I awoke one night with a start, my senses telling me that something or someone was near. Garlic popped her head up, yawned, and went back to sleep. Clearly, she was not bothered, but I felt the need to check our perimeter. The moon was nearly full and beautiful, casting an ethereal light as I moved silently through the jungle toward the freshwater spring. It could have been a hint of orchids, but I knew it to be the flowery aroma of a woman.

I stopped and hid in the underbrush a few paces from the spring's clearing, then caught the barest flash of a buckle glinting in the moonlight. A woman was moving softly and carefully. She stopped suddenly, and I knew she was aware of my presence, and I knew she was some sort of immortal.

I stepped out into the clearing with my sword drawn but by my side. "I mean you no harm," I called in Spanish. I could see her a little more clearly in the moonlight now. She wore a black jacket, even in this tropical heat, and men's breeches tucked into boots. I could not see her face clearly as she wore a hat low over her face. Her sword was raised in fighting position, and her crouch was defensive. "I mean you no harm," I called again, this time in English. Then, I tried French, German, Dutch, Italian, and even Greek.

She spat in my direction. "Quite the world traveler, aren't you?" she replied in perfect Cockney English. "There is no boat moored offshore and no skiff beached. Did you follow me by crystal? Why are you here? What do you want?" She stepped forward, leading with her sword, and it was then I saw her lean, unusually muscular frame, and that, coupled with her plentiful blonde hair, green eyes, and attitude, made me face-to-face with a female werewolf, and a beautiful one at that.

"You ask a lot of pointed questions," I said. "Didn't that bitch of a mother of yours ever teach you how to be nice?"

She scowled in the moonlight, and a low growl emanated from her throat. "You will answer me now, vampire, or I will take your manhood and add it to my collection."

I laughed. "That will weigh you down mightily, my dear girl," I said. "But, if you are nice, it is just you and me on this beautiful and romantic island, and maybe you could find another use for it, hmm?"

She reached into her shirt and pulled out a necklace that indeed appeared to be made of dried phalluses. She held one of these up. "This is all that is left of the last man that tried to touch me," she said. "Speak now, you wretch, or this will be your fate."

I'd had just about enough of this insipid creature who was souring my relaxed tropical paradise, and her war trophy collection certainly had quashed my playful mood. "The only touch I'd like to give you is a good spanking to your bare bottom," I said. "You need to learn some manners, and who knows, you might even like it."

My witty banter was rewarded with a vicious thrust in the direction of my aforementioned manhood. I parried her blade easily and quickly realized she was all sound and fury with the blade. Her strength and ferocity certainly were more than a match for any mortal, and even most immortals. However, I had learned from the best and was thankful for my recent months of practice. But what I really noticed as I toyed with this howling mass of blonde hair was that Persephone's work in the garden and the bedroom had made my strength and stamina greater than I had ever experienced before.

She stopped, her chest heaving in exertion, and wiped the sweat from her brow. She looked at the moon, now nearly full, and inhaled deeply, growing just a little bit larger and a whole lot angrier. She let forth a deep primal howl and rushed at me with uncommon speed. To be honest, before my visit to Paradise, I mean Hell, I am not sure if I would have been able to evade her blow. But now I chopped down easily on the hilt of her sword, snapping it in two, and swept her legs out from under her, sending her to the ground. She somersaulted in midair and rolled effortlessly to her feet into a defensive crouch.

"Nice trick," I said. "Have you had enough?" I looked down and realized I was still holding my sword while this howler was weaponless. "Well, I guess this is not very gentlemanly," I said. "I seem to have the advantage here." I thrust my sword into the ground, sinking it into the soft island earth. "Are we done here?"

But the Howler was not done and leaped forward, not going for my sword as I expected, but directly at my manhood with a dagger she had plucked from her boot. The Howler was apparently obsessed with getting to my phallus, but not in the way I liked. I stepped to the side and caught her wrist and, using her momentum, flipped her to the ground and disarmed her in one motion. Her eyes went wide as she hit the ground heavily, unable to brace her fall. Not letting her wrist go, I ratcheted up the tension, until I could see the pain in her face, and placed a boot on her throat.

"Listen to me," I said. "I do not want to hurt you. I do not want to kill you. I do not want to take you." I looked down at a face that was much prettier now that the owner was not trying to make me a gelding. "I want you to tell me just where on earth I am. If I let you up, do we have a truce?" I could see her eyes widen when I admitted that I did not know where I was. She nodded as Garlic scampered into the clearing and sat down at my feet, ignoring the Howler. "Oh, did you have a nice nap, Garlic," I admonished. "I could have been dead or worse yet, singing a few too many octaves higher!"

I had stepped back and let the Howler get to her feet. She could not take her eyes off Garlic. "Is she your pet?" the Howler asked.

Garlic now took notice of the Howler and growled in challenge. I laughed. "She is no man's pet."

"She is not just a dog. What is she?"

I realized the Howler's werewolf lineage gave her a little more insight into all things canine, but I certainly was not going to share Garlic's uniqueness with her. I shrugged, "She is just . . . Garlic."

I retrieved my sword, and with the Howler in front of me and Garlic trailing me, we walked back to my camp. As we walked, I realized the most important thing she could tell me was what year it was. If it was after 1690, my contempt sentence would have expired, and I was free to go and do what I pleased. Ironically, I had no idea what that really was anymore.

I cooked the Howler some freshly caught rabbit over a fire and ignored her rather unladylike table manners as she made short work of the little bunny. In between her bites, I thought to ask her some questions, and decided I would offer up only vague information about myself. "My name is Sirio Sinestra," I said. "I am a mercenary by trade and was the only immortal on a ship bound from Spain to India when a great storm came up, capsizing the ship. I was the only survivor and eventually washed up here, stranded without any crystals." I could see from her face that she did not believe me.

She stopped chewing for a moment and pointed at Garlic. "And your dog survived the storm too?"

"She does a rather impressive dog paddle," I said.

"Well, you both must be part merpeople, because you are on Saona Island," she said. "That island over there is Hispaniola. You are about a month's sail heading southwest from the Canary Islands. You are nowhere near India. This is the New World."

I looked away for a moment, realizing the nonsense of what I had said. "All right, that is not quite the way we got here. Let me make a deal with you. Tell me what year it is, and I will tell you our real story."

"It is 1692," she said. I could see she had stopped eating and was now quite interested in Garlic and me. But I could barely contain my excitement. My one hundred years had passed, and I was a free man! A broke and nearly penniless man, but a free man nonetheless. "How did you get here really?" she asked. "Be honest this time, we have a deal."

"You have never been married, have you?" I asked. She shook her head in the negative. "Well then, there is a court of law that governs the marriages of immortals, the Immortal Divorce Court. I was found in contempt of court and was banished to Hell for one hundred years. I escaped and ended up here. That is my story."

The Howler tossed a rabbit bone to Garlic, who snapped it out of the air with an audible crunch. "I think you should have stuck to the other lie," she said. "No matter, you are obviously a Spanish mercenary of some sort. Your sword and clothes are English, however. You could have easily left this island, crystal or no crystal, but didn't. So, clearly you are a man in hiding or a man with something to hide."

I looked her dead in the eye. "I was indeed a man in hiding until you told me what year it is—assuming of course that you are not lying to me," I said. "But I am now free of my obligation to stay here, if you were true to your word. So, what is a nice young lady like you doing skulking around this—what did you call it?—Saona Island? And does Spain control Hispaniola?" I asked the Howler.

"Spain had it all for a while, but now Santo Domingo is their only stronghold, which is on the east side of the island. On the north and west, you will find bases of English, Dutch, and French pirates," she replied. "And even farther west you will find Jamaica and the great city of Port Royal."

"The French?" I said. "Surely, you jest. French pirates, now you are the one telling stories."

She laughed, "A lot has changed in one hundred years apparently. If you didn't know, the Spanish Crown sent Columbus in search of a new route to India, but instead he discovered Saona Island and Hispaniola back in 1492."

"Columbus, I have had enough of that wayward traveler," I grimaced. That now long-dead explorer was following me wherever I went. To say nothing of his damned navigator.

The Howler was intent on giving me a history lesson. A lesson I had already learned the hard way. She continued, "He was looking for India but found this land, the New World instead. Mortal history does not even tell the most humorous part about that."

"Let me guess," I said. "His navigator, Martin, was ensorcelled by an evil bloodsucking female vampire, and he was so under her spell that he guided Columbus here not India."

"Do not play me for a fool, Mr. Sinestra," the Howler snapped. "If you know that, then clearly you know just where and when you are!"

"I can explain," I said, and told her the story of Martin, Bloodsucker Number One, and the courtroom drama.

When I finished, she nodded in understanding. "All right," she said. "That story is too farfetched for anyone to make up. I believe you. And I kind of feel sorry for you."

"So what is your story," I asked.

"My name is Anne Smith and I hail from Lancashire near the Irish Sea. My Pack has been sailors and merchants there for centuries, but a great crime has forced me to come here to seek a just and certain revenge," the Howler said.

You think I would have learned that a pretty face is not immune from lying, and that a woman's true motives are usually well concealed and known only to her own self. The Howler was lying to me, because through Harvis, I knew the names of all the families of werewolf Packs in England, and some of their members quite intimately. There was not a Smith among them. And Harvis had never mentioned that there were any werewolves in Lancashire. The Howler she would continue to be.

I feigned concern. "A great crime?"

She nodded, tears welling up in her eyes easily as if on her command. "Indeed," she said. "I am searching for the Moon of Madrid."

"What is the Moon of Madrid?" I asked. "It sounds like a Spanish ship."

The Howler knew she had me as her captive audience now. "The Moon of Madrid is a white opal of mystic properties that my sister Cornelia wears on a chain around her neck. The Moon of Madrid is sacred to werewolves."

I racked my brain, trying to think if Harvis, or any of his people, had mentioned such a gem. I sensed there was more to the Howler's story. But was she telling me the truth about this Moon of Madrid? "Do go on," I encouraged her.

The Howler nodded. "But the loss of the Moon is not the worst of it. My little sister, Cornelia, is as late-maturing a bitch as my Pack has ever seen, and she was born sickly and weak. My father entrusted her as the guardian of the Moon of Madrid to give her a sense of purpose. The poor thing cannot defend herself properly, or so we thought. Unbeknownst to us, she started a secret society that worshiped the Moon of Madrid. But she was betrayed by some goblins in her cult that served a different master."

"And if you find the Moon, you will find your sister," I surmised. "Why are you alone? Where is the rest of your Pack?"

"My three brothers went after the goblins, but . . ." The Howler put her head into her hands and sobbed.

I shook my head in disbelief. If the Howler's tale was true, her brothers were colossal imbeciles to mess with goblins. They actually made faeries look pleasant. Goblins were shape-shifters, generally appearing human to blend in with the mortal world. But in their quest to accumulate as much wealth as possible, the most elite of their warriors could turn themselves into semihumanoid versions of sharks, tigers, bears, or whatever deadly creature served their usually nefarious purposes. "Why in the world did your brothers mess with that evil ilk?" I asked. "They started a fight they could not hope to win. What happened to them?"

The Howler just looked at me blankly. Then it hit me like a bogeyman attack—her brothers had been killed or incapacitated by the goblins when they took Cornelia. Fighting goblins required strategy and even then it was bloody and usually fatal. "Sorry," I said. "What do they want with Cornelia, other than your father's money?"

"Someone is willing to pay the goblins more than all the gold in my family's coffers," the Howler said. "She is to be sold for the most nefarious purpose."

It was a very engaging story, I had to admit, and I felt myself drawn into the Howler's big wet doe eyes, or more accurately big puppy dog eyes. "What purpose is that?" I asked, raising an eyebrow and waiting for the big finish.

"Cornelia is going to be sold to an Aztec priest-king who is going to kill her while wearing the Moon of Madrid to complete a lunar-cycle death rite. Legend says he will get power greater than that of any mortal and be able to command the very tides to do his bidding. I have to stop him and save Cornelia!" She burst into tears, her body shaking violently with sorrow and pain. And either she was a much better actor than the faerie Pansy who had taught me a lesson so many years ago, or she was actually telling the truth. Garlic crawled over to her and licked her boot. Apparently, Garlic could not tell if the Howler was lying either.

There is nothing a man, immortal or not, hates more than a crying female of any species. "It is going to be all right," I said. "We will help you get Cornelia back." I ignored Garlic's yelp of surprise at being volunteered to help the Howler. Licking a boot was one thing, but taking on a horde of goblins? Not to mention a murderous Aztec priest-king bent on world domination.

The Howler stopped crying, and since I did not have a handkerchief, I did the next best thing and handed her another rabbit leg. "Here, eat this," I said. "You will feel better."

I braced for the leg to be thrown back at me, but after eating it, she gradually gained her composure. "You will help me?" she said. "Do you mean that, or did you just want me to stop crying?"

I smiled. "Actually, both." She feigned throwing the rabbit leg at me and smiled back. Yes, the Howler was quite attractive when she was smiling and not snarling, or trying to stab me in the man parts. Quite attractive indeed. Garlic growled at me again, and I realized I did not even know the Howler's real name. My eyes took in her shapely frame. There would be time for a proper introduction later, I mused. She had her reasons for concealing her true identity. If the situation had been reversed, I certainly would have done the same as the Howler.

My mind was already working on solving the Howler's problem. "What were you looking for on this island?"

She tossed the rabbit bone into the bushes. "Father had set me up as the captain of a crew of privateers, with the plan being to attack the goblin ship before it got to the Aztec priest. While the privateers were distracting the goblins, I was going to sneak aboard and rescue Cornelia. But once I got on board my ship, those bloody pirates, true scourges of the sea, had other ideas about who was in command. However, once I added to my necklace, they were nothing but respectful. We were on the trail of one of the goblin clan's minions who knew where Cornelia was being held, and just as we saw him land his sloop on this island, we were set upon by two Spanish warships. Outgunned, we ran and finally lost the Spaniards, but returned to find the goblin's sloop destroyed. Not to call any more attention to my ship, I sent it to hide out at our base in Hispaniola after it dropped me here to investigate."

"I see," I said. Her plan to take on the goblins would never have worked as she and her crew would have been slaughtered. The Howler really did need my help, and we needed a plan. I could see the pink fingers of dawn creeping over the horizon. We had fought and talked all night, apparently. "I think I know where to find your minion."

The Howler leaped to her feet and grabbed my arm anxiously. "Take me to him now!" she exclaimed. I was very conscious of her delightful smell of flowers with her standing so close to me. It made me want to nose her bouquet.

I shook my head for a multitude of reasons. "If it is him, don't worry, he isn't going anywhere, what with his head being separated from his body and all. Let us get some sleep. We will have better luck searching for clues when the sun is fully up."

CHAPTER 7

I had done the gentlemanly thing and given the Howler my makeshift bed and rigged up another piece of sailcloth far enough away that both she and I would feel safe. Trust was hard to come by on our little island. I did not think she would try to kill me when I slept. She needed me and, like most women, would take full advantage of any services I could offer, as long as they advanced her agenda. Besides, with Garlic curled up next to me not even an overly aggressive ant had a chance of harming me.

I awoke with the sun nearly at the day's apex to find the Howler curled up at my side, her arm draped across my chest. Garlic had kept vigil and was sitting next to my head. I was well practiced at the art of slinking out of a woman's bed and made my way to the spring for fresh water, harvesting some fruit on the way back. When I got to my camp, the Howler was lying in her own bed, and neither one of us chose to mention her sleepwalking.

"I got us some fresh fruit and water," I said, handing half of what I had collected to her. "It is a short trek to the body I found that might be your quarry."

"Thank you," the Howler replied. It seemed she did have some manners after all. "We don't have much time. My ship will be rendezvousing with me in the morning. Which begs the question—how am I going to explain to my English crew that I am consorting with a Spaniard?"

I laughed to myself. Consorting with her would need no explanation from any man. "That is an easy one," I said. "I am a mercenary sent from your father to help you. I have been following you the whole time." I paused while she considered this, then said in my best Cockney accent. "Sirius Sinister, at your service."

She was taken aback for a moment, then laughed. "Now that is a good pirate name if I ever heard one!"

We finished eating quickly and, with Garlic trailing us, made our way to where I had discovered the decapitated corpse. He was exactly where I had left him, his bony skull still resting in his hands, grinning eerily at us. "Do you know this to be the minion?" I asked. "Someone or something wanted to make sure he couldn't do any talking."

The Howler stared at him for a moment and then bent to rifle through his clothes, but found nothing other than a few stray maggots. "This is the man," she said. "I recognize those foppish clothes even after a few weeks in the jungle."

I peered at the man's neck and noted his spine had been severed cleanly with one swift blow. "No mortal can kill like that," I said. "He was meeting someone here, and once that meeting was over, so was his life."

The Howler began searching frantically around the body. I did not know what she was looking for, and clearly neither did she. She screamed in frustration. "There has to be something," she said. She grabbed the skull, and made to throw it into the jungle.

"Wait," I said, grabbing her arm and eliciting a growl of anger from her. "You obviously have not dealt with goblins much. His head was left in his hands, and before I took it, his sword leaned neatly against the tree. They are sending you a message."

"My sister's life is no game," the Howler said, slamming the skull into my open palm.

I nodded slowly, "Well, it is to them. If they can humiliate you, eventually torture and kill you, *and* make a deal netting them lots of gold in the process, it doesn't get any better for the horde. Now then . . ."

I replaced the sword where I had found it and dropped the skull neatly into the waiting corpse's fingers. I stepped back and viewed the scene with a different tack than when I first found it. Something was nagging at me about the corpse, and then it hit me. "Where are his boots?"

The Howler shrugged, "What difference does that make? The goblins probably took them. Or he took them off. So what?"

"He wasn't killed here. He was put here for you to find. The skull in the hands, well, that is just an assassin's sense of humor. The sword is the key."

The sword was pointing west, if I had replaced it in the proper spot, and I knew I had. "Come on," I said, and set off west through the jungle. I could see faint traces of where the minion had been dragged, and on one rock underneath a bush, there was the familiar stain of dried blood. Definitely mortal blood by the smell of it. Soon, we came into a clearing with another natural spring. A pair of boots stood propped up in the sand. I read the signs of what was a very brief struggle. The minion had come up to the spring and removed his boots to cool his feet. The moment he set foot in the spring, something had come out of the water and decapitated him. I could still see the dent in the sand where his head landed.

"This was not a meeting," I said. "This was an assassination." I caught a glimpse of something glinting in the sunlight in the clear shallow water of the spring. But before I could investigate, the Howler had gone over to the minion's boots and peered inside. Carefully, she went to reach down into the boot, but I caught her hand before she did. She looked at me quizzically, not mad but deferring to my assassin's expertise. I pointed at a needle halfway down the leather, barely glinting in the sun. "Goblins, remember?" I said. "I don't know what poison that needle is tipped with, but I don't think you want to find out."

The Howler's eyes grew wide at her near escape, and this time she took a stick and fished out of the bottom of the boot a tress of blonde hair identical to her own. "Cornelia," she said.

I nodded. "They want you to know she is still alive. Now, the question is, where is she being held?"

The Howler grabbed the other boot, inspected it, and more carefully this time, pulled out a kerchief. "This is not hers," she said. "This has the crest of the governor of Santo Domingo on it. That is it! She is being held in the governor's house in Santo Domingo."

"No," I said. "Your impetuousness precedes you. A trap lies set for you in Santo Domingo, but she is not there."

The Howler stood, angry and a little frustrated, and folded her arms across her chest and glared at me. "Well then, Sirius Sinister, if you think you are so brilliant, where is she?"

I decided two things at that moment. One, I definitely liked the name Sirius Sinister, and two, I found her pouty look to be quite fetching. Not answering her, I strode into the water, thrust my hand under the surface of the spring into the cool white sand, and brought up a shiny gold necklace. "Now, if you are going to swing your sword so bloody hard as to lop off a head," I said, "you have to make sure you don't leave evidence of who you just murdered." I pointed to the sand. "The head bounced there, and this necklace got caught on the blade for a moment and then was deposited behind the killer on his follow-through. He never even looked back in the spring. He poisoned the boot, and set his trap for you and your men. Then, just grabbed the head and the body of the minion and headed east to the tree. That is mighty sloppy work, if I do say so myself."

I peered at the necklace. "This is a badge of membership to something called the Gallows Club. Do you know where or what that is? Because that is where you will find Cornelia."

"The Gallows Club is a social club composed of the wealthy merchants, royalty, and such in Port Royal, which is the capital city in Jamaica," she answered. "That does make sense. It is a perfect place for goblins, and Aztec priest-kings. Port Royal used to be a haven for privateers, but now slaving, sugar plantations, and English money reign supreme."

I tossed the necklace to her. "Your ship will be here in the morning, and then we are off to Port Royal. I suggest we change our ship colors from privateer to merchant, or we will be real members of the Gallows Club."

We walked back to camp, and I felt hunger growing within me. All the overcooked rabbits had me hungering for some more substantial meat. I left the Howler at the camp, excusing myself to forage for a deer and to think. Garlic came with me and always enjoyed a hunt, that one did. I did not know what I was getting myself and Garlic into with the

Howler. There was that whole business with her lying to me about who she was.

Part of me still doubted her story about Cornelia and the Moon of Madrid, and that part of me wanted to backtrack to where I had hid the dugout and leave her and Saona Island long behind. But the image of her standing all distraught and pouty by the spring earlier in the day popped into my mind. The Howler needed me, regardless of her story, and as I crept silently through the jungle, I knew I was not leaving the island without her. I heard a crack in the underbrush far ahead, and Garlic and I froze instantly. We saw through the trees a red moon, low on the horizon. It cast a beautiful scarlet hue across the jungle, bathing the deer up ahead in a lovely shade of blood. We attacked silently and quickly, and dinner was soon ours for the eating.

Garlic and I returned to the camp, our kill draped over my shoulders, and the Howler grinned in anticipation of the feast. She deferred to me as I quickly got some venison steaks roasting nicely over the fire. One thing she was not lying about was being a city girl since she displayed no knowledge of properly dressing and carving a kill. As we ate, the moon grew big and full in the sky with nary a star in sight. It was a breathtaking sight to behold.

But there were other sights for me to behold at dinner, as the Howler had removed her ever-present black jacket, and rolled up her shirtsleeves to display tan, lithe arms. She had tied her hair back, and her eyes sparkled enchantingly in the moonlight. The Howler had uncharacteristically taken a seat next to me as we ate, and when she handed me fruit or water, her hand held contact with mine for a little longer than was necessary. When we finished eating, I looked over and noticed Garlic's white fur was stained completely crimson with the blood of the deer. She was a voracious little hunter. We would be traveling by ship tomorrow, and neither she nor I looked presentable with our recent bloodlust so evident on our clothes. The Howler did not seem bothered by our appearance, but her mortal crew would surely be less than welcoming.

I rose to my feet and stretched. The Howler followed my every move. "I am going to dispose of the carcasses and see if I can get Garlic's fur back to her normal shade of white," I said.

"Do you need any help?" she said.

"Thank you, but no," I replied. "We will be back in shortly."

Garlic and I set out for the far side of the island, where we deposited the deer carcasses in a copse of trees. As soon as we were out of sight, the island's scavengers would have a hearty meal on us, and none of the deer would go to waste. We then headed straight for the beach, and I stripped off all my clothes, dropped them on the shore, and waded into the surf. I was an excellent swimmer from my days on Sa Dragonera, and Garlic joined me in chasing minnows for a while. I came out of the water clean as could be and gave my clothes the same treatment. We made our way to a freshwater pool downstream from our drinking source and dunked ourselves and my clothes in the freshwater to remove the salt. Garlic came out of the water and shook herself dry. My clothes did not have that same ability, and I hung them on some branches, retreated to the pool, and waded in up to my thighs, enjoying the refreshing feel of the water. The Howler would have to fend for herself at our camp since this was likely my last time to focus my thoughts and energies on the mission ahead.

"It's nice," the Howler said, standing in the sand at the edge of the pool. "It looks lovely."

I looked back over my shoulder and realized she was talking about my bare rear end and not the water. "Yes, quite refreshing," I replied, barely suppressing a grin.

"Do you mind if I come in?" she said, pulling out her hair tie, and shaking her blonde mane loose.

I shrugged and turned slightly toward her. "If you would like to . . ."

"I would," she replied, and pulled off her boots. I turned all the way around now, and watched intently as she removed her shirt—and pants. She had my full attention now, and I could not take my eyes off her as her underclothing dropped to the sand. She sauntered into the water, her full hips and ample breasts illuminated by the moonlight. She was lean and incredibly muscular as was her kind, but as my burgeoning manhood agreed—she was all woman.

The Howler came into my embrace, and our lips met hungrily. She pulled away for a moment and looked downward. "You were not lying, Mr. Sinister," she said, putting her hands on me. "This is indeed a weighty proposition to handle."

I had always been rather generous in that respect, but now, in my first encounter with a woman since my days in Hell, it appeared that Persephone really did make things grow. "Well, if you are not up to the task . . ." I started to say, but her lips quickly covered mine, and we thrashed the water with our passion. She mounted me, wrapping her legs around me right there in the water, and I realized that the Howler was a perfectly fitting name for this lively werewolf. Again and again her body tensed with her pleasure, and I could feel the bite of her fingernails on my back and hear the slow drip of blood into the water. Not that it concerned me at that moment, as I could feel my own pleasure begin to build. She sensed it was coming and writhed even harder, taking all I gave her in one tremendous thrust before we collapsed exhausted into the water, spent with our exertions, and drunk with the pleasure of the moment.

We woke to the morning sun and the call of voices echoing from the shore. Garlic had appeared out of nowhere and stood at my side, a low growl emanating from her throat. I looked at the Howler and cracked a knowing smile, but she returned only a blank gaze, hurriedly pulling on her clothing and setting her hair back in a tight bun. Whatever passion had ruled her under last night's full moon had departed, and she was back to the business at hand. Still naked, I lingered for a moment, watching her dress, and was rewarded with an angry glare. "Get dressed," the Howler said. "My ship is here, and explaining a naked vampire to my men is not going to start the voyage to Port Royal on the best footing."

"All right then," I said. "Last night was something wasn't it, though?"

The Howler did not make eye contact. "Something indeed," she said, and walked off toward the beach.

I looked at Garlic quizzically. "Well, she certainly seemed to be enjoying herself last night," I said, feeling the skin tightening in my shoulders where the Howler's passion wounds were healing. Garlic ignored me, moving directly in front of me. She sensed danger was afoot, and I dressed in a second and retrieved my sword. "Okay, Garlic," I said. "Playtime is apparently over. Let's meet some pirates, shall we?"

I came out onto the beach and saw the Howler with her sword drawn in a standoff with three burly members of her crew. "What is this?" I said, breaking into a sprint. "It seems our girl has a little mutiny on her hands." As I ran, I saw a skiff pulled up high on the shore, and the Howler's well-armed sloop anchored off shore.

The pirates seemed surprised as Garlic and I were upon them before they even saw us coming. "What is the problem here, mates?" I asked, taking quick stock of our foes. The leader in the middle was a shifty-eyed fellow with a big belly, who stood favoring a right leg that had been injured in some fashion. He held his sword clumsily and was not a threat. The other two were a different story. Both men were lean and rangy, and held their swords a little too expertly for mere pirates. They had been classically trained in the blade and stood as light on their feet as acrobats. Each bore tattoos on their left forearms that I recognized instantly marked them as members of a prestigious mortal assassin's guild. They eyed me warily, recognizing my true nature.

When the silence continued, I addressed the Howler. "Captain," I said to her. "The crew appears to need a little discipline. Shall I take care of it for you? I can start with Big Belly Bart here first."

The man I had dubbed Big Belly Bart spat at me. "I'm going to eat your little dog for breakfast," he said.

Garlic lunged forward, and nipped his Achilles tendon, dropping him to the sand in a crying, sobbing heap. The assassins were stunned at the dog's speed and at their inability to react. They stepped back cautiously.

The Howler smiled coldly, looking down at the big man struggling to his feet. "It seems it is you that are the breakfast, Mr. James Sullivan."

Sullivan fell back to the sand and implored his mates to help him. "Don't just stand there," he cried. "Help me."

I took this opportunity to get the Howler's ear as they struggled to pull Big Belly Bart to his feet. "Why the mutiny?"

She shrugged. "They say they have a new first mate and captain, and I am not in charge anymore."

"That makes absolutely no sense," I said. "They would never have come back to get you if that was the case."

"Unless," she said, "the crew told them that I knew where to find an astoundingly valuable treasure like the Moon of Madrid."

"Ah, good old-fashioned greed," I said. "We could kill these fops now, but your sloop would be long gone before we could get the dugout and lay chase. What do you say we go meet the new master of your boat?"

The Howler hesitated for a moment, weighing the choices. "You are right," she said. "We have to get to Port Royal and the Gallows Club."

"Just follow my lead," I said to her, turning to the pirates. Big Belly Bart had an arm draped over each of the assassins, hindering any move they wanted to make. Garlic licked her fangs, hungrily eyeing Big Belly Bart's other leg. "Garlic," I said, "if these men make one move toward us on the boat, rip their throats out, okay?"

Garlic yelped her assent, and wagged her tail happily as she ran to and fro. "Now then," I said to the pirates, "drop your swords, and help Big Belly Bart to the skiff. We would like to meet your captain and first mate."

One of the assassins stared at me in shock. "Who are you?" he asked.

I laughed. "You don't know?" I said. "I am Sirius Sinister, the soon-to-be new first mate of your ship."

The two assassins helped the limping Big Belly Bart into the skiff. I assessed his wound as he moved and realized that Garlic had not crippled him. The bleeding had stopped, and by the look of his pudgy face, Big Belly Bart was managing his pain. He sat down in the boat and glared at Garlic, who snarled back and faked a lunge at him, causing him to fall into the boat. Big Belly Bart pulled himself up, and the look on his face was pure hatred as he stared at the prancing Maltese. Garlic was very pleased with herself.

Big Belly Bart was clearly now plotting how to turn this situation against us. But as the assassins rowed us back to the Howler's ship, the three men grew quiet and subdued. Then I sensed it, as did the Howler and Garlic.

"Well, that is odd," I said to the Howler. "Something immortal is on your ship. And it is making these mortals a little bit uncomfortable, to say the least."

"Indeed," replied the Howler, peering with her keen eyes up and down the deck of her ship. "It is not a werewolf. It stays hidden, and that is not our way."

I nodded and smiled. "I would stay hidden, too, if I knew that we were coming aboard."

Garlic did not seem to be bothered by the threat we all felt, other than sniffing quickly at the ocean air and growling ever so slightly. She kept her eyes affixed to Big Belly Bart and the assassins, waiting for their treachery. It would most assuredly come, but the gang of three was obviously waiting until we were on the Howler's ship, where the strange hidden immortal and the rest of the crew would—in their minds—overwhelm us.

I was betting on the Howler regaining control of her crew. And aside from a faerie with an attitude, I had not yet faced an immortal when I was sober that I could not defeat, especially with a vampire Maltese by my side! We were still a good distance from the Howler's ship. I could see just a few idle crew members on deck, and the man in the lookout's nest was either sound asleep or doing a passable job at faking it. I estimated there were twenty men below deck, plus the mystery immortal. Big Belly Bart began fidgeting in his seat and was no doubt trying to signal the lookout of the danger we represented. We were approaching from the stern of the Howler's ship, and I grinned as I saw the name of her craft—the *Moon Hunter*.

The skiff came closer, and there was now a flurry of activity on deck as Big Belly Bart had communicated his warning, or the lookout had found us suspicious. Either way, it was of no concern to the Howler, Garlic, and me. A ladder came over the side of the boat, and the assassins steered us toward it. The feel of the immortal was strong now, and I could sense its anticipation as it sprung its trap.

But I was never one for standing by idly while a plot against me unraveled ever so slowly. I stepped forward and pitched the two assassins headlong into the sea, then steered the skiff to the side of the Howler's ship opposite the ladder. I tossed Garlic up on the deck, and the Howler and I spun expertly up the anchor chain and somersaulted onto the deck. Big Belly Bart's cries from below had alerted a crew of nineteen rogues, who turned to find us in charge of the bridge.

The Howler knew she had to regain control of her ship and do it quickly. We could slay these men quite easily, but again would be stranded without a quick way to Port Royal. And we would rather have them on our side when the immortal made his appearance.

"Men of the *Moon Hunter*," the Howler called out to the crewmen, her voice unwavering. "This mutiny is no more. You have been promised riches beyond your wildest dreams. It is I who is your captain. My patron is a man of much means. Do not cross him."

I could see a few of the men begin nodding as she spoke. Clearly, her father had made an impression on them. But could she bring them over to our side before Big Belly Bart and the immortal played their hand?

Up from the ladder came the two assassins jumping onto the deck, and behind them with a series of grunts and much puffing of breath came Big Belly Bart. They stood in front of the crew, and Big Belly Bart cursed them angrily. A few of the crewmen shied away, and one cowered as the pirate raised a hand to strike him in the face. The feel of the immortal grew stronger, and oddly, it seemed vaguely familiar. Had I crossed paths with whatever strange creature lay in hiding, watching and waiting as Big Belly Bart did its work?

Big Belly Bart pointed his finger in our direction but did not take his eyes off the crew. "We don't need her," he said. "Our new captain and first mate take care of us, provide for us, and will make us rich men."

"More like they will make you dead men," the Howler said. "Bind these traitors and take them to the hold." But the crewmen did not move.

"No, milady," spat Big Belly Bart. "It is you that must answer to our first mate and captain."

Suddenly, the door to the hold was thrust open, and out from the belly of the ship emerged a mountain of a man. He was easily seven feet tall and built like a barrel. His eyes were vacant and dead, and a sneer was permanently etched on a scarred, misshapen face. A bloodstained cutlass hung on one side of his belt, and a short but deadly gun I would come to know as a blunderbuss from the other. The crewmen and Big Belly Bart stepped back from this monstrosity as he tromped toward us. I could feel the vibration of his heavy step, and the crewmen appeared to be quite terrified of this new first mate. Oddly, he seemed to grow larger as he walked, feeding off the collective terror of the crew.

"You want to parley?" I called to the monster. "Negotiate your surrender?"

He kept walking, took out his cutlass, and eviscerated the air with a couple of savage swings of his mighty blade. I looked at the Howler, nonplussed. "Not a very talkative one," I said. I turned back toward the approaching giant, who now stood just a few paces away. "I guess he rules by fear and that ugly mug of his."

The Howler put a hand on my arm for reassurance, losing her nerve for just a moment. She was scared, and the first mate inhaled deeply, as if savoring the odor of her fear, and then charged us, swinging his weapon and going for the death blow. But he was too late, for I knew just what we were facing and how to stop it.

"Garlic," I called, "bark this Bogeyman into oblivion!"

Garlic jumped forward into the path of the pirate Bogeyman and let out an earsplitting bark. The sound waves rushed over the Bogeyman like a tidal wave, stopping him in his tracks and then sweeping him backward across the deck and into the ocean in a million pieces of disintegrated fury. The Bogeyman's cutlass dropped to the ground with a resounding clang, and all around the *Moon Hunter* fish and birds descended on his remnants in a frenzied feeding.

The crew stood silent, some with mouths open in utter shock. Garlic padded over to stand in front of them and growled. One crew member fainted to the ground, while another soiled himself when Garlic looked directly at him. The bluster had gone out of Big Belly Bart, and he lowered himself to the ground and sat quietly.

I walked over to stand near Garlic. I knew it would do no good to explain to the crew what the Bogeyman was, and perhaps the world was now a little happier, less fearful place, what with the Bogeyman's new occupation as dinner for the local wildlife. "Your first mate is no more," I said. "The *Moon Hunter* is once again in the hands of its rightful captain. I am Sirius Sinister, your first mate. Any questions?"

One gangly pirate raised his hand. "What did that little white dog do to him?"

"Ended his reign of tyranny and oppression for starters," I replied. "What is your name, son?"

The pirate gulped awkwardly. "They call me Ishmael," he said.

"Well, Ishmael," I said, "once we complete our mission, you can tell the first mate's family and friends, if he had any, that he wasn't killed by a small white dog, but rather some sort of monstrous white whale that had it in for him. No one would believe a little white dog could kill a big, mean, old, nasty pirate, right?"

Ishmael nodded. "Okay," he said. "A white whale killed him, got it. So the dog won't hurt us?"

I grinned wryly, looking down at Garlic. "I can't promise that, but if you listen to the captain, you will have no problems at all."

The Howler had taken this opportunity to walk to the captain's quarters. She stopped suddenly and motioned me over. "Sirius," she hissed in my ear, "he is still here."

"Who is still here?" I whispered. There was a faint scratching from behind the door. Concentrating very deeply, I closed my eyes and caught the faintest smell of freshly cut flowers, clouded by the overwhelming smell of rum. My sword drawn, I pulled open the unlocked door and peered into the dark cabin. I could make out a small figure in a hooded cloak, sitting at the captain's table, armed only with a glass of rum. "Who are you?" I said, striding over to the table and slapping the glass out of a scrawny hand. When no answer came, I pulled the hood off the creature's head and found myself looking into a familiar face from long ago.

CHAPTER 8

To my amazement, sitting in front of me was Jova, whom I had left as a young boy in the charge of Harvis over one hundred years before, after my first encounter with the Bogeyman. He looked to be about eighteen or nineteen years old, and there was no mistaking his big gray eyes boring back at me in a drunken stupor, nor the streaks of red in his hair that with age had become even more prominent. There was also no mistaking that Jova was our mystery immortal.

"Jova," I said. "Do you remember me?"

The Howler looked at me in surprise. "You know this mutinous wretch," she said, raising her sword. "He had better do some quick explaining before I add more ginger to that head of his."

I turned to the Howler with a frown. "Settle down," I said. "I knew him long ago when I first tangled with the Bogeyman. But he was no more than a child then."

"That thing was the Bogeyman?" she exclaimed. "That explains what that weird feeling was I felt before Garlic destroyed it. It was fear!"

I knelt down in front of Jova, and his eyes followed me like limpid pools of quicksilver. "Jova," I said. "It is me, Sirio, although you can call me Sirius Sinister now." Just then Garlic padded into the cabin and came into Jova's view.

Jova reached out a hand to pet Garlic. "Sirio," he said, clearing his throat and the haze of the rum. "I love Garlic."

I laughed. "You always did," I said. "Now just what kind of immortal are you?"

He shrugged. "It is kind of hard to explain," he said.

"I know what you are," the Howler interrupted, growing impatient. "You are a thief and a vagabond. Why did you come on board, and what did you do to my crew?"

"I can explain," Jova said. "Really, I can."

"It is all right, Jova, don't worry about her," I said, glaring at the Howler, who made a face back at me. "She just gets a little bit overeager from time to time. Did the Bogeyman just find you again? Were you hiding from him?"

Jova swallowed long and hard, and reached for the bottle of rum, which I snatched away from him before he could grasp it and empty it. I needed a sober Jova to learn the truth about him and the Bogeyman. When the Bogeyman regenerated from the few remnants that survived being fish food, he was probably not going to be happy with me and my Maltese. Getting disintegrated by a vampire and his faithful pooch twice in one hundred years was surely going to make him one angry and vindictive bogeyman. I needed Jova for whatever information he could provide, since the last thing the Howler and I needed was the Bogeyman paying a visit to us, seeking its revenge while we were trying to rescue Cornelia.

"Come on now, Jova," I implored as Jova put his hands on his head. "What is it?"

"I have never told anyone this before," he said. "It is a family secret. I was not running from the Bogeyman. I *am* the Bogeyman."

The Howler's mouth dropped open in shock, and I noticed mine had followed suit. "You are the Bogeyman?" I repeated. "That is not possible. He lives on the essence of fear, until a vampire Maltese blows him to bits. Without fear, he does not exist. He is a monster. You are . . . are . . ." Actually, I wasn't sure just what Jova was.

"I am the monster, well, in a way," Jova said. "I didn't know it when I first met you and Garlic with my sisters back in England, but I was the one that animated the swamp to attack you."

"But the Bogeyman is not an actual person," the Howler interjected. "It is a thing, right?"

"No," Jova said. "From the dawn of time, the youngest male member of my family has inherited from his father the mantle of the Bogeyman. The rest of them are just ordinary witches and warlocks like Veela and Marmitte, who were taking me to see Hedley Edrick for training. That is why you didn't know who we were, Sirius. They had cast a spell that shrouded our true identities."

"So you didn't need my help that night," I said. "You were animating the swamp to destroy the ruffians that lay in ambush."

"Yes," Jova nodded. "That is, if my sisters didn't turn them into cockroaches first. Witches love turning deserving souls into cockroaches for some reason. But back to meeting you in the swamp, I was only a child, so my control over my power was raw and undeveloped, and once you took out the ruffians, I could not stop the swamp from hurting you. I am deeply sorry." Garlic had climbed up into Jova's lap, and he stroked her softly.

"It is okay, you did not mean to attack me. We all do things when we are young that we regret," I said, nodding in amazement at what I was hearing. "But I was not afraid of the swamp," I said. "Whose fear were you channeling, the ruffians'?"

Jova laughed. "I have no idea, might have been them, might have been your fear of my sisters and me being hurt by those common thieves. Now, I can focus on one person's slightest insecurities and animate something for whatever purpose I need. The first mate for example was made up of foodstuffs and old clothes in the hold, and the crew's terror did the rest."

The Howler had listened intently. From the look on her face, I could tell she was fascinated by his story, but her untrusting nature always lurked beneath the surface. Was this the same girl that I had such a deeply passionate interlude with on the island? "Okay, Jova," she said, her lips curling into a sneer that, in the back of my mind, I found quite alluring. "That is a lovely tale and all, but how come you were trying to kill us up on the deck. Didn't you see Sirius and Garlic and recognize them? And most importantly, what are you doing with *my* ship?"

Jova sighed and put Garlic down at his feet. "Sorry about that," he said. "When they sounded the alarm, I had already been drinking for a while. I am not a fighter. I let the Bogeyman do the fighting. I am all about my personal safety."

"You never even looked out of the cabin, did you?" the Howler said.

"Uh, no," Jova said. "But once the first mate was destroyed, I realized some immortals were on board and hid here, fearing for my safety."

I sensed this little exchange was not going to end well and jumped into the fray. "All right, all right," I said. "Why did you take the ship from her captain?"

"I am trying to get to Jamaica," he said. "Part of my education, I am doing a field study, if you will."

"Go on," the Howler said.

Jova took out a leather-bound book and showed it to us. I nodded encouragingly, but could not tell what language it was written in, or anything about it. When this adventure with the Howler was over, I resolved to learn how to read—in one language, at least!

"Hedley Edrick told me to learn as much about fear as I can to get total control over my power," Jova said. "If I get angry or lose focus, my power still goes out of control. I rage, it rages. If I do not get it under control, someone I love may get hurt or killed one day. I can't live with that, so I commandeered this boat to take me to Jamaica to study Obeah."

"O . . . what?" I said.

"Obeah," Jova said. "It is a mystical African religion, and its adherents focus on the strength of the mind. And there is a mystic in Port Royal who can show me how to better control my mind."

"Port Royal," I said. "Just so happens that is where we are going. And we need your help there."

Jova looked a little bit nervous. "Will there be any fighting?"

"Well, I hope so," I answered with a laugh. "But, your talents will help us even out the odds. After you help us, then you can go find your mystic, deal?"

"I don't like conflict," Jova said.

"You should have thought about that before you tried to kill us!" the Howler exclaimed.

"The lady does have a point," I said. "You owe me for the swamp, and both of us for what happened here today."

Jova nodded. "You are right," he said. "I will help you."

The Howler made eye contact with me, and then her gaze darted to the deck. She walked outside the cabin, and I joined her, leaving Garlic and Jova in the cabin. The Howler came close and put her lips to my ear.

"Do you think we can trust him?" she asked.

I could feel my manhood yearning to take her. The island seemed so long ago, and her standing so close to me was maddening, but she was all business at the moment. Perhaps we could break in the cabin a little later, I mused, casting my eyes downward to take in her body as I pretended to ponder what she had said.

"Good question," I said. "I don't know for sure. An immortal without full control of his powers may prove to be more dangerous than helpful. But I can tell you one thing."

"What is that, Sirius Sinister?" she whispered.

I kissed her quickly on the ear, and stepped away before she could react. "We don't stand a chance against the goblins without him," I said, and walked over to assess the crew and ready the ship for its departure to Port Royal.

"Aye," she replied. "Aye."

The Howler and I told the crew that the first mate was really an evil ocean spirit that had enslaved Jova to do its bidding and run the ship. We also presented Garlic with a leather collar studded with gold in front of the crew, telling them that Garlic was a good luck charm, and her bark had destroyed the first mate because, as an ocean spirit, it could not face land animals. Mortals will believe anything if it presents an alternative to believing in something they don't want to exist—like a bogeyman, for instance. For the most part the crew seemed genuinely happy to have the Howler back in command, except, that is, for Big Belly Bart, who failed miserably in hiding his dislike for me and Garlic. He was to be watched closely for treachery.

Pirates were not welcome in Port Royal since the antipiracy laws of 1687 were passed in Jamaica, unless they were being hanged, so we busied the ship for departure to Santo Domingo to outfit the *Moon Hunter* as a merchant ship and disguise our armaments. Jova moved about the ship more and more as the days went on, and once, I even caught him smiling as he played with Garlic on the deck. Our Bogeyman was in good spirits, an absolute necessity for what I had planned for him. The Howler and I deemed it unnecessary to tell him about our mission, and after being put off once, Jova merely shrugged, content to wait to learn of our mission and for the plan of attack when we were ready to tell him.

We decided to wait for morning to sail to Santo Domingo, and the crew bedded down for the night, except for a watchman, whom I made sure was not either of the two assassins or Big Belly Bart. Jova had been adopted by the crew, as his apparent slavery at the hands of an ocean spirit made him a sympathetic figure, and he was invited to bunk in the crew's quarters. I followed the Howler back to the captain's cabin.

"What are you doing?" she asked, putting a hand on my chest as I bent my head to enter the cabin.

I smiled coyly and raised an eyebrow. "What am I doing?" I said. "That would be providing a valuable service to my captain."

The Howler shook her head. "We can't."

"What do you mean, we can't?" I said. "You are the captain. You can do anything you want. And besides, I would just be following orders."

"It is not going to happen," the Howler said. "We cannot risk the crew losing respect for me by thinking you are bedding me."

"But, I have bedded you," I said. "And quite well, I might add."

She nodded, and finally the barest hint of a smile formed. "I know that, Sirius," she said. "But I am the captain now, and I cannot consort with my crew. You'll have to sleep in the crew's quarters."

I could see she was not going to be persuaded—at least not tonight. So I swallowed my pride and found a secluded spot to sleep on deck. After a few hours the ship was quiet, and all on board were asleep, including our faithful lookout. Only the moon's light followed me as I snuck back to the Howler's cabin. I was nothing if not persistent. Turns out I did not have to do much persuading as the Howler was waiting for me with her cabin door slightly ajar. I slipped quickly inside and pressed the door shut quietly.

"Are you ready to follow my orders, Mr. First Mate," the Howler said, her nightshirt dropping to the ground.

"Yes, Captain," I replied, tugging at my belt. "Sirius Sinister at your service."

"Good," she said. "I order you to service me."

"As you wish," I replied.

"But, quietly."

I folded my breeches and placed them on her nightstand. "But, of course."

I sneaked out of her quarters the next morning before dawn, and when the captain took the bridge a little later, she did so with a smile. We reached Santo Domingo and docked at a deserted wharf, then dispatched some of the crew to get supplies to ply in Port Royal. We did not need much since it was all for show, and other members of the crew busied themselves with changing out our sails, and Jova took it upon himself to repaint the name of our craft. We were the *Moon Hunter* no longer, as the goblins may have recognized that as the Howler's ship. Instead, we would sail to Port Royal as the *Dancing Swan.*

After a few short days, the *Dancing Swan* was ready for her journey to Port Royal. I took roll as we readied to set sail, and began cursing soundly.

"What is it?" asked the Howler as she and Jova came up to where I stood on the deck.

"It seems we are missing three crew members," I said. "Big Belly Bart and his two assassin friends did not return from town today."

"Maybe they are just running late," Jova suggested.

"Maybe," the Howler said. "Or more likely they are trying to tip off our enemies in Port Royal that we are coming."

"They can only travel by ship and cannot have much of a head start if any, so let's get the *Dancing Swan* underway," I said.

"Can you tell me now just who these enemies are in Port Royal?" Jova implored. "I would like to know who I am facing. Don't I at least deserve to know that?"

The Howler and I exchanged glances, and I shrugged, deferring to my captain.

"Sure," the Howler replied as she signaled the crew to set sail. "My sister was kidnapped by a horde of bloodthirsty goblins, and we are going to rescue her."

Jova nodded. "Oh," he said, suddenly looking a little pale and sitting down on the deck. "Glad I asked."

Unfortunately, as we made to leave Santo Domingo, the weather turned for the worse, and we were forced to harbor the *Dancing Swan* in the protection of the island rather than risk facing the perils of the open ocean and the storm passing just to our south. The weather relented after only a day, but it had seemed like an eternity even for the immortals on board. We had lost valuable time and did not know if James Sullivan aka Big Belly Bart and his cohorts had gotten off the island before the storm hit.

The Howler looked noticeably anxious, and as we finally steered the *Dancing Swan* toward Port Royal, I could only pat her shoulder reassuringly. In reality, it did not matter if Big Belly Bart had left before us or not—the goblins would be ready. But there was no way they could prepare themselves for the living embodiment of fear that was Jova the Bogeyman. But then I wondered—looking out upon the amazing clear blue-green waters of the Caribbean—just what did a goblin fear anyway? If we wanted to rescue Cornelia and escape with our lives, we had better figure that out.

The voyage to Port Royal was slow, as the wind was not in our favor, but finally the harbor came into view. We docked quickly, and Jova and I, with Garlic padding alongside us, headed for the harbormaster's office to register the *Dancing Swan* for trade. The crew made a great show of unloading semiempty barrels and crates, while a few key members readied the weapons belowdecks for the raid on the Gallows Club. Jova and I were in and out of the harbormaster's office in a few moments. The harbormaster did not question us or seemingly give us a second look, yet I sensed treachery in him as he gave us a cursory wave when we walked out the door.

"Something is amiss," I said to Jova. "That was too easy."

Jova shrugged. "Perhaps any trade at all is welcome in Port Royal. Gold is king here. Don't be so suspicious."

I glared at him. "Suspicion has kept me alive for a few centuries now," I said. I looked back and saw the harbormaster whispering in the ear of one of his minions. I thought he looked in our direction as he did so. My instinct told me that we did not have much time to find the Gallows Club and Cornelia.

Port Royal was truly bustling with activity as we walked back to the *Dancing Swan*. Huge brick homes, like ones back in England, lined the streets, and signs of wealth and opulence were everywhere. One house seemed to be three or four stories tall, and the huge gate in front of it looked to be painted with real gold. We passed a crew of laborers filling in some marshland in preparation for another manse. There were easily thousands of homes in this town, and the solution when they ran out of land was apparently to make more land. I snorted to myself—not the best idea to construct heavy buildings over what amounted to fill, sand, and water, but lots of gold tended to addle the brain like a fine wine where wealthy mortals were concerned.

"With all these houses, taverns, and stores, how are we going to find the Gallows Club?" I wondered out loud.

Jova shrugged. "I don't know," he said. "Maybe we could just ask someone." He nodded casually to sailors and others who passed by, staring a little too long at a beautiful woman whose services he could not afford, despite her inviting glances. "Hmm," he said. "She looks friendly enough. Let's ask her."

I fought off the urge to smack him in the back of his red-streaked head, instead tugging on his shirt to get his attention. "Really?" I said. "Ask a common harlot?"

"She seemed very willing."

"Jova," I said, "that might be true, but get focused here."

Who would have thought that I would be the voice of reason? I continued, "But there is a tavern a little way ahead that my instinct tells me is the place to find out what we need. Just follow my lead, don't call attention to yourself, and above all—do not provoke a fight, got it?"

"Spoken from the vampire assassin in the group," Jova said with a wink. "You have me confused for someone else—I am a frighter not a fighter!"

I laughed and put my arm around his shoulder. "True," I said. "And I have mellowed with age, haven't I, Garlic?" Garlic merely barked once and shook her head. The truth was that I was on a mission and would not jeopardize it by being out of control. I smiled—as long as there wasn't a naked woman around, I was actually pretty clearheaded. Just then, I saw the tavern I remembered up ahead. I glanced at the sign and grimaced at the painting of a smiling Death holding a drink with eerie smoke rising from it.

"Death's Door," Jova said with a nervous laugh. "These must be your kind of people."

I smirked, vowing to tell Jova of my trip to Hell someday. Now, Persephone was my kind of people. "Don't be a coward, Master

Bogeyman," I replied. "Just keep your head high and your mouth closed, and we will be fine."

Jova nodded, and we ducked into the tavern. Heads instantly swiveled on thick, ropey necks, and a host of unfriendly eyes were upon us. I sized up a mix of immortals and mortals in this dastardly place, all of whom were heavily armed and all very interested in their new bar mates. Garlic trailed behind us, a low growl in her throat, ready to draw blood from any that dared threatened her. None dared.

"Barkeep," I said, pounding my fist on the bar to get the attention of the hunched figure in the corner. "Two beers for me and my friend here to slake our thirst. And make it quick. We do not have all day."

The barkeep rose to his feet, and his gargantuan frame kept rising and rising until it seemed his big blocky head was brushing the ceiling. His black face looked like it was hewn from a single massive piece of obsidian, smooth angles shaping a face, mouth, and nose. Dark, thoughtful eyes bored into my own, and a deep intelligence lurked behind them. He pointed his stubby finger, the size of a blunderbuss, and rasped. "No service." The barkeep moved away, fingers deftly plucking empty glasses from the bar top despite their huge size. He collected gold from his patrons and, without even looking, tossed the coins over his shoulder where they clattered into his strongbox.

"Lovely," I said to Jova, perturbed at being ignored. "Of all the bars to walk into—we pick a troll bar." I turned back to the troll, who met my glare and extended a different finger. "What?" I said, ignoring his insult since picking a fight with a troll was literally like banging your head against a wall, and usually just as successful. "Is vampire gold not good here in Port Royal? Did you fall off your bridge and dent that stone dome of yours?"

The troll grimaced, or smiled, or maybe even frowned. I could not tell given the utter lack of facial expression particular to trolls. Jova on the other hand looked quite terrified as the troll lumbered back toward us. Reaching deep into his breast pocket and, I thought, glaring at me the whole time, the troll pulled out some reading glasses. I had expected a chicken bone or a club to bash my head in, so I was pleasantly surprised by Stone Brain's educated ways.

Stone Brain reached below the bar and pulled out a piece of parchment. "By the order of the governor of Jamaica, no animals shall be allowed in public houses, inns, or taverns," he read, looking down at me smugly. At least I thought his mug was smug.

"Why didn't you say so, Stone Brain," I replied. "She is not a dog—she is half vampire. So she can stay, and you need to get us some beers."

The troll consulted his parchment and was clearly conflicted as to whether Garlic was a vampire or a canine under the law of Jamaica. He scratched his head, which sounded like someone rubbing two rocks together trying to make a fire. I looked carefully for a spark but saw none. Finally, the troll, after deliberating with himself, slammed down two beers. "You can stay for one drink," he ordered. "You pay now. And my name is not Stone Brain, you ignorant boob, it is Oliver."

I quickly paid Oliver his gold and reached for my beer, and as Jova and I went to take a seat at one of the wooden benches along the wall, we found our way blocked by three rather unfriendly pirates. "You need to leave now," said one, pointing to the door. I assessed them quickly, seeing the three men were identical triplets. They wore cutlasses on their hips and stood with the easy confidence of men that did not lose a fight very often if at all. Two of them had straw-colored hair that was long, wild, and unkempt, but the middle brother had his blond bird's nest pulled back into a greasy ponytail.

"Oliver said we can stay for our one beer," I replied, staring into his eyes and causing him to look away. "And that is what we are going to do." I rolled my eyes at Jova, who looked rather green around the gills. Jova's hands were visibly shaking, drops of beer spilling out of his mug and into Garlic's waiting mouth below. But, beer notwithstanding, Garlic was ready to back me up and was eyeing a tasty pirate leg.

The leader of the triplets put his hand on my shoulder and drew close, exhaling breath that could wilt a flower, and bringing with him the collective stench of the high seas. Clearly, if these three bastards had been baptized, it was their last encounter with clean water. I glanced down at his hand and smiled unnervingly. "I suggest you take your hand off me, my good man."

Jova gulped loudly. "We do not want any trouble," he interjected.

The pirate suddenly dropped his hand from my shoulder and laughed. "No trouble," he said. "You are a funny man. You cannot walk into Death's Door without finding trouble. And you found us—I am Andrew, and these are my brothers, John and Little Jack, and we are the Trouble brothers." I did note, for what it was worth, that Little Jack was three inches taller and at least twenty pounds heavier than his two brothers.

Jova raised his hands, and his eyes scrunched up tight in his head. I leaned back against the bar in anticipation of the Bogeyman springing to action. What would it be—a sea monster composed of the alley sludge bursting through the door to send the Trouble brothers running scared for their lives with their tails between their legs? Maybe a ghostly spirit of their ancestors composed of the tavern draperies frightening them into an early grave? Either way, I rubbed my hands together happily. This was going to be a sight to see!

Jova opened his mouth, but no sound came out at first. "I-I-I don't understand," he sputtered. "We are just simple merchants looking for a friend who belongs to the Gallows Club."

If I wasn't so shocked at this turn of events, I would have punched my blabby bogeyman right in the face before the Trouble brothers did so. Because as soon as Jova said Gallows Club, the room went as silent as the aftermath of the Widow Jenkins passing wind in the front row of the Sunday service. I could see Oliver moving glasses and tankards away from us and sliding bottles of his finest wines to a safe place in a well-practiced routine.

With his beady eyes, Andrew Trouble stared at Jova and exhaled deeply, again to my great chagrin. "You don't say, funny man," he said. "I know all the members of the Gallows Club. I am a charter member. Who is your friend?"

Jova thought quickly. "James Sullivan," he answered coolly. "We are old chums."

Naming Big Belly Bart was brilliant, I had to admit, because Andrew Trouble looked quite astonished. His mouth dropped open far enough that I could see his dentition matched his bathing habits. "Well, now, I am in the presence of a friend," he said. "Because any friend of James Sullivan is a friend of the Trouble brothers." He reached into his pocket, took out a gold coin, and handed it to Jova. "Tonight at dusk go down to the House of Angels, three blocks west of here, across from St. Peter's Church. Show this coin to the man at the door, he will let you in, and I am pretty sure you will find old James. I heard he was back in town, but I have not run into him just yet. So, if you see him, tell him Trouble is looking for him." With that he guffawed loudly at his joke, slapped Jova hard on the shoulder, and the brothers Trouble departed Death's Door.

"Well, that was easy," Jova mumbled.

I put my glass to my lips and drank, ignoring Garlic's whine for a moment. "I guess bogeymen are good with trouble," I agreed. I relented and set my beer down on the floor to let Garlic finish it.

Oliver, seeing the coast was clear of trouble and the Troubles, came over and began replacing his glasses and set another beer in front of me. He kept his voice low so only Jova and I could hear him. "If you are friends with that scoundrel James Sullivan," he said, "then I am a dancing pixie."

I smiled and raised my glass to him. "You do look very light on your feet, Oliver."

"Quite so," Jova added. "Even if you are a little big for a pixie."

Oliver shook his head in mock disappointment. "Seriously, you are good men," he said. "Trolls can see an immortal or mortal's character by reading the expressions on their face. Vampires are easy to read—so emotional!" He looked at Jova with a steely glare. "You are a good man too," he said, "but I am still not sure what you are!"

"A friend," Jova answered, extending his hand.

"A friend is good," Oliver said, enveloping Jova's hand in his monstrous paw. "You can never have too many friends, especially in Port Royal. But, my new friends, you better have lots and lots of friends if you are serious about tangling with those nasty goblins at the Gallows Club."

I pointed down at Garlic. "She is our secret weapon," I said. Garlic licked her lips, looked up from her beer, and belched.

"I think you had better find some more friends," Oliver said, walking away to serve some more customers.

CHAPTER 9

When we returned to the *Dancing Swan*, the Howler, Jova, and I met in the captain's cabin to plan our assault on the Gallows Club. We decided quickly that Jova and I would enter the House of Angels using Trouble's gold coin and see how far it would take us. That would leave Garlic, the Howler, and the crew positioned around the House of Angels to back us up. The Howler was not completely convinced, however.

"I don't like this plan." She grimaced. "Once Sullivan sees you, the element of surprise will be gone, and you will be outnumbered and facing the goblin horde. Then what? We come in to retrieve your bodies?"

"Well," I said, trying to sound confident, "that is a possibility." I ignored a panic-stricken Jova. "But we are not going to lose the element of surprise before Garlic blows in the side of the House of Angels, and you, she, and the crew come in." I thought for a moment, then snapped my fingers. "Got it," I said. "We will go up to the House of Angels at quarter past the six o'clock hour. When the church bell of St. Peter's peals across the street at the bottom of the hour, Garlic will start the assault." Garlic barked happily. She liked the plan and the prospect of destroying the House of Angels one wall at a time.

The Howler nodded. "That only gives you a quarter of an hour."

"That is all the time we will need to breach the inner sanctum," I replied. I looked to Jova, who I hoped was ready to play the part that I had in mind for him. He had panicked at Death's Door, and we had a long and detailed discussion about fear and goblins on the way back from the tavern, but I neglected to mention that to the Howler just then.

Jova cleared his throat. "If there is one thing goblins fear, it's losing their hoard of gold," he said. He pulled a length of sailcloth from the deck and stuffed it in his rucksack, along with some gold ingots, and the pièce de résistance—a dragon's tooth. "Right around the time we walk up to the doorman of the House of Angels and present the Trouble coin, a golden dragon is going to bust through the doors. Those goblins will be so busy running to protect their riches from Goldie the Dragon here that finding and saving your sister should be child's play." He folded his arms across his chest and looked more confident than I had ever seen him before.

The Howler did not share my sentiment. "That is, if you don't lose your focus like you did on deck," she scowled. "Don't fail us, Bogeyman! Or our souls will be the ones haunting you!"

I reached out to place a hand on both of them. "We can do this," I said. I looked the Howler straight in her beautiful eyes. "Now," I said, "let's go rescue your sister."

At shortly before six o'clock, Jova and I had made our way to the House of Angels. I scoured the area for signs of the Trouble brothers or other peril. Oddly, I did not sense any danger. My assassin's brain started working—had the Trouble brothers set us up? Maybe the real Gallows Club was elsewhere, and when Goldie the Dragon and our crew crashed the walls of the House of Angels, we would find nothing but a deadly trap.

I looked over at a focused Jova who was spreading out the sailcloth and positioning the gold ingots and dragon tooth. He did not look fearful, in fact his eyes had a distant look in them—the Bogeyman was here! I left him to his own devices and crept closer to the House of Angels. The street in front of the building was oddly deserted for a lively town like Port Royal. Then, it hit me—the overwhelming stench of those gold-hoarding, bloodthirsty monsters of merchantdom. Goblins. "Do a deal or die trying" was their motto. At six o'clock on the nose, a burly pirate came down the street and perched himself in front of the House of Angels. I took a deep breath and returned to Jova's side. He nodded that he was ready, and we strode confidently around the corner and walked right up the doorman.

Jova extended his hand and showed the doorman the coin he had gotten from Andrew Trouble. The doorman did not even look twice at it. "Hurry up and get to the chapel," he said. "You are going to be late for the ceremony!"

"Uh, sorry," I muttered as we brushed past him. Ceremony? What horrific goblin embodiment of evil were we going to see? If the Howler only knew her sister was apparently to be tortured in some ancient goblin spectacle of sadism. Half past the hour could not come soon enough for us to rescue the poor crippled werewolf from unthinkable harm.

We began running down a narrow hall that dead-ended at a set of double doors that were suddenly thrust open from inside. Speechless, we found ourselves face-to-face with a bevy of unattractive female goblins with their faces powdered and lips slathered in rouge, and wearing full-length formal gowns and high heels, which incidentally did not improve their appearance whatsoever. You can put a hog in a ball gown but it is still a hog, after all.

"Come on, it's about to start." One of the goblins grabbed my hand and pulled me through the door into the chapel. "Take your seats, quickly," she hissed. "Confounded pirates," she said to her friends. "And I bet they are not even going to dance tonight."

Jova and I slunk down the side of the chapel and squeezed into some empty seats in a pew filled with a goblin family all dressed in their finest livery. Instead of raising the alarm and trying to kill us, they nodded and smiled. I looked around the chapel and marveled as sitting together in rows and rows of seats were finely dressed goblins, mortals, and immortals of all kinds. For a moment, I felt Jova and I were a bit underdressed, until my eyes fell upon the altar at the end of the aisle and the hooded figure standing there. It had to be the evil priest-king! I looked at the goblin mother who was reapplying rouge to her lips. I shook my head sadly. What kind of mother brought her children to a sacrifice? I estimated we still had ten minutes or so before Garlic and the Howler would make their grand entry, and we were no closer to finding Cornelia.

Jova looked at me, now clearly quite unsure whether he should summon Goldie to bust down the front doors. Quite honestly, I was not sure if he should do that either. If only I could get a signal to the

Howler to hold their assault until Jova and I could figure out just what in the world was going on. Suddenly, everyone stood, and Jova and I followed the gaze of the crowd, and we heard the unmistakable sound of—a fiddle?

Down the aisle the fiddler came, followed by the bevy of goblin "beauties." Following them was a veiled woman dressed in white, holding flowers, the long train of her gown flowing behind her. She limped noticeably and paused once for a few moments as if in great pain. The Moon of Madrid hung around her neck, its iridescent beauty reflecting the many candles in the chapel. She reached the end of the aisle with some difficulty, and the hooded man came up to her and bowed. So nice to be polite before he killed her, I thought. A man wearing all black with a white collar had come out to stand with the hooded man while we were looking at the poor girl—was it even Cornelia?

The crowd grew silent, and I readied myself for action. I looked at Jova, and he was trembling nervously, and Goldie was nowhere to be seen. The hooded man reached up and pulled back the woman's veil to reveal a face similar to the Howler's, although a whole lot less attractive.

"Cornelia?" Jova said out loud, causing the goblin family in our row to look at us.

Cornelia reached up and pulled back the hood of the mystery man, revealing an immortal who was clearly part goblin. He smiled at Cornelia, who rolled her eyes in obvious disgust.

"Murfield," Jova yelled. "Andrew Murfield, you bastard!"

Murfield and Cornelia and the entire congregation now turned to look at us. "Jova! You came for me," Cornelia exclaimed, clapping her hands excitedly.

I turned to Jova. "You know Cornelia and that fellow?" I exclaimed.

Jova stepped out into the aisle. "You are darn right I do!" He began walking down the aisle toward the altar, and a great hush fell over the crowd. "Andrew Murfield," he said. "I have told you since the first day of class at Hedley Edrick's College of Immortals that Cornelia is *my* betrothed. You will marry her over my dead body."

"That can be arranged, Jova," Murfield sneered, motioning to the wings of the chapel for his groomsmen to assemble. They were a mix of goblins and warlocks, and soon Murfield was backed by a host of wand-carrying warlocks and, to my chagrin, elite goblin warriors who had shapeshifted into a lion, a tiger, and a bear.

"Oh my," I said from my seat. But Jova did not stop walking down the aisle and reached the end, where he held out his hand for Cornelia, who rushed to his side. "You don't scare me, Murfield," he said. "Unlike school, I have lots of friends now. Meet my sweet pet, Goldie."

Bursting through the sidewall of the chapel strode the biggest, fiercest dragon I had ever seen. Venom dripped from Goldie's long fangs, and her angry roar drowned out the screams of panic as the chapel guests pushed to escape this malevolent menace. I looked once, looked twice, and as I calmed my nerves, I could see Goldie was nothing but sailcloth. But to the congregation, she was pure terror. I made my way to the altar through the throng of terrified wedding guests and saw Murfield turn to urge his groomsmen to attack. The warlocks were having none of this conflict, pocketing their wands and sprinting for the exit with the reverend in tow, leaving the goblins alone with Murfield. Jova was whispering in Cornelia's ear, and quickly the look of fear on her face abated and turned to a wry smile.

"You call yourselves goblins," Murfield implored his groomsmen. "It's a dragon. What of it? Kill it." Goldie turned in his direction and roared deeply, swinging a mighty claw at his face. Murfield stumbled backward in terror, tripping over his robes and falling headlong into Jova and Cornelia, sending them all to the floor in a heap.

"Jova!" I called, reaching for him too late. I hoped he would keep his concentration, and thus, Goldie stalemating the goblins, but the back of Jova's head had struck the floor, and Goldie instantly collapsed in a pile of sailcloth, gold, and dragon tooth. The three remaining goblins turned to face me, their faces contorted in angry scowls. Apparently, they did not like uninvited guests.

Murfield rose to his feet and kicked an inert Jova in the ribs, causing Cornelia to scream. "You have learned a few tricks," he said to Jova with a sneer. "But they are not going to help you now." Cornelia lunged at him and spit in his face. "That is no way to treat your future husband," he said, sweeping her injured leg out from under her, sending her to the ground once again. He plucked the Moon of Madrid from her breast and drew his hand back to strike her.

"Murfield, that is no way to treat a lady, now is it?" I said, sword in hand. The goblin groomsmen had not moved to attack me, waiting for a signal from their leader. "No wonder you have to kidnap them to get them to marry you. Maybe you should simply try being nice. It might suit you."

Murfield stopped his hand in midair, and his eyes found me. With his sword drawn, he fell in with his groomsmen. "A vampire pirate?" he said. "That is about as likely as Jova having friends."

I smiled. "Jova has plenty of friends," I said, wondering if I was experiencing the longest quarter of an hour in recorded history. All of a sudden, I heard the distant peal of the bell of St. Peter's. "And I think you are about to make their acquaintance."

Murfield and his goblin cohorts made a big production of looking around the now empty chapel and then laughed heartily. "I think you are mistaken," he said, pulling Cornelia to her feet and shoving her violently forward. "Kill the vampire, and after you beat this miserable wretch, pathetically knocked-out cold on the floor within an inch of his so-called life, bring him with you so he can watch me marry the love of his life."

From the back of the chapel, the Trouble brothers had walked in while Murfield was talking. "Sir," Andrew Trouble said. "Your carriage is ready."

"Excellent," Murfield said. "You can stay and help kill the vampire."

"With pleasure," Andrew Trouble said, motioning his brothers into position. "I remember you from Death's Door. You are no friend of James Sullivan. And you are no friend of mine." His brothers nodded in agreement and cracked their knuckles in anticipation of putting their fists in my face repeatedly. They would not get that chance, I mused. The goblins on the other hand . . .

"No, he certainly is not," said a familiar voice from the eaves. In walked James Sullivan aka Big Belly Bart with his two assassin friends in tow. He looked at Murfield. "Sir," he said, "I owe this wretched vampire some payback for what his mangy mutt did to me leg. I beg of you, let me be the one to deliver the killing blow."

"No need to beg, my good James," Murfield sneered. "You can all have a turn with him, or shall I say what is left of him after my grooms-men have a go."

I had a whole lot of trouble at my back and angry goblins in front of me. "Don't you blokes know it is rude to talk about someone in front of their face like they are not even there?" I exclaimed, quickly surveying the scene and my odds. I was severely outnumbered. My best chance was to take out as many of the goblins as I could before the mortals even drew their blades. That was no easy task.

I exhaled slowly and readied for the battle of my life, and for my life. Then, a tremendous explosion rocked the back of the chapel, blowing a huge hole in the wall. Garlic leaped through the smoke and debris, the Howler and the crew trailing her. I took advantage of the distraction to deliver a mighty blow on the bear goblin, who fell back, blood running from a deep killing wound to his chest. There were only two goblins left, I thought, before I watched in amazement as the bear goblin healed from that massive death blow right before my eyes. What strange magic was this? Goblins were incredibly tough and resilient, but this was something entirely different. I knew that the goblin should have been dead, but he stood up and unsheathed a long, wicked blade, shook his head, roared in rage, and charged me. I decided that warlock magic and elite goblin warriors that could take animal form were a really unfortunate combination.

The battle was joined. I sidestepped his rush, and cleaved his ankle nearly clean off his foot, but he only paused momentarily to let his foot reattach before he came at me once again. I was faster than him, but eventually I would tire, and this the goblin knew. I jumped to the altar and surveyed the scene, grinning for just a second as I saw Big Belly Bart on the ground, blood spurting from his other, formerly healthy, leg courtesy of Garlic. The Howler was a whirling blur of steel, her hair streaming like silk, and green eyes flashing in anger as she sliced clean through the lion goblin's leg, en route to her sister. Just as she reached Murfield and Cornelia, the lion goblin stretched out and grabbed her ankle, pulling her to the ground. She reached back with her blade and chopped the goblin's hand off, then pried the hand from her leg and threw it in rage toward the exit. "Get your hand off me," she said. Her gorgeous eyes went wide as the hand crawled down the aisle on its fingertips to rejoin its owner. "Sirius," she called, kicking the hand back into the main chapel with a grunt. "You have to do something here!"

"Why, you seem to have things well in hand," I answered. On came the bear goblin to the altar. I somersaulted off and sliced his hamstrings to buy myself some time. "I am thinking," I said, returning atop the altar. How could we break this spell? "I am open to suggestions, however, Madam Captain."

Murfield took advantage of the chaos and frantically pushed Cornelia toward the exit. But Jova barred his path. "No illusions, no magic, just you and me, Murfield," Jova said. He rolled up his sleeves, and all I saw was Jova throwing the most awkward punch in the history of fisticuffs before the bear goblin's next charge forced me to vacate my perch.

The crew was battling admirably, stalemating the Trouble brothers and Big Belly Bart's two assassins. Where was Garlic, I wondered. Then I saw her and the tiger goblin squaring off. Clearly, the tiger goblin did not know what to make of Garlic, because every lunge it made at the Maltese resulted in opening the many now-healing gashes on its legs. Garlic had enough of playing tag with the goblin and let out a tremendous bark, but the tiger goblin was already in midair in an attempt to crush Garlic. The bark clipped the goblin, sending it head over heels into a pillar, its head ending up in the rather unnatural position of facing backward. What seemed like mere seconds later, it rose to its feet, and grabbing its head, pulled it around to face us.

The three goblins broke off their assault and huddled together, and the Howler, Garlic, and I did the same. I surveyed the scene. The assassins had apparently limped off, carrying Big Belly Bart once again, but half of the crew was dead at their hands. The Trouble brothers had indeed run at the first sign of trouble, choosing not to face the other half of our crew, who had set out after them in pursuit.

That left Jova and Murfield still trading blows—if you could call it that. Cornelia had crawled behind Murfield, and Jova took the opportunity to push him over her, and they both clapped with glee as he toppled to the ground. "Now," Jova said, getting on top of Murfield, "remember what I said to you? I told you Cornelia is mine!" He reared back to hopefully smear Murfield's nose across his bloody face, but Cornelia was an angry bride and smashed Murfield over the head with a Bible before Jova could finish him off. Cornelia tossed her bouquet at Murfield's chest and smiled as his eyes rolled back in his head. "Hey,"

Jova said. "I was going to do that . . ." But Cornelia's lips on his own soon drowned out his protest. That just left us and the goblins.

I rallied my troops, which consisted of Garlic and the Howler. "If Garlic uses her bark too much, she will probably bring down this whole building on our heads," I said.

"And we would not want to kill the lovebirds over there," the Howler sneered. "If I live through this, I am going to have a few short angry words with your friend Jova."

I glanced at the positioning of the couple, seeing Cornelia astride Jova. "Well," I said. "You are going to have to remove your sister's tongue from his throat first so he can answer you. Must run in the family . . ."

The Howler opened her mouth to retort, but the goblins had now turned with swords drawn. "Your master is defeated," she said. "Leave this place, and you will not be harmed."

Her words drew laughs of derision. "It was worth a shot," I said, patting her arm. "They look very intimidated. Scared, even." Actually, they kept looking at Garlic, and it was clear to me that they viewed her as the biggest threat of the three of us. Their meeting was not about the Howler and me, but about how to navigate the bark of the vampire Maltese. Garlic barked, and the goblins jumped slightly. Garlic looked to me, wanting to attack, as standing idly did not suit her one bit.

The goblins separated and surrounded us as the Howler and I stood back-to-back with Garlic by our feet. Good strategy on their part, I mused. Garlic could get one, maybe two with her bark, if she didn't take the Howler or me out in the process. One of the three would get us, if not this time, when we tired and made that one fatal mistake.

"Sirius," the Howler exclaimed. "We need a plan!"

"Try this," said Oliver, walking down the aisle with wine bottles in hand. He sidestepped the oblivious Jova and Cornelia and came up to the altar. In such time of peril, those two were in their own little world! It was not like either one of them could be any use against the goblins anyway.

"Now is really not the time for a drink, Oliver," I said. "Perhaps after we get out of this little predicament?" The Howler looked quite exasperated, shifting her weight from side to side, ready for the goblins' attack. Garlic licked her lips, wondering if Oliver had that oh so tasty beer, and seeing and smelling none, turned her attention back to the goblins.

The goblins paused, unsure if the mighty troll was friend or foe. They knew him to be the barkeep at Death's Door, the Trouble brothers' favorite drinking establishment. But no matter, they would find a different place to slake their thirst, and they raised their swords for the attack. They had killed trolls before, and they would kill this one and take his wine to celebrate.

But this was no ordinary troll, as this one had a plan. I watched in amazement as Oliver leaped forward and broke a bottle of wine over the lion goblin's head, dousing him with the vintage. The other two goblins retreated suddenly, looking scared. "We have to get the other two," Oliver said, tossing me some bottles.

I threw the bottles in the air over the goblins. "Garlic," I called, "make it rain!"

Garlic jumped in the air and barked, shattering the bottles and drenching the other two goblins. "What kind of wine is that?" I called to Oliver.

"It is the wine made from the Apple of Cain," Oliver replied. "Now the goblins can't heal from their wounds. The wine breaks that spell! Hell, the wine breaks all spells! Attack them now and save yourselves, because the wine's effect only lasts a short time!"

The Howler and I did not waste a second and dispatched the lion goblin and bear goblin with what I thought was amazing teamwork. That girl could certainly handle herself in a fight, I realized quite impressed, wanting to discuss some more intimate strategies with her when the first chance arose. The tiger goblin saw the blood slowly seeping out of its two comrades and turned to flee, but Garlic had other ideas, barking the evil creature into tiny bits.

I turned to Oliver. "Why did you help us?" I asked, curious why a notoriously neutral troll would take a side in any conflict.

Oliver shrugged. "Andrew Trouble has been promising to pay his and his brothers' tabs for months," he said. "I came here to collect."

I exchanged a delighted glance with the Howler. "And you did so carrying enchanted wine that can stop a goblin in its tracks?"

"Yes," said Oliver. "Yes, I did."

I reached for the last bottle of wine, which Oliver handed to me. The bottle was very old, and the label was in Spanish and inscribed in gold. "Perdición del Monstruo," I said. "Bane of the Monster." I looked closer at the name inscribed in the very tiniest of print at the bottom of the bottle—"Don Indigo." "It can't be," I said. "I knew a man named Don Indigo, years and years ago."

Oliver nodded, "Don Indigo was one of the most famous winemakers in all of Europe," he said. "Though he was a great vintner, he was an even better man."

I thought back to my act of mercy so many years ago in Segovia. I had let Don Indigo live that day, and centuries later his work had saved my life. "I could live to be a thousand years old," I said, "and I will never understand how this world works."

Oliver smiled at me. "Those might be the most intelligent words you have ever uttered."

Something caught my eye over his beefy shoulder. When Garlic had blasted the last goblin into oblivion, her bark had also sheared off the lock of the goblins' vault behind the altar. I pushed by Oliver and pulled the heavy door off its hinges, and had to squint to protect my eyes from the sheer brilliance of the chests and chests of gold, jewels, and other assorted baubles that filled the room. I turned back to the group. "To the victors," I said, "go the spoils."

The Howler had run to Cornelia, interrupting her reunion with Jova. The two sisters embraced tightly, and whatever words Jova whispered to the Howler appeared to work, for soon he was brought into the sisterly hug. The riches of family were many, but paled to me in light of the contents of the goblins' treasure.

"Hey," I called, "come see this vault. We are all rich beyond our wildest dreams."

But the Howler had stood and was looking at Murfield. "First, Sirius," she said, "there is some unfinished business with this one." She kicked him in the crotch with her boot, and he moaned in pain though unconscious. "This cretin is not a corpse—yet . . ."

I shrugged my shoulders, looking again at the wonders of the vault. "So kill him already. Come on, we have more gold here than I have ever seen."

The Howler measured Murfield's throat with her blade, and her face hardened in anger. "You killed my spy by taking his head," she said to a stirring Murfield. "So now I am going to take yours. See how your people like that when they find it on the altar!" The blade came down, rushing for Murfield's throat, but there was a clang as her blade was deflected by another.

"No," Jova commanded, holding a sword with surprising firmness and resolve. "There has been enough bloodshed this day."

The Howler glared at him, but backed down, seeing Cornelia had clutched Jova's arm, standing with him. "Suit yourself," the Howler spat. "But you are making a big mistake." She looked to me to get involved, and grimaced, seeing I was content in idly flipping some gold coins in the air. Frankly, I did not care whether Murfield lived or died. The Howler growled and walked away, holding up her hands in defeat. "Doesn't anybody *kill* their enemies anymore?"

Jova searched around for something to tie up Murfield with and settled on the strips of sailcloth that had made up Goldie the Dragon. With Cornelia's assistance, Murfield was quickly trussed up, looking rather like a fly caught in a spider's web. Satisfied, they moved to join us, when Cornelia turned. "Wait a minute," she said, reaching into Murfield's breast pocket and removing the Moon of Madrid. "I nearly forgot this. That would have been bad, to say the least."

"Okay, then," I called. "We really must move this along, shall we? No offense meant to you, Cornelia, but there are probably a hundred jewels in this vault that put that little bauble of yours to shame."

"It's sentimental," she said, quite ignoring me as she and Jova walked up to the vault. Jova peered in and shrugged. "That *is* a lot of gold," he said. He turned and took Cornelia in his arms. "But I have what I came for. I have had enough of Port Royal, pirates, and treasure."

I rolled my eyes. "You can never have enough treasure." The memory of seeing the shower of my hard-earned gold pouring down on Bloodsucker Number One in the courtroom entered my mind. Looking around the room, I saw there was ample gold for all of us, and in my mind, my kindness in helping the Howler and rescuing Cornelia was about to be repaid, courtesy of the goblins.

Jova started to protest, but spied on the floor of the vault a ring that had a diamond the size of a walnut, set in an intricate setting of yellow gold. "Cornelia, dear," he said. "Can you come over here for a second?"

"Sure, what is it, my love?" she answered. "Do you need some more of my sweet kisses?"

"Indeed, your lips are too far away," he responded.

Cornelia wandered into the vault and found Jova on one knee, holding up the ring. "And thus, I would like them to be nearby forever." She gasped and dropped to her knees to join him. She began wiping tears from her eyes, and seeing Jova was tearing up, too, reached to caress his blubbering face. These two were going to make me ill, I mused. Did they really love each other *that* much? Was it possible for love to be like Jova and Cornelia's—where you could actually see it?

"I almost lost you once," Jova said. "I am not going to let that happen again." He placed the oversized ring on Cornelia's ring finger. "I don't care what your father says. Will you be my wife?"

"But Papa was the one that arranged my marriage to Murfield," Cornelia exclaimed.

"He was?" I shouted, looking to the Howler.

The Howler nodded. "He was," she said, gritting her teeth. "Murfield's family is incredibly wealthy, and they are one of the biggest landowners in all of Europe. They are politically connected in England, France, Spain, and Portugal. They have the gold to bend the ear of any king. That is the kind of power that Papa wants access to. He'll never approve of Jova. Papa is all about appearances. All men that marry his daughters are men of means and substance and, usually, fame."

"And you knew this too, Jova?" I said, staring down the Bogeyman.

"It really was not a concern," Jova said. "Either way, we were fighting goblins, whether you knew the truth or not."

"True," the Howler agreed. "I needed your help, Sirius, and breaking up a wedding is a little less enticing a pitch to a cynical vampire assassin than the kidnapping of your baby sister!"

"But, you lied," I said to her. "Actually, you both lied."

"Yes," Jova answered. "My apologies. But, I did it for love—true love."

The Howler put her arms around my neck. "Me too," she said softly. "Can you ever forgive me?"

"Fine," I said, losing myself in her eyes for a moment. Did she mean she loved me, or her sister? Women were so damned complicated. Could have used Oliver's face-reading skills to translate here! "But *you* owe me."

I turned to Jova. "Now, you and me?" I said, grabbing his shoulders and glaring at him. He looked panicked, until he saw me smile broadly. "We are good, Jova," I continued. "You are a good man. But what are we going to do about Cornelia's father? Hmm, can we find a better use for all this loot? I wonder . . ."

Jova looked around the vault and began nodding in understanding. "I changed my mind on the treasure," he said. "I think I know where to find quite a dowry. And besides, who wouldn't want the world-renowned Bogeyman in their family? So it is settled. Cornelia, will you be my wife?"

"I will," Cornelia said, tears of joy streaming down her face.

Oliver clapped his big hands together. "I just love weddings," he said. "It would be an honor to supply the wine. And since I am going to have to close down Death's Door this very night, because of the goblins, I will be heading back to London anyway."

"That would be lovely," Jova said, his eye catching the bottle of Don Indigo's wine. "Oliver, is that what I think it is? Is that a Don Indigo?"

"Yes, Master Bogeyman," Oliver said. "Now that I know your secret, here is mine. This particular wine was crafted by Don Indigo over one hundred years ago from the fruit of the strawberry tree. Some call the fruit Cain's Apple. Only the trolls and Don Indigo have known about its power to break enchantments. Oh, and it has no effect on us trolls, other than making us smile a whole lot more."

"Not that we can tell the difference," I uttered to no one in particular.

Jova ignored my comment. "Did you know the great Don Indigo?"

Oliver nodded. "I met Don Indigo when he was in his later years and helped him expand his vineyard in the Tuscan region of Italy. As repayment, he gave me these bottles and many even more rare ones that I have back at Death's Door."

"Don Indigo was a genius," Jova exclaimed. "We must get your wine back to London! Cornelia and I will rendezvous with my ship down at the docks and take our share of the gold and your wine back to England."

"Your what?" I said, fearing my ears had deceived me.

"My ship, boat, craft, vessel," Jova said. "Come on, the goblins are going to come back for the hoard. We do not have a lot of time to waste."

"You never said you had a boat and crew!"

Jova shrugged. "You never asked." He could see I was getting angry. "It was for true love, Sirius, remember?"

Garlic suddenly began yelping and whining as she pawed through a treasure chest, sending gold doubloons and jewels through the air while she dug frantically. "What are you looking for, girl?" I wondered out loud. "You are getting gold and gems everywhere." Then, with a triumphant arf, Garlic pulled a black leather collar studded with red crystals from the chest.

"What do you have there, Garlic?" the Howler asked, bending to examine the collar Garlic had brought over to her. "Are those the kind of crystals I think they are?"

Jova peered at them curiously. "If so, they are probably the smallest transportation crystals I have ever seen."

Oliver nodded. "Probably just some sort of knockoff that the goblins took, and found useless, so it was dumped here with the rest of this stuff. I mean no offense to Garlic, but it's not like dogs can transport like us immortals anyway."

"She does really seem to like it for some reason," I said, not thinking at that moment if it was necessary to let him know that, again—one, she was no ordinary canine, and two, she actually had transported via crystal before. "No harm in letting her wear it that I can see," I added.

Garlic whined and tried to jump through the collar that the Howler was now holding. "Okay," the Howler said. "I get it. You really do want to wear this." Garlic yelped in assent, and the Howler fastened it around her neck.

"She has claimed her part of the booty, making her a true pirate," I said. My eyes found Jova once again. "You and I will take this up in London. Does anyone have any crystals? We could try to transport the gold that way."

Garlic barked loudly and ran back and forth. "Okay, girl, I know it was a good idea, but hush for a second," I said to her. Garlic rolled her eyes and put a paw over her nose, clearly frustrated, but I had no time to decipher her canine commentary.

"I do," said Oliver. "But the House of Angels is protected from anybody or anything getting in or out by crystal. And unless it is a really special crystal, you can only transport so much with you. It would take time we do not have. So we are going to have to do it the old-fashioned way—we need some wagons."

The church bell of St. Peter's struck midnight. "We cannot count on the goblins waiting until tomorrow to regroup," I said, noting the moon, though not full, would give us plenty of light to work under but not betray our actions. "We have to move the treasure now."

We'd need to retrieve wagons from the docks, so Cornelia and Oliver set out for Jova's ship, and the Howler set out for the *Dancing Swan*, leaving Jova, Garlic, and me to guard the treasure. I viewed Cornelia as a liability with her leg, but Oliver was an able protector. No one messes with a troll, except an enraged goblin, but since Jova was happy to have her out of harm's way, I chose not to mention that. The Bogeyman had clearly found peace within himself, apparently buoyed by Cornelia's love. He looked ready and willing to levy his powers of fear on any who approached the House of Angels and the treasure that would serve as his dowry for Cornelia.

Jova was not much use moving the treasure out of the vault, in fact Garlic pulled twice as much as he. When I set the treasure chests on sailcloth, she tugged it along easily on the smooth wood floor. Finally, Jova collapsed in exhaustion, so I took a moment and peeked outside to check the streets. They remained deserted.

"It is a good thing the moon is not full tonight," I said. "There is no bright light to reveal our position. Of course, the last time I had Madam Captain under the full moon, I had her in a most enjoyable position."

Jova looked at me in abject horror. "You did what?"

"Oh, I get it," I said. "You have never been with a woman. Well, no one should be a virgin on their wedding night. When you get back to London, you might want to find some strumpet to show you what to do so Cornelia won't be disappointed. Let me tell you, if her sister is any indication, get her on a full moon, and you can really make her howl, if you know what I am saying."

Jova's mouth opened and closed as he searched for words. Poor kid, I thought, he could only imagine what being with a woman was like, and the Howler was quite the impressive creature—and it was good that Cornelia was not nearly half as pretty as her, or poor Jova's little bogeyman might be too frightened to make an appearance.

"Did you know what you were doing, being with her on the full moon?" Jova finally sputtered.

I put a knowing hand on his shoulder as Oliver returned with the wagons. "Jova, I always know what I am doing when women are involved, especially beautiful naked werewolves in the light of the full moon. Come on, we have wagons to load."

"Right," he replied. "Wagons . . ."

For all of the earlier bickering, I was happy to see our group working together as impressively as any army regiment or assassin's squad. When Jova's wagon was nearly full, Oliver and Jova bid their adieu, with a plan to stop at Death's Door to load Oliver's prized wine into the space that was left. I questioned them if the wine was really worth the risk, but Jova merely chuckled and said I should know the value of rare wine was absolutely priceless. Damn haughty Bogeyman, I thought. He would fit in very well with Cornelia's snobby family.

As they left, our crew arrived with our wagon, and as we loaded the last chest of gold, I could smell very faintly the dastardly odor of goblins. It was nearly daybreak, and I shoved the Howler into the wagon. She protested until she, too, caught the scent of approaching death, and took the reins of the wagon in hand, and we sped back to the *Dancing Swan*. We encountered no trouble or Trouble brothers on the way, but Port Royal was beginning to come alive as the first hints of sun peeked over the horizon.

"Quickly now," I said to the crew as they unloaded the wagon and deposited the treasure chests safely in the hold. This operation was going surprisingly smoothly, I thought as Garlic and I stood watch on the pier to scent any approaching goblins. The Howler looked at the brightening sky and looked relieved to see the last chest disappear into the hold.

"Let us shove off," she said. "Cornelia and Jova should be safely on his ship by now and on course to London. It is time for us to do the same."

I thought of all the lovely gold in the hold. "We are rich," I said. "But we have to be prepared to fight off the goblins if they come after us."

"They won't," she said.

"How do you know that?"

"Because before we joined you back at the House of Angels, Garlic barked some new portholes below the waterline of their ship and sank it rather quickly," the Howler said. She smiled and went to hop down on the dock to help with the ropes when her eyes rolled back in her head and she fainted, falling right into my open arms.

"Water, water," I yelled. "Get me some fresh water and a cloth for our captain!"

Instantly, the crew circled around her, concerned, and I held her in my arms and dabbed at her face with the cold cloth. The Howler awoke with a sputter and a curse. "Get back to work, you scurvy rats!" she yelled.

"Some space for the captain," I said, helping her to her feet. The crew went back to finishing the ropes, and we were ready to leave Port Royal. "What was that all about?" I asked. "Werewolves don't faint. You aren't sick, are you?"

The Howler threw up her breakfast onto my boots. "No," she said. "I am fine. There must have been some wolfsbane in one of those chests. Damn those goblins. Just leave me alone." She wobbled to the ship's railing and proceeded to empty the rest of her innards into the bay.

"Sirius!" a voice called—a voice that should have been on the way to London long ago. I turned to find Jova, Oliver, and Cornelia sitting in a very empty wagon.

"What are *you* people still doing in Port Royal?" I screamed. "You should have been gone hours ago." Garlic padded over and cocked her ear, then sat at Jova's feet, waiting for his explanation.

"Right," Jova said. "It seems Oliver underestimated the number of wine casks he had at Death's Door, and . . ."

The Howler, still looking a little green around the gills, had managed to walk over to us. "And . . . ?" she repeated.

Cornelia looked at the Howler's face, and a look of fear came over her own. "Oh," she said. "This is not good. Not good at all."

"You are right this is not good!" I exclaimed. "Get to it, Jova. Now! Or your face is going to be very not good because of my fist!"

Jova remained silent, so Oliver spoke up. "When we ran out of room for the wine, we started unloading the treasure, and before we knew it all the wine was in the wagon and all the gold was at Death's Door. So we hurried to the dock and unloaded the wine into Jova's ship. And . . ."

"And that is when we discovered we had a problem," Jova finally said. "My ship is small and built for speed, well, and the rest of the gold won't fit on it. I sent my ship back to London with the wine. But I need that other treasure for Cornelia's dowry. The *Dancing Swan* has room for it all."

"So here we are," Cornelia added, her eyes still on her sister, who was doing a good job of leaning against the rail to hold it up.

I stood rubbing my head with my hand. "So, let me get this straight," I said. "You offloaded gold for wine and sent your ship to London with nothing but wine on it."

"But priceless wine," Cornelia said with a smile. I rolled my eyes. She was clearly drinking the Bogeyman's elixir.

"And now you want us to go with you through likely goblin-infested streets in the middle of the morning, load treasure into a wagon, come back to the dock, load it onto the *Dancing Swan*, and then go to London?" I said, making eye contact with Jova and his wayward pirates.

"So you will do it," said Cornelia as she took her sister's arm and helped her into the wagon.

"She is not going," I said. "She can barely move. She must have touched some wolfsbane."

Cornelia looked at her sister. "Wolfsbane, right, that explains it," she said. "Then she needs to get away from this ship. Let the crew search for it, or it will be a long trip to London for us."

"She can stay on the dock away from the boat while it is searched by the crew," I said. The Howler gave me a cross look. "Fine," I said. "Just try not to throw up on my boots again." I turned to see the crew ready with their cutlasses, all of which would be useless if the goblins approached. Then I saw them priming the cannons and turning them toward the docks. Still not likely to stop the goblins, but if it made them feel better, that worked too.

"Find the wolfsbane," I said to the first mate. "And if anything comes down that pier besides us and this wagon, blow it up, and leave for London," I said. "In fact, if you see anything that resembles trouble or the Trouble brothers—go. Understood?" The first mate nodded, and with a deep breath, I took the reins of the wagon and steered the horses toward Death's Door.

I guided the wagon through now crowded streets, but the going was slow as it seemed all of Port Royal was out doing their morning errands. There was a tremendous crash ahead of us, and I slowed the wagon to a halt, which gave the Howler a chance to poke her head out the back and vomit once again. She did not seem any better being away from the wolfsbane, I thought, but my attention was diverted by a cloaked figure flipping over wagons in the middle of the street. I spied sinewy hands reaching out from under a cloak, and inhuman strength at work. Goblin! The merchant whose path the goblin had just blocked jumped out of his wagon for a confrontation, and there was a sickening crunch of facial bones being pulverized. The merchant crumpled to the ground, and the crowds scattered.

"Go that way." Oliver pointed down an alley marked by where the Howler had just thrown up.

I backed up the horses and peered down the alley. "It is too narrow," I said. "The wagon cannot clear it."

Oliver waved his hands in sweeping circles. "Look again," he said.

To my great surprise, I now looked upon a deserted cobblestone alley, easily big enough to allow us to pass. The cobblestones appeared to be made entirely of wood. I nudged the horses down the alleyway, delighted that I saw no goblins or traffic, and was shocked to hear the horses' hooves made absolutely no sound. "How did you do that?" I asked.

Oliver smiled. "That alley is my backdoor bridge to the loading dock of Death's Door," he said. "A warlock might be able to find it, but it should give us enough time to load the gold and get back to the ship, especially with all the commotion that goblin is causing."

It was an hour before noon when we pulled up to the loading dock of Death's Door. Color had returned to the Howler's face, and she placed her hand on my own and squeezed it. "Are you ready?" she said with that delightful but oh so rare smile of hers.

"Indeed," I replied. "Let us get ourselves a dowry."

She gave me a rather pained look, perhaps the wolfsbane again? "For Jova," I clarified.

Cornelia set watch at the front of Death's Door, as Oliver, Jova, and I moved the treasure chests into position. "Oh no," she screamed. "Not him. It cannot be."

"What is it?" cried the Howler. Cornelia did not answer but merely pointed. I peered outside to see Murfield standing with the entire goblin horde, all, to a man, carrying flaming torches in one hand and assorted death-dealing weapons in the other. They backed a wagon piled high with hay against the entrance of Death's Door and ripped the wheels off, sending it crashing to the ground. We would not exit that way.

"Forget the gold," I said. "Oliver, let's head to your bridge."

I was the first one to the back entrance and flung open the door to find myself staring at a brick wall where there should have been an alleyway. "I guess they found your bridge," I said. "You got any other secret trapdoors out of here?"

He shook his head. "All I have is this one crystal," he said. "It will get me out of here, but is not big enough for all of us."

"Give it to Cornelia," I said. "We can go out the windows and fight them, but she cannot."

"I am not leaving Jova," Cornelia said, and the look in her eyes said she was not going to be persuaded otherwise.

I could smell smoke and feel heat coming from the front wall. Maybe I had only delayed my time in Hell, I mused for a second. "This place is about to come down on top of us," I said. "We have to go out the windows and fight them."

The Howler took that moment to pass out and fall to the floor. "What is wrong with her?" I said, looking to Cornelia. "The wolfsbane has got to be out of her body by now. Good Lord, I didn't think a person could actually expel that much bodily fluid by puking."

Not waiting for her to answer, I picked the Howler up, and motioned for Garlic to bark a hole in the wall.

"It is not wolfsbane," Cornelia said. "She is with child. Your child."

The floor began to shift and wobble beneath my feet. I stumbled and struggled to hold the Howler. "My child," I stammered, trying to regain my composure, but a crack formed in the floor, and the walls began to buckle. I was picking one heck of a time to start seeing things, and possibly faint.

"It's an earthquake!" Jova shouted. "We have to get out of here, or we will be crushed!"

Garlic barked loudly, and in front of her formed a great swirling wormhole. Her collar fairly shimmered as the ruby-red crystals on it were stirred into action by the most amazing vampire Maltese. "Garlic, why didn't you tell us earlier that you can use those crystals on that collar," I yelled over the din to her. "Oh yes, that whole can't-speak-like-a-human thing . . ." The floor tilted up right under the treasure chests, and soon we were under an aerial assault by the wealth we had so dearly coveted. A treasure chest slammed into the backs of Jova and Cornelia, knocking them sideways before it disappeared through the wormhole. The rest of the treasure quickly followed.

"Let's go," I screamed, dodging falling beams with the Howler and my unborn child in my arms. "I don't know where that hole leads to, but anywhere is better than here!" Where did a vampire Maltese focus on going when she was in certain danger? We were about to get our answer.

Oliver swept up Jova and Cornelia in his massive arms and dove for the wormhole, with Garlic, the Howler, and me right on his heels. There was a great rush of air reminding me of passing through the hidden gate of Hell, and the Howler chose that moment to wake up, and pull away from my arms. I flailed around in the wormhole but could not see or feel her before I found myself hurtling headfirst into a massive pile of hay. Were we only just outside Death's Door? Yet I smelled no fire and heard no goblins, and no sword pierced my chest. I pulled my head from the hay, wiped the dust from my eyes, and found my face an inch from Harvis's naked, hairy behind. And he was not alone.

"Hello, Molly," I said to the beautiful naked werewolf under him. "Did I interrupt you all taking a roll in the hay?" Molly's mouth dropped open, and her hands went across her breasts. Her eyes went wide with horror, and I looked up to see a swirling gray cloud rotating above the hay loft. The wormhole!

"Sirio Sinestra," Harvis sputtered. "I am going to have to kill you."

"I go by Sirius Sinister these days, Harvis. And it is great to see you too," I said. "Perhaps not so much of you, but you can't kill me," I said, "I am going to be a father." I looked around for the Howler, but did not see her in the hay, nor any of my companions from Port Royal. Were they still in the wormhole? Had they gone somewhere else? I heard a faint bark coming from the wormhole. "Garlic!" I exclaimed.

Harvis's ears perked up, and he rolled to his haunches and looked up at the wormhole. "What in the hell is that, and what is it doing in my barn?" he said. "Did you say you are going to be a father?"

Garlic's bark grew closer. "Yes, yes, I did," I replied.

"Congratulations," he said, looking up as a screaming Jova flew out of the wormhole and landed in his naked lap. "Jova?" he said.

"Hello, Harvis," Jova said. "It has been a while. Have you been well?" Jova then noticed that he was sitting in Harvis's naked lap. "Oh, this is awkward." Jova coughed loudly, and moved to safer territory faster than I had ever seen him move.

Molly had scrambled off the loft and into her clothes. "What is that?" she screamed. "Something big is coming through . . . Look out!" But it was too late, and Oliver tumbled out of the wormhole, barely missing crashing into Jova, Harvis, and me, before sending a huge cannonball of hay flying into the air when he finally landed.

Harvis turned to look at me. "Um, Sirius, is it now?" he said. "There is a troll in my hay loft."

I nodded. "That's Oliver—he is with us."

"I kind of figured that part out," Harvis replied. "You got any more friends coming through?"

"Actually, yes," I replied. I was beginning to wonder if the two sisters were going to make it out of the wormhole. I wished I had been able to keep the Howler in my arms, but had not expected her to fight me from holding on to her in the wormhole's disorientating twists and turns. What had happened to the werewolves, one of whom was carrying my child?

Cornelia came cartwheeling through the wormhole, and Jova dove to catch her. They rolled to a stop in front of Harvis and began kissing passionately until Jova pulled back and looked at his betrothed.

"I was afraid you were lost forever," Jova exclaimed, stroking her hair, and looking deep into Cornelia's eyes.

"The Bogeyman was scared," she teased. "You are not going to lose your future wife so easily."

Harvis sat, processing out loud what he had just heard. "Bogeyman? Wife?" he sputtered. "Cornelia? Is that you?"

"Harvis," she said, seeing the gruff werewolf for the first time. Then realizing that he was not wearing any clothes, she blushed the finest shade of red and turned her head quickly away, and that was when she spotted Molly. "Oh, hello, Molly, nice barn you've got here. It has been a while, hasn't it?"

"Yes, Cornelia, it has," Molly said politely, and eyed the wormhole with suspicion.

Harvis scrambled around the loft, looking for his breeches. "Let us hope there are no more surprises," he said.

Before I could open my mouth to reply, I heard Garlic's bark, and coming through the wormhole in a tangle of arms, legs, soon-to-be swollen belly, and paws came the Howler and Garlic. Harvis's face turned a lovely shade of crimson as he realized he was holding the Howler in his arms while wearing not a stitch of clothing. Garlic was happy to see the big werewolf and began licking his toes. That is when I was glad that Garlic was a vampire Maltese and not a vampire Great Dane, and I was wagering that Harvis felt the same way. But Molly was not so happy, or perhaps was simply feeling the urge to let loose the most primal of angry screams.

"You!" screamed Molly, pointing a finger in my direction.

"Me?" I said. "What did I do?"

"Not you," she screamed. "Her." Her gaze rested squarely on the Howler.

"You know each other too?" I said, looking from the Howler to Molly and back again.

"Yes, we do," said the Howler. "How are you, Molly?" She looked downward at Harvis's nether regions and, grimacing, slid over toward me. "Better put some clothes on, Harvis—it looks like you are catching a cold."

An eerie silence came over the barn as the two female werewolves stared each other down, low growls emanating from their throats. Then a single gold doubloon shot out of the wormhole, flew through the air, and plunked Harvis right in the middle of his forehead. "Ouch," he said, bringing his hand to his head. "What madness is this?"

"Move, people, move," I shouted, as more and more doubloons shot from the wormhole. "The treasure chests are coming next!" Jova helped Cornelia off the loft, and I did the same for the still weakened Howler. No more than seconds after we vacated the loft and got to safety, the wormhole jettisoned the final bit of its cargo from Port Royal, the massive weight of the treasure sending Harvis's loft crashing to the floor. A fine mist of gold dust hung in the air, and gold coins covered the floor wherever the eye could see. Jewels dotted the landscape along with various necklaces and bracelets of unimaginable value. But all Harvis wanted was his peace and quiet and his loft back in one piece. He held his breeches in one hand and a piece of wood that was all that remained of the ladder up to the loft and frowned sadly.

I was relieved to see that the wormhole had closed and had brought only treasure and no goblins. "Sorry about the loft, old chum," I said. "But I think we have the means to rebuild you another." Harvis said nothing, but I had a feeling that he was about to build the nicest hayloft in London, courtesy of the treasure. I looked over at the Howler, who stood next to me, staring daggers at Molly. "Come on, now," I said to her. "No reason to be angry. You are going to be the mother of our child. What is the problem here?"

The Howler took the moment to faint once again into my arms. Molly fixed an evil gaze on me. "She is the mother of your litter?" she said with a sneer.

"Yes, she is," I replied, slowly lowering the Howler to the ground. "What of it? And just what is your problem with her? Wait a minute. Did you say litter?"

"You are still a fool, Sirio—I'm sorry, Sirius, or whatever your name is now," she said. "Werewolves don't have just one baby—we usually have eight or nine at once."

Eight or nine at once?

I awoke to Harvis splashing water on my face and Garlic licking my nose and the droplets of water that remained on it. "What happened?" I asked, seeing we were not in the barn any longer but in Harvis's farmhouse. I could hear the laughter of Oliver, Jova, and Cornelia coming from a different room.

"You fainted," Harvis said casually. I was relieved to see him now wearing the breeches he held earlier. Then it hit me again—eight or nine little whelps?

I shook my head, choosing to process that later. "A man can only see your nakedness for so long," I said. "All right, what is the deal with Molly and my sweet innocent little flower of a werewolf?"

Harvis looked like he was about to be violently ill, and I could see he was struggling to find his words. "Molly and your new friend are distantly related. Their fathers are third cousins twice removed, and they lead two rival Packs that stand for two very different ways of life. My dear father-in-law leads the werewolves that honor the old ways by cultivating the earth and living off the land. Your lady friend's father has abandoned the old ways. He is focused on acquiring as much wealth, power, and riches as he can, just like mortals and goblins do."

"Is that really so bad?" I interjected. "Not the goblin part, of course."

Harvis shrugged his massive shoulders. "It is for a werewolf. They go around recruiting the young pups with promises of wealth and shouting odd phrases like "free trade for all" and "merchants are not just mortals," and building ship after ship so they can compete with mortals, goblins, and whoever else is trying to profit from this great earth of ours."

"Times change even for immortals," I said. "Look at the mortals. They have changed this world much even in the few hundred years I have been alive. Again, is that a bad thing?"

"Is it a good thing?" Harvis answered back. "The old ways say no. There is a word these new werewolf merchants are using. They call themselves capitalists."

It was as though even saying the word *capitalist* was painful for him, but I did not understand why. Actually, I did not understand what the word *capitalist* meant, but I wasn't going to admit that. If being a capitalist meant going for the gold, then that was exciting. To me, simple was not better, it was dull and boring. The reality was that a simple life was not going to enable me to support my family. Besides, vampires were generally pretty bad at trying their hands at farming, as we were good at killing things, not growing them.

"And that is why the mother of my unborn child and your wife hate each other?" I said, eyeing my big friend.

"Yes, that is it," Harvis said, not making eye contact.

I heard more laughter from the other room. Something did not sound right to me. "Well, how come Molly does not hate Cornelia with the same amount of venom I saw directed at the mother of my litter in the loft?" I asked.

"Uh, yeah, that . . ." Harvis said. "Well, I mean look at Cornelia. She is as homely as they come, not at all like her attractive sister, and all the werewolves feel bad for her with that crippled leg. Can't hunt. Can't farm. Can't defend herself. Probably useless to her father as a merchant. What can she do? And, she is just so nice—how can you not like her?" He finished and looked at me, assessing my reaction.

"You have been with her, you oversized mongrel!" I hissed.

"With Cornelia?" Harvis said.

"You know who I am talking about," I said, trying to keep my voice low. "The other beautiful female werewolf in this farmhouse that is *not* your wife—her!"

Harvis sighed. "Yes, I have," he confessed. "But, that was two hundred years ago."

"Before you were with Molly."

"Yes, we all were at Hedley Edrick's College of Immortals," Harvis said. "They both liked me, but Molly was a little shy about it, the other one . . . not so much."

"That is her style," I replied.

"It was just one time," Harvis said. "'Course, it was my first time . . ."

"And Molly knows this," I said.

"Yes," he sighed. "That is the problem with female immortals," he said, gritting his teeth. "When an immortal woman tells you she is never ever, ever, going to forget something, she really, really, means it. Oh well, it could have been worse."

I laughed. "How is that?"

"Well, first off, I had her before you did. No man likes to follow you vampires in the sack what with your legendary stamina," he said. "And, second, unlike you, I was not a big enough imbecile to have relations with a female werewolf during a full moon."

We laughed and clasped hands. "I guess I really do need that education," I said.

Harvis chuckled. "My friend, I think ready or not—you are about to get one."

CHAPTER 10

We spent the next two weeks rebuilding Harvis's loft, and it was of no surprise to me that Oliver was as good at building a loft as he was at pouring a glass of wine. Harvis had built his barn, the loft, and his farmhouse, and even he was impressed with the ingenuity and attention to detail the big troll gave to the new loft. Truth be known, we had it built in three days, or Harvis and Oliver did, with Jova and me just trying to stay out of the way. The last week and a half, with Oliver's help, Harvis expanded his barn, farmhouse, and outbuildings. The Howler was holed up in a side room of the farmhouse, while Cornelia tended to her. I had tried to see her several times but had been intercepted by Cornelia, who insisted it just wasn't a good time. Garlic had taken to lying outside the door of the Howler's room, occasionally padding in to see her before returning to her post. Molly merely rolled her eyes with a practiced air and busied herself with the chores of the farm and feeding her guests.

One night we found ourselves by the hearth in Harvis's now expanded great room, sipping wine and enjoying a late dinner to celebrate the completion of the farmhouse renovations. Cornelia had come to us, telling us that the Howler was not well again, and after kissing and stroking Jova's face and whispering in his ear promises for later, she departed back to her sister's room with a bowl of soup. Garlic snatched up a hunk of meat and followed Cornelia to resume her guard duty. I made eye contact with my canine companion but said nothing, since I felt it was an honor to have such a loyal and deadly creature protecting my unborn children from harm. Did Garlic know something that I did not?

"Tomorrow, I shall take my leave," Jova said. "I appreciate the hospitality, Harvis, but I need to go to London to meet my ship and then to Lancashire to ask Cornelia's father for her hand in marriage."

I nodded, wondering if Cornelia would be going with him, and so, too, the Howler, or if they would be staying here. I was a bit frustrated at being shut out of the planning. The Howler after all was carrying my issue, and I felt that she should be deferring to me. She wasn't.

"And I shall join you," Oliver replied. "Your craft should be landing at the docks in the next day or two, and I am anxious to recover my wine. From there, I need to return to the Meats and Cheeses, my pub on Fleet Street, and see if my brother has managed to not run it into the ground in my absence."

"Why were you in Port Royal?" I asked. "We never did get that part of your story."

"Now that is a story as old as the world," he said. "One day I was walking down by the Thames with nary a care in the world. There was the flash of a tail, and then out of the water popped up the most beautiful mermaid I have ever seen."

"A beautiful mermaid? You must have had too much wine that night!" Harvis scoffed. "Mermaids have the face of groupers, the personality of river trout, and their privates reek like rotting seaweed. You are telling us one big fish tale!"

"Come on, Oliver," I said. "Why were you really in Port Royal?"

Oliver chuckled and took a sip of his wine. "I know you think I am pulling your legs, but I am telling you the truth, lads," he said. "Her name was Iyonna. And she wasn't beautiful, you say? Please! Her hair was the color of sea foam, while her skin was as pure and white as the silkiest sand. And her eyes? Well, her eyes were the green-blue of the Caribbean Sea. She had never seen a troll before and wanted to touch my face to see what it felt like. So, I let her."

Jova was hanging on Oliver's every word, and had inched up to the edge of his seat. I stifled a grin, for the Bogeyman was in love with love. "And, and . . ." Jova asked. "What happened?"

"You mean after she bruised her soft little hands on his rocky face?" I said.

Jova and Oliver each gave me a look, and Harvis merely laughed. "Go on, go on," I said.

"Well," Oliver continued, "every day after I closed the tavern, I went walking by the Thames, and she met me and we talked. She was from the Caribbean Sea and had swum all the way to London, following a young mortal sailor she had fallen in love with. He got old and died, and she stayed, too heartbroken to go home."

"Aww," Jova exclaimed.

"Until she met me, that is," he said. "One night, she pulled me into the river, and kissed me, and pulled off my clothes, and . . ."

"And you were quite hard, were you not?" I interjected.

Oliver turned to look at me, and I braced for the stony punch of the big troll. "Come on," I protested. "How could I resist? That was funny!"

Then Oliver tilted his head back and roared with laughter that sounded like an oncoming avalanche. Harvis, Jova, and I joined in— me more out of relief than anything else.

"Yes, I was, vampire," Oliver said. "And that little mermaid sang like she had never sung before. But, Iyonna wanted to go home and convinced me to go with her. So I did."

"Why did you leave Port Royal then?" Jova asked. "I get the goblin thing. But it doesn't sound like you are going back to the Caribbean."

Oliver shook his head. "I am not," he said. "Interspecies romance is not easy. We were doomed from the start. Once Iyonna returned to her home, her parents saw to it that she broke off the relationship. It turns out mermaids are prohibited from consorting with land folk. So that was that—I was already making plans to close Death's Door and return to London when you two louts walked into my bar. Sometimes things just work out. What can I say?"

Jova sat in silence, staring at the floor. "What if her father doesn't let me marry Cornelia?" he said, looking up at us with tears in his eyes.

"Well, you can scare him into next week," I said. "That will do the trick, I am sure. Once you make a man relieve himself in his drawers, it kind of changes the balance of power."

Harvis nodded. "Shockingly, Sirius makes a good point," he said.

"Thank you," I said, raising my glass. "Hey, what do you mean shockingly?"

Harvis ignored me. "Werewolves respect power and can smell weakness a mile away," he said. "When you go to Lancashire to meet him, you cannot do it as Jova, but rather you must do it as the Bogeyman in all his fear-inducing fury."

"I agree," said Oliver. "And I will give you a nice bottle of wine to take with you—a rare vintage he will know and appreciate. Wine is always a good way to loosen up a person's hesitations."

"What are you going to do, Sirius?" Jova asked. "How are you going to approach her father?"

"Approach him about what?" I replied.

Jova looked taken aback. "She is with your child," he said. "Are you not going to do the right thing and make her an honest woman?" Harvis and Oliver hung on his words. I could see from the look on Harvis's face that he already knew how I was going to answer.

"Gentlemen," I said, "marriage was not very kind to me on the last go-around. To be perfectly clear with you, I do not have any intention of getting married, whether she is carrying my issue or not." I ignored Jova's flabbergasted expression. It was like he could not comprehend what I was saying whatsoever. Maybe if he had a little taste of Immortal Divorce Court, he would be singing a different tune. "And since we returned to England, she has been holed up in that side room," I continued. "So it is not like I have had a chance to see what her plans are at this point, babies or no babies. She is not acting like the woman who slayed ensorcelled goblin warriors with me in Port Royal these many days ago."

The conversation came to an abrupt and awkward end, and Harvis banked the hearth for the evening. Then I heard the faintest rumble of hooves pounding the earth. "We've got company," I announced, reaching for my sword and dropping a pair of knives into my belt. Garlic had heard it, too, and raced from her post and out the door, facing the dark forest. She bared her teeth and growled menacingly.

"I don't hear anything," Jova said. But he was the only one that didn't. Harvis moved with a speed belying his size and snatched up a massive mace as Molly readied her pistols and crossbow. Oliver wielded a large iron crowbar like it was a piece of kindling and smiled down at Garlic as he took his place next to her. "Is it the goblins?" Jova asked. His face grew pale as he finally heard the hoofbeats, which to me now sounded like so much rolling thunder.

I shrugged. "I don't know," I said. "But from the sound of it, they are in a hurry, are well armed, and there are at least twenty of them." Garlic barked in disagreement. "Right," I said, "At least twenty-five." I turned to Jova, who now had streams of sweat running down his face. "Go to the sisters—any help they can lend would be most appreciated." Jova ducked back into the farmhouse—he would be Cornelia and the Howler's last line of defense. I did not smell the stench of goblins, so against what enemy?

Harvis began scenting the air, taking deep breaths as the riders came closer. "No, it cannot be him," he said, looking to Molly, who frowned in disgust. "He never leaves his castle."

Molly looked up at her husband. "We are harboring members of his Pack," she said. "What did you expect him to do? I am surprised it took him this long. Well, Angus always did like to make a big entrance."

Bursting from the forest, twenty-five werewolves appeared astride the biggest black Percherons I had ever seen. The leader rode at the forefront, his long platinum hair splaying out behind him like a great mane made of moonlight. A black sword bounced on his massive oak tree of a leg, and at this short distance, I realized that he was even bigger than Harvis. His companions were equally impressive-looking warriors, split evenly between bowmen, musketeers, and swordsmen. He slid down from his horse with an agility that defied his immense stature, and walked deliberately toward the farmhouse. Garlic's lips peeled back, and a low growl resonated into the silent night.

The werewolf smiled, revealing a full set of shiny white teeth as he assessed the snarling vampire Maltese, who wisely chose not to attack. "Harvis," he said in a voice deep and cold as a winter night. "Is this little runt bitch from your and Molly's latest issue?"

"You are charming as ever, Angus Blackheart," Harvis replied, clenching his jaw in anger. "Tread carefully now, as that little bitch has slain bigger prey than you."

Taken aback by Harvis's boldness, Angus sniffed the air and looked at me with his steely blue eyes. "Vampire there," he said, and took another look at Garlic. "Odd that I also smell another vampire there.

Well, no matter, she had better mind her manners and stay up on the porch and not tangle with the big dogs. That goes for you, too, vampire assassin."

I said nothing but wondered why Angus was here. There was no way he could know the Howler was pregnant. Or was there? I scanned each warrior carefully, looking for some sign of weakness in their stances or lapse of concentration in their bearing. But I saw none. These men were trained professionals, each separate fighting group within the main one focusing on Oliver, Harvis, Molly, or me without using any spoken language whatsoever.

"Why are you here, Angus?" Harvis said, hefting his mace. "Because if you've come looking for a fight, we're ready to give you one."

Angus threw his head back and laughed deeply, although to me it sounded much more like a howl—like father, like daughter. "Bold words from a man outnumbered six to one," he said. "As much fun as it would be to make a pin cushion out of your mangy hide, Harvis, I am not here to teach you a lesson. I am here to take my daughter home."

I moved ever so slightly, drawing the attention of the werewolves assigned to me. Helpful information if a fight was to break out, but what I really wanted to know was what daughter he was talking about. If he knew I had besmirched his little flower, I figured he would have no reservations about showing me his displeasure.

From the doorway, a figure appeared, and I breathed a sigh of relief when I saw by its slightly crooked stature that it was Cornelia. Jova stood next to her, shaking ever so slightly as he tried and failed to quell his internal terror. She stepped forward into the moonlight, walking boldly up to her father without any hesitation. Jova had started walking with her, love giving him a small measure of courage that, unfortunately for him, ran out at the edge of the porch.

Angus saw his daughter and smiled. "Good girl, Cornelia," he said. "You were wise to come to me." He raised his hand as if to strike her, and Harvis, Oliver, and I tensed to attack in spite of the odds against us. Jova remained paralyzed on the porch as Cornelia turned her face away. Angus dropped his hand. "If you stayed in that house one minute longer, I was going to have to give you a little reminder not to disobey me again. Come, it is time I return you to your rightful future husband so I can get the dowry he has promised me."

Cornelia looked her father right in the eyes. "There isn't going to be any dowry—from him, at least," she said. "He is not the one I am promised to, Father." Cornelia held out her diamond ring, which glinted exquisitely in the moonlight.

Angus was taken aback by her boldness as he assessed the size of the ring. "Oh, you will be married, Cornelia, and that marriage will be to Andrew Murfield," he said. "I don't care who gave you that little bauble. You will do as I say and marry Murfield, or suffer the consequences." A slight wind began blowing from the east, and the trees swayed ever so slightly. A distant peal of thunder echoed faintly, and a flash of lightning lit the night sky. A storm was coming. Angus sniffed at the air uncomfortably, but I could see he was confused. "I don't care what magic this is," he spat. "You will be loyal to the Pack."

"That is my big sister's onus—not mine," Cornelia said. "Remember me, Daddy? Your second-born cripple? You never took me to your cult—I mean Pack—meetings. I wasn't good enough for you, but I have found someone that thinks I am more than good enough."

"Now, now, pumpkin," Angus said, actually looking like he was feeling bad, or it could have been the unease in his stomach as the storm raged closer. "You are plenty valuable to me, actually quite the commodity, which as you know is something I know a whole lot about!"

"I am in love, Father—something you know nothing about." Cornelia sniffed. "There is nothing you can do or say that will ever change that."

"Is that so?" Angus said, a smirk creasing his face. "Who among these degenerates is your so-called love? Is it the troll? Please don't tell me it's the vampire."

"What do you have against vampires?" I said, ignoring his glare and stepping closer to Cornelia. Garlic jumped down off the porch and joined me, sitting at Cornelia's feet. "You wanted her to marry a half goblin, half pompous ass, and you are complaining about vampires? Well, don't worry, I am not the marrying type."

"Who in the hell are you? Did I tell you to speak, boy?" Angus said.

I was happy to see the clouds cover the moon and cast darkness across the farmyard. If this confrontation went the way I thought it would, I would have a chance against the werewolves, as a slippery, wet, dark farmyard would even out the odds in my favor. Thunder boomed ever closer, and I could smell the rain approaching. Come on, storm, I thought, facing Angus.

"My name is Sirius Sinister, you babbling buffoon," I said, flashing my fangs in challenge. "And I don't need your permission to speak." I could see Harvis and Molly rolling their eyes, and I think the expression on Oliver's face was one of displeasure. But I'd had enough of Cornelia and the Howler's blusterous sire. And Angus Blackheart had apparently had enough of me.

He turned to his assembled troops. "Kill the vampire," he said. "And any that oppose you. I am taking my daughter—"

"You are not taking Cornelia anywhere, sir," Jova said, coming to Cornelia's side. He took her hand in his, looked her confidently in the eye, and winked. "This meeting is certainly not how I thought our introduction would be, but my name is Jova Hopkins, and I would request the honor of your daughter's hand in marriage."

Angus leaned forward, looming over Jova. He burst out laughing and slapped his beefy thigh. "Hold on, hold on," he said. "We can kill a vampire anytime. Whoa, this is truly superb. Cornelia, this pauper is your love?"

"I am no pauper, sir," Jova replied. "And I can pay a more than ample dowry."

Angus puffed out his chest and gave Jova his most penetrating glare. He poked Jova in the chest and sneered, "No grandchild of mine will have a red-striped head like some kind of crimson skunk, I don't care how much gold you have." His soldiers roared with laughter, but Jova stood his ground, holding Cornelia's hand even tighter. Angus sniffed the air around Jova and frowned with the unease he clearly felt. "Hmm, what hole did you crawl out of?" he said. "Not a mortal, not a warlock, you smell like . . . like . . . what is that?"

"It's fear, sir," Jova replied calmly.

"I don't know fear," Angus scoffed, looking back to his troops for approval.

"Well, you are about to," Jova answered.

A massive peal of thunder drowned out Angus's answer, and lightning flashed across the sky, illuminating the farmyard like it was daylight. Down came the rain in a deluge, and I rejoiced as I anticipated the battle was about to be joined. A bloodcurdling scream came from

Angus, and his troops scattered as their horses reared in sheer abject terror. I blinked through the heavy rain and saw that covering Angus were not drops of rain but rather hundreds of small black spiders streaming down from the night sky onto his hair, beard, mouth, and down into his armor. He backpedaled, clawing blindly at his eyes and mouth, and slapped at his arms as he choked and spit up bits of spider, but more kept coming down in a never-ending stream to take their place. He fell back into a pile of manure and lay covered, convulsing under a river of blackness until finally the rain of arachnids let up. Deserted by his troops and covered in manure, Angus threw up his dinner on himself, and looked up to see Jova standing over him. "Who . . . who are you?" he gasped.

"I am the Bogeyman," Jova replied. "And I am going to marry your daughter."

Angus's eyes rolled back in his head, and he fell back onto the manure pile.

"Well, that went well, don't you think?" I said to our assembled group. I looked to Jova and Cornelia. "I don't think you are going to have a problem getting married now. And you might not want to mention that bit about a dowry again." I looked at the now completely unimposing figure of Angus Blackheart stretched out in the manure, and wished I had the chance to mention that little issue I had with his other daughter before he fainted clear away. The smell of the wet manure was overpowering to my sensitive nose—perhaps after Angus's bath, we would have a chat. But what would I say to him, because I had absolutely no intention of marrying the Howler. I sensed that now was the perfect time to take my leave.

Harvis and Oliver had grabbed Angus by the arms and were hauling him in the direction of the farmhouse. Jova looked to Cornelia, and both of them seemed confused as to what to do next. Molly however had no doubts. "Where do you think you are taking him, Harvis?" she called to her husband.

Harvis and Oliver stopped in their tracks. "To the house," Harvis offered.

"I don't care if he is family," she said. "He stinks of manure, and a ten-day ride. Take him to the barn with the rest of the animals, throw a bucket of water on him, and fetch him some of your clothes."

"My clothes?"

"Yes, your clothes," she said.

"Aye," Harvis assented, and he and Oliver turned and dragged Angus toward the barn.

Jova turned to Cornelia and looked nervous all of the sudden. "I am sorry about what I did to your father," he said. "That was not very nice."

"It wasn't very nice of Father to basically sell me to Murfield, now was it?" She snorted. "He deserved everything that you did to him. Maybe, just maybe, that pompous sire of mine will finally learn a little humility."

"What was all that Pack nonsense Angus was babbling about?" Jova asked. "Is the Pack just a name for your family unit, and him trying to make you feel guilty?"

"I am not sure why he mentioned the Pack to me, actually," Cornelia said. "I have always been the odd werewolf out. The Pack is indeed the family, whose leader is Father. The Pack is strength in numbers, and, well, I am a single bit of weakness."

"Maybe if he thought you were finally going to be accepted by him, that you would ditch Jova, and do what he said," I offered. "He thought you should be loyal to the Pack above all things, even love."

Cornelia shrugged. "That is where dear Daddy failed in ever really knowing who I am," she said. "I don't give a pile of manure what he thinks of me. I don't need him, or his Pack. I don't need anyone!"

"Okay, then," Jova replied. "When he comes to, I will press my advantage, and even though *you* don't care about it, I am a traditionalist. I *will* get his permission to marry you, even if it costs me my share of the treasure. The gold is not important to me because poor is all I know. I used to think I didn't need anyone either, but then I met you. I need you. Like, *need* you, need you!"

Cornelia fairly melted into his arms, and I watched rather enviously as Jova and Cornelia stood off to the side of the farmhouse, lost in their own private world of kisses under the now clear night sky. Molly grumbling under her breath had disappeared into the farmhouse. Now was my chance to leave without anyone seeing me and asking me questions that I didn't have answers to. Harvis would keep my share of the gold safe, and the Howler, well, she would understand if she even cared.

"Come on, Garlic," I whispered. "Let's go." I motioned in the direction of the road to London. But Garlic pointed her nose in the direction of the farmhouse and barked softly. "Oh, right," I said. My backpack lay just inside the doorway, and contained some gold, provisions, and my assassin's kit. We snuck into the house, and Garlic pointed down the hallway to the Howler's room. "Not a chance," I hissed. Before I could say anything else, she barked loudly and raced down the hallway. I froze momentarily, backpack in hand, trying to decide whether to leave in true assassin fashion and let Garlic try to find me . . . or face the Howler. I turned and took one step toward the door to make my exit.

"Going somewhere, Sirius?" asked the Howler.

I whirled on my heel to find the Howler standing in the dark hallway. Garlic sat at her feet, looking up at me with what I could have sworn was a doggie smile. "No," I answered. "You mean other than going back out to the barn to help Harvis and Oliver with your father's bath?" I heard a great splash of water coming from the barn, followed by a veritable flood of cursing.

"Hmm, sounds like they have things well in hand," she said. "Father so hates bathing. You are better off with me. And besides we have to talk . . ."

We retired to the spare bedroom, where she had been holed up since our return from Port Royal, and closed the door for some private conversation. The room was lit by four candles perched on the nightstand, and the Howler looked as beautiful in the flickering warm light as she had back on Saona Island when we had sat by the fire, what now seemed, so long ago. I shuddered involuntarily as I walked close to the warmth of the room's hearth, where a fire roared invitingly. "Let me help you with your shirt," the Howler said sweetly. "You are going to catch a cold all soaking wet like that." She did not stop at my shirt, and her hands roaming all across my body raised my heat even more. She kissed me deeply on the mouth and stepped away, invitingly holding onto my manhood for a tantalizing moment as she did. She blew out the candles, slipped into the bed, and dropped her nightshirt to the floor. I slid quickly into the bed, and she was on top of me, her mouth covering mine, and her tongue darting and probing as she sighed with pleasure. Her breasts were full and bountiful, bigger than I had remembered. She moaned as I caressed her nipples, and she thrust my manhood deep inside her right as I noticed the swell of her belly.

She saw where my eyes had gone and grabbed my hands and placed them on her belly as she took me in ever harder and deeper. "Marry me, Sirius," she said. "For the children, for *our* children—marry me."

The blood was rapidly emptying from my brain, and my swollen member was nearing its bursting point. "Marry you?' I gasped. "But, your father hates vampires." It was the only thing I could come up with at the moment, and the Howler had the answer.

"Jova took care of Father," she said. "And besides, you don't want your four little bitches being bastards, do you?"

"How do you know you are having girls, and four of them to boot?" Four girls, seriously?

"Simple, you do it on a blood moon—you get girls," the Howler said. "And, I feel four distinct little fighters in here.

"Okay, fighters, huh?" I said. "Fine, I . . . I . . . I . . . I . . . will . . . marry . . . you . . ."

The next morning we all found a frantic Angus in the kitchen, staring out into the forest. "My soldiers will return in moments," he said. "No one can know of what happened last night. If my men find out, they will lose all respect for me. And worse, all of Lancashire will know of my cowardice. I'll be ruined, if not killed! The leader of the Pack cannot show any weakness!"

Jova was filled with newfound confidence and seized the moment. "Then you will give me and Cornelia your blessing in marriage, Angus, won't you?" he said, patting his future father-in-law on the face.

Angus thought quickly and craned his ear for the sound of hoof-beats. "Jova, you have my wholehearted blessing to marry Cornelia," Angus said. "You will be a powerful ally. I could use your consider-able talents against my enemies in Liverpool. With your help, my new docks will revolutionize the merchant world in Liverpool, Lancashire, and for that matter—all of merry old England. Murfield will be coming to our family for money!"

"I'd like that a lot, sir. Anything I could do to humiliate Murfield would be a blessing," Jova replied. "But, there is one thing . . ." He dropped his voice low and waved his hands in wide circles for effect. Angus drew back, looking outside for any spider-carrying clouds. "To be truly effective, my gifts must remain known only in this small circle," Jova said. "Fear is most effective when it operates from the shadows. But rest assured, Angus, I have a sizable dowry to offer you, sir. It is the right and proper thing to do."

But Angus would have none of it. "It is an honor to have the legendary Bogeyman as my son-in-law," he said. "Even if no one knows that secret but me. And my enemies will be your enemies, and together we will change the world. I have a country house being built down by the River Mersey. I bequeath it to you and Cornelia and your children for all time."

Cornelia and Jova embraced and pulled the gruff and cantankerous Angus into their hug, and I thought I saw the harder-than-forged-steel werewolf wipe a tear from his eye. The Howler chose that moment to make her entrance. I gasped, for by daylight, she was very obviously with child. And I was with her again last night. I wondered . . . Could she get pregnant again? Would that mean eight little bitches to contend with?

Angus screamed in terror when he saw the telltale sign of her pregnancy, and the Howler's face grew a little ashen. Had she misjudged the effect Jova's little lesson in fear had had on her father? But Molly leaped forward and snagged a tiny brown spider hanging from a silky thread in front of Angus's paralyzed face. "Get out of the kitchen, you little crawler," she said, "to the garden where you belong so you can eat all the vegetable bugs."

"Father, I am with child," the Howler announced to her sire. "And Sirius Sinister is the father."

"Are you bloody kidding me," Harvis grumbled, motioning Oliver to get between a soon-to-be enraged Angus and me. "Molly's new kitchen is just perfect, and I will not have it destroyed by the likes of you two," Harvis stated calmly. "If you are going to kill him, Angus, I will have you do it outside."

But Angus stood leaning against the counter, his hand on his chest, which was still heaving with the terror caused by the minute arachnid. "Is it gone?" he asked. "Is that horrible little creature gone?"

The Howler came closer and grabbed her father's free hand as his eyes wildly cast about the room. "So Sirius and I have your blessing?" she said.

"Blessing?" Angus said, looking from her belly to me and back to her belly again. "You cannot marry that vampire. Are you sure that the troll is not the father? Even that would be better than *him.*"

I really wondered what this cantankerous ball of dog fur had against vampires, but I heard the unmistakable sound of many hooves beating the ground—Angus's troops were approaching. "I'll be outside while you and your daughter work this out," I announced. "I've got the most amazing story to tell those men of yours. I bet they are going to love that part where you faint like a little girl right into that pile of manure. I know that's my favorite."

"Stop!" Angus raised his hand. "You may marry my daughter. I am not sure what is more offensive—children born out of wedlock or those born to a vampire. But, I know that I cannot live with having blood of mine be illegitimate *and* from a vampire."

"Thanks, I think," I replied. "So what great house do we get?"

Angus rolled his eyes. "You can stay in the barn for all I care, vampire," he said. "I have no house for you or your ilk. And I want gold from you, lots of it."

"I am not giving you any gold," I replied. "And we will settle for a nice cottage."

"You are an enterprising fellow, so use some of that pirate gold and buy yourself a nice place in Liverpool," Angus sneered. "Consider yourself a lucky vampire, for were it not for last night, there would not be enough gold in all of England for you to offer me as a dowry. And as to a cottage—that is positively unthinkable."

"Well, I think I will talk to your fellows after all," I said with a smile.

"Fine," Angus seethed. "A bloody cottage it will be. Now, see if you can manage to keep that fanged mouth of yours shut."

Cornelia looked outside and saw the troops riding up. "So it's settled. Jova is a powerful warlock, and he and Daddy came to a truce after a fierce battle. And we'll say that Sirius is a prince from a wealthy Spanish family. Sister and Sirius are to be married with me and Jova. Can we do a double wedding, Father?"

"Him a prince? That is rich, because he certainly isn't," said Angus. But then he nodded begrudgingly, likely thinking about the expense of two separate weddings. "Your sister is not going to be able to walk down the aisle, much less waddle like a river duck if we wait much longer. And it will be cheaper to do this just once . . ."

"Daddy!" the Howler protested. "I will not waddle one bit!"

"We can do a double wedding, but on one condition," Angus said.

"What is that?" I asked. He wasn't going to try and get my gold again, was he?

"Someone has to go through every inch of that dusty old church of St. Mary's from its basement to its rafters," he said, "and clear out each and every blasted spider!"

The next day the Howler, Garlic, and I rode in Harvis's old wagon with Oliver, Jova, and Cornelia. Harvis and Molly agreed to take my gold and store it in the underground vault that Harvis and Oliver had built under the barn. Jova left half of his gold with Harvis for safe-keeping, even though I assured him that no highwaymen would be so foolish as to challenge our well-armed wagon.

The Howler seemed to be growing bigger by the day, and I questioned if she really was going to be able to walk not waddle down the aisle of St. Mary's. Angus and his troops had set out ahead of us to prepare the church and castle for the Lancashire event of the year— per Angus, all of Liverpool's most important were invited. It was truly going to be quite a show.

Our first stop was London, where Jova rendezvoused with his ship and crew and offloaded Oliver's wine, which the big troll then stored at the Meats and Cheeses, except for several choice barrels, which he loaded into the wagon to take to Lancashire for the wedding. Jova had wanted to pay Oliver for his wine, but Oliver showed him a vast underground cavern beneath the Meats and Cheeses, where casks of wine stretched out on great wooden racks for as far as the eye could see. "This cellar is but a small replica of the one at Don Indigo's vineyard," Oliver exclaimed. "Perhaps we can travel to Tuscany on your honeymoon, and I can introduce you to his heirs, and we all can sample his amazing work while staying at the House of Indigo."

Jova and Cornelia clapped their hands with glee. I caught the Howler's eye, and I knew from the curve of her belly that there was to be no honeymoon for us. Just as well, I mused, dealing with what was to come was more than I could likely handle anyway. In reality, I still could not fathom whatsoever the responsibility of this new family. I knew I was not going to be able to stay in Lancashire for very long with the cheery bit of vampire-loving happiness that was Angus. But just where would the Howler and I go? Maybe, just maybe I could convince her to return with me to Sa Dragonera.

We covered a surprising amount of distance each day and made it to the outskirts of Lancashire in what seemed like no time at all. The Howler knew the shortest and safest route, and we stopped at several inns at night, and with Oliver's huge head hooded by day, we drew no unwanted attention.

I could sense the Howler was growing more and more anxious as we approached greater Liverpool. One night I pulled her aside from the others and attempted to both interrogate and console her at the same time, but it was to no avail. The Howler was not talking. And with all of us sharing space at the inns, there was certainly no ability to steal any intimate moments. At least that applied to me and the Howler. Jova was getting quite a premarital education from his betrothed, judging from his smiling, chipper face every morning at breakfast. Quite honestly, it made me want to smack the red streaks right out of his hair.

At the border of Liverpool proper, we were greeted by an honor guard sent by Angus Blackheart to welcome his daughters home. Soon the narrow dirt path we had traveled widened considerably, and Cornelia fairly jumped out of the wagon trying to contain her excitement. "We are close, Jova," she squealed. "This is the old Northwich Road. Castle Blackheart is just a little ways off."

"Yeah," I said. "Must be named after your people, but I think it is a bad omen to name a road after a witch. I don't care where she is from."

"Not North Witch," the Howler said. "Northwich. It's a town east of here."

"Oh," I replied. "Tell me, do you really have a castle, or is it just a little field house with some stone walls?"

"No, it is a castle," she said. "You'll see. Father purchased it some years ago from the penniless heirs of Nigel, the first Baron of Halton. It was originally called Halton Castle, but Daddy likes to put his name on everything. Every one of his ships is named some version of Blackheart. I have not been here in a few years, but Cornelia tells me Father has been busy expanding and making it, in his words, 'fit for a king.'"

"Oh my!" Oliver exclaimed as the wagon came around a corner, and Castle Blackheart hove into view. "Now that is a castle." I nodded in agreement while Jova, who clearly was trying to muster the courage to stand up to Angus in his home territory, merely gulped. High up on a wooded bluff, Castle Blackheart sat, its many spires and turrets forming a great crown on a massive stone face looking down on the beautiful countryside and the Mersey River. We crossed Blackheart Brook, and I noted someone had taken great pains to grade the roadway so it was smooth as polished wood, and our wagon fairly glided along. When we reached the outer gate of Castle Blackheart, we were greeted by cheers from the farmers and the other castle workers, and I basked in their adulation, waving my hands with glee. Then a sinking feeling washed over me, and I frowned, unsure of what was causing my unease. Jova noticed, and looked at me with concern, so I shrugged and waved my hands even more vigorously. Yet the foreboding did not fade. What was bothering me?

At last we reached the castle, the horses fairly straining at their reins, seeking the comfort of the stables they could smell so tantalizingly close at journey's end, and their hooves thundered across the drawbridge, finally stopping in front of the inner battlement, flecks of foam flying from their nostrils. Greeting us in his full battle armor perfectly shined and gleaming in the noonday sun was Angus Blackheart and every single inhabitant of Castle Blackheart dressed in their finest garb. Etched on Angus's face was a smile that did not fade one moment, even when he laid eyes on me and the Howler, or even when I kissed the hand of my soon-to-be mother-in-law, Anne Blackheart, for just a little too long. Not that she minded, of course, like mother like daughter, apparently, judging from her seemingly inadvertent squeeze of my backside as our party crowded into Castle Blackheart's great hall. She presumably was quite fond of vampires!

We were ushered to seats at the massive wooden table that occupied the hall, painstakingly carved with great care from a single gargantuan oak and painted with the Blackheart family crest of a snarling black wolf cradling a black heart in its massive jaws. Music started up, and a great banquet was served. Oliver had managed to get a barrel of his wine to Angus, who sampled it and roared with approval. We were all ravenous and tore into the most magnificent meal of lamb, deer, cow, and pig. "No scouse in my house," Angus shouted, and the hall roared in approval. "To the Pack!"

I turned to the Howler. "What is scouse?"

"It's a stew made from leftover meat with vegetables and potatoes," she answered. "It's all father ate as a child, so now that he is prosperous, he refuses to eat anything but a fresh kill."

"I can relate, though we seem to have different definitions of what is a fresh kill," I said, wishing my meat was a heck of a lot bloodier and less cooked than the werewolves seemed to like it. Garlic was not so picky, tearing into a leg of lamb with a vengeance. She caught my eye and woofed in approval. I laughed out loud—she would have no problem staying in this castle, as long as the food kept coming. But that was the thing, I mused. After the wedding, Angus said we were on our own, and in my mind that meant leaving this place. I bit into a delicious lamb chop, overlooking the fact that it was a tad overcooked, and took a sip of Oliver's fine wine and savored it. I would enjoy this life while I could, and I turned and smiled at the Howler. I leaned over to ask her what the deal was with all this Pack nonsense. Cornelia had said that it was the Howler's onus, not hers. What was the onus of the Pack that the Howler bore like the children of ours she carried in her burgeoning belly? But my words failed me because she looked sick to her stomach, was white as a castle ghost, and excused herself to retire to her chambers with her mother and ladies-in-waiting holding her by her arms.

Angus did not seem to notice his daughter had left, and stood with his goblet while the room went silent. "Tomorrow," he said, "we are going to have a wedding like Lancashire has never seen. Two of my daughters shall be given away in marriage at St. Mary's, then we shall all return to Castle Blackheart for the feast of all feasts. And now let me introduce the grooms." The crowd burst into a deafening applause, and much wine was drunk or, more aptly, chugged.

Jova leaned over and whispered in my ear. "Tomorrow? Did he say tomorrow?"

I nodded, "Yes, he did. So enjoy your last night as a single man," I said. I noticed he, too, was looking a bit pale. Cornelia's face was flushed with wine, and she did not seem to notice her groom was looking a little green around the gills. Was Jova actually nervous about marrying his one and only true love? Not possible, I thought. "Don't worry," I said with a grin. "Getting married is easy. In fact, the last time I got married, I did not even know it!" Jova did not look remotely comforted by my words, so I raised my goblet and drank, wondering if the Howler would be too sick to make it down the aisle.

Angus held up his hand, and the crowd grew silent. "Good people of Lancashire proper, this man seated at my table is a legend among his kind. He is a warlock beyond compare," Angus said. "We battled in the outskirts of London for hours, nay, I say days, before we came to a truce. We found common ground, and Cornelia has found love—true love." A whispered hush came over the crowd, and I could hear the people repeating "true love" to each other. Was it really that unusual? "Rise, Lord Warlock Jova of Hopkinshire and join me."

Jova stood and walked over to Angus, who clapped him a little too enthusiastically on the shoulders amidst cheers from the crowd. I laughed to myself, as Angus was certainly full of bluster. Hopkinshire? Lord Warlock? I could not wait to see how he was going to explain me, and I wasn't disappointed. When the cheering faded, Angus continued his presentation to his minions, arm still draped around Jova's shoulder, which flung Jova around like a rag doll with every movement Angus made.

"And from the far reaches of fabled Spain comes Prince Sirius of Madrid, fifth in line to the throne of the Spanish Empire. Cheer, good people, for we have royalty among us," Angus commanded. "Join us, fair prince, so we may toast your brides."

I could not have been more shocked at Angus's sincere platitudes. Royalty? Well, that certainly worked for me, so I put on my best royal face and did not make eye contact with the commoners as I joined Angus and the Lord Warlock. I put my arm around Jova and said, "Lord Warlock."

"Prince Sirius," he replied, stifling a grin.

Angus raised his goblet, and the Lord Warlock and I followed suit. We looked out into the cheering, drunken masses. "To the brides," Angus said. "To the brides," Jova and I echoed. After our toast and some more wine, Cornelia departed with her ladies after sharing one last prewedding kiss with Jova.

"The next time I see you," she said, "I will be walking down the aisle at St. Mary's to be your wife forever!"

"Right . . . forever," he repeated. Had the aforementioned Lord Warlock of Hopkinshire drank too much, or did he look like he was going to lose his dinner for some other reason? Like marrying Cornelia, perhaps . . .

Cornelia kissed him one more time before a stern look from Angus sent her on her way. I pulled Jova over to the hearth, where we sat down to warm ourselves and share one more goblet of wine next to Garlic, who was reveling in the heat of the fire and the fullness of her belly. With great effort she crawled over to me and promptly fell asleep in my lap. "Now, that is a good idea," I said. "We should get some sleep." Jova merely nodded, and I could sense he was feeling nervous about the following day. "Don't worry," I reassured him. "It will be over before you know it. Now, go to bed." Again, the Bogeyman just nodded and stumbled his way to his bedchamber. Oliver followed, shaking his head. Garlic and I, seeing the great hall was clear, were in no hurry to depart from the warmth of the fire and, finding a few plush furs, decided to bed down for the night right where we were lying. We both found sleep came easily and deeply that night for, in the wine-clouded recesses of my mind, the unease from earlier in the day was unable to muster any strength to disturb me, and for that I was grateful—or was that grapeful?

CHAPTER 11

I awoke refreshed and ready to face the day, and I was even getting a little excited about the prospect of getting married and actually knowingly participating in the ceremony. Jova and I were ushered out of the castle proper to avoid the slightest possibility of running into our brides and casting some serious bad luck upon our nuptials. Jova looked a little better, so Oliver and I took him into the village to get him some air. Garlic loped along beside us, sniffing at each new scent. Suddenly, she took off running, and I followed her, breaking into a sprint to keep up and drawing the attention of a few merchants, who could not fathom my rather unnatural speed. I slowed to a more mortal pace, and spied Garlic sitting next to a tavern. As Garlic happily lapped from a bowl of beer, a young serving wench was bending over to pet him, giving me an unfettered view of her ample bosom.

"Is this your dog, good sir?" the girl asked, looking up at me and pushing her long blonde hair away from her face and patting a long comb of pink flowers back into place. She looked to be about eighteen or so, and I found myself staring into inviting brown eyes flecked with bits of green and gray. "What is her name?" she asked.

"Her name is Garlic," I said, stooping down next to my new friend, and noticing the stark contrast of her lips, which were the color of crushed strawberries, against her pale, milky-white skin. I fought to keep from gazing down her open blouse at my eye level . . . and failed miserably. "I am Sirius. What is your name?"

The girl smiled coyly. "I am Heather," she said, rising, thankfully, to her feet as Jova and Oliver came up. "I have never seen you three here before. Are you here for the wedding?"

Before Jova could wax poetic to this lovely creature about his true love, I interjected. "Yes, yes, we are," I replied. "Would it be possible, Heather, to get a beer to quench our thirst and a bit of breakfast before the ceremony?"

"Absolutely," she said. "Follow me."

My eyes did follow her pert posterior as she stepped into the tavern. I sighed—my days of bedding tavern wenches had come to an abrupt end. Oliver had followed my eyes and accurately read my sigh. "Ah, poor Sirius," he said. "I guess that will leave one wench in all of England that has not known your charms."

"Right," I said, feeling a bit annoyed. "Let us get a beer, some breakfast, and get Jova married." Jova had not said much at all on our walk, and was very much lost in thought. "Jova," I continued. "You are actually going to have to speak during the ceremony. You think you can manage that and a little conversation with your mates right now?"

Jova shook his head as if he was waking from a deep sleep. "I am okay," he said. "Just thinking, that's all. Tell you the truth, I am not feeling very hungry. I think I am just going to go down to St. Mary's and wait for Angus's tailor to bring me my waistcoat and breeches."

Oliver nodded. "I think I will look after him," he said. "We will meet you at the church when the bells toll four o'clock—that should give you ample time before the ceremony to get ready." At that moment innocent little Heather came over and placed a frothy mug of beer and a warm plate of scouse in front of me. I would have preferred some fresh deer, but my growling stomach indicated this would do. She bent down and placed a bowl of scouse and some more beer on the floor for Garlic. Oliver had noted I had followed Heather's every move like she was, well, prey. "And, Sirius," he said, "your days of hunting are over. So make sure you keep your weapon sheathed until tonight."

I ignored his disapproving look. "My weapon has already done its work—fourfold if you must know. Go take care of Jova and leave me to my drink. I will be fine, and so will young Heather. Don't you worry, I have Garlic looking out for me." Garlic looked up at Oliver and burped, then put her face back into her bowl. "See?" I said.

"Right," said Oliver. "A word of caution, my good man. I cannot read her intentions because all I see is a big open smile on her face, so she is either a complete simpleton, or—"

"Or what?" I cut him off, digging into my scouse and watching Heather flit about the tavern like a pretty, blonde, cleavage-baring butterfly.

"That is just it, Sirius, I don't know," Oliver said. "That would cause the wise man to worry and have caution. But I can see from your face that your intentions are not pure. That alone on your wedding day is not wise."

I took a long draught of beer and sat back in my chair. "My intention is to enjoy my beer in peace, so if you are finished with your sermon, you may go."

Oliver took Jova by the shoulder and steered him out of the tavern, leaving Garlic and me to admire Heather's work around the kitchen. Indeed, she did not talk much to the other guests or engage in any idle conversation with the other workers. She took customers' orders, got the food and drink, and smiled at everyone with the most pleasant of bearings. Perhaps Oliver was right, and Heather was not the quickest mare in the pasture. But she sure was quite the filly to look at, and I fancied a ride. It wasn't like I was married yet, and the Howler was certainly not going to be howling at the moon with me anytime in the near future.

The noon hour passed, and the tavern emptied out, and I saw wagon after wagon passing, filled with goods and decorations that were destined for the wedding banquet at the castle. The tavern workers left for other tasks associated with the wedding, and I found myself the only occupant of the hall. Garlic was lying content by my feet, studying the wagons as they passed and taking inventory of their contents. Heather had disappeared into the storeroom of the tavern some time ago, and it was just as well, for I decided to leave and head to the church to join Jova and Oliver. I placed a generous amount of gold coin on the table.

Garlic and I had walked several paces back toward Blackheart Castle and St. Mary's when my sharp ears picked up the sound of a tremendous crash that came from the direction of the tavern. "Hold on, girl," I said to Garlic. "That sounds like a bit of trouble. Let us go see if we can lend a hand."

We quickly retraced our steps and saw right in front of the tavern that two wagons had collided, and one had tipped sideways, and the barrels being held in place were bursting at their ropes and threatening to come loose. The drivers of the wagons had escaped unscathed and had drawn a crowd, who cheered raucously as the drivers exchanged blows in an argument over who should have yielded the right of way. Then from out of the inn, drawn by the utter commotion, walked sweet innocent Heather, right into the path of dire peril. "Get out of the way," I called. "Heather, move!" And that was the worst thing I could have done for poor simple Heather turned to see who was calling her, right as the ropes gave way, sending several barrels of rolling death toward her.

I was Heather's only chance at survival and sprinted with Garlic running beside me to save her. Luckily, the crowd was completely engaged in the fisticuffs so I could sprint at top speed. Heather turned back to the oncoming barrels and froze, one hand over her mouth, the other held out uselessly for protection. Garlic got to her a split second before I did, and careened into the barrel nearest to Heather, splintering it into a thousand pieces and sending a fountain of beer skyward. I leaped and landed in front of Heather, sweeping her up in one motion before I backflipped over the barrels, which crashed harmlessly against a stone wall outside the inn.

The bloodthirsty throng had not even turned around at the sound of the barrels. Garlic stood dripping wet from her beer bath, which she did not seem to mind, and went to liberate the rest of the beer from the broken barrels. I stood with Heather still in my arms and realized her arms were around my neck and mine were about her waist. Neither one of us made a move to disentangle from the embrace that danger had forced upon us. "Sirius," she exclaimed, her heart beating so fast and so strong I could feel it with her still pressed so tightly against me. "You saved my life. How can I ever repay you?"

But I did not answer, as my mind was somewhere else. A tiny shard of the barrel that Garlic had detonated had grazed Heather's temple, causing a small cut from which a drop of crimson blood began to run slowly down the side of her pale white face. The smell of her innocence was irresistible, and before I knew it, my hands were on her face, and my thumb daubed the blood sympathetically.

"There is no need to repay me," I said. "I was just doing what any other person would have." I released her from my grasp and guided her in the direction of the tavern. As soon as her head turned, I put my thumb in my mouth and reveled in the deliciousness of her blood.

Heather turned back to me as we entered the tavern. "But no one could do what you just did," she said, her not-so-nimble brain trying to process what she had seen. "Would you like another beer?"

"Yes," I replied. "I would like that very much indeed." Since Heather's shift was over, we retreated to a back room of the tavern, and she poured a beer for herself to settle nerves that still had her shaking visibly and jiggling deliciously. She downed her beer in several quick gulps and held out her hand, looking at it with concern, for it had not stopped its tremors. "You will settle down in a moment," I said. "Take it easy on the beer."

"You are right," she said, standing up and going to the kitchen. She brought back a bottle of whiskey and poured a glass for each of us. "I know this is not very ladylike, but I need this right now."

A small white cat with pretty green eyes had followed her out of the kitchen and now nuzzled its head against my legs. "Scat, cat," I said, reaching for the glass Heather had poured me and pushing the cat away with my boot. The cat gave me a slight hiss and sat down by Heather's feet, licking its paw defiantly. I was not a cat lover.

"But kitty is so nice," Heather said, putting a hand down to stroke the cat ever so gently. "Don't you want to touch my kitty?"

I absolutely did want to touch her kitty. Down went the first shot of whiskey, its fire warming my throat and my belly. A second shot had a similar effect, and Heather seemed much calmer and was no longer shaking. The cut on her temple had stopped bleeding, but she still had a line of blood down the side of her face. She saw me staring at her face and brought her hand up to feel her wound. "It still stings a little, and I am a mess," she said, dropping her hand back to the table. She had reopened the cut, and the blood began to trickle tantalizingly once more. That blasted cat rolled to her feet, and licked its lips at the sight of Heather's blood. That was the problem with cats, I mused, because if they were big enough, they would try to eat you.

I slid my chair closer to Heather, and our knees touched. I looked around for a cloth and, seeing none, put my thumb to her temple and held it. I could feel the quickening beat of her heart at my touch, and stroked her hair reassuringly. "This will stop bleeding in a moment," I said. "Your hand just started things going."

"You mean like this?" she said, placing her hand on my inner thigh and rubbing it. Her eyes were so soft and sweet as she looked at me, and she licked her lips ever so slightly. She took my hand off her face and put my thumb in her mouth and sucked hard, while the hand on my thigh cupped my manhood and squeezed delightfully.

"Aye," I gasped. "Like that." Her hands went to my breeches and freed the beast yearning to get out, and her eyes widened as she saw its size, but that did not stop her from taking it into her mouth, where I found she was as adept with it as she was with my thumb. I lay back against the wall, thankful that the tavern was deserted, but frankly not caring if an entire legion of Angus's men walked in at that very moment. Heather stopped what she was doing, and lifted up her skirt and bent over the table.

"Take me now, Sirius," she moaned, her fingers touching her womanhood as she looked back over her shoulder at me. I slid inside her, and Heather inhaled deeply and began clawing wildly at the table as I brought her to climax easily and often. Her mouth opened wide, but no sound came out as I pulled her back against my body, my hands on her firm breasts and my mouth on her neck and shoulders.

I felt the cat by my feet again, and a well-placed boot sent it hurtling into the kitchen. Fortunately, Heather's eyes were closed, and she did not seem to notice or care, as her own moans drowned out the mew of the punted pussy. She was the first mortal to experience my enchanted phallus, and what Heather lacked upstairs, she clearly made up for in her nether regions. Finally, it ended, and Heather collapsed on the table. Suddenly, I heard from outside the faint peal of four bells, or was it five?

I cinched up my breeches and wiped the sweat from my brow. "Where are you going?" Heather asked.

"I have to get to the church," I said, noting with a bit of pride the deep grooves in the table's wood that Heather's fingernails had made. She must have had some strong fingernails, or I was that damn good! "There is about to be a wedding I need to attend, and I can't be late."

Heather turned around on the table and lifted up her skirt and spread her legs. "Are you sure you can't be late?"

"Quite," I said, and sprinted with all immortal speed to the church. Garlic awoke from a beer-induced sleep under a tree and caught up to me quickly, in spite of being unable to run in a straight line. I sure hoped that I had not heard five bells because that was when the ceremony was supposed to start. I came up to the church and found only a frantic Oliver.

"Where have you been? It is nearly a quarter past the hour," he said. Then he looked at my face a little more clearly. "Really, Sirius, you had to on your wedding day? Come on now, we have a real problem with Jova."

I don't know if I was more relieved that it wasn't time for the ceremony or that Oliver had dropped the issue of my little dalliance so quickly. But then his words sank in. "What problem is that?" I asked.

Oliver motioned toward the church. "Jova's wedding clothes arrived, and as he went to put them on, he completely lost his mind," he said. "He is curled up, naked as the day he was born, in a tight, little Bogeyman ball in the back room of the church. He is mumbling to himself, and I cannot get through to him."

"I have seen that type of behavior from him before," I said. "Garlic helped last time to bring him back to us." I looked to Garlic, who had just finished lapping dry the basin of holy water by the door of the church. "Garlic, I need your help," I said. Garlic looked at me, hiccupped, and promptly vomited a nasty mix of beer and holy water all over the doorway of the church, then lay down looking quite under the weather.

"I will take care of that mess," Oliver said. "One thing about running taverns, you learn how to clean up after drunkards—even canine ones."

I scooped up my wayward pup. "I will go see what we can do about Jova."

I nodded to the workers who were busy putting the final touches on the church for the wedding of the year—a wedding that would not come to pass if I could not get Jova's naked backside into his breeches and to the end of the aisle! I chuckled when I saw a whole team of people dedicated to removing every single cobweb in the old church. One would wipe a corner, and another would follow right behind in case they had missed the barest hint of web. St. Mary's was indeed going to be arachnid-free, and Angus Blackheart would have no fear of soiling his drawers when he walked his two daughters down the aisle.

I heard a strange muttering as I walked into the back room of the church, and there indeed was Lord Warlock Jova of Hopkinshire, in all his natural glory, huddled in a corner with his pale posterior pointed up in the air. I remembered how he was in a similar state when the Howler and I confronted him on the *Moon Hunter*, though then he at least had given me the courtesy of being clothed. Then it was the *Moon Hunter*, and now it was just the moon. I looked around and saw no wine, rum, or whiskey, just Jova's wedding clothes draped over a chair. "Jova, it is me, Sirius," I called to the huddled mass of Bogeyman. "Snap out of it, man, there is a wedding about to begin, and it is yours!" He did not move, so I set down Garlic and motioned for her to go to Jova. She belched, threw up in her mouth, and walked over to Jova and proceeded to enthusiastically lick his posterior. "Garlic, really now!" I called to her. "Stop that right now, no man needs that much love on his wedding day!"

Garlic sat down and looked at me sheepishly. Clearly, she was not sure what I had wanted her to do, and she just comforted Jova by licking the nearest body part she could—what was *my* problem? But as Garlic and I engaged in a vampire stare-down, Jova rolled over, and slowly rose to his feet. Garlic's magical tonguing had awakened the Bogeyman from his trance. "Sirius," he said, "I am glad you are here."

I looked down at his nakedness. "Well, I am not sure I am so glad of that, to tell you the truth. Put your breeches on, man . . . we have to get married soon!" The church bell pealed half past the hour, and I knew I had no time at all to get him to the altar—preferably with clothes on, but at this point, that was becoming optional.

"I am scared, Sirius," the Bogeyman said. "Really, I am absolutely terrified! I don't know if I can do this."

"Scared of what, Jova?" I asked. He wasn't the one marrying the girl who had four half werewolf, half vampires rolling around in her pregnant belly. What were they going to be called anyway? Werepires? Werevamps? "What do you have to be scared about? You are marrying the love of your life, and she is absolutely positively in love with you!"

"What if I am not good enough for her?" Jova said. "What if she decides at the last minute that I am not a worthy suitor?"

I held out his breeches and said, "That is not going to happen. I have lived a long time and been with many a woman, and only once have I seen the look that Cornelia gives you, and you give Cornelia. Frankly, you can see it and feel it. The rest of the world can see the true authentic love that you two have, and that you are lucky to have found it in a mortal lifetime, let alone an immortal one."

Jova took his breeches from me. "Really?" he said.

"Without a doubt," I said. "Look into her eyes as she is coming down the aisle, and I promise you, there won't be anyone else in the church but you two. You are gifted by love with being in your own private world. So enjoy it, have faith in it, and take strength from it."

"Sirius," said Oliver, who had stepped into the room for the last moments of my speech, "that was quite an impressive discourse on love, considering your colorful history, my friend."

"Thanks," I replied.

Jova, still naked and with his breeches in his hands, leaned forward and embraced me. "No, thank you, Sirius," he said, squeezing me in a rather intimate full-body hug. "I will never forget what you have done for me."

I stepped out of his manbrace. "I will never forget this image, my good man, because it is seared into my noggin forever," I said. "Come on now, there are some brides to wait for." We changed into our wedding wear and walked out to wait for Cornelia and the Howler. I could not get out of my mind the nagging realization that the Howler and I did not remotely feel about each other the way Jova and Cornelia so obviously did. Ours was a marriage born out of lust and then out of the necessity for, frankly, legitimizing four unborn children. Jova and Cornelia's was one that embodied love and honesty. I noticed Garlic's mood had changed, and she was no longer the drunken fool, but rather was picking up on my thoughts. She whined and paced, and I shushed her. "I'll be all right, girl," I said. "Do not worry."

The church was packed with all of Angus Blackheart's well-to-do friends, and any major and minor member of the nobility within sixty miles. I also spied Harvis and Molly some ways back, and he smiled at me. Molly, too, had a wide grin on her face, which I realized came from her seeing me about to get hitched, which she knew made me extremely uncomfortable, and because the Howler was soon to be officially off the market. Jova caught Harvis's eye and waved frantically. The Bogeyman was finally ready to get married!

The processional entered, led not by an ordinary fiddler but a full company of musicians playing Angus's favorite march. I counted at least ten musicians wearing fine gold silk uniforms that matched the ribbons on the sides of the pews. The music reverberated a bit too loudly in the old stone church, and I was thankful when they stopped playing. The church was silent, that is until Garlic let out a single forlorn howl, drawing chuckles from the assembled congregation, and I shushed her once more. "Any more out of you," I snapped, "and you are going to have to go outside. What is it, Garlic?"

But we did not have a moment to spare for conversation because coming down the aisle, led by a single flutist, was the bishop of London, Horatio Ignatius Sturgeon IV. He wore a huge hat that must have loomed three feet into the air and was adorned with gold filigree, as were his bejeweled robes. He had come from London for this very event, and I only wondered how much money my wily soon-to-be father-in-law had to have to be able to bring this walking testament to decadence here before us.

Bishop Sturgeon took the crowd in as he walked, making eye contact with only a chosen few of the nobility. He was simply too important to see anyone who was less than a baron, duke, or earl. Garlic growled as he approached, but the bishop glared at her, and her growl subsided. He took his place in front of Jova and me, and it was all I could do to keep from coughing from the immense amount of perfume he wore. It seemed to bore deeper and deeper into my lungs with every wave of his hand and haughty movement of his chin as he nodded his head, soaking in the adulation.

The crowd stood as one, and yet another procession began. Jova leaned over and whispered in my ear, "Finally!" he said. And I had to agree, but was so much pomp and circumstance really needed for a wedding—a wedding that cost who knows what in pounds? But Angus Blackheart cared nothing about cost, for this day was just as much about him as it was about his daughters.

There was a collective gasp as the two brides began their walk down the aisle, each clutching onto one of their father's meaty arms. And it was a good thing Angus was such a gigantic creature, for on one side of him, Cornelia leaned heavily into her sire for balance as she did not want her bad leg to be a hindrance to her graceful wedding march. She was dressed rather elegantly in a dress snug at the waist and corseted with a beautiful lace bodice that forced what little breasts she had into prominence. I heard Jova gasp in awe. "I have never seen her look more beautiful then she does this day," he declared. I nodded and had to agree—Cornelia radiated an inner beauty imbued with the confidence of a woman marrying her true love.

I have eyes that rival that of the mountain eagle, but I had to look once, twice, and yet again at the woman on Angus's other side to make sure it was indeed the Howler. Her face was swollen and puffy. Had she been stung by a thousand angry bees last night? Her abdomen stretched her billowy dress way out, forming a great tent of cloth over her feet as she walked—no, lumbered—down the aisle, leaning with all her weight onto Angus's other arm. A bead of sweat formed over his brow, but the smile never left his face, and he was completely in the moment. Garlic began to whimper slightly, but I did not shush her. I agreed with her sentiment at that moment. Jova leaned in to my ear to whisper some platitudes about the Howler and then, apparently being unable to say anything complimentary about her, retreated awkwardly to his spot on the altar. Finally, after a brief eternity, which included one stop about halfway down the aisle for rest, they reached the altar, and the good Bishop Sturgeon was ready to proceed.

"Marriage," the bishop stated, looking out at the assembled masses hanging on his every word, which for right now totaled one. In my opinion, his dramatic pause was way too long in the drama department, for in the silence that followed His Bishopness, all I could hear was the labored breathing of the Howler next to me. Maybe she was trying to blow a bug away from her mouth? Or a spider? I dared not look and kept my face pointing straight ahead, fixed on the blustery bishop.

"Marriage," the bishop began again. "Marriage is the sacred union of a man and a woman joined by love, blessed by heaven above, and is a treasured institution since the very dawn of civilized history." I guess he had not heard of Immortal Divorce Court, which had apparently been deciding marital disputes since shortly after the great seas cooled.

"Without marriage," the Bishop said, "we could not have unions between a man and a woman so that they can produce progeny to honor God's name and carry on our great traditions." His eyes tried hard to ignore the Howler's swollen belly, but failed, and briefly found mine and were clearly filled with his moral displeasure. The bishop reached into his vestments, jiggled some gold coins, then found Angus's gaze with a knowing nod. Angus frowned and then smiled back at the bishop, whose fee for performing this service had clearly just gone up. So, I had skipped a step in the bishop's mind. So what?

But I knew I was here for Angus Blackheart's mortal and moral appearances and for my unborn children. I heard the Howler stifle a slight moan of pain. I looked around—surely, someone could bring the poor girl a chair. Or a block and tackle, perhaps? Angus was as strong as a proverbial bull, but the Howler was threatening to bring even him to his knees. Out of the corner of my eye, I could see her squeezing her father's hand so hard her knuckles were white. And still not the least bit of a reaction on Angus's face. Or so I thought.

"Speed it up," Angus hissed in a voice so low that only those of us at the altar could hear it. "Consecrate these marriages, now!" Indeed, the Howler's moans were coming more and more frequently, and the assembled congregation was beginning to whisper audibly.

The bishop snapped into action. "Er, now then, do you lovely brides of the House of Blackheart, daughters of the honorable and esteemed and courageous Angus Blackheart, and his wife, the caring and sweet and innocent Anne Blackheart, take these noble men, Lord Warlock Jova of Hopkinshire and Prince Sirio Sinestra, heir to the throne of Spain, as your husbands, and masters, and centers of your universe, so help you God?"

"I do," said Cornelia, beaming like the morning sun at Jova, who stifled a tear of joy.

"Ungh," grunted the Howler, leaning over for a moment and clutching her abdomen.

The bishop paused, looking at the Howler, not sure what she had just said, and he opened his mouth to ask her again. Angus was having none of that. "She said 'I do' clear as day," he said.

"Uh, are you sure?" the bishop asked.

"Ungh," moaned the Howler, even louder.

"Uh, quite," Angus replied. He lowered his voice. "Continue this ceremony right now, or I am going to shove your precious gold right up your vestibule!"

"Yes, I did hear her say it," the bishop suddenly agreed. "And do you, Lord Warlock Jova of Hopkinshire, and Prince Sirio Sinestra, heir to the throne of Spain, take these daughters of the House of Blackheart as your lawfully wedded wives, to procreate in the name of God and protect as your property, so shall you swear?"

"I do," Jova said, barely letting the bishop finish.

I paused for the briefest of moments, and between Garlic's whines of concern and the Howler's grunts of pain, I could barely think to speak aloud, since I was just trying to block out an awful, visceral feeling of impending doom. But what could I do at this point, other than to say . . . "I do"?

Looking relieved that his role in this travesty of a service was nearly complete, Bishop Sturgeon raised his hands. "Then, by the power vested in me by His Holiness in Rome and our good and loving king, I hereby pronounce you man and wife. You may now kiss your brides."

Jova nearly knocked me over in his quest to get to Cornelia and take her in his arms. He kissed her long, deeply, and passionately, drawing a collective murmur of sweetness from the congregation. I turned to the Howler and reached my arms around her. Her stomach was so big it pushed into my own, and yet it seemed we still stood quite far apart. I looked at my new spouse's glazed-over eyes and saw her lips curling back for a kiss, or perhaps a snarl. Then all of a sudden, her face went white, and there was a great rushing of liquid from under her dress onto my boots, breeches, and the floor of the church. She leaned back hard and howled in absolute agony, collapsing to the floor. Anne Blackheart and her bevy of ladies-in-waiting rushed the altar, and I found myself thrust to the background.

"These babies are on the way," Anne declared. "Help her to the back room. She is not going to make it to the castle this day." She looked up with disgust at the speechless Bishop Sturgeon as he stood taking up space in her maternal domain, saying nothing and doing nothing—not even giving a well-timed blessing. "Clear out of the way,

Your Holiness," she ordered. "And you had better start praying for this good woman and her newborns, or you will be doing your own last rites and not the baptisms of the lovely little ladies that are coming into this world right damn now!"

In a moment, the church was cleared by the ladies-in-waiting, and Jova, Cornelia, Angus, and the congregation retired to the castle to begin the wedding reception to end all receptions. Garlic stayed inside with the ladies-in-waiting. That left me and Oliver standing by a tree out in front of the church, waiting for the birth of my children. "You don't have to stay," I said to Oliver, who merely shrugged.

"There are not a lot of mortal or immortal ladies that fancy dancing with trolls," he replied. "Unless Angus's moat has a mermaid in it, I am probably out of luck. Besides, I can't leave you here all alone, now can I?"

"You can," I said. "But I am glad you have not done so." A blood-curdling howl of pain came from the church, cracking one of the stained-glass windows near the door with its volume. I had never felt so helpless. I could do nothing to help the Howler and my daughters. Inaction did not suit me.

"Here, try this," Oliver said, handing me a flask. "It will settle your nerves."

"I am not nervous," I said, watching my normally calm hand shake like a leaf on a windy spring day as I took the flask from him, accidentally spilling half of its contents into the dirt. Another shriek, this one longer and louder, came from the church and shattered the remaining stained-glass windows, leaving a rainbow path of glass shards across the entrance that glistened in the setting sun. I put the flask to my lips, and the fiery liquid ran down my throat, sending a peaceful calm throughout my body. "Thank you," I said. "I needed that. Do you think everything is going well in there?" Another long scream answered my question, bursting the church doors from their very hinges and sending them clattering to the ground.

"I think so," Oliver replied, eyeing the doors. "Your children are quite the fighters, it seems."

"Right," I said. After a few minutes, a great cheer rose from inside, and Garlic padded out to the front entrance, barking once, and made for us to follow. Anne Blackheart met us halfway down the aisle, barring our way as Garlic disappeared into the back room.

"Sirius," she said, "Oliver must wait for the formal introduction of these children to Lancashire proper. But you are the father of four unique wonders and may see the spectacle of their beauty."

Oliver nodded in understanding and stepped back. "I am going to go to the reception at the castle and leave you with your new family," he said. "And besides, I have a special bottle of wine to deliver for Jova and Cornelia's first night as husband and wife."

He bowed to Anne Blackheart and departed the church, and I followed my new mother-in-law into the back room, my blood rushing through my veins so fast that I could feel my ears burning crimson. My throat had a dryness that no liquid could quench, and my heart threatened to pound itself right out of my chest. I had no earthly idea what to expect.

Behind a curtain and buried deep in a warm nest of blankets, I glimpsed the Howler. Piled near her were many blood-soaked cloths, and her face was pale, and her breathing faint and shallow. Anne caught my concerned eye. "She lost a lot of blood with the biting and sucking of those newborns," she said. "Your ladies have a taste for it, even so young. But we got them out of her and feeding on something that wasn't their mother, just in the nick of time, and so she will be all right in a few days."

I was so stunned I could not even speak and merely nodded. Then my eyes took in the four little swaddled bundles, each held by a lady-in-waiting, who rocked them ever so slightly. I dropped to my knees and took them in, each as beautiful as her sister with tousled wet hair and red little faces. One was bigger than all the rest and slept the most contentedly. Two were the same size, and the last little beauty was smaller in stature than her sisters, yet she mewed the loudest. It was by her lady-in-waiting that Garlic sat, keeping vigil over her new charges.

I rose to my feet in utter awe and wept openly, as first one then the others were passed to me so that I could hold them close to my heart. Each in turn flashed her beautiful eyes at me as they were placed in my arms, cooing ever so softly and contentedly in the safety of fatherly love. I looked up at Anne, beaming with utter joy, and Anne returned my smile and placed a hand on my shoulder.

"You need to go now, and join the revelry at the castle," she said. "Your daughters need to feed and sleep—as does your wife. All will be fine, Sirius Sinister, so do not worry."

I gazed down at my littlest child more in love with her than I had ever been with anyone or anything in this world. "But," I said, feeling so cold and lost as she took the baby back from me, "these girls are not properly named. My wife and I must talk and name them."

Anne had handed off my little girl to her lady-in-waiting as I spoke, and my eyes longingly followed her every move. "There will be plenty of time for that tomorrow," she said. "Now you celebrate with your friends and let your women rest. Garlic will be here with them."

I nodded and let her usher me out of the back room into the nave of the great church. She said goodbye and returned to the back room, leaving me feeling more alone than I had ever felt. But then, a strange new feeling came over me.

It was responsibility. The Howler and I were going to raise these girls into amazing young women. For the sake of these girls, this marriage was going to work and be as loving as that of Jova and Cornelia. I stood outside in front of the church, comforted in knowing my family was safe and secure, and my future was as bright and permanent as the great moon above. So focused was I on my thoughts, that I never even saw the blow coming to the back of my head—but I sure felt it as I was pitched face first into the ground fighting to stay conscious. I was dragged to the back of the church out of sight of any rescuing eyes. If only I had known what was transpiring just a few feet away from me.

In the back room of the church, Anne Blackheart picked up the largest pup in the litter and held her up to the sky with the approval of her nodding husband. "Are you sure she is the one that came out first?" Angus said.

"I caught her myself, my liege and husband," Anne replied, not risking the wrath of the leader of the Pack in a moment like this, of all times. She knew all too well the feel of his harsh hand across her face and the pain of his boots in her ribs. She was worried she sounded insubordinate and spoke quickly to compensate. "Look at her size compared to the others, Lord Blackheart," she said. "She is clearly the product of your line."

"Our seed is indeed strong in her," Angus agreed. "We have created the perfect weapons for the Pack. They will have all the coordination and stealth of the vampires, and all the muscle, power, and resources of our kind. It is time, my wife, to begin the ceremony of the firstborn . . ."

Anne Blackheart nodded, and brought the baby's ear to her mouth. "Your loyalty is to the Pack . . ."

CHAPTER 12

I faded in and out of consciousness, hearing muted voices and laughter and feeling my body lurch to and fro. I tried to scream in anger but found myself tightly gagged. I saw nothing but blackness for I was hooded. I strained hard against bonds that I could not break, but that did not keep me from trying again and again, until I could feel the blood dripping from my wrists.

Finally, I gave up and lay still and listened for any hint of the identity of my captors or location. When my senses calmed, I smelled the salt of the ocean and felt rounded wood at my back, and I realized that I was in the hold of a ship. A ship I knew was heading out of Liverpool, and with every moment getting farther and farther away from my baby girls. As the waves steadily slapped against the hull, and the occasional gull cried, all I could do was conserve my strength and wait.

The thud of heavy boots on the deck above woke me from a brief slumber, and I soon found myself hoisted in the air by gloved hands and deposited unceremoniously in the back of a wagon. We had only sailed for a day or so at best, and I felt the air was mild for July, so I knew I was still in the British Isles somewhere. I listened intently for a clue but heard only the rhythmic clack of hooves on cobblestones, which soon turned to dirt. I tried to scent the identity of my captors through the hood, but it was perfumed so heavily that I could only catch a whiff of the freshly cut hay I was buried under.

The wagon lurched to a stop, and I was again carried aloft, but this time the journey was shorter, and the air grew colder. We were going underground, and deep, by the feel of it. I could hear a faint drip of water in the distance and felt my body tilt increasingly down at a steep angle as my captors walked. I was placed on the ground with my feet shackled, and pushed roughly against a stone wall. I could hear the clink of metal on metal as my chains were attached to the wall. My hood was ripped off, and I blinked in the darkness, lit by a single torch, and took in my surroundings.

I was in a dungeon, hewn out of red sandstone. Iron chains covered the walls, but the ones binding me shone with an eerie gold hue emitting more light than the torch. Iron I could break, but these chains were made of something entirely foreign to me, and no matter how much I tested them, they failed to yield the slightest bit. The dungeon could have held a whole company of soldiers, but it seemed that I was its only prisoner. But the real question was, who were my captors? And why had they taken me? I had made lots of enemies over the last several centuries, so many that I couldn't even begin to hazard a guess as to who intended to even the score against me. I was not concerned, in spite of these seemingly insurmountable odds. After all, I had survived Hell, and even it did not ultimately hold me. So then, what could an immortal do? Standing guard over me were five gigantic humanoid creatures, dressed head to toe in black, and each wearing a different color mask over their faces. I could not tell if they were vampires, werewolves, goblins, trolls, or something else entirely. Their scent was apparently masked by their uniforms, but there was no mistaking that they knew how to use the deadly swords hanging from their waists.

The leader wore a gold mask, and he motioned for two of the soldiers to leave the room. They returned with a long red carpet, which they unrolled from the entrance of the dungeon right up to my feet. The leader pointed at an insubordinate wrinkle in the carpet, which was quickly smoothed out by his lieutenant. Satisfied, the leader left the room and returned with two large golden shields, which he set on the floor on either side of the carpet. In the center of each shield a great red gem sparkled in a familiar way—transportation crystals! It seemed like I was about to meet my warden. The leader looked to the ceiling, down to the floor, and all around the room, finishing with moving around my chains. A great hum filled the air, and I could see a curtain of energy forming in between the shields. A hulking figure appeared, hazy at first, then crystal clear, and stepping into the room still wearing his finest wedding wear, was my new father-in-law, Angus Blackheart.

"You have a pleasant boat ride, vampire?" Angus said with a sneer, sauntering up to me. "I much prefer traveling by crystal if I can, don't you? Oh, I am sorry you are still gagged. Let me help you with that." He pulled the gag from my mouth and slapped me hard across the face. "Oops, sorry about that—actually no, I am not." He glared, looming so close to me I could smell the stench of wine on his breath, and his nose almost touched mine. I remained quiet and looked at him calmly.

"You've got nothing to say, vampire?" Angus said, stepping back again. "Now that is a surprise. I do remember how you like to run that mouth of yours. Which reminds me . . ." He lunged forward and punched me in the face, bloodying my lip. "That's for insulting me in front of my troops." He paced back and forth in front of me. "Still nothing to say?"

I spat out some blood, and looked up at the smooth, carved ceiling of my new home. "I was kind of hoping a spider would drop on your head so I could watch you soil your breeches again," I said.

Angus screamed in rage and launched an off-balance punch into my right side. I could only move ever so slightly, and winced, hearing the crack of one of my ribs. He was not done, and soon my left side was equally in pain. "That is for your insolence," he said, breathing heavily.

He could torture me all he wanted, and even kill me if he could, but I was not going to give him the pleasure of crying out in pain. But even I could not take the full brunt of an enraged werewolf the size of Angus for very long. Was there a reason for his kidnapping me other than simple torture, or did he have a more nefarious plan?

"You have a funny way of welcoming people into your family," I said, breathing through my rib pain. "You might want to skip this part of your Blackheart family initiation with Jova, because either he will be dead, or you will be eating spiders again."

That last comment earned me a punch in the stomach that would have dropped me to my knees but for those damned chains, but it was worth it. "Jova has nothing to fear from me," Angus said coldly. "His powers will serve my empire well. He has brought celebrity and fame to my house, and one of his progeny, my grandchild, will take over the mantle of the Bogeyman one day. Half werewolf, all bogeyman is a combination my enemies cannot overcome."

"I have given you heirs as well," I pointed out. "And I will take care of your daughter. I . . . I love her."

The next punch went straight to my groin, and I nearly vomited, blinking back tears from my eyes. "Like you loved that tavern wench?" Angus replied. His fists flew to my face, his punches blackening my eyes.

Damn those small towns! Right, there was that little indiscretion, but Angus was a man, surely he would understand. "I can explain that," I said, not really knowing what I could say to get Angus to stop his beating. But he stepped back of his own accord, and I breathed a sigh of relief.

"I would like to see you try and explain that to my daughter," Angus said. "But it doesn't really matter. I knew about that tryst the moment it happened, but I needed you to marry my daughter and legitimize those children. I cannot have any daughter of mine with a bastard litter. Do you know what that would do to my reputation? But now that you are married, and my grandchildren are here—neither I nor my daughter need you anymore."

"Your daughter and I are going to work things out," I said. "I am a changed man. Those little girls of mine need their father, and their father they shall have!"

Angus grinned evilly. "Poor vampire misses his babies. What a sweet and tender moment this is! It is such a shame you abandoned your wife and newborn babies and disappeared for parts unknown—oh well—such a sad story . . . But it ends happily, for the girls shall be raised by the Pack."

There was a hum in the air as he spoke, and the curtain of energy formed over his shoulder, and I tried to peer through my swollen eyes at the figure coming through the crystal. "She is not going to believe I just left, and neither will Jova and Cornelia," I said, craning my neck to see who it was that had joined the torture session.

"Believe it?" said the Howler, taking her father's side and looking remarkably well recovered from how I last saw her. "It was my idea.

Perception is reality, Sirius, and everyone knows you run from commitment. It is a perfect plan, the last piece being put into place when Garlic imprinted on the girls. It is so cute how she doesn't leave their side. She certainly won't be coming to look for you."

"But why? You begged me to marry you. For the girls, you said."

She snorted in derision. "The girls will be fine. I will see to that," she said. "I needed you to marry me to save Father's reputation and my inheritance. If I had birthed my girls while unmarried, Father would have disowned me from the sheer embarrassment of the whole ordeal."

"True." Angus nodded. "I probably would have." He patted her sweetly on the arm. "You were quite the soldier getting through that ceremony," he said. "I am so proud of you!"

"Listen," I said, "I don't want to break up your special father-daughter bonding moment, but seriously, didn't we have something back on Saona Island? Didn't you feel the passion?"

"Of course I felt something, you imbecile," she said. "I was in heat—not in love. I never loved you. I just needed you right there, right then, on the island. If Big Belly Bart had come one day earlier, he would have done the trick. And I needed you to marry me, and you did, and now, Sirius Sinister—we are through." She feigned like she was about to cry, putting her hand to her face and scrunching it up. "It is now time to go practice weeping for my husband, who has deserted me with all of those newborn children. I feel so alone." She turned on her heels, kissed her father on the cheek, smiled that ever-so-evil Blackheart smile, and departed back through the curtain.

"Breaking up is so hard to do," Angus said. "I think she took you leaving her quite well, don't you?"

"I will break these chains eventually," I said. "You can't hold me here forever."

Angus laughed. "Actually, I can," he said. "We are on the Isle of Man, in a private dungeon I had built especially for you. We are two hundred paces below Peel Castle, so no one is ever going to hear your pathetic, whimpering cries." He walked over and picked up a link of the golden chains. "I am surprised you do not recognize these little beauties," he said. "But, I guess it has been a century or so since your little visit to Immortal Divorce Court."

That explained why they had transported me by boat, since nothing ensorcelled with magic from the IDC could pass through a crystal. It also was the reason that I could not break the chains, and for the first time in my life, I felt utterly defeated. No immortal could break these chains. Peel Castle would become my tomb because, at some point, I would starve to death.

Angus must have been reading my thoughts. "Don't worry, Sinister, my friend at Immortal Divorce Court says they have improved the chains, so now, not only can't you escape, but the chains will also keep you alive, sustaining your body, and eliminating your need to eat, drink, and even sleep. You will be alone in your thoughts forever and ever. And the last thing you will hear, other than your own screams of insanity, is my voice telling you that you will never, ever, ever, see your daughters or the outside world again."

He stepped through the crystal and was gone, and his henchmen packed up the crystal shields and locked the door. All I could hear was the steady drip, drip, drip of unseen water that mirrored the drip, drip, drip of my tears.

I do not know if I had been in my private hell—real this time—for an hour, a day, a week, or even a year, when I heard footsteps approaching from afar. They were light and soft, which effectively ruled out the lumbering gaits of Harvis or Oliver. My heart lightened. Had Jova come to rescue me? A blue light flashed outside the door to the dungeon, and the door slowly opened to reveal a hooded, shadowy figure.

Stepping forward into the dim light emitted by the chains was simple Heather, who smiled at me ever so vacuously. She wrung her hands nervously. "Sirius," she whispered, "what has happened to you? I thought I would never find you!"

My heart had sunk at her appearance, but I realized quickly that, even though she could not shatter the chains that bound me, she could certainly return to the village and get the help of Oliver or Jova. But, I wondered, how did this simpleton get here in the first place? "Heather," I said. "How did you find me? Did you stow away on the boat that brought me here? And how did you open that door? What was the blue light out there?"

But helping me was not what Heather had in mind. "So many questions, they are hurting my poor wittle brain. I am here now, and that is all that matters. I like you all chained up like this, Sirius," she said, moving close to me and nipping my ear none too gently with her teeth. "I can do whatever I want to you."

I had to get her one-track mind focused on something else—like saving me from an eternity of misery! "Sweet, sweet Heather," I cooed, trying to catch her eye. "Later! Later, you can do anything you want to me," I pleaded. "But first you must return to the village and find Jova or Oliver and bring them here to me."

"Is that the kind of party you want?" she asked, thinking about it for a moment. "Hmm, tempting, but that is a no. I don't want you and friends, I just want you. And I don't want to wait. You don't need anybody else—because lucky you has me!" She bent over in front of me and ground her backside hard into my manhood, but did not get the reaction she was hoping for. "What's wrong?" she said—her voice turning all cross. "Don't you like me anymore? Maybe I should just leave you here to rot if you don't want me!"

"No, no, please don't go!" I exclaimed as she backed up to the entrance of the dungeon. "Please stay, I want you, I want you so much I can't stand it, but . . . but . . . It's these chains. They are hurting my arms and legs so much I can't feel a thing!"

"Oh," she said, happy again, bounding over like some kind of crazy lovesick puppy. "Why didn't you say so?" She pulled my breeches to the ground. "Does that feel better?"

I grimaced. "Yes, quite, thank you, so very nice of you to do that," I replied. I had to get her to go get someone that could actually rescue me! "Heather, get some help for me, and I promise we will be together again, and it will be so amazing!"

"You promise?" she said, her mouth hovering near my hesitant manhood, looking up at me with those big wet eyes that I realized radiated pure madness. How had I not noticed that before? She removed her blouse, and then I remembered. She put her face so close to mine she was practically breathing into my mouth, but it was dank, fetid air. I did not find it remotely erotic as her once warm brown eyes were turning cold and white as a winter night, and the set of her jaw was positively carnivorous. "Promise?" she repeated.

"Yes, yes, I promise," I said, seeing with dismay all traces of color vanish from her eyes. Heather was not the simpleton she appeared to be, and instead of a "who," she was probably going to turn out to be a "what." If only I had listened to Oliver!

"Well," she said, her voice low and rough. "I don't believe you. And if I can't have you, then no one can." She took a silver knife from her belt and held it high in the air, and her pale white skin grew even paler, until the only traces of color on her entire body were the blood-red of her nipples and lips. She pulled out the comb from her hair and shook her mane from side to side, and in the process it became as white as new fallen snow. She advanced on me, and her free hand shot out and captured my manhood roughly in its grasp. Her fingernails dug into me like five little jagged icicles, and were it not for the enchanted chains, I would have fainted mercifully away. But mercy was not on sweet Heather's agenda.

"You thought me stupid?" she sneered. "Thought you could just have me, and then run down to the chapel and marry another?"

"No," I replied weakly.

"No," Heather repeated. "But that is what you did, and no man who rejects the Winter Witch gets to remain a man." She muttered a few incantations, and I yanked on the chains with all my strength but only succeeded in sending twin streams of blood down my forearms, which the Winter Witch promptly licked away. "Mmm, I love the vintage that is vampire," she said. "Always so darn tasty. It must be that you guys are so absurdly high in iron, and you know us girls are always losing blood now and again. Oh, how ironic, because you are the one that is going to be losing a whole lot of blood from the place where your cock used to be!"

She assessed my manhood once again and raised her blade high in the air. "It is going to be a shame to destroy something so beautiful, and useful," she said. "At least I was the last one to have it." Down came the knife, and I closed my eyes and braced for incomprehensible, unimaginable pain . . . but felt nothing. The Winter Witch screamed in surprise, and my eyes snapped open, taking in the joyous fact that I was still whole for now.

"What magic is this?" she screamed, releasing me from her hold. "It is not possible. No immortal can best my Dagger of Despair—least of all a weak-minded vampire like you." She tried again and again, and to her utter chagrin, she was unable to inflict any harm on my apparently enchanted member. Once the shock of her attempts wore off and I knew she could not harm me, a rather satisfied smirk came over my face. Persephone, I thought, it had to be—one of the only creatures on this fair world, or Underworld, with powers that made this vile creature pale in comparison. Pun intended.

The Winter Witch stood to the side and, without warning, jabbed her Dagger of Despair successfully into my bare ass cheek, which was not apparently protected by the enchantment of Persephone, and I stifled a cry as the blade burned and then turned cold. "If I can't take your pride, I will leave you with a lesson," the Winter Witch said, grabbing her blouse and walking away. "I am leaving you with a hundred-year-old boil, and combined with the power of those lovely IDC chains, it should keep you company for about one thousand years or so. Have a nice life, Sirius Sinister." The door slammed shut behind her, and the wound on my backside began to heal instantly, forming into a nasty pus-filled boil that spit pus down my legs and, in between spitting fits, proceeded to berate me in seven different languages. But all things considered, I was much happier with a talking boil on my ass than being turned into a gelding by the Winter Witch.

I cursed out the boil, the Winter Witch, the Howler, and Angus Blackheart, using every curse word I knew in every language I knew, even inventing a few new ones along the way. Not to be outdone, the boil kept up with me, cursing my life, my courage, my intelligence, and yes, even the very posterior on which it resided. I soon grew tired of the game. "Boil," I said, gritting my teeth and wrinkling up my nose at the growing and rather stinking yellow pile of pus at my feet. "Why don't you just shut the fuck up?"

"No, you shut up!" said the boil. "You think I asked to be stuck to the ass of an ass like you?"

I sighed—it was going to be a long one thousand years if this continued. But somehow my encounter with the Winter Witch had oddly raised my spirits. There was nothing like keeping your manhood intact in a situation where there seemed to be no hope at all. I had new resolve to get myself out of these chains and find a way to see my daughters. There just had to be a way to free myself or get help!

Not being hungry or thirsty or having the ability to see outside was playing havoc with my sense of time. For all I knew one hundred years had passed outside my prison walls while I had traded insults with the boil. Then my ears detected faint footsteps growing closer and closer, and my heart leaped because they were far too heavy to be those of the Winter Witch or the Howler, but heavy enough to be those of Oliver or Harvis, or so I hoped. The dungeon door crashed open, momentarily silencing my babbling boil. A large figure appeared at the door, brandishing what I hoped was a weapon that could free me from this infernal prison. Into the light stepped a familiar face, wielding not a weapon, but a sheaf of papers embossed with an iridescent wax seal.

"Sirius Sinister, by the power vested in me by . . . ewww . . . how revolting," stammered Buttercup the faerie, jumping back and scraping his boot on the floor to remove a well-aimed spit of pus. "Now that is just nasty!"

"You are the nasty one, you stupid faerie," said the boil. "Come a little closer, and I will get one in your eye."

Buttercup looked to his papers, then at me and, shrugging his shoulders, looked back at his papers. "Sirius," he said. "That is you, isn't it?"

"Yes, Buttercup, it is," I replied. "I guess you are here to serve me. I should have known I would be seeing you rather soon."

"Between the total absence of breeches, and not getting peed on by your little white dog, for a minute there I thought the IDC had got one wrong," said Buttercup.

"But that doesn't happen, does it," I said. "Well, sorry about the boil."

"I'm *not* sorry!" announced the boil.

"Not a problem," said Buttercup. "And yes, I am here to serve you."

"Serve this!" shouted the boil, spitting in Buttercup's direction and succeeding in getting the faerie's other boot blemished with pus.

Buttercup wiped his boot on the floor. "At least it can't move as fast as that dog of yours," he said, looking around the dungeon for Garlic. "Where is she anyway? In spite of the pee thing, she was a cute little puppy."

"It's a long story," I said. "But I guess even you haven't served a man chained to a secret dungeon's walls, with his breeches at his ankles, and cursed with a talking boil on his ass."

"Talking boils are funny!" opined the boil, spitting pus happily.

"You know I don't have time for a story since I am on court time," Buttercup said. "And not to disappoint you, my friend, but this doesn't rate as even in the top one hundred of my weirdest service assignments."

"You said ass," howled the boil. "It takes one to know one!"

Buttercup thought for a moment. "Well, maybe it is in the top one hundred, because that boil is brutal. Oh well, back to the matter at hand." He held out the sheaf of papers and stood a safe distance from the boil. "By the powers vested in me by the Immortal Divorce Court, you are hereby *served*."

I watched nonplussed as a rainbow shot from the wax seal and struck my money pouch on the floor, magically lightening it by ten gold coins. "After the time I've had lately, I couldn't care less about the gold!" I exclaimed. "Did I just say that about the service fee?"

"You did," Buttercup stated. "Did you actually marry the woman serving you this time?"

"Yes," I said. "This time I actually did marry her. We had a big church ceremony and everything. What was I going to do? She was pregnant with four of my babies!"

"So the children are really yours this time?" Buttercup queried. "Actual children, you know, babies, not just some old curmudgeon clinging to his life by a mortal thread?"

"Yes, that is what happens when you have relations with an apparently in-heat werewolf during a full moon."

"You did that?" Buttercup laughed, slapping his knee. "Really, Sirius? No one could be that stupid . . ." He saw the look on my face and stopped talking. "Can you read the summons?" I raised my hands, and the chains clinked loudly. "Right," Buttercup said, quickly perusing the paperwork.

"He can't hold the papers!" said the boil. "But, I can between my lips, so why don't you come a little closer?"

Buttercup ignored the boil. "She is divorcing you on the grounds of abandonment," he said. "She claims that after your wedding, you left her and the children without even saying a word. Wow, you must be a real dick to do that . . ."

"Would you like to hazard a guess as to who kidnapped me and imprisoned me here?"

Buttercup shook his head. "Oh no," he said. "That is something for your lawyer to hear. I am just the messenger. And, you know what they say, don't spit pus on the messenger."

"I would if I could," the boil spouted, clearly disappointed. "That would send the messenger a message—fuck off."

"You know I have to agree with him there," I said. "I mean, come on now, Buttercup, just how am I going to find a lawyer to represent me in Immortal Divorce Court since I am chained to the walls of a hidden dungeon on the Isle of Man?"

"That is a good question," he said. "But I am afraid I do not have any answers. Well, I have to go, Sirius, but I'd like to wish you luck. In spite of the dog and the boil, you seem like a rather pleasant fellow."

"Thanks," I said as he headed for the door.

"Faeries suck bull pizzle!" the boil yelled as the dungeon door clanged shut. I was starting to like the way the boil talked. Faeries did suck bull pizzle. At that moment, I wished for another visitor to come to this dungeon—a visitor by the name of Maximillian Justice. But I had no way to contact him, and he certainly didn't make dungeon visits outside of the IDC jail. What was I going to do?

I heard footsteps outside the dungeon, and Buttercup's familiar face hove into view, keeping his distance this time from the spitting boil. "Aww, come on, faerie," the boil taunted. "Are you afraid of an itty bitty boil?"

"Something like that," Buttercup replied.

"Did you change your mind and decide to help me after all?" I asked. "You could not have gotten far as it has only been a few minutes since you left."

Buttercup frowned and held out a new sheaf of papers. "Being locked up is completely addling your sense of time," he said. "I am afraid I have to serve you again. She got a default judgment entered when you failed to appear in court."

"Fault?" I exclaimed, clenching my fists in anger. "How is being chained to a wall my fault?"

"Because you were stupid enough to not look behind you and got knocked on the head, you ignorant ass," the boil said. "And your bedding the Winter Witch didn't work out too well for either of us!"

"Not fault," Buttercup explained. "Default. It means because you did not show up in court, whatever the other side says is pretty much deemed to be the whole truth and nothing but the truth." He opened the sheaf of papers and read quickly. "It appears she got her divorce on the grounds of abandonment, full custody of the children, and you have one month to pay the child support and alimony ordered, or you will be arrested."

"But," I protested, "that is not fair."

"I didn't say it was fair," said Buttercup. "I said it was divorce law."

"This sounds like some kind of cruel joke."

"The only joke I see is the one chained to the wall," said the boil.

"I am deeply sorry," Buttercup said. "But I must serve you with the judgment. By the powers vested in me by the Immortal Divorce Court, you are hereby *served*."

I watched, stunned, as that accursed rainbow shot from the wax seal and struck my money pouch. "Can you at least give a message to Justice, or Harvis, or anybody?"

Buttercup shook his head slowly, looking quite sorry for me. "I am forbidden from interfering in any proceeding," he said. "If I do anything to help you, I will be stripped of my office and banished to Hell. And word around the IDC is that you are persona non grata in Hell, for some reason—so helping you would, no pun intended, be doubly damning to me." I watched Buttercup leave, and the boil fell oddly silent. Maybe even it felt sorry for me.

It seemed like only minutes had passed, but I knew it was a month's time, for coming through the door were three heavily armed faerie deputies of the IDC. Their sergeant was a brutish lout with a cruel sneer permanently affixed to his face, and he spat at the ground at my feet as his eyes adjusted to the dim light of the dungeon. "Sirius Sinister," he called, "step away from that wall and surrender." He spat again and stepped forward into the range of the boil.

"Oh yeah?" the boil answered in challenge. "Right back at you, you fat faerie fucker."

"What madness is this?" the sergeant shouted, wiping gobs of yellow pus from his face. "Sirius Sinister, you are under arrest for failure to pay child support and alimony as ordered by the IDC, and now I am going to file additional charges for assaulting a deputy with your foul vampire spew."

"Why don't you charge me, you idiot?" the boil spouted. "Because I am the one that just *ass*aulted you!"

"I am charging you," the faerie said. He was apparently unable to discern that the boil and I were two different entities. Well, we were sort of two different entities. "Raise your hands, drop your weapons, and come with us," the faerie continued.

"My hands are raised, and that is a rather permanent condition right now. And my weapon is unfortunately in full view for all to see. However, I cannot rightfully claim the spew adorning your face . . . still . . . since you missed a spot," I said. "Nice aim, though, boil."

"Thank you, Sirius," said the boil. "I've had plenty of practice on that other stupid faerie. Well, no sense in leaving the other two all nice and clean." The other two deputies soon had faces full of pus and danced around, desperately trying to wipe it out of their eyes.

"Who speaks?" shouted the sergeant, looking high and low for the assailant. "Sinister, I warn you, any allies of yours are subject to immediate arrest and imprisonment. Show yourself, you foul, invisible demons, so we can punish you with all the might and power of Immortal Divorce Court!"

"Listen, boil," I said, "if they can get us out of here, we might be able to sever our little relationship. So let us let them try. Ease off with the spitting, all right?"

"Sure, it's no skin off my ass," the boil said. "Truce, you stupid faeries!"

The sergeant and his men approached gingerly, finally getting a good look at my predicament without getting pus in their eyes. "Sinister, why did you chain yourself to that wall?" the sergeant asked. "You cannot escape us that way. It has been tried before." The sergeant reached for the chain, turning his body into diamond and yanking with all his might. Clearly, he expected the chain to splinter into a thousand shards at his slightest touch. He let go of the chain and looked to me.

"Where did you get these Immortal Divorce Court chains, and what magic have you put on them?"

"Let me get this straight," I said. "You think I chained myself to this wall with these IDC chains, two hundred paces below Peel Castle, just to avoid getting arrested by the likes of you?"

"Yes," said the sergeant. "That is exactly what I think."

"And after I chained myself to the wall, how did I manage to pull my breeches down to my ankles?"

"Loose breeches?" one of the other deputies suggested.

"And I cursed *myself* with a talking boil on my ass, right?"

"Nope, that was the Winter Witch," said the boil.

"The Winter Witch did this to you?" said the sergeant. "That makes a little bit of sense now. What did you do to get on her bad side?"

"He gave it to her but good, then left her to get married to a werewolf bitch the very same day. And it was the werewolf bitch, along with her daddy, that chained him up," the boil said.

"Is that true?" the sergeant exclaimed. "Wow, now I say *that* is a great story!"

I nodded. "Yes, it is. You fellows want to be my witnesses in court?"

"I am not a witness," said the sergeant. "I would be merely repeating what I heard the boil say about what you said in its presence. That is hearsay, actually double hearsay, and is completely inadmissible in court."

"Hear me say what?" said the boil. "What are you rambling on about, faerie?"

"And the boil is not a witness for the same reason," finished the sergeant.

"Witness?" said the boil. "I am too a witness! You wouldn't believe what I have to witness down here."

I realized what the sergeant said made sense, sort of. And I had caused enough of a ruckus in Immortal Divorce Court without dropping my breeches in open court so that the boil could testify. The only ones that could testify on my behalf were the ones that imprisoned me here in the first place. "I understand," I said with a frown.

"Sorry," the sergeant said. "We are the arrestifiers and not the testifiers." He motioned to the other two deputies, and they changed to pure diamond and grabbed on to one of my chains, yanking with all their might. I thought I could feel the ground beneath my feet begin to waver and shimmy, but the chain still remained affixed to the dungeon wall. The sergeant released the chain and stood back, scratching his head. "We should still be able to break these Immortal Divorce Court chains since we are on official business. I find this highly unusual. Sinister, we shall return. Don't go anywhere while we are gone, all right?"

"Who knew?" the boil said. "Faeries can be funny!"

I could do nothing but wait for the deputies to return and, hopefully, free me. I was just beginning to grow a little bit crazy, trading insults with the boil, when I heard footsteps approaching. Through the door came a broad-shouldered figure wearing a traveling cloak as blue as the sky with a large cowl draped over its head. It moved slowly but deliberately, like its knees had suffered many an injury, and stopped suddenly just out of the boil's range.

"Drat," said the boil to our mysterious guest. "How did you know to stop just outside of spitting range?"

"I've read Bartholomew's *Treatise on Enchanted Boils*," the deep voice behind the cowl said. "Save your pus for a less well-read guest."

"Who are you?" By this point I'd had so many guests that I was not remotely bothered by my privates being on full display. "Are you a special warlock envoy of Immortal Divorce Court, sent to try your magic on these accursed chains?"

"Well, Sirius Sinister," said my guest, "I have actually been waiting a few centuries to make your acquaintance. I grew tired of waiting for you to come to me, so I decided to come to you. And seeing how you have been on the wrong end of a few bad decisions, I figured now was the perfect time." He drew his hood back, revealing a perfectly clean-shaven head that glistened in the eerie light of the chains. "I am Hedley Edrick, but you can call me 'the Teacher of Teachers,' 'the Master of Masters,' 'the Scholar of Scholars,' 'the Sage of Sages,' and yes, you guessed it, I am the most learned creature on this amazing planet of ours."

"What a cocky cock!" opined the boil.

I smiled wryly. "It is a pleasure to finally meet you," I said. "I always meant to attend your school at some point in the last two hundred years. But instead I seem to have wandered off onto an all too different path." I rattled my chains. "Of course, I have been getting some hard lessons all the same, though."

"So I see," Hedley replied, his eyes twinkling. "But it is never too late to find the proper path. Sometimes life is like making sausage—the process is not something that is pleasant to look at but ends up as something you really wanted all along."

"What I really want is to be free from these chains so I can go to Immortal Divorce Court and fight for my girls," I said, feeling a tear come to my eye, which I fought unsuccessfully to blink back in.

"I will free you from those chains," Hedley said. "If you promise that you will do just one little thing for me."

"Anything!" I said. "Just name your price!"

"No matter your result at the IDC, whether you are jailed for a thousand years or are free to live unfettered with your girls, you must promise to come to my school and study for as long as I say," he said.

"I will," I said. "Not a problem. Now get me out of these chains!"

"Swear," Hedley said.

"Shit!" said the boil. "Are we free yet?"

"Fine, I swear, I swear," I said. "Now come on, Edrick, get a move on, those faeries will be coming back any minute now. I can feel it."

"Swear also to never give up in trying to find the purest love that lifts your heart up and makes all well with the world."

Damn, that certainly wasn't a question I wanted to be asked while chained to a wall with my breeches at my ankles and some strange hooded man in the room. But hopefully, this wasn't that kind of party. So why was I questioning anything the Teacher of Teachers said? The reality was that I would promise anything just to be able to pull my breeches up.

Hedley interpreted my desperate inner dialogue as confusion at his request. "I read a lot," he said. "You are actually featured prominently in Eros's *Book on Love*. So promise." He looked at a strange crystal strapped to his wrist. "And you had better hurry up with the promising, because the faeries are mere minutes away, by my calculations."

"I promise to always seek the purest love that lifts my heart," I said.

"And makes all well with the world," he prompted.

Really? "And that makes all well with the world," I repeated. "Are you happy now?"

"More than you know," Hedley said. "Boil, if you choose to spit pus at me, both of you will rot in the Immortal Divorce Court jails for eternity. Got it?"

"Aye," said the boil. "My lips are sealed."

Hedley reached into his robe and pulled out a bottle of wine. "This rare vintage is courtesy of Don Indigo, my only mortal student, and a man who was worthy of many lifetimes on this earth."

"Don Indigo! He studied with you?" I exclaimed. "That is completely amazing. We had a chance meeting so long ago, but I keep finding myself the recipient of his gifts centuries later."

"I know," Hedley replied. "He told me about your act of mercy. Remember this, Sirius—mercy knows no mortality. This wine is called Amor Lo Conquista Todo."

"Love conquers all?" I said, perplexed. "What can it do?"

"Why, everything, of course," Hedley said. He reached up and poured some of the wine over one of my chains, and then the other, and before my amazed eyes, the chains dissolved in a rush of golden liquid and pooled on the ground at my feet. My arms dropped to my sides, and I happily grabbed for my breeches and pulled them up.

"Hey," shouted the muffled voice of the boil. "I can't see."

"It doesn't matter, boil," I said, extending a hand of thanks to Edrick. "We are free."

"Not for long if you don't get out of here," Hedley said. "You cannot travel by crystal because the deputies will track you wherever you land. You have to do this the mortal way. I have a small boat called *Patty's Folly* moored by the dock. The crew is expecting you and will take you to London. There you can get your gold and see if you can rustle up old Justice to help you fight for your children."

"Thank you so much," I said. "I don't know if I will ever be able to repay you."

"Just come see me when you are done with your business at the IDC," he said. "The last place they will be looking for you is the IDC courthouse."

We hurried out of the dungeon, and I was thankful to see Peel Castle disappear from view as we headed to the docks. The sun was coming up, truly a beautiful sight, and one I thought I would never ever see again. The chill of the morning was welcome, and it felt so good to do something as simple as walk after being confined for so long. Winter was clearly fast approaching, but I needed no overcoat, being fully warmed by my vigor. How long had I been locked up in Peel Castle?

The sea air had never smelled so clean, and I inhaled deeply, filling my lungs with its refreshing briny breath. Even though I had no weapons, and just the clothes on my back, and thankfully the breeches around my waist, I was ready to go fight for my children. I could see *Patty's Folly* ahead and turned to Hedley Edrick. "One more thing, Hedley," I said. "How much time has passed?"

"It's the twenty-third day of November, 1703," he said. "Not so long for an immortal."

"Still, I have missed a lot." I climbed on deck. My little girls were now eleven years old. A strange sadness came over me of having missed their first words, first steps, first everything—indeed nearly their entire childhood. Did they even know I existed? I could only imagine the horrible things the Howler had told them about me.

"Years pass ever so slowly for us," Hedley replied. "But even an immortal cannot go back in time to experience what has been utterly and irrevocably lost in the present, though now that I think of it, I should probably work on that." He remained on the dock deep in thought.

"You are not coming with me?" I said.

"I have to see an old friend by the name of Finn McCool," he said.

"All right then," I said. "Wish me luck."

"We are going to need it," the muffled voice of the boil said from the depths of my breeches. "We are not going on a boat, are we? Are we?"

"Yes, you are going on a boat, boil, and yes, you will," Hedley replied. "Yes, you will indeed. Good luck, Sirius Sinister. I will you see you soon." With that he walked away and disappeared into the morning mist.

CHAPTER 13

The crew of the good ship *Patty's Folly* were all mortals except for the captain, who, judging by his long greenish-brown hair and eyes as brown as the newly tilled earth, had at least some elf in him. They moved as one casting off, and the *Patty's Folly* left the dock and the Isle of Man behind, heading out upon the Irish Sea, heading south. "Good riddance," I said out loud, watching the island disappear behind us.

"You can say that again," said the boil. "But I don't like boats."

The captain came up to me while the boil was chattering. "You seem to have some talking hose," he said. "Hedley told me about your little problem. Do not worry about it. This crew, though they are mortals, are plenty used to strange sights, or sounds."

"Who are you calling strange, fat boy?" my breeches stated.

"Boil," I said, "please don't get us thrown off this boat, unless you can swim well."

"Nooooo!" the boil screamed. "Not the ocean. Anything but the ocean. I'll be good, I promise." And with that the boil went silent.

"My name is Seamus," the captain said. "You are the one they call Sinister?"

"Yes," I replied. "You can call me Sirius. How do you know of me?"

"I am a quarter water elf on my father's side," he answered. "My grams is a full elf, and a friend of hers recently was at Immortal Divorce Court, attending to some family business. Apparently you are quite the celebrity there. It was something about your dog?"

I laughed. "That is a long story, my friend. I'll be sure to tell it to you on the way to London. What route are we taking?"

Seamus sniffed at the wind and looked troubled for a moment. "That is odd," he said without explaining his concern. "We are going southwest toward the coast of merry old England. We will come around past Holyhead, Bardsey Island, Ramsey Island, and then once we hit Skomer Island, we will be able to blend in with the traffic coming into Bristol. From there it is just a short ride to London. It shouldn't take us long at all."

Our small sloop cut through the calm sea like a hot knife through butter, and I took a spot on the deck out of the way of the crew, and reveled in the feeling of the wind in my hair and the rise and swell of the waves. I heard a small moan of anguish and wondered where it was coming from, and then felt wetness running down my leg. The boil was apparently seasick. Grimacing, I wadded up a cloth and nonchalantly rammed it down the back of my breeches. "Easy now, boil," I said. "This journey will be but a short one. I'll have you back on dry land in a jiffy."

Seamus came by with a piece of bread and some cheese, which I gladly took and devoured like it was a hunk of dripping bloody meat. Soon I would be back on dry land, and soon I would have some exceedingly rare meat from some four-legged frolicker. I really missed Garlic, thinking of the many kills we had together. What was she doing now with my girls? I comforted myself thinking that she was watching over them, and thus, I was participating in the raising of my daughters through my pup after all.

We passed from the Irish Sea into the Atlantic and *Patty's Folly* swung well wide of Skomer Island, where the character of the ocean changed, and what was once a smooth and, dare I say, fun ride got a whole lot rougher.

"We are catching the will of the open ocean, as bonny Ireland no longer shelters us with her fair skirts," Seamus said with a grin as he exhorted the crew to battle through waves that sent *Patty's Folly* deeper and deeper into the troughs only to rise up again undaunted against the might of the ocean. Finally, as the boat made the turn for Bristol, the waves lessened to an eerie calm, and the wind simply stopped, causing the sails to hang limp and powerless. "What madness is this?" Seamus exclaimed to no one, peering back at the open Atlantic, and sniffing the air. The crew grew nervous as their captain reached over the bow and swished a hand in the calm water and sniffed again.

"Mistress is coming," the boil screamed from my breeches, now wet with the boil's tears. "She is coming to kill us."

"Easy now, boil," I said. "She had her sport with us and surely has moved on to greener pastures."

Seamus stared at a massive black cloud that loomed high on the horizon, and the wind began picking up as the sea once more came to life. Thunder boomed, and an eerie green lightning illuminated the cloud for a moment, giving it the appearance of a ghastly skull. "Pray tell," he said, "who is this mistress your breeches speak of?"

"The Winter Witch," I said.

Seamus cursed under his breath and made every single mystic sign he knew, then added a few more he made up on the spot just in case they would help. "Edrick never told me that she was part of this journey," he said. "If I had known that, I would have charged him a lot more gold!" A lightning bolt shot out of the cloud and struck the ocean, and a great wave formed, heading straight for our craft. "Like a whole lot more gold!"

We sat dead in the water, but rushing in front of the wave blew a great wind filling our sails and turning the ocean into an angry mass of foam and waves. "Hold on," Seamus said, leaping for the rudder as his crew expertly trimmed the sails. "I am going to need your strength, my fanged friend," he said. "We must stay the course. If this windstorm spins us sideways, and a wave hits us broadside—we are done for!"

The wind howled and ripped what sail remained on our masts into tattered shreds. I could no longer hear the whine of the boil over the fury of the ocean. I stood with Seamus and held the rudder fast, as waves crashed over the bow of the *Patty's Folly* onto the deck and into our position, threatening to send us into the angry sea. And each time we came up from the depths of a stormy trough, the wind seemed to howl ever angrier. Lightning bolts sizzled and crackled all around us, and one great wave thrust Seamus and I together. "What did you do to that witch to piss her off so damn bad anyway?" he shouted above the din of the storm.

"I plowed the field with her right before I married my second wife," I said.

"Like, *right* before, right before?" Seamus exclaimed.

I nodded, hanging on to the rudder for dear life. "Yeah, I kind of just made it to the church on time."

Seamus looked up at the dark cloud that was nearly upon us, and we both could see amidst the swirling darkness the sneering angry face of the Winter Witch. "We are surely doomed," he said. "Or, more accurately, your getting fucked is going to get us fucked. Like completely fucked . . ."

A lightning bolt shot out from the cloud and struck our main mast, snapping it in two and setting the bottom half on fire. If the storm did not get us, the fire surely would, as the crew scrambled to put out devilish green flames that grew larger by the second, feeding off the rain of hate coming from the cloud. I did not think I could drown, and Seamus, being part water elf would survive, but his crew of mortals would surely die. I only had one choice.

I stepped back from the rudder. "If it is me you want, it is me you shall get, witch," I screamed to the furious firmament, and dove from the ship into the frothing sea, powering deep into the ocean with the broad strokes of a youth spent on Sa Dragonera. The water felt so cold I half expected to see ice floes. No matter, my lungs were strong and my purpose was true. I had to pull the attention of the Winter Witch away from the *Patty's Folly*. I surfaced a good distance away from the ship, and caught on to the remnants of another ship whose passengers had not been so lucky. My heart felt a deep sorrow for my actions with the Winter Witch, because her rage at me had killed many innocents. If only I had walked away from that tavern, these people would be alive. A child's shoe floated by me, and the salt of my tears joined that of the ocean. A wave thrust me high into the air, and far off I could see the *Patty's Folly* at the edge of the storm as the Winter Witch sought to find me. "Bitch," I shouted into the wind. "I am here. Bring whatever foulness you have, but it is not going to be enough to slay me this day!"

Down from the cloud came a streak of lightning growing larger and larger as it neared the ocean, slamming into the waves and sending a geyser skyward. I rode a wave high in the air again, and saw bearing toward me the large white dorsal fin of a shark. It was a massive creature easily as long as the *Patty's Folly*, with a mouth that could swallow several men whole at once, but it only had eyes for me. Green lightning shot up and down its body, churning the ocean as it came for me. I would not survive in the caustic acid of that demonic gullet and dove down deep, swimming with all my might.

Suddenly, up ahead I saw the hull of another ship, and stopped swimming. There would be no more mortal souls lost today on my account. The shark changed course, and instead of bearing straight for me, it headed right for the ship, and its purpose was obvious. One strike to the hull, and it would surely be breached. Hundreds would die unless I acted. I looked around frantically for some sort of flotsam that would serve as a weapon, but saw none. A voice called from the ship, and someone hurled a golden sword to me, which I snatched right out of the air.

I had speared many a fish off Sa Dragonera, but the beast bearing down on the ship was no guppy. I would have a single chance to stab it through one of its dastardly green eyes and hope that the blade would reach the brain. But to get the leverage to do that, I would have to be practically sitting on top of the shark. I took a deep breath and dove down into the depths as the storm currents buffeted me to and fro in the water, and the white death appeared. I was in perfect position, but then a swift current pulled me back into the shark's path. I saw nothing but teeth and death, and twisted my body and thrust at the shark at the same time. I felt sharp teeth rake down my back and legs, opening deep wounds that sent red tendrils of my blood all around me. But my aim had been true, and crimson spewed out of the shark's eye, joining my own blood as I held on for dear life, driving the sword deeper and deeper into its primeval brain. I did not have much breath left, and I could feel my strength ebbing with the effect of the wounds and the icy grip of the North Atlantic. The shark began its death roll, spinning deeper and deeper, the pressure tearing most of the remaining air from my lungs.

I kicked away from the shark, straining for the surface, but all I saw was an eerie white light. I had swum in the wrong direction and had gone ever deeper, and the Winter Witch had apparently found me. Her white arms reached out to grab me, and I struggled away, spitting out my last breath in the process. I would die before I would yield to her. A small, white hand found my own, and I felt not the cold chill of the Winter Witch but something else entirely. Amidst a swirl of bubbles, warm lips found my own, and I stopped struggling, realizing I could breathe, and found myself eye to eye and lips to lips with a mermaid.

With a flick of her powerful golden tail, the mermaid propelled us under water, away from the dead shark and the boat filled with innocents. The sharp sting of the wounds on my back and legs told me they were quite serious. I would heal, but I had to get out of the icy cold of the Atlantic that, moment by moment, was stealing the life from me. If I became fish food, there was no possible way I could recover from that. The mermaid grabbed my other hand, and we zipped through the depths, partners in an aquatic dance, with our hands gripping tightly and our bodies thrust together as my legs hung useless, her tail thrashing the water between them. In spite of the dire circumstances, I could not help but enjoy the feel against my own cold body of the full breasts and amazingly soft, warm skin that was the color of the whitest sea foam that belonged to the lovely golden-haired creature that was saving me.

Finally we surfaced, and I reluctantly broke our kiss, staring deep into eyes bluer than any perfect sky I had ever seen and that sparkled with an unyielding intensity. Curly golden hair framed her beautiful face and then cascaded over her shoulders. The conventional wisdom was that mermaids were quite unattractive, even ugly. I remembered Oliver's story of his encounter with an attractive lady of the sea, and realized that either he and I had met up with the only two beautiful mermaids on the entire earth, or conventional wisdom was dead wrong. I grimaced as the cold air struck my skin, and pain shot down my legs, and she pulled me close once more. "Thank you," I said. "Why did you help me?"

"You could have saved yourself," my rescuer said. "That shark would have been unable to resist all the mortals in the water and would have feasted on them for hours. From the looks of you and your uncommon ability to swim, even for an immortal, you surely would have made it to the coastline. So why did you help them?"

I shook my head. A boom of thunder drew my attention to the edge of the storm, which seemed to be changing direction to intercept us. "My actions have caused me to have much mortal blood on my hands," I answered. "I simply could not bear the thought of any others losing their lives because of me."

"That is quite noble," she said, smiling in approval. "And that was no ordinary shark. That was a familiar of the Winter Witch."

"I know," I said. "Sure would like to know who threw me that sword I stuck into her familiar. He deserves a thank you as well."

"Not he—she," the mermaid said.

"You, you were on that boat!" I exclaimed. "But, who are you?"

She did not answer, for the swell of the waves had suddenly picked up, and the storm was drawing closer by the second. Green lightning crackled, and the sky swirled in a menacing fashion. "The witch is coming for us with full hurricane force," the mermaid said anxiously. "Our only hope is to make it to Lundy Island."

I nodded, remembering Lundy Island was just off the coast of Devon. Had the storm pushed us that far south of the channel into Bristol? What little adrenaline I had left began to ebb. Now, I only felt pain. "I don't have much strength left," I said. "How far is it?"

"Not far," she said. She drew me into her embrace once more and pushed her lips against mine. I gasped, losing myself in their sweet softness. Her hands gripped my face, and we kissed deeper, and despite my condition, I felt myself responding. But then she grabbed my hands, and we dove beneath the waves, racing the Winter Witch's hurricane to Lundy Island.

I closed my eyes and held on to my aquatic angel as best as I could. I had lost a lot of blood, and even for a vampire with a constitution like mine, I was in trouble. The Celtic Sea was being fairly churned by the hurricane as it sought to overtake us, but the mermaid was not to be denied, and soon we were in the shallows of the island. The closer we came to the water's surface, the rougher our passage became. The hurricane was nearly upon us. All I could hear was the howling scream of the wind even from just below the surface.

But the Winter Witch would not have us this day, as the mermaid swam us into a small grotto at the base of a cliff. Back we swam into the darkness, where the waves and wind could not follow, and slowly the sound of the wind faded. Blindly, the mermaid navigated through a narrow passage into a lagoon and, with a kick of her tail, dislodged a crude lever that dropped a stone over the passage, thwarting the storm surge. All was quiet but for the light wash of gentle waves upon a sandy beach lit with a warm blue glow from strange underwater plants. She pulled me through this undersea garden and pushed me gently onto the beach.

I felt the soft touch of sand on my face and reached out with my hands to clench two dry fistfuls in victory. But I lay groggy in the grotto, with the mermaid embracing me and warming my body as it healed from the wounds of the shark familiar—safe at last.

I awoke facedown in the sand and turned to find the mermaid lying in the water beside me. She smiled comfortingly and swished her tail in the water at my feet. My body was wrapped in oddly sweet-smelling, brown seaweed from head to toe. It was warming and as comfortable as the softest goose down. The chamber in which I lay was still lit from the warm blue glow of the underwater plants. "Is the Winter Witch gone?" I asked.

"Even she cannot wield power over the elements forever. She has lost control of the storm, and all of England is feeling the brunt of her desire to see you dead. You must have really got on her bad side," the mermaid replied.

"Yes, I sure did," I replied, offering nothing else to this delightful girl. Took the Winter Witch from her backside was a more apt description, but I remained silent, taking stock of my wounds. Strangely, I felt absolutely fine. I reached over my right shoulder and peeled back a layer of seaweed and found my skin bore absolutely no sign of the jagged wound I recalled being there from the shark.

"After such a colossal use of her magic, we are not likely to see her for a long while," the mermaid said.

"No one has infinite power, right?" I said.

"Even a heroic vampire like you," she replied. "If not for me, I am not sure you would have survived."

"I would have," I said, not so confident that I would have. "But, all the same I am glad the Winter Witch is not all-powerful."

"She will lick her wounds for some time. How are you feeling?"

I turned on my side still bound in my seaweed blanket and was taken aback at how incredibly beautiful this mermaid was to my well-trained eye. I stole a quick glance at her breasts and taut stomach. I had been with many a woman, but this creature of the sea could catch any man she wanted, hook, line, and sinker. "Surprisingly good thanks to you, considering the shark nearly had me for a meal," I said. "This seaweed is miraculous. I have never seen it before in all my travels. Where did you come by it?"

The mermaid smiled. "Now that is my secret, and the ocean does not like giving up its mysteries to those that walk on land," she said. "Rest assured, without it, you would be looking a whole lot less pretty back there than you are now. That shark had taken a nice bite out of your back and shoulders, and well, half of your backside was nearly ripped off, you know!"

"The boil!" I exclaimed. "I completely forgot about it!" In the chaos, the last thing I had been thinking about was the pus-spewing entity occupying a prime spot on my ass. I reached back and gingerly pulled a piece of the seaweed off my posterior to let the strangely silent boil get some air, wincing as I waited for my not-so-favorite pus spitter to utter some obscenity-laced tirade to ruin this incredibly pleasant moment. Miraculously, I saw only the smooth olive skin I had come into the world with. The boil was gone, ironically excised by the Winter Witch's familiar. Being in mixed company, I patted the seaweed back into place.

"The what?" the mermaid asked.

"Just a nasty old curse, courtesy of the Winter Witch," I replied. "It is a relief to have it gone, as entertaining as it was!"

"We need to get the seaweed off you," she said, reaching for a strip. "If you tarry in it too long, it turns your skin a lovely shade of bright green—permanently. And I don't think that is your color! Here, hold still, I want to make sure you are completely healed." She rolled me on to my side, facing away from her, and gently pulled the seaweed from my body. Her soft hands caressed my back, bare backside, and legs, and it was all I could do to not make a sound hinting at the pleasure it gave me.

"All right, that is great," she said. It sure was. "Everything looks good to me. Now lie on your back," she said, and I readily complied. "Your wounds seem to have healed amazingly quick, even for a vampire." She looked at me a little oddly, and I wondered if Persephone's gift had translated in ways I had not discovered. The truth was that I had never in my life suffered wounds that severe. Even that blasted faerie Pansy had gone a whole lot easier on me!

The mermaid reached for my chest and drew the seaweed from it, thrusting herself out of the water and onto the beach, rising up on her golden tail. I could see her skin ended a few inches below her navel, and from there lustrous golden scales that sparkled iridescently in the blue light took over all the way to her life-saving tail. Her hands moved down to my abdomen, touching it ever so softly, and I could feel my manhood threatening to burst through the seaweed that bound it. Had the mermaid ever seen such a thing?

I had never seen a mermaid up close, let alone a merman, and frankly did not know how they propagated their species. Down came the wrap and up I came, but the mermaid gave no reaction, continuing to unwrap me until I lay fully naked on the sand with her on my side. She thrust with her tail slightly and landed at an angle, her delightful breasts resting atop my chest and her face even with my own. She looked down at my excitement. "You still seem to have a good bit of swelling," she said. "And it's all red. Do you think it is infected? Because I can get some more seaweed and wrap it up for a while."

"No, no," I replied. "It is normal for it to look like that when . . . I am . . . uh . . . happy." I paused. How could I tell this mermaid that I was aroused by her? The awkwardness of this situation was beginning to cure me of my "swelling."

"Are you feeling sad now?" she asked. Before I could answer, she reached down and curled her hand around my manhood and stroked it. "Oh," she said, watching the effect of her hand. "I like it much better this way when it is happy, and now it looks positively overjoyed! Now, I think you need to make me happy." She leaned forward, and brought her lips to mine and kissed me softly.

I had no idea what she had in mind—I had not actually noticed any parts on her that could accomplish her happiness—and believe me, I had looked. But as she rubbed me, she began moving her tail side to side, and in a burst of white light, her tail changed into a pair of lithe, white legs. Mystery solved—for framing her womanhood were the same beautiful curls that she wore upon her head. She straddled my legs, and I could feel the warmth of her womanhood pressing against me.

"That is better," she said. "Much, much better. Do you like my land legs?" She squeezed her legs against mine and ran her fingers up and down my chest.

"Matter of fact, I do," I said. I reached up and pulled her to me, bringing her lips to mine and licking the barest hint of salt from them. I kissed her ever so deeply as my hands found her breasts and pinched her nipples, and she pushed harder against me.

I gasped as she took me inside her. I realized that I didn't even know her name. She leaned back and began rhythmically thrusting down on me with her hips. I realized that I didn't care what her name was. A moan escaped those full soft lips of hers, and I could feel the wetness of her pleasure bathing me. I realized, squeezing hard on her firm buttocks as she rode me, that I should have asked her a whole lot of questions. Her screams of pleasure reverberated around the grotto, and her hands dug into the sand next to us. I realized I didn't care about the answers to those questions. Her pleasure built, rolling like great waves and crashing on me with warm, foamy delight. I realized that time and time again I had gotten myself in trouble doing this so wonderfully pleasurable act. I felt my own tidal wave of joy cresting ever so powerfully, and she sensed it, riding her own wave of pleasure with me, and we screamed out in unison as we reached our apex together. She collapsed upon me, her chest heaving as she tried to catch her breath. I realized as I fell into a deep slumber that I did not care one damn bit about how much trouble I just may have gotten myself into. Two words—worth it.

I awoke many hours later, and she was gone. The only trace that she had been there were small footprints leading from the sandy beach to the edge of the lagoon. I smiled to myself as I was usually the one beating a hasty retreat after an encounter such as this one. I rose to my feet and brushed the sand from my buttocks. I was feeling quite used by the mermaid, but I couldn't have been happier. We both got what we wanted, and she departed without requiring anything else from me. Now, that was a perfect relationship—I thought for a minute—unless there was something I did not know about doing it with a mermaid at high tide, or in the sand, or after being wrapped in magical seaweed. Blast it! Why were women so damn complicated anyway?

I saw a path that led from the beach to an alcove, where I discovered a cache of clothes, weapons, and a few bags of gold. I was going to have to get passage from Lundy Island to Bristol, and then on to London to get my gold, and then pay Justice a visit and see if there was anything he could do about the arrest order, and getting me time to see my daughters. They would be on the cusp of womanhood now, and being fed who knows what mindless drivel by the Howler and the rest of the Blackheart clan. I sure hoped that Jova was still with Cornelia, and maybe, just maybe he had told them that I would never ever have left them.

For a moment I considered going to Lancashire to confront the Howler and Angus but stuck to my original plan. I would be a fool to beard the alpha Pack leader in his den. Angus probably had half the werewolves in England guarding the perimeter to Lancashire County. Plus, I had no guarantee that the Howler had not spirited the girls off to some undisclosed location far away. So to London and then to Immortal Divorce Court I would go.

I dressed quickly, finding clothes that, oddly, fit me just perfectly. Was this mere coincidence or a knowing present from that beautiful mermaid? I sighed. It would have been nice to give her a proper good-bye kiss on those salty lips of hers, but that pleasure was not to be mine. Armed with a trusty sword and blunderbuss, I found a path leading upward that terminated in front of a circular rock set on a strange lever. I pulled the lever, and the rock slid open, revealing a copse of trees and thick underbrush.

I stepped into sunlight and bright blue sky. The Winter Witch's hurricane was gone, but I could see down to a small pocket beach, where a number of vessels crammed in just offshore with repairs aplenty being made to the damaged crafts. It was destruction that I was ultimately responsible for because of my selfish actions. I climbed down to the beach and blended in easily with the rest of the survivors of the hurricane, and after a few days of good, clean, hard work, hired on to the crew of an English merchant ship bound for Bristol.

I could not believe my good fortune. No one asked who I was, or where I was going, or even for any gold for passage. All they wanted were my willing hands and strong back, of which I freely gave. It was my penance and my disguise all at once. I was amazed at how, in the face of such utter disaster, mortals could come together to achieve a common goal—survival.

But when I got to Bristol, I saw anything but good fortune. I made my way inland, heading toward London, and all around me were signs of great flooding and misery. From the looks of what I saw, hundreds of people must have died in the flooding, all of whose blood was now on my hands. My heart was heavy. If this trip to Immortal Divorce Court returned me to Hell, there surely would be some tortured and rather angry souls to greet me for some personal payback. I passed a ship, easily fifteen miles inland, and wondered if it was the one that I had tried to save in, perhaps, what now was a futile act. If only I had done more. Actually, if only I had done less and acted honorably, and not consorted with the Winter Witch. So I decided to do all I could and again lent my back and hands, and when I could not do that, I gave my gold to all who were in need that I passed on the way to London.

I found Harvis on the outskirts of his farm, stripped to the waist and wielding a huge axe that he was using to successfully turn the many fallen trees on his property into winter firewood. Old Man Tyler was with him, scooping the wood up dutifully and hauling it off in the direction of the farmhouse. "Need some help?" I said, coming out of the woods behind him.

"I thought I smelled coward," he said, not turning to face me. Instead, with several powerful blows of his axe, he proceeded to add to his firewood collection.

"What are you talking about, Harvis?" I said, walking toward him. Old Man Tyler had returned from his trip to the farmhouse, and speaking of smelling things, indeed he still had not apparently found the time in his busy day to have a moment with some foamy soap bubbles. Tyler tipped his cap to me and waited for Harvis to split some more wood.

But Harvis spun, axe in hand, and poked a powerful finger sharply into my chest. It was so hard and violent that for a moment I wondered if my old friend was trying to split me into so much kindling. "The woman I get," he said. "I knew she was trouble when I had her. That is why I never went there again. But your children? Come on. How could you just leave them? What were you afraid of?"

I grew angry at my old friend accusing me without hearing me out. "I didn't leave them."

"Well, what's it been, eleven, twelve years, since I have seen you?" Harvis said, still poking me in the chest, which was frankly beginning to hurt, though I stood my ground and felt my fists balling up. Old

Man Tyler backed away slowly. The wood could wait until this dispute among old friends was settled. "I know you haven't been in Lancashire. Jova said you disappeared right after the girls were born. Sounds just like you, don't you think?"

I unclenched my fists and calmed down, because it did sound just like me—the old me. "It does," I said. "But there is a reason I disappeared."

Thankfully, Harvis stopped poking me and leaned on his axe. He nodded. Old Man Tyler nodded with him. "Sure there was," Harvis said. "This ought to be good. Really good. Talk."

And talk I did. "My dear beloved wife and her father kidnapped me, imprisoning me with enchanted Immortal Divorce Court chains to the wall of a dungeon below Peel Castle on the Isle of Man. Then the barmaid I had relations with before the wedding turned out to be the Winter Witch. She showed up in the dungeon and found me chained to the wall, tried to cut off my manhood, and when that failed, cursed me with a talking boil on my ass . . ."

"A talking boil on your arse? Come on," Harvis said, "that is ridiculous!"

"You too, Sinister?" Old Man Tyler croaked. "She did that to me once. 'Course she left my manhood alone—she said it was so small it was a punishment all on its own. That wasn't very nice, was it? I mean, I am part gnome, you know. What did she expect?" He stood looking at an astonished Harvis and me. We did not have an answer for him, so he went back to stacking firewood. Neither one of us wanted to know just how he had managed to have an intimate encounter with the Winter Witch. I mean, when it happened, did he smell just like he did now?

"Okay, so now the talking boil on your arse has been spoken for," said Harvis. "But what about the dear Howler and Angus, what did they do?"

"Well, in typical devious Blackheart fashion, my dear beloved Howler divorced me on the grounds of abandonment and got an order for my arrest," I said. "Finally, eleven years later, Hedley Edrick showed up and freed me with magical wine from Don Indigo that melted away the enchanted Immortal Divorce Court chains . . ."

"Oh, Don Indigo," Harvis said. "Well, that part makes sense."

"But on the way back to London by way of Bristol, the Winter Witch, realizing I was still alive, conjured up the Great Storm of 1703 to try and kill me . . ."

"Aha! I just knew this disaster was your fault somehow." Harvis surveyed all the fallen wood. "I just had that feeling!"

"Do you want to hear about my nearly death-inducing battle with the Winter Witch's demon shark and the gorgeous mermaid who saved me, healed me, pleasured me, and then left me passed out naked in the sand of a hidden grotto on Lundy Island?"

Harvis laughed. "You are certainly catnip for crazy pussy, my good friend."

I thought for a minute. "The mermaid was not crazy," I said. "At least I don't think she was, but she left before I woke up, so it doesn't matter. Anyway, how'd the farmhouse and barn take the storm? And how is that sweet Molly?"

"Molly is fine other than another litter growing in her belly," Harvis said. "And the house and barn are fine—nary a scratch. Oliver and I have been making some improvements."

"Good," I said. "I need to pay a little visit to the barn vault and get some of my gold. I need to hire Justice to help me get my little werepires back."

Harvis looked around carefully behind me. "That explains why I have smelled faeries around this farm lately," he said. "I think they are looking for you. Of course, the storm has bought you some time, but they will be back. No one evades the IDC, my friend."

"I am not going to run and hide, Harvis," I said, sniffing the air for a sign of anything other than a big sweaty werewolf and his rather odoriferous companion. Perhaps it was a blessing that Old Man Tyler and his grand funk were waylaying the senses of any that were trying to scent this fugitive vampire. "I am going straight to the IDC. Actually, I am going right to Justice's office. But if I show up without any gold after the last experience with him, I can tell you that cantankerous demon would probably hand deliver me to the court himself."

"All right then." Harvis put the massive axe over his shoulder and reached for his shirt. "It's probably best that you don't greet the lady of the farm. I don't think she is too fond of you after you interrupted us in the barn, and then—in her mind—left one of her sisters, so to speak."

"They hate each other," I exclaimed. "You'd think she'd congratulate me for leaving that bitch if that was really true."

"Uh, that would be a firm no," Harvis replied. "When there are pups involved, the instincts of a momma wolf overcome sheer visceral hate quite easily. So let's sneak over to the barn, and you can borrow a crystal to get you as far as the outer gates of the IDC. I have a big enough one to get you through with one, maybe two, chests of gold, but that is about it."

"That will have to be enough," I replied. "If not, I can always try and rely on Justice's good graces."

"He's a demon and a lawyer, so forget the good graces thing."

"Oh, right," I replied. "Hopefully the gold is enough for him."

We walked into the barn, and I realized we were not standing on dirt, but something else entirely. The floor was now hard and smooth and as white as snow, with drains spaced out in key places and in all the stalls. "What is this stuff?" I asked.

Harvis shrugged. "Oliver said it is called concrete, with a few choice bottles of wine added to the mix," he said. "I call it barn rock."

"Where is the vault?" I asked.

Harvis led me to what looked like an ordinary horse stall, and pulled on a rope. I was amazed to see the floor rise up on its own to reveal a hinged staircase that descended into the farmyard earth. I followed him down into the vault and saw gold and jewels piled neatly in storage areas as far as the eye could see. "Wow," I said. "This is amazing!"

He led me to a section and pointed to several chests. "These are your share from the goblin hoard," he said. He handed me a large oblong red crystal. "This little baby should be enough to get you close."

I held out my hand, which he clasped firmly. "Thank you," I said.

He shrugged. "What are friends for?" he replied. "But don't let it be another eleven years before I see you." He smiled warmly. "And yes, I do want to hear about the mermaid!"

"I'll be back," I said. "You can count on that!"

I sat down on one chest of gold, and put my feet on the other. I felt more focused than I had ever been. I thought of the road on the way to Immortal Divorce Court and remembered the outcropping overlooking the Gulf of Corinth, where I had stopped for lunch so many years ago. It was well hidden and, hopefully, was not presently occupied or fallen into the Gulf of Corinth, or I would be in for quite a surprise.

I focused on that spot as my destination and, this time, heard no howling vampire Maltese bidding me adieu as the Greek coastline popped into view. The outcropping was empty save for a few gulls that spread their wings and took to the sky, startled by my sudden arrival. I slid the chests holding my gold back into the brush, covered them up as best as I could, and pushed my way through the underbrush to the road. More than a decade of growth made this no easy task, and it was all I could do to make my way silently, but thankfully the road was deserted. Could the faeries sense my presence this close to them? I didn't have much time. I would have to get this gold and myself to Justice's office. But how?

My keen eyes picked up a small dust cloud coming down the road toward the village. It was a small wagon pulled by a single horse struggling to pull its load. The wagon was traveling alone without any kind of advance guard. Which, come to think of it, was not unusual, since anyone traveling this IDC-forsaken road to the outskirts of Hell either had no gold or was about to be stripped of all the gold they had left. No one went into Immortal Divorce Court *with* their gold in hand. That would be insane. Or at the very least, a not very well thought out plan. The wagon drew closer, and I saw a single driver with a cowl draped over its head to protect from the sun. I could not tell if it was a man or woman, mortal or immortal. And quite honestly it did not matter, for this wagon was soon to be mine.

It was nearly even with my hiding spot, and as it passed, I leaped from a rock onto the wagon and slipped my arm around the neck of the driver and incapacitated it. It bleated loudly and struggled quite feebly. Bleated? I snatched the reins from its hands with my spare hand and yanked hard, slowing the horse, and pulled back the cowl of the sputtering driver and instantly released my grasp.

"Cabernet!" I exclaimed, slapping the flushed cheeks of the poor satyr to bring him back to consciousness. He tended bar at the Golden Rule, the inn right across the street from the IDC courthouse, and clearly he was not used to being assaulted by the likes of me. "My apologies, good bartender! I did not know that it was your wagon I was intending to borrow and not return. It is me, Sirius Sinister—although you might remember me as Sirio Sinestra."

The old satyr sat next to me on the wagon, rubbing his throat, peering at me through the same worn spectacles he wore the first time we had met. He looked even more weathered, more tired, and definitely more mange-covered than since I last saw him over a century ago. Finally, he nodded. "I remember you, Sinister," he said. "The business with Feminera and Justice and the lady vampire, right?"

"Yes, but the vampire was no lady," I said. "You remember that?"

Cabernet's eyes became more focused, and he wagged his finger at me. "Yes, yes," he said. "The Zombie Pope came to your trial, which went quite poorly for you. And then your little white dog destroyed the jail, and you got sent to Hell!"

I nodded. "You have a good memory for an old goat."

"Memory, nothing," he exclaimed. "That was the talk of the town for at least half a century. That is, until we heard about your business with Persephone . . ." He bleated frantically and jumped out of the wagon, looking at the ground and the sky for who knows what. All I could smell was the sea air and a hint of fire and brimstone wafting to us from down the road. I frowned, wondering if the Lord of Darkness had forgotten about my dalliance with his ex-wife.

"He is going to kill you!" Cabernet screamed, dancing around on his shaky cloven hooves and wringing his hands in exasperation. "Really, really kill you. Probably in a way that no mortal, immortal, or god has even thought of yet."

That would be a no, apparently. "Cabernet, come on. You are overreacting," I said. "You don't really know that, do you? Well, do you?"

Cabernet put a hand on his chest and looked away to compose himself. "Yes, as a matter of fact I do," he said. "A demon creature of some sort came into my bar and, after a few too many drinks, began rambling something about putting a mark on a vampire for the Lord of Darkness."

"A vampire," I said. "He could mean any vampire in the world. How do you know he meant me?"

"A vampire that had the stupidity to sleep with the Lord of Darkness's ex."

"Oh, that is me," I said. There was nothing I could do about that little tidbit of information, assuming it was true and not the idle ramblings of some drunken demon. I had other tasks at hand, and I needed Cabernet's help to do them. "But I can't do anything about that now," I said. It is not like I could have a heart-to-heart with the Lord of Darkness, what with him not having a heart. "I need you to get me inside the IDC and to Justice's office."

"I thought you were already divorced," Cabernet said, confused.

"It's a different girl," I said. "At least the children that I am planning on fighting for are actually mine."

"You don't learn, do you?" Cabernet asked, an amused look forming on his long face. "You could be part satyr since you are so prolific."

I sighed deeply. Maybe Harvis was right about me being catnip. "Apparently not," I said. "And I am nothing but pure vampire." I bared my fangs for effect, and Cabernet took a few steps back nervously. "Now will you help me?" I pleaded.

"He is going to have my hooves," Cabernet protested, climbing back on the wagon. "The faeries are going to get you anyway, unless . . ."

"Unless what?" I asked the old goat.

"That must have been what he was talking about," said Cabernet, scurrying to the back of the wagon, where three large barrels were stacked.

"What was who talking about, Cabernet?" I asked, climbing to the back of the wagon to meet him.

Cabernet popped off the top of one of the barrels. The aroma of wine drifted to me. "Do you know a fellow by the name of Hedley Edrick?" he asked.

"I am starting to think that everyone does," I said. "Why?"

Cabernet gestured at the barrel of wine. "He said I needed to take this wine to the Golden Rule, and that it would help protect someone from being discovered by the faeries. I guess that someone is you, huh?"

"Do you have a goblet?" I asked.

Cabernet shook his head. "You could drink the whole barrel, but the faeries would still see you. Get in the barrel. The wine will keep you from being discovered. It is the only way to get through the gate. I will put your gold in the other barrel. When you hear the faeries at the gate, dunk underneath and hold your breath."

"So what is in the third barrel?" I asked.

Cabernet shrugged. "Don't know. He didn't tell me, and I didn't ask. It is going to the Golden Rule just like Hedley Edrick asked. You ready?"

I stepped into the wine barrel clothes and all, and dipped myself down. When my body went into the wine, the level rose perfectly to a few inches below the top of the barrel, leaving just enough room for me to breathe. Cabernet put the top back on, and I closed my eyes and steadied my breathing. The wagon lurched forward, and I got a mouthful of wine for my troubles. Though it was quite tasty, I focused on staying quiet and keeping calm, for the gates to Immortal Divorce Court were just a few minutes down the road.

"Once you hear them, hold your breath," Cabernet said again, "and I will get you to Justice's office."

Cabernet's horse maintained its deliberate pace, and I hoped we would get through the gate without any trouble. But one particular ornery faerie must have felt something odd as Cabernet passed through the gate. "Stop," he commanded. "What do you have there, you old goat?"

Cabernet slowed the wagon to a halt. "Wine for the inn," he replied.

The faerie came up to the wagon and sniffed around. Right before I dunked down in the wine, I heard him say, "What is that smell?"

I waited to feel the wagon move, but felt nothing. I waited for the lid to the barrel to come off, and a spear or two to be thrust into my hiding place. But nothing pierced my vampire hide, and slowly the wagon came back up to speed and passed through the gate. I waited as long as I could and surfaced slowly, breathing in the stale air of the barrel with great difficulty. Finally, we lurched to a stop, earning me another mouthful of the wine, and the top of the barrel came off. I rose out of the barrel, and found myself looking at Maximillian Justice.

"Sinister," he said, puffing on a long cigar. "It has not been long enough since I have seen your face. I hear you have been one busy vampire. Persephone? Really? Talk about having a death wish. But at least you actually had issue of your own this time. Nice work."

I stepped out of the barrel and realized we were standing in one of the outbuildings attached to his office. "I need your help," I said. "I have to get my children back."

Justice continued chomping on his cigar and spat on the ground next to me. "I wouldn't represent you for a whole chest of Spanish gold after that last fiasco."

I motioned to the barrel containing my gold. "Well, I have *two* chests of Spanish gold stowed in there," I said. "Will that work?"

Justice smiled, and golden sparks shot from his teeth. "Of course," he said. "Why didn't you say so in the first place?"

CHAPTER 14

It was like a bad dream, finding myself back in Justice's office, although gone were the stacks and stacks of dusty law tomes along with any traces of dust and rubbish whatsoever. I sat down on a chair so clean I could have eaten off it, and looked to Justice's desk where every quill, parchment, and file had its place. The claws on the dragon's legs that served as the supports to his desk glinted evilly, looking razor sharp and newly honed. I took a second look at Justice and noted his fiery hair was also in place, and his robes had no evidence of wine stains, food, or other detritus. He flipped open a book as old as he was, and strangely no dust welled up in a great storm of neglect.

Behind me I heard a flitter of activity, and into the room fluttered two angelic beauties flying on gossamer wings that sprouted from their shoulder blades and sparkled iridescently. The one flying closer to me had skin as dark as the night with flecks of shimmery gold in it, and she wore nothing but a single black pearl pinned in hair that was pure sunshine. That same lustrous hair crowned her womanhood, and her breasts were tipped with nipples of the softest honey. Her eyes were almond pools of bronze, and her cheekbones were high and regal, and she flashed a smile of approval from behind soft golden lips as she saw my jaw had dropped, and I was staring at her with my mouth wide open.

Her companion had skin the color of liquid sunshine with flecks of diamonds running through it, and she wore only a single diamond that glinted like a small sun in her hair, which sparkled like a rainbow, all colors and none at the same time. She blew a kiss to me with lips that shimmered in the light along with her nipples, which made for a delightfully dizzying effect, to say nothing of her womanhood that was framed by that same eye-catching rainbow hair that surely would drive any self-respecting leprechaun wild with passion.

Justice seemed oblivious to the two enchanting creatures as they replaced books on the shelves that spanned floor to ceiling in Justice's office, and snared every stray mote of dust that dared invade this hallowed space. I could not take my eyes off these lovely helpers of Justice. I strained my ears. Did I hear harp music playing? From time to time, they each met my gaze with coy looks and smiles of their own, and when their work was complete, they fluttered down to my side. I kept looking from one incomparable creature to the other, unable to decide which one I fancied the most. They smelled of fresh flowers and honey, and began running their fingers through my hair, and rubbing my shoulders. I closed my eyes and thought of the many naughty deeds I could do with these creatures.

"Sinister!" Justice shouted, snapping his fingers in front of my face, breaking my trance.

My eyes snapped open to see a slightly bemused Justice staring at me. I motioned with my head to either side ever so slightly as to not interfere with the treatment I was receiving from his helpers. "Aren't you going to introduce me?" I asked.

"They are my research assistants, Wisdom and Knowledge," he answered. "And they are quite capable of introducing themselves."

A small black hand with perfect tawny nails reached out and turned my face toward its owner. I was instantly lost in those gleaming eyes. "I am Wisdom," she said, her voice clear and strong.

Her companion touched my arm, and I turned to find myself staring directly at her rainbow-hued womanhood. She laughed and settled into my lap. "I am Knowledge," she giggled. Wisdom soon joined her, and they began rubbing their faces against mine.

"Well, you have certainly improved your customer service," I said to Justice. "What made you get some helpers? I sure wish they were here last time."

"You are such an idiot," he replied. "You have met these ladies." I scoffed at him. Like I would have forgotten these beauties? Was he kidding me? Wisdom turned my face to her and licked my lips ever so lightly with her long golden tongue. I gasped—what that tongue could do. Not to be outdone, Knowledge licked my ear, sending chills up and down my spine.

Justice shook his head. "You remember my bookworms?" he said. "You know, I am talking about those creepy crawly things that had you jump and scream like a schoolgirl? Well, they are all grown up now."

I glanced at their bountiful bosoms and shapely, round posteriors, and could not fathom that these lovely ladies were once . . . worms. "But, those things were just oversized caterpillars." I said. I looked at Wisdom, who winked back at me and licked me softly on the cheek. She had one incredibly long tongue, I mused. Not that I found that to be a bad thing—on a woman. "Now they are . . . are . . ."

"Research assistants, law clerks," Justice said. "But who needs labels? They do whatever I need, and I take care of them." They flitted over and kissed him on his ears and patted his head lovingly. "Okay, ladies," he said. "That is it for now, thank you." We both watched them flutter out of the room. "And they still like you," Justice said. "What is it about you that makes females just fawn over you?"

I shrugged. "I guess it's my blessing and my curse," I said.

Justice fixed a steely gaze on me. "That might be the most intelligent thing you have ever said. Now then, let's talk about your case. I am pretty sure I can prove that you did not abandon that Blackheart bitch, and that she and her ignoramus of a father conspired to trap you in Peel Castle, and that should free you of any financial obligation to her."

"Pretty sure?" I asked. "How could there be any doubt?"

Justice laughed and lit a clove cigarette with his index finger and puffed happily as the smoke twisted upward. "If you haven't learned anything from your last go round," he said, "nothing is certain in Immortal Divorce Court but *uncertainty.*"

"What about me being able to see the girls?"

Justice sighed and nodded. "Well, I said I should be able to free you of any financial obligation to the mother of your children," he said, "and I believe I can. Tomorrow I am going to file all the necessary paperwork on your behalf in Immortal Divorce Court, requesting your case be placed on the emergency docket."

"That's great, thanks," I replied. "So the emergency docket gets me in court in what . . . four or five days, right?"

"Try four or five years most likely, by my check of the last court calendar," he replied.

"That's ridiculous!" I spat. "How can the law move that slowly?"

"We are immortals, so we get a lot of divorces, and thus, the court docket is always full," Justice replied. "You'll have to wait your turn like everyone else. Hmm, I can't even imagine how the mortals feel about their divorce courts, which from what I understand, move as quickly as frozen molasses."

"So, they are going to be sixteen years old and a little bit more by the time I even get into court?" I said incredulously. "Is that what you are telling me?"

"Yes, and if they are still with the Blackhearts as their property, and haven't been married off for whatever alliances Angus needs to cultivate, I will fight to get you into their lives. But if they are considered legal adults, or have husbands, then you are going to have to track them down and make peace with them all on your own. And I can only imagine what madness and hate the Blackhearts have filled their souls with about their dear old dad."

"Maybe Garlic has put in a good word for me," I said, hoping it was true.

"That is a good point," Justice said. "That little pup of yours has stayed with them for a reason. A reason we are soon to find out." He rose to his feet and yawned. "All right then," he said. "Well, it is to bed for this lawyer, for I will need my rest for filing your paperwork tomorrow."

His servant showed me to an impressive room with a massive bed hewn from a single pine tree, draped under a canopy of live greenery that smelled of rosemary and thyme. I spied a porcelain tub steaming with hot, soapy water, and stripped and bathed the wine and dust of many days travel from my body. With a clean body and a clear mind, I settled under the soft down comforter and closed my eyes, hoping to drift off into a sound and restful sleep. I heard the sound of harp music and smelled fresh flowers and honey and felt soft wet kisses on either side of my neck. I opened my eyes slowly and saw that Wisdom and Knowledge had flitted ever so silently into my bed.

"Hello, Sirius," Wisdom said, her golden eyes glinting in the light of the many candles that lit my room. "Maximillian said he is filing for you tomorrow, and we are to provide whatever support we can."

Knowledge shimmied down to the end of the bed, reached under the comforter and began massaging my toes. "The legal research is done," she said with a dazzling rainbow smile. "Maximillian is ready to win your case for you."

Wisdom nodded, rubbing her fingers through my chest hair, stopping at my nipple to caress it ever so lightly. "Knowledge and I sometimes cannot agree on the best way to solve a problem," she said, pulling the comforter down.

"Indeed," I said, completely over the fact that my bedmates were once, well—worms. "So what do you do?"

Knowledge winked at Wisdom, and they both licked their lips. "Well, we do the only logical thing. We meet in the middle." And with that, Knowledge began kissing my legs gently, working gradually upward, and Wisdom started at my neck and chest and headed lower. The harp music grew louder as they met in the middle and cooed with great satisfaction, intent on giving my swollen member an education with those long, supple tongues of theirs.

The two girls had no problem sharing what I had to offer them, and after a while Wisdom slid back and dropped her gilded honey into my face, and I was only too happy to taste her sweetness. Knowledge settled in on my manhood and found pleasure instantly, singing out to the world of her orgasmic joy in knowing me. After one final crescendo for Knowledge, the girls switched places, and I knew Wisdom intimately and licked up all the Knowledge I could. When Wisdom had had enough of me, they met at my middle again, and Knowledge and Wisdom then intertwined their tongues, kissing each other and me all at the same time. I could feel the beginning of my glorious end building with each touch and lick of their tongues, and I sang my own song of utter joy as my lesson from Wisdom and Knowledge was complete. They curled up, one on each side of me, their gossamer wings blanketing me softly, and I slept the deepest most peaceful sleep I had experienced in ages.

When I awoke, Justice, Knowledge, and Wisdom were all gone from his abode, but the servant who had shown me to my room made it clear that I was forbidden from leaving Justice's home under the pain of death. Just how was I going to pass the time during the next five years? The servant showed me into Justice's library, where my counselor had preselected some of his favorite law books for me to read. And I thought lawyers didn't have a sense of humor. I shrugged, picked up a book, and promptly fell asleep at the table, only to be awakened by Knowledge and Wisdom, who had some excellent suggestions for how to pass the time. It was going to be an amazing five years. The next day I practically ran to Justice's library for my nap and to get ready to enjoy some more Knowledge and Wisdom. I was disappointed to find Justice there, who clearly enjoyed telling me that time did not pass in his library the same way as it did outside it. Five years had passed, and my hearing in Immortal Divorce Court was tomorrow. I did get one last night with Knowledge and Wisdom, however!

I awakened refreshed and ready. Next to my bed a full breakfast was laid out, which I hungrily devoured. I smiled when I reached for the last bowl and found some blood oranges. "Thank you, Persephone," I said out loud, devouring the blood oranges with renewed hunger, and the leafy bower atop my bed seemed to answer back as it swished in the slight breeze that had suddenly entered my room. I dressed in the clothes that had also been laid out for me, as my own had been discarded, and I went to find Justice.

He was waiting for me in the atrium, dressed in his finest gold robes. Fire shot from his eyes as his intensity literally smoldered below the surface of his massive intellect. "Ah, there you are, Sinister," he said. "I trust you slept well?" He let the barest trace of a knowing smile creep across his steely countenance.

"As a matter of fact I did," I replied. Actually, I felt incredibly calm and collected in spite of the uncertainty facing me in court. "Thanks for the clothes and breakfast."

"Not a problem," Justice said. "Just do me a favor this time."

"Sure, what can I do?"

Justice put both his hands on my shoulders. "Whatever you do, whatever happens, you have to remain as calm and relaxed as you are right now." He looked at me very carefully, as if trying to examine the deepest part of my soul. "Hmm," he said. "I guess a little dose of wisdom and knowledge really does change a man."

On cue, Wisdom and Knowledge flitted up, dressed for court in matching gold tunics with cut-outs in the back from which their iridescent wings protruded. They landed, and each looped an arm around me, while in the others, they each held a sheaf of writing papers. "Hello, Sirius," Wisdom said, patting my bottom.

"Good morning, Sirius," said Knowledge, sneaking a kiss on my cheek.

Justice laughed and shook his head. "Ladies," he said, "I am trusting both of you to help me keep this randy vampire calm in court. The last time he was in open court, he did not do so well and ended up getting sentenced to Hell for contempt for one hundred years."

"Oh my," said Wisdom, putting a petite hand over her mouth.

"The horror!" Knowledge exclaimed, holding me just a little bit tighter. "How did you ever survive such a dastardly and evil place?"

"That is a story for another day, ladies," Justice said. "Mr. Sinister is in your capable hands. Let us go." I followed Justice out the door, and we walked in the direction of the IDC courthouse. Justice had taken some of my gold and posted a bond, and although the faeries scowled menacingly at me while at the same time ogling Knowledge and Wisdom, they could do nothing but let me pass. I sighed and felt my nerves begin to rise and my stomach tighten. Would anyone notice if I vomited my breakfast?

"Easy now," said Wisdom, rubbing my arm gently.

"You are among friends," said Knowledge. I breathed deeply and focused on the harp music and was once again calm. We reached the courthouse steps, and I followed Justice up to the door, while Knowledge and Wisdom more flitted than walked. The faerie deputy guarding the door barely gave Justice and me a second look, saving his gaze for the two ladies. I couldn't say I blamed him, but found myself pulling Knowledge and Wisdom a little closer to me to try and protect them from his outright leer. Men really are lascivious louts, and now I had four ladies of my own to protect from the assembled phalluses of the world. I sighed because, hopefully, Justice would give me the chance to do that.

Justice turned to have a word with me as we reached the courtroom, but I had already stopped, stunned by what I saw pictured on those awful obsidian doors. Amidst the many moving faces of past litigants, I saw Bloodsucker Number One and Angus Blackheart. The Howler, too, revolved around to make an appearance. But what unnerved me was my own angry face spewing silent words as I sat chained to my seat, awaiting the Head Magistrate's order. I could not let that happen again. Knowledge and Wisdom each tightened their grip on my arms and pulled me into the courtroom behind Justice. My spirits were lifted by the sight of Garlic's little head popping up on the door, clearly satisfied with having left the Head Magistrate a present on his bench.

I took a seat next to Justice at one of the counsel tables and carefully examined my chair for any signs of magical gold chains. "Don't worry," Justice said, reading my mind. "They are there and ready for use. Just make sure that doesn't happen, got it?" Knowledge and Wisdom smiled reassuringly from the bench behind our table, and I felt better and calmer instantly.

"I got it," I said. I saw that the clerks and deputies were pointing at me and whispering, and looking all around the courtroom. What were they saying? Was it that little contempt issue?

Justice leaned in and, half chuckling said, "They are looking for Garlic." So that was what they were doing! "Not everyone can say they nearly destroyed Immortal Divorce Court," he added. "You are a local celebrity of sorts. But a word of advice—don't get yourself thrown in Hell this time. Word is the Lord of Darkness has some payback planned."

That was the second time I had heard of my dalliance with Persephone creating a problem—a big, angry, demonic Lord of the Underworld kind of problem. "Are you telling me what Cabernet said is true, and big, bad, and soul crushing wants me dead?"

"Oh yes," Justice said. "He wants you more than just dead if he can manage it. But you can't worry about that now. The Blackhearts and their attorney are about to enter the courtroom, so get some color back in your face, will you? Here, eat another blood orange."

I hurriedly gulped one down and felt instantly better. Persephone's gifts were many, and I mused some of them weren't even fatal! I turned as the courtroom doors opened, and in strode the Blackhearts. Angus came first, wearing his finest robes of black silk, his blond hair hanging loose over his massive shoulders. He glared at me, and I met his stare with my fangs bared. How I wanted to kill this man who was responsible for taking me away from my children and robbing me of countless irreplaceable memories. I stood up and pushed out my chest, and a low growl came from my throat, prompting the faerie deputies to get between us.

"Easy now," Justice warned, and Knowledge and Wisdom each rested a hand on one of my shoulders, gently trying to get me to sit down.

"Yeah, you don't want to get hurt, do you, boy?" goaded Angus, flipping directly at my scowling face a link of the enchanted gold chain that had kept me bound and away from my girls for years.

With a dual wave of their gossamer wings, Knowledge and Wisdom created a miniature tornado, which sucked the chain into its vortex and sent it whizzing right back into Angus's grinning face. He stumbled backward, putting a hand on the railing to catch his balance. He whirled to attack, a mighty growl bursting from his lips. He reached for his massive broadsword, which was notably absent from his waist, then stopped, looking sheepishly at the frowning deputies who barred his path and pointed for him to take a seat—which he wisely chose to do. I smiled and shrugged my shoulders, taking my seat next to Justice once again. I would have given anything at that moment for a spider to have dropped smack dab onto his pompous head.

Next into court came the Howler, dressed in her finest pirate leathers, and upon her head, a plumed black hat with a single peacock feather protruding from its top. She looked at me and rolled her eyes in disdain, smirking as she held up a small silver baby rattle and shook it in my direction. The Howler strutted down the aisle to meet her father. Gone was the weight of childbearing from her face and body, and back was the brash attitude. She looked as good as I remembered from that brief idyllic time on Saona Island, but radiated such haughty indifference that I felt nothing for her but anger.

Knowledge and Wisdom gave her their own looks of disdain, and each placed a hand lovingly on my arms. The Howler clearly did not like being outshone by these two beauties, and her smile turned quickly to a pouty frown. I was happy to disappoint her once again by giving her no reaction whatsoever. I was not going to give her the satisfaction. The deputies and Justice seemed much relieved at my choice to remain calm.

What did I ever see in that girl, I wondered. I pulled my eyes from her and leaned in to Justice. "Where is their attorney?" I asked.

"Oh, he is coming," said Justice, not looking up from his papers. He sniffed the air and wrinkled his nose. "Yes, definitely on the way."

Into the courtroom pranced two young mortals wearing sleeveless purple leather vests adorned with pink ostrich feathers. They looked to be twins, with matching high cheekbones and long wavy blond hair. Copious amounts of rouge reddened their cheeks, already flushed with the vigor of youth, and they also wore too much rouge on their full, pouty lips. They were so pretty they had to be girls, yet had a little too much girth in the shoulders not to be boys. Frankly, I could not tell if they were young boys or young girls, but I looked downward at their matching pink breeches drawn so tight that I could see their man parts unpleasantly and quite clearly. What was this? "Law clerks," whispered Justice. "*No* accounting for taste . . ."

In came a herald, a whole lot fatter, a whole lot balder, and definitely a whole lot older than the two prancing pixies that were law clerks to the Blackhearts' attorney. Unfortunately for him and everyone else in the courtroom, he was wearing the same purple and pink ensemble as the young, lithe boys. "That is Evan," said Justice with a smirk. "In his younger days, he used to be a law clerk. But he got old, as mortals do."

I felt sorry for Evan, as his belly was straining the ostrich vest to the bursting point, which, on second glance, was missing quite a few feathers. Fortunately, his girth was covering his nether regions. The rouge on his lips and face gave him the appearance of a court jester or a man that had lost a wager—badly at that. "I am afraid to ask what he does," I said, seeing him whip out a small trumpet.

Justice put his fingers into his ears, and I quickly did the same. "He is now a herald." And with that, Evan blew with all his might on the small horn, his face getting ever redder in the process. The two pretty ones had retreated to the door to await the coming of their master. Their smiles seemed permanently etched on their faces, and they made me want to smack them right in their ruby-red lips to see if their expressions would change. I bet that would be a firm no.

Evan finished his trumpet playing and, after a brief coughing fit, cleared his throat, and announced, "Hear ye, hear ye. Now presenting to this honorable court and all who seek to try their business here, the one, the only, Sir Gareth Flockingham the Third!"

The two clerks immediately began jumping up and down clapping quickly, and their smiles grew even greater, if that was humanly possible. Wisdom leaned over and put her lips to my ear, which I found quite reassuring. "Happy little fellows, no?" I nodded and craned my head to see the door opening and in striding a gigantic peacock. No, not an overly glamorous man—it was literally a gigantic peacock on a pink leash. And holding that leash was the man I assumed was Sir Gareth Flockingham III.

Sir Gareth was dressed in lavender robes of the finest silk, and he wore atop his long, curly black locks a lavender hat garnished with a single pink and purple peacock feather. The robes were tailored to his form and barely hid the massive shoulders and thick body particular to werewolf kind. Whereas Angus Blackheart and his daughter radiated a primal seething anger, Sir Gareth's gray eyes flitted around the room, focusing on everything and nothing all at once, betraying no emotion or stray thought. We locked gazes for the barest of moments, and a wry smile creased his lips, reminding me of the look a fox gets when he enters the henhouse without being spied. No mangy mongrel was he, but rather a dangerous and cagey old carnivore.

Sir Gareth handed off the peacock to one of the clerks and walked, nay sashayed, to the Blackhearts' counsel table. He made a big show of shaking Angus's hands and of kissing the Howler on her cheek, not once, not twice, but three times for effect. From the look of him, I thought he would rather have fancied trying that greeting on Angus. Sir Gareth turned and placed one neatly manicured hand on Justice's shoulder. How did Sir Pretty Hands make his fingernails look so sparkly, I wondered. "Justice, so good to see you. old chum," he said, his voice clear and projecting like his every word was a bit of operatic prose.

"Yes, it is, isn't it," Justice replied, flashing his golden fangs ever so slightly. "You look well, Gareth, although perhaps just a teeny bit stouter since I last saw you." Justice cast a glance at Gareth's midsection, and Wisdom and Knowledge tittered like schoolgirls.

Gareth's face grew dark, and his gray eyes drew into slits as he stared evilly at the two girls. "I should have crushed you two beneath my boots when I had the chance," he said, turning on his heel and taking his seat next to the Blackhearts. His clerks ran to him, spritzed his face with perfumed mist, and patted a stray black curl back into place.

"What was that all about?" I asked Justice. "Does he have a relationship with Knowledge and Wisdom?"

"Knowledge and wisdom aren't exactly his thing," Justice said. "He is more of a cunning and guile kind of fellow." He pointed to the names of Sir Gareth's law clerks, stitched on the back of their pink breeches. "See, that one is Cunning, the other is Guile—please learn to read by our next courtroom escapade."

"No, I mean our Knowledge and Wisdom," I said.

"Oh, right, yes, Sir Gareth clerked for me for just one day when he was in law school," Justice said. "He couldn't handle the bookworms and kept fainting every time he saw them. So he had to be let go, and to tell you the truth, if he saw them the way you have, I bet he would still faint dead away on the spot."

The faerie deputy snapped to attention and took a small brass horn from a shelf. He expertly played a long series of notes, holding the last one for dramatic effect. I glanced over and saw Evan looking at the deputy lovingly, but I wasn't sure if it was the horn playing or something else. "All rise—hear ye, hear ye," the deputy boomed. "May this honorable court come to order."

I rose to my feet and looked at Justice, who gave no expression, as always. Wisdom and Knowledge each grabbed an arm of mine and stood so close to me that their hips were touching mine. I looked over at the Howler's table, and Angus returned my gaze with a wave, although he chose not to use all his fingers. The Howler sneered and shook her dried phallus necklace at me to send the not so subtle message that she intended to take my heart, my manhood, and my gold, in no particular order.

The deputy ignored the peacock that chose at that moment to let out a great caw, and continued his introduction. "Please remain standing for I present to you, Head Magistrate Jane Dough." The deputy blew on his horn once more, and with her frail frame blanketed under a gold robe that easily looked several sizes too big for her, in walked Jane

Dough, Head Magistrate of the Immortal Divorce Court. Though her frame was slight, her eyes were ever bright and her intelligence obvious to all that met her gaze. She pushed a stray strand of blonde hair off her face and, hitching up her robe, stepped up to the bench and settled into her seat.

"She's the head magistrate now?" I hissed in disbelief to Justice, who shushed me loudly. "But, she testified in my first case. Isn't that against the rules?"

Justice turned to me and smirked. "I am actually impressed that you thought of that all by yourself," he said. "But no, that was a different case. She was not a magistrate then, and I assure you she has absolutely no connection to the Blackhearts or to their foppish counsel."

Head Magistrate Dough fixed her eyes upon me, and looked to the Howler and then back to me. She gave no indication that she knew me or, more accurately, had testified against me. "Mr. Justice," she said, "we are here on your motion to dismiss the charges against Mr. Sinister."

"Yes, we are, Your Honor," Justice replied. "And also, there is the matter of the children. The Blackheart woman, in a conspiracy with her father, Angus Blackheart, both seated over at yonder counsel table, has kept my client from seeing his rightful issue."

"Sir Gareth, what say you?"

Sir Gareth stood and straightened his lavender robes. He cleared his throat, held his head high, and began to speak. "Justice's motion to dismiss is mere folly and poppycock, Your Honor. I have never seen the like of it in my four hundred years of practice."

Justice gnashed his teeth, and this time red sparks flew from his mouth. "I concede Sir Gareth is well versed in folly and certainly poppycock, or any sort of cock, for that matter," he interjected. "But this is a court of law, and we have rules here, and this is my motion to dismiss, not his opportunity to spout operatic babble."

The Head Magistrate barely suppressed a smile. "Indeed, counselors, indeed," she said. "Let us get to heart of the matter. Sir Gareth, please take your seat and know that you will get your turn, but I expect to hear a bit more from you when you do, other than pomp and idle ramblings. Justice, you may begin the prosecution of your case."

"Thank you, Your Honor," Justice said. "We call Angus Blackheart to the stand." Justice caught both Sir Gareth and Angus by surprise, and Angus kept waiting for Sir Gareth to object, pontificate, or do something to save him from testifying. Instead, Sir Gareth merely nodded to the deputy and to the Howler and Angus like there was no problem at all with the elder Blackheart testifying. Angus had to tell the truth, and the deputy who brought over that crystal globe with the raging fire within it was certainly going to ensure he did!

"Place your hand on the perjury globe," the deputy said with a scowl. "Do you swear to tell the truth, the whole truth, and nothing but the truth, or risk incineration in the tenth level of Hell?"

Angus shuddered. "I do," he said, his voice cracking ever so slightly. I realized I was perhaps the only creature on the planet, with the exception of dear Garlic, that had fond memories of Hell!

Justice peered over his spectacles at Angus, whose oversized body looked quite uncomfortable squeezed into the witness stand. "State your name for the record," Justice commanded, walking up to the witness stand.

"I am Angus Blackheart."

Justice turned and pointed to me. "And that man, Sirius Sinister, was married to your daughter, who sits here in the courtroom next to Sir Gareth Flockingham the Third, correct?"

"That is correct," Angus agreed, looking to Sir Gareth for approval and receiving none.

"And it is true, Mr. Blackheart, is it not, that no sooner had Mr. Sinister married your daughter and she gave birth to their four daughters, that you kidnapped him and imprisoned him in a dungeon at the bottom of Peel Castle?"

Angus stared for a moment at Sir Gareth, who nodded ever so slightly, a smile creasing his face in a manner that unnerved me. What was running through the mind of that wretched gray fox? Angus could only answer yes, couldn't he? Angus's eyes went to the fiery globe, and he swallowed hard. "Yes," he said. "That is true, absolutely true." Angus looked down from the witness stand at me and continued. "I left that poor excuse for a son-in-law chained down there to rot for what I hoped was all eternity."

"Disappointed, are you?" said Justice.

"Clearly," Angus replied.

Justice peered at Angus, placing his hand on the witness stand. "And Mr. Sinister was imprisoned there for twelve years, isn't that so, Mr. Blackheart?"

"Objection," said Sir Gareth, sounding a bit bored. I noticed that when he objected, he hadn't even bothered to look up at the Head Magistrate or Angus, but was busy shuffling through his papers. One of his assistants leaned forward and spritzed him with perfume as Sir Gareth rose slowly and dramatically to his feet. I decided Sir Gareth could make even picking his pompous ass look dramatic and showy.

"Grounds, Sir Gareth?" said Head Magistrate Dough.

"The witness stated he kidnapped Mr. Sinister, chained Mr. Sinister to a dungeon wall in Castle Peel, and thereafter left Mr. Sinister," said Sir Gareth. "There has been no testimony that he has any knowledge of Mr. Sinister's whereabouts since. The only one to have testified about that is Mr. Justice, and that is thus not evidence, Your Honor."

"Your objection is sustained, Sir Gareth. Continue, Mr. Justice," said the Head Magistrate.

Justice nodded and looked like he had expected the objection. I felt the light touch of Wisdom and Knowledge upon my shoulders. I sure hoped he had expected it. But the truth was that Angus and the Howler had chained me up, then left for Liverpool. They really did not know if I had stayed chained to the wall or not. It is not like they came back to check on me!

"Mr. Blackheart," Justice said, "is it true that the chains you bound Mr. Sinister with were enchanted?"

"Yes, that is true," Angus bragged, puffing out his chest. "A werewolf couldn't break them, so a puny vampire like him had no chance in Hell—" Angus stopped short as Sir Gareth had fixed his best withering gaze upon him. I smiled. Angus did like to talk. I had learned the hard way the lesson of talking too much, while testifying in court my last time.

"And those chains came from right here," Justice said. "You got those chains from someone at Immortal Divorce Court, did you not?"

The Head Magistrate perked up on the bench. She was more than just a little interested in the answer. And so was I.

"Objection," said Sir Gareth. "It is immaterial, and quite irrelevant, where those chains came from. The witness has admitted he chained up Mr. Sinister. Asked and answered ad nauseam."

"Overruled," said the Head Magistrate. "Answer the question, Mr. Blackheart."

Angus gulped. "The assistant to the Immortal Divorce Court's blacksmith owed a lot of gold to me for gambling debts," he said. "To forgive those debts instead of me taking his wife, his house, and his life, he procured some extra unused links and made me the chains. He said they were just going to be burned in the forge anyway, and thus, no one would ever notice they were given to me."

The Head Magistrate nodded and turned to the deputy. "Place the assistant blacksmith under arrest for questioning. Mr. Blackheart, I am not done with you yet either. Those chains are Immortal Divorce Court property and, thus, not to be used for personal gain. Continue, Mr. Justice."

"You don't know of any way to break those chains, do you, Mr. Blackheart?" Justice said.

"No," Angus replied, glaring at me. "I meant for him to rot in that cell forever."

"Besides you and your daughter and henchmen, who knew Mr. Sinister was there in that cell?" Justice asked.

"There was no one else," Angus started, staring at the globe, which began to heat to a white hot glow. "Wait, wait, I remember. Give me a minute! It was the Winter Witch! She knew he was there!"

"And how did the Winter Witch know that?"

Angus shrugged, looking at Justice like he was an idiot. "I told her," he said. "She was still all mad about Sirius Sinister having relations with her before the wedding, and leaving her before she was done with him."

"Wasn't your daughter angry with him?" Justice asked. "And that's why you imprisoned him, isn't it?"

"Oh no," Angus replied. "Our plan to imprison him was hatched long before he stuck it in at the inn with that witch. My daughter was done with him. He served his purpose. Sinister being with the witch is of no consequence to her. Me, well, I was not so happy. That is my sweet and innocent little girl over there, you know? So I let my fists give

Sinister a little goodbye lesson before I left him. And I have not seen him since, until today."

Angus was looking to Sir Gareth for approval. But I turned to see Sir Gareth's head in his hand, rubbing his eyes in disbelief at his client's testimony. Justice merely smiled. "Why did you tell the Winter Witch where Mr. Sinister was?"

"Because she said she wanted to go torture him," Angus replied. "Which, I have to say, sounded pretty good to me."

"Did the Winter Witch go to Peel Castle?"

Angus shrugged. "You would have to ask her. I don't know, but I sure hope she did."

"I have no more questions of this witness," Justice said, taking his seat. Wisdom and Knowledge patted my shoulders, and Wisdom made a face at the Howler, who turned her head and rolled her eyes. I thought things had gone well. Angus had admitted he planned to imprison me all along. Nice father-in-law. Not exactly a welcome-to-the-family moment.

Sir Gareth strolled over to Angus, stopping for a moment to let one of his clerks brush a bit of lint off his robe and smooth the back of it. "Now then, Mr. Blackheart," he said. "You chained Mr. Sinister and left him?"

"Yes," said Angus.

"And is it your sworn testimony that neither you nor your daughter have seen Sinister until today?"

"Yes, that is true."

"So you cannot tell this court where Mr. Sinister has been these last nearly twelve years, other than he was not in Liverpool, being a good husband and father?"

"Yes, that is true, all of it," said Angus, looking around the room for approval from any that would meet his gaze.

Sir Gareth walked to his table, pulled out a length of chain, and held it out to Angus. "Is this a piece of the chain you bound Mr. Sinister with?"

Angus peered at the chain. "It looks to be, yes."

Sir Gareth walked back and forth in front of Angus, swinging the chain in a circle. "Mr. Blackheart, do you know what Mr. Sinister's chosen trade is?"

"He is an assassin."

Sir Gareth nodded as if pleased. "Would it surprise you to know that he was trained in all means of escape and concealment by the esteemed and revered Master Assassin Ernesto Sinestra, who also happens to be his father?"

"I did not know that," Angus said. "Ernesto is a legend. I did not make that connection. His father! But that's where I sent—"

"Thank you, that's enough," Sir Gareth interrupted Angus. What was Angus about to say? What did he send to my father? "So it is possible that Mr. Sinister escaped those chains right after you left him and has, thus, purposefully and intentionally abandoned your daughter and grandchildren these last sixteen years?" Sir Gareth continued.

"Yes, it is," Angus replied. "We never saw him in Liverpool. Truth is, I do not know if the chains were to have bound him for eternity or not. All I know is that when he failed to return from Peel Castle, we had no choice but to file for divorce."

Sir Gareth returned to his table and picked up a small silver plate onto which he placed the chain. "Have you ever heard of Amor Lo Conquista Todo, Mr. Blackheart?"

Angus shrugged. "I have not." He looked confused, and I felt the same way. How did Sir Gareth know about that? He pulled out a small flask and pulled off the stopper, dumping the contents upon the chain, which melted into a small puddle of gold liquid and dripped over the plate to the floor.

"Amor Lo Conquista Todo, which means to the English speaking, 'love conquers all,'" Sir Gareth said. "It is a rare vintage of wine with even rarer properties. Look at your enchanted chains, Mr. Blackheart. Are they gone?"

Angus could not believe what his eyes had just witnessed. "Aye," he said. "Where did you get that?"

Sir Gareth ignored Angus and continued with his questions. "So, Mr. Blackheart, if Mr. Sinister had access to some of this wine, he could have easily freed himself, correct?"

"Objection," Justice said. "Leading."

"Sustained," said the Head Magistrate. "Sir Gareth, rephrase your question."

"Of course, Your Honor," Sir Gareth said with a smile. "Please excuse my silly little direct examination mistake. Did the wine dissolve the chains just now, Mr. Blackheart?"

"It did," Angus said.

"If you, or Sinister, or anyone poured this wine on those chains, would it dissolve them?"

"Yes," Angus agreed. "It would seem to be the case."

I was convinced that Sir Gareth was pulling one over on the court, since love was required for the Amor Lo Conquista Todo to work. Out of the corner of his eye, Justice could see me getting worked up. "Don't worry about it," he said in a well-practiced whisper. "It worked because Sir Gareth is in love with himself and with being a lawyer. Now, shhh."

"Do you know who all the guests were at the wedding of Mr. Sinister and your daughter?" Sir Gareth continued, waving a finger in the air like he was conducting an orchestra. I realized that Justice was right, and Sir Gareth really thought he was an artist when he worked.

"Of course not," Angus snorted. "There were hundreds of people there. I mean, I know all the important ones, if that is what you mean."

"There was a troll at the wedding, correct?"

"Objection," Justice shouted. "If he leads the witness any more, they might as well be dancing."

"Withdrawn," said Sir Gareth. "May I have a little latitude, Your Honor? I am just trying to move this along. Was there a troll at the wedding?"

"Yes, there was," said Angus. "A big black troll with a prodigious taste for wine. I think his name was Oliver. He supplied the wine for Mr. Sinister as a present."

"Would it surprise you to know that Oliver's surname is von Cliffingham?"

"You mean the von Cliffingham family of famous wine vintners, purveyors, and importers/exporters?" Angus spurted. "It would surprise me. But that would explain the fine taste of those vintages."

Sir Gareth handed him the empty flask of Amor Lo Conquista Todo. "Read the bottom of the bottle to the court, if you will, Mr. Blackheart."

Angus peered at the bottle, squinting at the small gold letters embossed on the bottom. "'Imported from Parts Unknown by OvC,'" he said.

Sir Gareth looked like a violet viper all coiled up and ready to strike, but waited until Angus had finished. "Do you know what the OvC signifies?"

"Yes, I do," Angus said proudly. "It is the insignia of Oliver von Cliffingham!"

"No more questions," said Sir Gareth. "May we take a short recess, Your Honor? My nose needs some rather liberal powdering."

"Let it be so," said the Head Magistrate. "We shall reconvene at the top of the hour." I rose with the others in the courtroom as the Head Magistrate left the bench. So Sir Gareth had shown that Oliver was the one that had made the bottles of the Amor Lo Conquista Todo. What of it? Just because he was my friend did not mean that I had used it to free myself. Actually, I did use it, or rather Hedley Edrick did—oh, blast that infernal Sir Gareth.

Justice led me to a conference room outside of the courtroom. "Wait here," he said. "I need to go see the head deputy. I need a special warrant sworn out."

I had so many questions to ask him and blurted them all out. "How did it go? What about Oliver and the wine? It looks like I freed myself with the wine, doesn't it?"

Wisdom put her mouth on mine and kissed me long and deep. Justice smiled. "That is one way to shut up a vampire, I suppose," he said. "Do not concern yourself with Sir Gareth's smoke and mirrors, and a little, shall we say, circumstantial evidence?"

"Circumcision-what?" I asked, quite confused.

"Coincidence, whimsy, luck of the draw, happenstance," said Knowledge, patting my shoulder. I opened my mouth to speak, and Wisdom closed it for me with another kiss. That fantastic long golden tongue of hers wrapped all around mine for a titillating moment, and I felt myself rising to the occasion.

"Hold on, vampire," Justice said. "Not now, focus. Focus!"

I reluctantly broke the kiss and focused on Justice. "Angus has testified that they chained you in Peel Castle, and he told the Winter Witch where you were," the demon lawyer said. "So, we need to summon the witch to testify—no easy task, mind you, hence the special warrant. She fills in the blanks."

"The Winter Witch?" I gulped. "Testify? But she cursed me with a talking boil on my ass the last time I saw her!"

"Exactly," said Justice. "Now, stay here and don't move." He shut the door, and I heard the lock click shut.

Wisdom and Knowledge shimmied out of their robes, and my eyes fell upon their incredible naked splendor. "You look tense," said Knowledge. "Or perhaps the word is *rigid*."

"He told you not to move," Wisdom stated, reaching for my breeches. "But don't you worry, sweet Sirius Sinister, because we will do all the moving for you."

CHAPTER 15

By the time Justice returned from his errand, it was nearly the top of the hour, and we were due back in court. As I entered the courtroom this time, I really did feel more relaxed, thanks to the ministering of Knowledge and Wisdom. It was enough to want to make me go to law school.

The Head Magistrate took the bench and looked to Justice. "I have no more questions for Mr. Blackheart," he said. "Thus, I do not wish to recall him to the stand."

"Your next witness, Mr. Justice," the Head Magistrate said, peering down at him.

The courtroom doors opened and in walked the head deputy carrying a bejeweled scepter. "A special warrant is necessary for our next witness, Your Honor," Justice said. "She is not going to come willingly."

The head deputy tapped the scepter on the floor once, twice, and a third time, causing a beam of bright green light to shoot from the scepter toward the courtroom doors, where it disappeared into their murky ebon darkness. "Call your witness, Mr. Justice," the Head Magistrate commanded. "The special warrant is hereby *served*!"

"By the power vested in me as counsel of record appearing in this honorable Immortal Divorce Court, I call the Winter Witch by her true name, Victoria Jones, to the stand to tell the truth, and nothing but the truth. This I decree!" cried Justice.

Ordinary-sounding Tori Jones was the boil-inducing creature that cursed me and then tried to have me eaten by her shark familiar? The temperature in the courtroom dropped, my breath frosting the air. She was coming all right, and she was not happy about it. Wisdom and Knowledge huddled close to me for warmth, and that I was happy about. I looked over at the werewolf contingent, and true to form, they did not even bat an eye at the temperature change. Sir Gareth yawned and held out his hands to his clerks, who immediately and expertly began buffing his fingernails. Justice pointed a finger at the ashtray on his table and summoned a small fire to the delight of his law clerks and the dismay of the Head Magistrate's clerk.

Suddenly the courthouse doors flew open, pushed by an angry blizzard of snow and wind that pelted all in the courtroom with its wintry fury, including the Head Magistrate, who immediately stood up at her bench and peered through the frosty precipitation to identify just who was invading her courtroom. Sauntering down the aisle strutted the Winter Witch, also apparently known as Victoria Jones, with snow forming a regal crown about her head and covering her body like a formal ball gown. In her arms she carried that accursed white cat, which, to my great pleasure, was wearing a patch over its right eye—the eye that I had stuck a sword in not so long ago when the cat familiar was in shark form. It saw me and hissed angrily, spitting and struggling in the arms of its master.

"Cease your magic, Miss Jones," commanded the Head Magistrate. She motioned to the head deputy to approach the Winter Witch, and he began sweating profusely in the arctic cold at the prospect of doing just that. "Or I shall find you in contempt of court, and rest assured all your winter magic is no match for the fires of Hell!"

Just as quickly as the snow had come upon us, it vanished, leaving the Winter Witch in a staring contest with the Head Magistrate. The Winter Witch shook out her long white hair and pursed her blood-red lips, finally smiling wickedly at the Head Magistrate. "As you wish," she said. "Why have you called me to this accursed place known as Immortal Divorce Court? And you people call *me* evil? Judgmental, no?"

She looked at the occupants of the courtroom for the first time, now that her snow show was over, and laid her eyes upon me and the

Howler. "Well, that explains it," she said. She turned to the Howler. "Honey. He is a cock in every sense of the word, but a good lay like that cannot be found just anywhere. Divorce—were you sure about that? I hate him for what he did to my sweet kitty, and would have gladly made him a gelding, but since his parts are enchanted beyond even my magic, I would still have him in the sack. Heck, even right here, right now."

"Miss Jones!" said the Head Magistrate. "Show some proper decorum. You will follow my rules. This is my courtroom. You are here to provide testimony in this matter. You will take the stand. You will tell the truth. You will keep your magic in check. Do you understand?"

"Fine," the Winter Witch answered. "Way to take all the fun out of it, Head Magistrate," she muttered. She continued down the aisle and gave an exaggerated wink to Wisdom and Knowledge. She pushed through the swinging gate separating the gallery from the counsel tables and witness stands, and stopped as she passed our table. That stupid cat of hers was practically frothing at the mouth in its attempt to get at me, but the Winter Witch held her pussy fast. She reached into her cleavage and pulled out a small gold pin, which she flicked in my direction. "I believe that belongs to you," she said. "Or better yet, you can return it to the sea whore that saved your ass. Or, most of it anyway."

What was she talking about? As I grasped the pin, it morphed into the golden sword I used to wound her familiar. There was a collective gasp of shock from all the court personnel, Wisdom and Knowledge, and lastly—me! Weapons were not allowed in Immortal Divorce Court, and somehow the Winter Witch had gotten this sword into the courtroom—a sword that was about to shatter into a million fragments. Instantly, I draped my body over the sword, trying to protect Wisdom and Knowledge from the blast, and waited for the incredible, incomprehensible pain to come.

But all I felt was a tap on my shoulder, and Knowledge beckoned for me to get off the table, which I did sheepishly. "What happened?" I whispered. "Why didn't this get destroyed?"

"I can answer that, Mr. Sinister," said the Head Magistrate. "You really need to learn how to whisper properly. That weapon is known as the Blade of Truth. Its powers are many, and hopefully they are not lost on an assassin as unlearned as you."

"Thanks," I muttered. Did the Head Magistrate think I was that big of an imbecile? My question was quickly answered.

"It is more than just a sword. The Blade of Truth cuts deep and serves no master," the Head Magistrate continued. "Wield it with care."

I held the sword out and looked at it closely for the first time. Were there strange runes embossed deep within this blade? I peered at it and saw only my own confused expression staring back at me. The simple truth was that the Blade of Truth had me utterly befuddled.

Justice cleared his throat. "Head Magistrate, since this is one of the Seven Sacred Relics, I presume that my client will face no charges or a contempt sentence from being in possession of such a weapon in this court?"

"You are correct, Mr. Justice," the Head Magistrate almost grumbled. "As you know, as one of the Seven Sacred Relics, it is immune to the powers of this court." She looked at me with definite irritation. "Since you apparently know nothing of what we speak, Mr. Sinister, allow me to enlighten you. The Relic now in your possession chooses who wields it—and apparently, it has chosen you. But once its purpose has been served, and you are no longer in need, it will vanish, to be conveyed to its next rightful possessor." The Head Magistrate sighed, then looked with great irritation at the Winter Witch. "And unfortunately for me, Miss Jones, and lucky for you, I cannot find you in contempt for that little stunt of yours, since you were returning one of the Seven Sacred Relics to its lawful possessor."

The Winter Witch smiled at me and then bowed down deep and ever so mockingly to the Head Magistrate. "Glad to be of service to the court. But it wasn't the first time I've given it to a hero," she replied, adding, "The blade, I mean. I was certain that blade was his to possess." Her words dripped with sarcasm, and she waited until the Head Magistrate glanced down at her papers, then looked to me, shaking her head and mouthing a definite no.

"Take the stand, Miss Jones, and you may consider yourself sworn," said the Head Magistrate. "Mr. Justice, this witness is yours."

Justice stood and took in the Winter Witch, who smiled at him. Clearly, she was enjoying herself. Justice was not amused. "Miss

Jones," he said, "did Angus Blackheart tell you where Mr. Sinister was imprisoned?'

"Yes, he did," she said. "I just *had* to pay Mr. Sinister a little visit when I heard I had a captive audience."

"So, he was chained when you arrived?"

"Delightfully so," she answered. "And he was chained when I left."

"Objection," shouted Sir Gareth. "Move to strike her last retort as unresponsive. Justice never asked her that!"

"It is stricken," said the Head Magistrate. "Continue, Mr. Justice."

Justice nodded. "When you found him chained, what did you do?"

"I tried to cut off his manhood because I was mad at him," she said.

"And you failed."

I wiped a bead of sweat from my brow. Just hearing about what the Winter Witch had tried to do was making me perspire. Damn right she failed. Thank you, sweet Persephone.

"I did," the Winter Witch said. She locked gazes with me. "No hard feelings? Well, that was ironic, because if I had succeeded . . ."

"Miss Jones!" shouted the Head Magistrate. "This is your *last* warning!"

"Was he chained when you left him in Peel Castle?"

The Winter Witch nodded. "He was."

Justice nodded and came back to our table. "I tender the witness to Sir Gareth," he said.

Sir Gareth rose and came forward to stand near the Winter Witch. Foolishly, he reached out to pat the now sedate kitty, which lay half sleeping in her lap. It whirled instantly and slashed at his hand with a sharp claw, opening up a cut, which began to bleed profusely. One of his law clerks let out a shriek and fainted, falling to the floor with a thud, while the other came forward quickly with a handkerchief to staunch the blood. Sir Gareth hopped back and forth in silent pain and shook his hand, covering the wound with the handkerchief that soon grew red with his blood. "Sorry about that, Sir Gareth." The Winter Witch's look made it clear she wasn't remotely sorry. "Though it does explain why you like dick so much, since this is how pussy treats you. And you are clearly more of a dog person, or persona, as it were."

"Do you need a moment, Sir Gareth," the Head Magistrate queried.

He shook his head no, but did pause for a moment to collect his thoughts before glaring angrily at the cat. "Miss Jones," he said, his voice even and calm, "you did not see Mr. Sinister at any point after you left him chained him in the dungeon at Peel Castle sixteen years ago until now, correct?"

"No, that is not correct," she said. "I came after him about five years ago with a little winter storm." She looked at me this time with a look that remarkably resembled respect. "He is an able adversary. I magicked my pussy familiar into a great shark beast, and despite its best efforts, kitty could not kill him." She stroked the cat's eye patch regretfully.

"But you cannot tell this court that he was chained to the walls of the dungeon in Peel Castle for the whole twelve years before that, can you?"

"I cannot."

Sir Gareth had recovered from the cat's slashing, and pompousness had replaced pain on his face. "Very well, Miss Jones, very well," he said. "I have no more questions for you." He turned to walk to his table and then paused and turned back to the Winter Witch. "Actually, I do have one more question for you. You don't have *any* knowledge of *any* person that can place Mr. Sinister in that dungeon for those twelve years, do you?"

The Winter Witch's eyes sparkled like tiny drops of ice in the sunlight. "No, Sir Gareth, I do not—unless, that is, you consider a boil a person."

Sir Gareth's face grew pale, evident even through the copious amount of rouge that adorned his face. I looked to Justice, who merely sat with his hands folded, enjoying watching Sir Gareth squirm at this apparent error. But how did the Winter Witch bringing up the boil help me? It is not like that pus-spewing pustule could testify. Could it?

"Boils are not people, but very funny indeed, Miss Jones," Sir Gareth said, sitting down.

Justice rose to his feet and could now barely contain his mirth and good fortune. "Perchance did you curse my client with a talking one-hundred-year boil?"

"Yes," the Winter Witch answered. "Yes, I did. Right before I left him. If I couldn't take his manhood, I was going to give him a living, breathing pain in the ass."

"So the boil is sentient?"

The Winter Witch nodded. "Well, it was sentient," she said.

"What happened to the boil?"

"As I said, I sent kitty in shark form to try and kill your client, and she failed to do so. But in the process she took from Sinister a large chunk of his backside, thus removing the boil."

"So, the boil is dead—never to be seen or heard from again?" Justice said.

The Winter Witch scoffed at his seeming ignorance. "I did not say that, Mr. Justice. The familiar is a creation of my magic and, therefore, absorbed the boil, which was another creation of my magic. The boil is not dead, but merely in hi-boil-nation, so to speak."

"Can you summon the boil again?"

Sir Gareth jumped to his feet, not liking where this line of questioning was going. "I object," he said. "This is highly irrelevant. It does not matter if she can summon the boil or not. It is not a recognized sentient entity capable of testifying, even if she could summon it, and therefore, the boil cannot testify."

"Your Honor," Justice said. "It is entirely within your discretion to determine the competency of the boil to testify."

The Head Magistrate nodded. "I agree with Mr. Justice," she said. "And I am inclined to hear what the boil has to say about what it saw those years it was with Sinister. Miss Jones, can you bring forth the boil?"

The Winter Witch looked at me with absolute glee. Surely, I did not have to suffer that horrid indignity once again? The thought of dropping my trousers in open court made me feel ill. The witch felt about her person and realized she did not have her Dagger of Despair. "Drat," she said. "Stupid, stupid, stupid court. I will have to put the boil on kitty, Your Honor."

She muttered a few incantations under her breath, and the cat leaped from her lap onto the rail of the witness stand with a terrified yowl. A shower of cat hair cascaded onto the floor of the courtroom, and forming on a patch of new pink skin on kitty's backside was the nasty two-lipped, pus-spitting menace that was the boil. "I am back!" shouted the boil, spitting pus happily. "But, on kitty? Mistress, but why?"

The Winter Witch looked at the boil with pity. "You are at the mercy of the Immortal Divorce Court, boil, so try and behave."

The boil became more aware of its surroundings as the cat whirled to and fro in a futile effort to dislodge the boil from its backside. "Werewolves, demons, and vampires, oh my," it said. "Whoa, who are those lovely creatures? Why couldn't you have put me on the ass of one of them?" Knowledge and Wisdom looked absolutely disgusted and tried to sink down behind me. Then the boil realized it knew me. "Sinister," it said. "Figures this mess was of your creation. Sorry I didn't recognize you sooner, perhaps if you had been bent over?"

"Enough with your rambling, boil," the Head Magistrate said. "Clearly you are capable of testifying, and I find you competent to do so. Deputy, swear in the boil."

"Oh, you don't have to swear me," the boil said. "I can do it myself—bitch, shit, bastard, asshole, fuckface—how is that?"

The Head Magistrate hung her head for a moment, seemingly frustrated by her limited ability to control her courtroom this day. What was she going to do—threaten a talking boil that was living on the backside of a cat familiar with contempt? I would have loved to see the Winter Witch's familiar become a whole lot more familiar with Hell. "Boil," she said, "you are going to need to tell the truth."

"Why didn't you say that the first time?" the boil said, sputtering an increasingly nasty amount of pus all over the cat, the railing, and the courtroom floor. "What do you want me to tell you?"

"Mr. Justice and Sir Gareth are going to ask you questions," she said. "All you have to do is answer truthfully. Mr. Justice, the boil is yours."

"Boil," he said, "where have you been these last sixteen years?"

"Oh, that is an easy one," the boil said. "I was worried that I wasn't going to know the answers. I was stuck to the ass of that ass Sirius Sinister up until the time kitty here in shark form took a bite out of said ass and ate me." The boil paused for a moment. "Odd, and now I am on the ass of kitty, who knew? Life sure is strange! Full circle from ass to pussy, though truth be told, since I am under oath, tain't a lot of space between the two!" The boil broke down in a spitting pus-fest of hysterics. "I am still hilarious!"

"Where was Sinister in the time you were attached to his backside?" Justice asked when the boil had regained what passed as carbuncle composure.

The boil chuckled and then spit a huge gob of pus that landed just shy of Justice's foot. "That fool was chained to a wall in Peel Castle for just about all those twelve years, except maybe a week or so," the boil said. "And I had to listen to his idle ramblings the whole time, with only those stupid faeries coming to visit to serve him or whatever. I did spit pus on them, but good though!"

"How did Sinister get free?"

"That man that knew not to come too close freed him with some kind of magical wine," the boil said. "Sure wish I could have gotten a gob of pus on that pompous ass—he kept saying he was some kind of teacher or something."

Justice looked at the boil, hesitating for a moment. "Do you know who this man was?"

"Mmmm," the boil said. "Bad knees, bald head, reeked of goat sausage—was it Edly Headlick? No, no, that is not right. I know, give me a second. I know—it was Hedley Edrick!" A collective gasp echoed around the courtroom, and I could hear the clerks and deputies whispering loudly.

"Silence," the Head Magistrate ordered. "Just because the name of the Scholar of Scholars is mentioned in this courtroom does not give you an excuse to titter like a bunch of washerwomen!"

Justice continued when the tumult had died down. "So, once freed by Hedley Edrick, the Master of Masters, Sinister did what?"

"He got on a boat to come back to London to get some gold and go hire you so he could get his children back," spouted the boil.

"Objection, leading, nonresponsive, irrelevant," shouted Sir Gareth. "Move to have that answer stricken!"

"The boil clearly knows where Sinister went, and it can thus answer," Justice said.

"Overruled," said the Head Magistrate. "Overruled."

"And when Sinister got on the boat," Justice asked, "what happened?"

"Mistress—I mean the Winter Witch, um, Miss Jones, came after him, and the shark got him and me in the process," the boil said. "And that is all I know of Sinister until seeing him in the courtroom just now."

"Your Honor," Justice said, "I have no further questions for this witness."

"Very well," the Head Magistrate said. "Sir Gareth, do you wish to try your hand at the boil?"

"Your Honor," Sir Gareth answered, "of course I wish to cross-examine the boil, or perhaps I will just lance him . . ."

"Wait a minute," piped up the boil. "I don't want this perfumed pus licker to touch me!"

The Head Magistrate ignored the boil's outburst without even the barest hint of a smile. Sir Gareth was indeed a perfumed pus licker! "Sir Gareth," said the Head Magistrate, "can you call any witnesses to refute the boil's testimony? Or are you just going to waste my time and get a whole lot of pus on that nice lavender robe of yours by questioning the boil?"

Sir Gareth looked down at his robe as if considering what the Head Magistrate had said. "One quick moment, I beg Your Honor, while I have a word with my clients."

"Make it a very quick moment."

I observed a heated but quiet argument between Sir Gareth and the Blackhearts, but in the end, Sir Gareth rose and announced that he would not question the boil. Justice smirked as he stood and also indicated that he would rest his case and await the court's ruling. "I have a good feeling about her ruling," he whispered in my ear as he sat back down. Knowledge and Wisdom were confidently patting me on the shoulder. I was not so confident—I had heard that before!

"Now then, first I have some housekeeping issues," said the Head Magistrate. She looked to the Winter Witch, who sat on the witness stand with her familiar still trying to shake the boil off its backside. "Miss Jones, please bear with me for a moment," she said. "I may need you to help me complete my ruling in this case."

The Winter Witch merely nodded, and even the boil did not offer a pus-covered protest. Clearly, everyone but the infernal cat was waiting with bated breath for the Head Magistrate's ruling. What did she need the Winter Witch for? Surely the boil was not going to be reattached to my ass? The Head Magistrate looked up at me as if reading my thoughts and smiled. My heart sank. I was surely doomed.

"First off," said the Head Magistrate, "I have never seen such a clear and blatant case of conspiracy to perpetrate a fraud upon this court and alienate a father from his children. Blackhearts, you should be ashamed of yourselves, and Sir Gareth, perhaps you should choose your clients a little more carefully."

Sir Gareth rose gingerly. "Your Honor, if I may . . ."

"No, you may not!" the Head Magistrate scolded. "I suggest you sit down and mind your tongue. And to top it off, your clients conspired to create an abandonment charge that, ultimately, they were guilty of—and with Immortal Divorce Court property to boot!"

Sir Gareth sat quickly, seeing the withering gaze of the Head Magistrate and the approaching deputies. That lavender robe would not protect him very well from the inferno of contempt, I mused. I could hear Justice snickering under his breath ever so quietly, as he was clearly enjoying the proceedings.

"Mr. Sinister, I find you not guilty of abandonment," said the Head Magistrate, looking me in the eye reassuringly. "In fact, the one that is guilty of constructive abandonment is your now ex-wife, Miss Blackheart. You do not owe her any alimony, and I hereby decree any of your marital obligations to her as dissolved."

No alimony? I wanted to kiss Justice, but instead settled for a double kiss with Knowledge and Wisdom. I could not wait to really celebrate with them later.

"The problem the court faces is that, even though Miss Blackheart committed constructive abandonment, and Mr. Sinister was the victim of said abandonment, she did have sole custody of the issue of this marriage during the entire time of the abandonment. And during this time, Mr. Sinister did not contribute anything to the welfare and maintenance of the children."

Justice rose quickly to his feet. "Your Honor, there was no way he could contribute anything to the children's welfare. He was chained to a wall in a dungeon in the bottom of a castle, with a talking boil on his backside."

"I am aware of that, Mr. Justice," the Head Magistrate said. "But that does not cure his duty to support his children, and Miss Blackheart, though committing constructive abandonment, never waived her right for support. Isn't that correct, Sir Gareth?"

"It is quite correct, Your Honor, thank you," said Sir Gareth grinning evilly and nodding knowingly to the Blackhearts.

"I am afraid I have no choice, Mr. Sinister," the Head Magistrate said. "As much as it pains me to do so, Miss Blackheart is due back child support these last sixteen years for your four girls."

"But, Your Honor," Justice protested.

I felt my ire raising and stood to give the Head Magistrate a piece of my mind.

"Sit down, Mr. Sinister," the Head Magistrate commanded. "I don't think you would find a second go-around with the Lord of the Underworld as pleasant as the first time." I sat. Quickly.

The Head Magistrate shuffled some papers. "Your assets," Justice hissed. "Stay calm, and whatever you do—don't talk." What assets did I have other than the gold and jewels of the goblin hoard?

"Ah," the Head Magistrate said. "Perfect. I hereby decree your house in Paris, recently decreed to you by one Oliver von Cliffingham, to be deeded to Miss Blackheart for a period of sixteen years for the collection of rents on said property, after which time, it falls to your children in equal shares." So, Oliver apparently gave me a house, and now it was to go to the Howler and then the girls? That absolutely worked for me. But what of the girls—just where were they?

"I have but one question, Your Honor," I said, rising to my feet. I ignored Justice's plaintive glance of panic and the approaching deputies. "With your permission, may I speak?"

The Head Magistrate nodded. "You may."

"I have not seen my girls in sixteen long years, a mere glance at them in swaddling clothes is all I have ever had. Can you order them to tell me where the girls are?"

"Absolutely, Mr. Sinister," the Head Magistrate said. "Mr. Blackheart? Where are they?"

Angus Blackheart stood and addressed the court. "From an early age, the girls displayed physical gifts and skills that made them uniquely suited to follow in Mr. Sinister's profession. So, we did what we thought best and recently sent them for advanced training to the best teacher we knew of." He paused, and looked to Sir Gareth, who shrugged.

"So, where are they?" the Head Magistrate queried again.

"With the esteemed and revered Master Assassin Ernesto Sinestra."

"With Father?" I shouted. "That is amazing. Your Honor, may I have leave of this court to return to Sa Dragonera?"

"Yes, in one moment," the Head Magistrate said grimly. "You will want to hear this, I promise you. The court will not tarry one minute longer than necessary and keep you from your children. I caution you it has been sixteen long years. They do not know you, and you cannot guess what the Blackhearts have said about you. Proceed with great caution and a well-protected heart."

"I will, Your Honor, thank you," I said. "May I go now?"

"Yes, you are free to go," she said. "But first, I hereby order Victoria Jones to transfer the boil to the face of Angus Blackheart for a period of one hundred years as punishment for misappropriating the property of this hallowed Immortal Divorce Court and using it for an evil and nefarious purpose."

"I would much rather stick with the pussy than end up on that dick, if you know what I am saying," the boil said.

"I know what you are saying," the Head Magistrate addressed the boil. "But sometimes you are the one spitting the pus, and sometimes you are the one getting spit on. Or, in this case, I will order your mistress to have you absorbed back into the being of this all-too-wicked pussy here." The cat smiled at the Head Magistrate, loving to be called a wicked pussy, and loving even more to be able to show it with a well-timed hiss. "So, the dick sounds like the better option if you want to stay out here in the world and spit some pus from time to time."

"Fine," the boil agreed, hawking a huge yellow glob of pus in the direction of Sir Gareth, narrowly missing his shoe. "The dick it is. Bring me dickface's kisser. I am ready!"

Sir Gareth popped up like a daisy. "But, Your Honor," he pleaded, wringing his hands in anguish. "My client throws himself on the mercy of this honorable court and knows the error of his ways. I beg of you to reconsider your punishment, reduce the term of years, or pick another spot for the boil—perhaps his elbow or big toe."

"Your Honor," the boil interjected, "he is getting punished, so how can his lawyer, Sir Loose Anus over there, run his gums? You promised me his face just now! What kind of fun is a big toe? Unless, of course, Sir Loose Anus can confirm, or deny, that his client dickface has a foot fetish, then maybe . . ."

"The boil is completely out of line," Sir Gareth exclaimed. "I protest."

The boil was a bit more successful with his next pus launch, which landed right on Sir Gareth's nose. "I think I was right on the line, if you ask me," it said happily. "Protest that!"

The Head Magistrate managed to barely stifle her smile as the yellow pus dripped off Sir Gareth's nose and right onto his fine lavender robe, which caused him to retch impressively on himself, soiling his august robe even more. "You get the face of Angus Blackheart, boil," she said. "And Mr. Blackheart, I am putting in my order that if you should ever dare to misappropriate the property of this honorable court again for your own nefarious purposes, so help me, you will have the boil attached to your phallus while you are bound in the bowels of Peel Castle for all perpetuity by the very Immortal Divorce Court chains you purloined—and that means forever and ever!"

A recovered Sir Gareth wiped his mouth with a ruined handkerchief. "My client understands completely," he said. "You will have no more trouble out of him." But to me, the look on Angus Blackheart's soon-to-be boil-marred face said something exactly the opposite of his attorney's words.

"Is it too late to choose the lifetime of pussy?" the boil asked, and seeing that it was, he sighed. "Great, here's to hoping I don't end up eternally on the dick of an eternal dick."

I walked out of the courtroom not in chains but yet still utterly bound by trepidation about the journey ahead to be reunited with my girls. I did not even crack a smile when I heard the screams of Angus and the boil as they, too, were united. Justice put a hand on my shoulder. "You leave in the morning," he said. "I will get you a crystal to get you where your heart needs to go."

"Thanks," I said. "But I will leave now. I've waited sixteen years and cannot bear waiting a moment longer."

Justice nodded, and I wiped a tear from Wisdom's long lustrous lashes. "Understood," Justice said. "Now let us get you to your children!"

I could barely stop myself from breaking into a full run back to Justice's abode. I found myself shaking in anticipation or nervousness, or most likely both. Knowledge pulled my face close to hers as we walked. "You will do fine," she said. "You will know just what to say and how to say it. And besides, your own father will be there to help you." I nodded, although my heart was not entirely convinced. What if they did not want anything to do with me? Or hated me with every fiber of their sixteen-year-old beings?

Justice broke into my thoughts as we arrived at his office. "All right then," he said. "You are now well-equipped with one of the most powerful weapons ever forged, and I can get you a day or two's worth of supplies. Just in case the fickleness of the crystals combined with your troubled, unfocused mind, deposits you somewhere in Spain, or Majorca, and not at your intended destination."

"I do not know how I can ever repay you," I said.

He scoffed. "Well, for one thing—I really don't need to see you anytime soon, or ever again, for that matter. And you have paid me, remember? Two chests of goblin gold are always welcome in this office." He handed me a star-shaped, red crystal, which I took with a sense of dread. Something was causing the hair on my neck to stand up. I embraced Wisdom and held her tightly.

"What is wrong?" she asked.

"I have no idea," I answered. "Must be my nerves."

Knowledge joined our embrace. She reached up to stroke my hair gently and put her hand on my chest to feel my steady heartbeat. "It is not your nerves," she said. "Be careful and trust your instincts."

I looked to Justice for guidance, and he merely shrugged. "You've made a lot of enemies in the last couple of centuries. They are probably standing in line for a chance to repay you. Don't wander into a goblin camp, and you'll probably be fine."

I smiled and adjusted the Blade of Truth across my shoulder. "I can live with the 'probably fine' part because that is better odds than I face most of the time!" I kissed Knowledge and Wisdom long and passionately, and stepped back, focusing on Sa Dragonera. Finally, for the first time in what seemed to be eons, I was going home!

I looked down at the crystal, thinking only of the comforting views of Sa Dragonera. But the strangest thing happened. The red, star-shaped crystal turned to black in my hand and began melting into nothingness. There was an audible pop and strange pulling sensation as the office of Justice and the tearful faces of Knowledge and Wisdom faded from view, and I found myself spinning out of control through space. A huge black fist came out of the ether and struck me full in the face, sending me tumbling head over heels, until I crashed hard into a stone wall and rolled down a sandy embankment, my head landing in seawater. I licked a mixture of blood and salt from my lips and rose to my feet, taking in the squat stone tower that I had tried to knock down with my face. I knew instantly that I was not on Sa Dragonera, and a second look at the tower and my surroundings confirmed this.

The owner of that ebon fist had deposited me in front of the Aragonese tower at La Pelosa off the island of Sardinia. I had come here centuries ago to train with my father, and it was on this very spot on the beach in front of the Aragonese tower where I had finally bested him in swordplay. Fond memories indeed, but who had brought me here and, the real question was, why?

I opened my hand to look for any remnants of the charred crystal, but it had either completely melted away, or I had lost it in my collision with the tower. I had never heard of a crystal going bad, but that was clearly what had happened. Of course, I never heard of getting punched in the face by a disembodied fist as you traveled by crystal either. I was not sure what bothered me more, but I did not have time to think about it. I was not far off from Sa Dragonera, and I would have to catch a boat on Sardinia. The sun was high in the sky, and with luck I could make it to Sardinia before nightfall and find someone willing to part with a fishing vessel or give me passage to Majorca. Nothing was going to stop me from seeing my children—not a messed-up crystal—not a phantom fist—nothing.

I wiped the sweat from my brow, and steeled myself against the heat radiating off the sand. A fierce wind came out of nowhere, whipping the sand in front of me into a small hurricane. The sand bit deep into my skin, and I dropped to my knees, shielding my eyes. I felt a great heat from below, and the sand beneath my knees began to give way as if it were melting. I rolled quickly away in the direction I knew the water to be, my eyes still closed, and I breathed a sigh of relief as I entered the cool water of the sea. I rose from the sea with my blade drawn and eyes wide open to find four helmeted and well-armed horsemen facing me.

"Oh, bloody hell," I said to no one in particular. "You got that right," a deep voice rumbled behind the riders, from the hole in the sand leading to the Underworld.

The biggest of the riders, clad in crimson armor, was astride a well-muscled red horse with flames flickering from its nostrils and sparks shooting from its hooves as they struck the sand. The red rider raised an immense bloodstained blade, seemingly too large to be wielded, and pointed it directly at my heart. The second rider wore bright gold armor and rode a horse so black it seemed to suck in the very light of the sun. The gold rider nudged its horse forward and raised a huge golden scythe, turning its point toward me. The third rider wore dull-green armor made of interlocking plates of crocodile scales, rode a creature that was more lizard than equine, and raised a bow and arrow that dripped with poison so vile that the very sand hissed in protest as the venom landed upon it. The fourth rider was smaller than the others, wore dull-gray chain mail, and was astride a horse that had seen better days, for its bony ribs were poking out from its sides, and foam dripped from its mouth and nose. But this horse was no creature to be trifled with, as it snorted evilly and pawed the sand, sending a bevy of crabs rushing for the safety of the ocean only to be crushed beneath those bony hooves with frightening speed and intensity. The gray rider did not wield a weapon that I could see, which made me all the more wary of what danger it brought to bear. The Lord of the Underworld had indeed called in his mark, for facing me were his elite warriors—the Four Horsemen of the Apocalypse, or some version of them. An evil laugh echoed up and down the beach, reveling in the vengeance that was soon to be wreaked.

I scanned the waters behind me, considering a nice swim to avoid combat with these emissaries of the Dark One, but spied a bevy of circling black dorsal fins that encouraged me to stay just where I was. If I could get to the tower's entrance, a narrow stone doorway would enable me to face my enemy without getting outflanked, which was an inevitable consequence if I stayed on the beach. So I did the last thing these creatures from the abyss expected—I attacked.

But they were just as quick to react, as no sooner than I had reached the red rider, a volley of poison-tipped arrows came in my direction courtesy of the green rider. I swung the Blade of Truth and caught the arrows flush on the blade, deflecting them into the gold rider's saddle, unhorsing him. The horse was startled and jumped sideways into the sickly looking horse of the gray rider, who somersaulted easily to the ground, landing with effortless grace that I would have appreciated in another time and place. The red rider swung that massive blade and engaged me in fierce swordplay from astride its mount. As my sword clashed with the red rider's, I was momentarily unnerved by a vision in the blade of me fighting myself. What was this sorcery? I jumped to the side, avoiding another hail of arrows by the slimmest of margins. The Blade of Truth almost had me turned into a pincushion, and I focused ever more closely on my adversaries. I dodged inside the red rider's blade and aimed a blow at his leg, making him leap from the saddle onto the sand, landing next to the gray rider.

All four riders were now on foot, the gold rider recovering its scythe, and I was struck by one surprising observation: aside from the red rider, who was nearly my height if not taller, all these warriors were, well . . . small in stature, the gray rider particularly so. "I would think you would all be a little bit bigger," I said to them, backing slowly away as they spread out on the beach. "I guess the Lord of the Underworld will have no complaints when I make short work of you." As I talked, I studied their stances, how they held their weapons, and even how they walked. I grimaced—there was something very familiar about what I saw. Father had apparently trained these very creatures that were now trying to kill me, which meant I was not fighting demons, but immortals of some kind. And that made the odds quite even after all. Or so I thought. I parried sword and scythe, dodged arrows and well-aimed punches all the way down to the water's edge, where the sharks circled ever so close, their great teeth bared and their tails whipping the water into a foamy frenzy. "Damn it, Father," I muttered as sweat poured down my face. "Did you have to train these creatures this bloody well?"

"Have you had enough?" I asked the riders, who were bunched uncharacteristically close together. I sensed that they were growing tired, having never faced a creature with my fighting skills. My blade was light as a feather, and I felt I could go on with this all day, but I had places to go and four little sweet teen darlings to see. And a father to curse out, but that could wait. I leaped forward, catching the gold rider by surprise, grabbing the scythe, and slamming its grip into the green rider and sending him flying backward. The gray rider was upon my back, small arm around my neck, holding on most expertly in an effort to choke the life out of me. But I had practiced defending that move for a couple of centuries, and the gray rider soon found himself flying through the air to collide with the red rider, sending them both to the ground in a tangle of arms and legs.

The gold rider was unarmed, but that did not stop him from attacking. I swept his legs out from under him with the scythe, and he fell hard to the ground. As I hovered above, hesitating for a moment before I decided on delivering the killing blow or showing mercy, I heard a familiar barking. Could it be? Was it possible? Racing toward me across the sand, a white blur of paws and fluff, was Garlic—a low growl coming from her throat. "Well, where did you come from, girl, because I have sure missed you all these years," I yelled out to her, all the while keeping my eyes on my now leery combatants. "You are a little late to help. But better late than never." I bent for her to sniff my hand, but Garlic never stopped running, slamming into my side and knocking me off my feet, and dislodging the golden scythe and the Blade of Truth from my hands in the process.

I landed hard on the sand, losing my breath for a moment, and when I recovered, I found pointed at my throat a golden scythe and a red sword, and atop my chest was a white vampire Maltese licking my chin. "Infernal Maltese," I said, spitting sand from my mouth. "Now, now, dear Garlic, you have got me in a bit of a mess. We will talk about what is considered a proper battlefield greeting later—assuming there is a later." As I spoke, the riders looked at each other in confusion and stepped back from Garlic and me to huddle together. I rose to my feet and retrieved the Blade of Truth. Garlic took this opportunity to put her paws up on my knee and hug me as only she could. I noticed she was still wearing her red-jeweled collar, complete with wormhole-inducing crystals. But I was certain that her summoning a wormhole would gain us no escape, seeing that the Lord of the Underworld had managed to circumvent my trip to Sa Dragonera once already. That collar would turn blacker than night in the Underworld, I was certain of it. This time we would surely end up as permanent residents of the tenth level of Hell. And I thought Sardinia was hot? I scratched Garlic behind her ears and called out to the horsemen. "Do you wish to parley?"

The red rider stepped forward, its voice muffled behind its visor. "How is it that you know our dog, and our dog knows you?"

I laughed. "Your dog? The Four Horsemen of the Apocalypse with my vampire Maltese? Now that is rich." I began to grow wary. Was this another trick by the Lord of the Underworld, who had grown strangely silent in all the commotion? I glanced back at the hole to the Underworld, but only a single snaky wisp of smoke emanated from it. Odd. Very odd.

"Who are the Four Horsemen of the Apocalypse?" the green rider called out. That sealed it—this was definitely a trap.

But now I was the one that was confused. If it was a trap, why didn't the horsemen take my life when they had the chance when Garlic had knocked me off my feet? "That would be you men—or maybe you are mere boys, since some of you are not yet full grown," I said.

"We are no mere boys," the gray rider scoffed. "Boys are no match for the four of us. And neither are you."

More smoke began coming from the hole to the Underworld, and I could feel a low rumble beneath my feet. Something big and ugly was coming to crash our little beach party, and I did not know if these riders were friend, foe, or something in between. But depending on what the Lord of the Underworld was sending from the netherworld, it might not remotely matter.

"You are able fighters nonetheless," I said. "Without a shadow of a doubt, I'd hate to fight all of you in a few years. But tell me, when did you train with the esteemed and revered Master Assassin Ernesto Sinestra?" I had to make these warriors my allies and forge some common bond. "I, too, trained with Ernesto Sinestra."

"I would believe you," said the green rider. "But our master said in this test of tests that there would be a trap. He said he sent his own son to this place for such a test."

I did not remember any such trap from my father at this place when we fought so long ago. But maybe he was hidden in the Aragonese tower, although he would surely be given away by his unmistakable low chuckle. Perhaps that is what he meant, or perhaps this was more trickery from the Lord of the Underworld.

The gray rider sauntered forward. "Admit it, you imbecile, you are the trap the master sent. Bow down before you are defeated." He pointed to the smoking hole on the beach. "And when you have surrendered, you can watch us dispatch whatever foul demon spawn comes forth from your foul nest of evil."

"I see your bluster does not match your size, small one. Perhaps you and Garlic are kindred souls after all," I said, smiling as the gray rider raised his fists. "But I lie not. I do not come from that devil-spawning hole, and I did train with the Master Assassin Ernesto Sinestra."

The green rider rubbed a hand across his chin. "You may be truthful. For you fight just like him and have much of his skill."

I laughed at the irony of his comment, ignoring the low hiss coming from the hole and the now steady rumble from below that made Garlic growl low and show her teeth. The riders turned back to the hole and looked uneasy, clearly trying to assess what was more dangerous—me or whatever was about to make a rather unholy appearance. I had originally thought that they had come from that hole, but I'd been clearly mistaken since they were just as unnerved about it as I was. Perhaps the Lord of the Underworld had snagged these warriors in his scheme of revenge. "Well, I should fight like the master," I said. "He is my father, after all."

"You speak blasphemy!" screamed the gray rider. "Quiet your devil tongue!"

"No, I certainly do not speak blasphemy—only the truth," I said calmly. "Do you not see the family resemblance?"

"I certainly see a family resemblance," said the red rider. "I know who you are. We have heard a lot about you."

"Excellent," I said.

"That is not a good thing, assassin," said the gray rider.

I smirked. "Do not believe everything you hear, young warriors." I pointed at the smoking hole, noting the rumble growing ever louder. Time was drawing short. "We must parley and face what comes from the demon hole together if we are all to live!"

"You are Sirio Sinestra, also known as Sirius Sinister," the red rider continued, reaching for his visor and quite ignoring the danger of the hole. The gold and green riders gasped and stepped backward, reaching for their weapons. The gray rider was silent, arms folded across his chest, and I imagined quite a scowl beneath its mask. What had Father said to beget such a mixed reaction?

The red visor came up, and my jaw dropped, as I was looking into a face very much like my own, except with the softer features, fuller lips, and higher cheekbones of a young woman. "But Granddaddy would not lie," she said. "Would he, Father? I am Contessa, your daughter." Our eyes met, and instantly we sensed each other's kindred souls. She was truly the blood of my blood and the soul of my soul. She stepped forward, and we embraced, her head on my shoulder, and I barely stifled a tear.

"No, Contessa," I said, stunned as she drew back. "He would most surely not." I turned to look at each of my daughters and saw that the green and gold riders had also unmasked themselves, and they each had hair the color of their mother's and most of her features, but stared back at me with my own eyes. They looked like twins, appearing so very different from Contessa. But while Contessa was warm and welcoming, these two were guarded and unsure of me. They did not approach and merely raised their weapons in salute. "I am Adelaide," said the green rider with formal seriousness. "I missed you with my arrows," she said. "My aim will be true next time to honor our family."

"Let's hope that next time I am not the target, Adelaide," I answered with a smile.

"I am Beatrice," said the gold rider. "I see I have much to learn."

"Indeed, the journey never stops, Beatrice, but if you are willing, I will teach you," I said. "There will be time." Beatrice nodded and stepped back, placing her mask upon her face once again.

"You left us," said the gray rider, her mask still on her face and her arms still crossed. "I have nothing to say to you."

"That's Mary Grace," Contessa said. "If you haven't figured it out, Father, she is the discontented runt of our litter."

"I have had just about enough of your insults, Contessa," Mary Grace howled. "This ends now!"

She charged at Contessa, who was grinning happily as she egged her diminutive sister on, only to slide to a stop in the sand as a blood-curdling roar came from the hole. Mary Grace and Contessa and I would all have to work out our differences later—if we got a later, that is. Four sharks surged in from the ocean and beached themselves on the shore, changing into something long ago forgotten on this planet as they thrashed upon the sand. "All right, ladies, get to your mounts. We have an enemy to engage," I said. They listened and instantly were on their horses and ready to attack—all but Mary Grace, who stood facing me with her arms still crossed. "Who are you to give us orders?" she said. "I am not listening to you."

"Mary Grace, get on your horse—now!" Contessa hollered.

"Like you are any better?" Mary Grace retorted. "Who made you the boss of me? And don't give me that Pack nonsense either. Firstborn is not the best born, my not-so-sweet sister!"

I shrugged and chose silence as Mary Grace begrudgingly took to her mount and got in line with her sisters. I was an only child and had no idea how to handle this obvious and heated sibling rivalry. They would surely have to get over themselves if they wanted to survive. Why was everything so damn personal with women, even little ones?

Garlic took her familiar place by my side and looked up at me for guidance. I sensed she wanted to be with the girls, and that was okay by me. Her loyalty to our "family" was unquestioned. "Go ahead," I said to her. "Keep them safe." She gave a solitary woof and leaped upon Contessa's horse, which started for a moment but quickly calmed under Contessa's able hand.

A great blast of fire vomited from the hole, and out of the darkness came stomping into the sunlight a huge chimera, part lion, part goat, part snake, and all bloodthirsty death. I had only heard of this vile creature in stories told to me by my father, and it was supposedly defeated long ago by the warrior Bellerophon atop the winged horse, Pegasus, but apparently the stories of its demise were greatly exaggerated. It was supposed to be the size of a normal lion, but this creature had enjoyed what the Dark Lord was feeding it, and it was easily taller than I was at its shoulder. Forget a winged horse—not that there were any of those left in the world—we needed an army!

"Contessa," I called to my daughter in red, sitting so strong and brave in her saddle. "You girls engage the shark beasts, and I will take care of the chimera."

"Be careful, Father," she said. I laughed. For the first time going into battle, I felt an unfamiliar emotion—fear. Not for myself, of course, but for these girls of mine who I did not even know, yet would mourn for the rest of eternity if something happened to them. And sweet Contessa was worried about me. "I will be fine, Contessa!" I saw the shark beasts—a strange mix of shark and crab, with a hard carapace balanced on immense pinchers and a shark's great maw with deadly jaws—were girding for an attack. "The underside is where those things are vulnerable," I yelled. "Take out their legs, flip them, and kill them. Got it?"

Off the riders went thundering down the beach, leaving me with a huge lump in my throat. Were the girls ready for this test of literal life versus ocean-borne death, and would they survive the first pass? Of course they were, I thought. The Howler and I had created quite the quartet of natural-born fighters with werewolf muscles and channeled rage, combined with the speed, balance, and stratagem of vampires. It was the beasts that were in trouble, not my daughters!

Contessa's red sword expertly sliced through the foreleg of one beast, and Beatrice's scythe clipped its back leg clean off. Adelaide sent a hail of arrows low and deadly, impaling one of the creatures and dropping it to the sand. I felt another wave of heat and leaped high in the air as the chimera had almost got to me. I had better start paying attention, or I would be the hero meeting his tragic end today!

I dodged to the side, away from the flame-spitting lion head, and delivered a mighty blow to the tail end and the snake head, severing the head from its body and dropping it to the sand. But it wasn't dead and thrust itself at my leg, and I barely kicked the venom-spitting creature away from me before its fangs nearly found my leg. I wasn't so lucky with the goat head, which rammed hard into my chest, sending me rolling back into the path of the lion's fire and claws. I came up quickly, flipping a double handful of sand into the creature's lion eyes, and leaped to the side, trying to see the action on the other side of the beach. I heard Garlic bark once, then twice, and saw two shark beasts explode in an impressive show of shell, claw, and teeth. So things were going very well for my girls. Only one shark beast remained alive—I wish I could have said the same for the chimera!

Strange runes appeared on the Blade of Truth as I swung my sword hard and opened a deep wound in the chimera's side. What was the blade doing? Was it a warning? I had no time to guess, instead thrusting a kill shot deep in the wounded beast's side, dodging one last feeble bit of fire as the chimera collapsed to the sand defeated. I saw the girls riding toward me—all four none the worse for the battle—and I lifted a hand in greeting. Contessa whipped off her mask and screamed, and I turned just a moment too late as the snake head of the chimera was upon me. But Adelaide's aim was true, and her arrow appeared in the snake head, staking it into the sand mere inches from me as the last bits of its life ebbed away in a slow green drip of chartreuse-ochre onto the beach.

"I told you I would not miss next time," Adelaide said, a slight smile creasing her face.

"Indeed, you did not." I surveyed the beach. The girls had been impressive in battle and, aside from a few scratches and bruises, had been able combatants. The runes on my sword were glowing, and there was a slight hum as the blade was actually vibrating. Garlic looked out to the sea and began pacing uneasily, a low growl coming from her throat.

"What is it?" Contessa said.

A huge tentacle broke the water just off the beach, reaching up to the sky with its many suckers dripping with ooze and covered with bits of flotsam. "It's a kraken!" I said. "Let's retreat to the tower. It won't come on land." More and more tentacles broke the water's surface, and finally a great mouth came into view, snapping at the air with great ferocity, then another mouth, and finally one more. Great yellow eyes the size of infantry shields accompanied each mouth, and when they spied us, the creature shrieked out of those three horrible mouths in unison, causing us to cover our ears. On it came, rushing toward the beach, its huge tentacles thrashing the water, and pulling itself onto the sand.

"It *is* coming on land," Mary Grace said. "I knew we shouldn't listen to you. If we go into the tower it's going to bring it down on top of us."

"Show some respect, Mary Grace," Contessa said, defending me.

"Eat excrement and die, Contessa," Mary Grace snapped back.

I weighed what Mary Grace had said, and since the kraken was easily twice the size of the tower, and this island was not all that big, she was probably right. I glanced at the entrance to Hell. Clearly, the Lord of the Underworld was going to try and force our hand. It was not like going in there was an option! Only a small bit of smoke streamed from the entrance. He was waiting to play his next card. "Choices, vampire, choices," a deep voice boomed from the hellish hole.

"To the tower!" I yelled, hopping behind Contessa on her steed. "The farther we get the kraken out of the water, the better chance we have!" Garlic jumped up behind me, balancing expertly on the hind end of the horse.

Even Mary Grace chose not to belabor her point, and we made for the tower, but right as we came close to Hell's hole, a host of slobbering hellhounds burst from it, attacking our mounts and causing us to jump from our horses and engage them. Their demonic eyes glowed red like hot coals, and their jaws dripped with venomous bile. They were the size of cattle and moved with a sinewy speed that belied their size—they were simply black blurs of rampaging death. But they had no interest in fighting us and were focused on attacking our horses with savage ferocity, ripping into horse flesh with a sickening crunch as fang struck bone. We attacked these whirling, howling creatures with equal ferocity, Garlic barking into smithereens any hound that threatened the fair steed she was still perched atop of. The hounds retreated to the edge of the tower, flanking us, and putting us between them and the kraken, which was now half on the beach and half in the water. The hounds closed ranks and marched toward us—choices indeed.

Only Contessa's horse had survived the hellhound attack, thanks to Garlic's barks, my magical blade, and Contessa's swordswomanship. Adelaide and Beatrice sniffed back tears behind their masks, while Mary Grace took a knife from her boot and slit her mount's throat to end its suffering. That was one tough girl, I thought as we made eye contact. Her face said that I could be next if she had the opportunity, almost like she blamed me for her horse dying, then I realized that she actually did!

"I told you that going to the tower would be a bad idea." She sniffed. "Good thinking, Master Assassin."

"You really do have a lot to learn, Mary Grace," I said, calmly surveying the beach. "Battles are never without their surprises, and in all my years of master assassinship, these are the first hellhounds I have ever encountered. So, if you stop talking and start listening, you might just survive this living nightmare, got it?"

On the hounds came, and the girls, including a put-in-her-place Mary Grace, looked to me for guidance. "All right then," I said. "Let us get back-to-back. We cannot let the hounds outflank us, or they will cut us down one by one." I looked at the sheer size and power of the approaching kraken. "Remember, the hellhounds want no part of that vile beast either. It will just as soon attack them as us, if they get in the way." The girls nodded, and Contessa took to her mount with Garlic again riding point on her saddle. "One last thing," I said. "I love you girls more than you will ever know."

"I know. I love you too," Contessa called from her saddle, but the others grouped around me had remained silent, and right then my heart hurt in ways I never thought possible. That wound cut deeper than any blade could, but I could not blame them. It was not their fault. I held the Blade of Truth high in the air, and saw Adelaide, Beatrice, and Mary Grace hugging me in its reflection. That was the reality as to how my reluctant daughters felt about me—they were just not allowed to love me. If they would only come to be as loyal and loving as Contessa—if we had another day together, that is! I cursed the Howler and Angus for the hundredth time.

We found ourselves pinned between the kraken and the hellhounds, and I briefly considered a rush at the hounds, thinking maybe one of the girls would get to safety. But that safety was an illusion, as the kraken would destroy the tower stone by stone, until all of us were dead. My sword glowed bright white like a mini-sun on the beach, and the hounds stopped with a painful yelp, turning their heads from us. A great horn sounded from the ocean, and then others joined it in a concert. Garlic howled long and loud, sending a welcome to those that were coming. I looked to the sea, and astride great orcas, a host of trident-bearing merfolk set upon the kraken with great ferocity.

Leading them was a mermaid of uncommon valor, her long golden hair flung out beneath her jeweled battle helm as she weaved her orca in and out of the kraken's many tentacles, slashing at the kraken's body again and again. "Look at her," Mary Grace exclaimed. "Now *she* is a warrior!" The other girls murmured their agreement. "Who is she?" Mary Grace asked, looking in my direction as if somehow I should know the answer. I shrugged. Now, of course I was pretty sure that I had met her before in the see-a-seaperson-naked kind of way, but she had left Lundy Island before I learned her name.

Again and again the orcas came away from the beach with great tentacles in their mouths, returning a moment later to do it again. The kraken shrieked in rage and pain, wrapping its tentacles around a great orca and heaving it and its rider high in the direction of the tower. The merman leaped from the orca, heaving his trident at one angry yellow eye, dodging tentacles as he fell back to the ocean in a dizzying series of twists and flips. The orca fell short of the beach, landing in the water near the shore with a great splash, and a few of the hellhounds attacked. But the orca fought back, snapping and biting at them as it rolled toward the water. A great net, flung by a group of mermen, snared the orca's tail, and they pulled it back to safety, dispatching the hellhounds they had caught in it with their tridents.

The merfolk seemed to have the kraken well in hand, so I rallied my girls to face the hellhounds. "Come on, ladies," I yelled, wanting to take advantage of the confusion. "Let us avenge your mounts!" Mary Grace had hopped on Contessa's horse, and on they charged with the rest of us right behind them. Adelaide's hands were a blur, as arrow after arrow found the throat or heart of a hellhound. Not to be outdone, Beatrice cleared a path to the tower with her scythe, and the sand soon ran red with the blood of the hounds. We chased them back into the entrance to Hell and rejoiced at our victory. Garlic was running circles around us in the sand, yelping happily in spite of the fact that her white coat had turned a fine shade of crimson from the blood of the hellhounds. The kraken moved off the beach with the merfolk in pursuit. It plunged beneath the surface of the ocean and was seen no more.

The mermaid with the jeweled helm walked up from the beach on her land legs, and Mary Grace began to get excited. "It is her—the warrior woman," she said, doffing her mask. For the first time, I saw Mary Grace was fairer than any of her sisters with reddish-brown hair and the green eyes of her mother, complete with the smoldering anger and snarky attitude—but not at the moment, since her eyes, and all of our group's, were on the mermaid.

The mermaid removed her jeweled helm, which sparkled in the sunlight, and I found myself staring into familiar blue eyes. "It's you!" I exclaimed, giggling like a proper English schoolboy. "And here I thought I was never going to see you again!

"These are my daughters," I said proudly.

"How do you know her, Father?" Contessa said. "She is amazing—tell us, tell us!" Yes, she was amazing, I thought. I took a deep breath, prepared to give them a highly abridged story of our meeting. But, thankfully, the mermaid took charge once again.

"Hello, Sirius Sinister, it is good to see you," the mermaid said. "And hello to all of you brave young lady warriors! Never before have I seen so much fighting skill from such young women. But as daughters of the legendary warrior Sirius Sinister, I should not be surprised." I saw my daughters hanging on her every word, thrilled at being praised by her as legendary.

"What's your name?" Mary Grace excitedly blurted, interrupting our new friend. "Are you somebody important?"

"Mary Grace!" I scolded, ignoring her all-too-familiar look of disdain. Indeed, Mary Grace had inherited much from the Blackheart side of her family.

The mermaid laughed at Mary Grace's impetuousness, and then she and I locked gazes, and I fell deep into her beautiful blue eyes. "My name does not have a translation into any land-walker language," she said. "Underwater, we communicate in a language that has no equivalent on land. It would sound like a series of clicks and such to you. But on land I do speak French, Italian, Spanish, Greek, and of course, now English."

Our little reunion was interrupted by one of her soldiers. "Forgive my intrusion, my Queen," he said, bowing his head. "But we are tracking the kraken to the north as it flees to colder and deeper waters. It appears to be on the run and shows no signs of return."

"Excellent," the Queen said. "Thank you for your report."

"Queen?" I exclaimed. "You are a queen?"

"I knew it," said Contessa. "She had to be a queen! Daddy knows royalty!"

I noticed that Mary Grace, Adelaide, and Beatrice were now more focused on the young soldier, who looked about their age, though he stood easily a head taller than me. Mermen were usually pale, like the Queen, and of average height, but this soldier clearly did not fit in with the under-the-sea contingent. He was wearing only a mesh loincloth and weapon belt that failed to cover any of his tan, bare, chiseled muscles—all of which I could see in well-defined fashion, as apparently could my girls. He looked like he was cut from a single piece of tan marble. I found myself wishing I had a spare cloak to offer him, to say nothing of a pair of voluminous breeches! Was Mary Grace really staring at his loincloth that was not doing such a great job clothing his loins?

"I beg your pardon, my good land folk." His voice was strong and melodic. He paused, not sure what to make of Garlic, who was happily licking the saltwater off his calf. "Queen of the Seven Seas, and the entire underwater realm of this world, would be more accurate."

Garlic looked up at him and continued licking his leg. "Get off him, you wretched Maltese," I admonished her, and banished to the deepest part of my mind the very real possibility that my daughters would want to do the same thing to this adolescent Adonis. "Why didn't you say you were the queen of the merfolk last time?" I asked the Queen, wishing the soldier would go back to the ocean, and his flowing blond hair would stop moving in slow motion in the wind. Did he really have to look all glistening like that? I thought I heard Adelaide and Beatrice sigh in concert. Damn.

"It never came up," the Queen answered. "We were a little occupied with trying to escape the Winter Witch, if you remember. And then . . . well . . . things . . ." She cast her eyes downward and flushed slightly. Contessa was watching everything, as she seemed to be wont to do, and she pounced quickly.

"What things?" Contessa asked, trying to guess what the Queen meant. "Tell us about fighting the Winter Witch!"

"Your father was swimming in the open ocean when I saw him, and he nearly slew the Winter Witch's familiar, who was in the form of a great shark beast. He saved a whole ship full of people," the Queen said. "But he was gravely wounded, and I swam him to safety."

"How did he breathe underwater?" Mary Grace asked.

"Oh, that is easy," the young soldier interjected. "I can show you how we do that."

"What kind of idiot do you take me for?" I bowed up. "Breathing underwater is not something a young, chaste woman should just do!"

"With all due respect, sir, the earlier they start, the better they get at it, and the more they enjoy it," the soldier replied, pursing full lips that looked all too ready for the job.

My eyes grew wide and my temper rose, and I found myself trying to look the young and all-too-pretty soldier in the eyes, in spite of the height advantage he had. "I don't think so, young man," I said, staring into his big sea-green eyes and feeling my fangs coming out. "She is only sixteen years old. Don't you have a whale to go feed or some shells to collect?"

The soldier stepped back and looked a bit confused, his eyes going to the Queen for guidance. "I meant no offense, sir," he said. "Should I take my leave?"

"How utterly embarrassing," Mary Grace said. "We don't see you for our entire lives, and in the first hour you decide to play father. I am in need of some air, so no, you impossibly pretty thing, I am going to take *my* leave!" She walked away in a huff, and I honestly had no earthly idea what to do.

"Oh, so, so, so rude," Contessa said. "The runt of ours has just offended the Queen. I don't know how you are ever going to forgive her, Daddy."

But the Queen was far from offended, and instead she laughed long and hard. I had no idea what was so funny. "Sirius, the way we traveled underwater is not what he meant. There are other ways. Soldier, please demonstrate for Mr. Sinister and his daughters."

The young soldier held up a strange shell he had taken from his belt. "If a land walker puts this shell on their mouth, they can breathe for nearly an hour underwater without coming to the surface," he said. "We have used them for centuries to help rescue people from shipwrecks."

I nodded, feeling a little bit embarrassed. "I am sorry for the misunderstanding, soldier," I said. "What do they call you? I guess we couldn't understand your real name. But what do land walkers call you?"

The soldier thought for a moment. "Well, sir," he said, "I have not been around land walkers much. But one day last week, I awoke from a nap on the beach and found myself discovered and in the company of several young maidens. I fled instantly into the ocean, but they kept calling, 'Come back, lovely,' so I guess that is my land-walker name."

"You have got to be joking!" I said, grimacing. "Seriously. Lovely?"

"Yes, sir?" he answered. "How may I be of service?"

The Queen, Contessa, Adelaide, and Beatrice failed to contain their mirth, and I could only smile in defeat. "I think the name Lovely very much suits you," said Adelaide in total mock seriousness. "Yes, suits you very much indeed."

"I second that," said Beatrice. "Thank you for the explanation." She paused. "Lovely." Beatrice and her sisters collapsed in a heap of giggles, and Lovely and I stood awkwardly together as he awaited his orders from the Queen.

"May I have a word with you in private, Your Highness," I said, changing the subject.

"Yes, of course," the Queen said. "Soldier, you may stand sentry here with the girls."

We stepped away, and I saw Mary Grace come back from the beach and join them. They formed a semicircle around Lovely, who was quite clueless as to the attention they were showing him. "So why didn't I get a shell?" I asked, giving the Queen a coy glance.

She shrugged. "I wasn't sure how long we would be underwater," she said. "And we might not have had the time to surface and switch shells without the Winter Witch catching us. As it turned out, we barely made it to Lundy Island at all if you recall. Besides," the Queen added, "you have great lips."

We both burst out laughing. I looked over to where the girls had apparently talked the innocent Lovely into showing them, one at a time, the proper way to hold a trident. "And apparently Lovely does too," I said with a sigh of anguish as each of the girls took turns having Lovely reach around them to properly place their hands on his trident. "I am not sure I am cut out to be a father with guys like him coming around."

"Nonsense," the Queen said. "They love you instinctively. Contessa adores you almost too much, considering today was the first day she met you! But sometimes girls with daddy issues try to overcompensate."

"Daddy issues?" I said. "Ah yes, absent from their lives through no fault of my own."

"Yes, and that's the sad part," the Queen said. "Contessa, well, she seems okay, and the others, well, they have sixteen years of negative words to overcome. They will get there. But remember, they have never had permission to love you."

"It is that obvious, isn't it?" I said. "Do you have children? If you don't, you should, you would make one heck of a mother." The Queen's face grew flushed, and I instantly regretted my words. I seemed to have touched on a subject that drew great embarrassment from this iridescent creature. Drat it all!

"Why did you help us?" I asked, changing the subject. "And how did you know of Hades's nefarious scheme to exact revenge on me by getting me to kill my daughters, or having them kill me?"

The Queen's face had thankfully returned to its normal color, and she did not seem angry with me. "Well, it is kind of complicated," she said, her blue eyes soft, wet, and inviting.

I rolled my eyes, wondering if a woman existed that *wasn't* complicated. "Of course," I said. "I wouldn't have expected anything else. You rescue me from the Winter Witch. And . . . and"—I lowered my voice—"we are together. And then you disappear. I think you are the one who tricked the Winter Witch into giving me the Blade of Truth. And then you show up here in Sardinia with a legion of merfolk to save me once again. Oh, and you are a queen. Of course, it is complicated!"

The Queen put her hands around my neck and pulled me closer, and this time those soft wet eyes did take me in. She kissed me ever so gently, drawing the attention of my girls and of Lovely, whose big green eyes nearly bugged out of his head. Apparently the Queen was not known to kiss. "When I saw you that day in the Irish Sea, I had been looking for you for a hundred years, Sirius Sinister," she said.

"You had been?" I exclaimed. "But why?"

And that was the moment when all Hell simply broke loose, or more accurately, bursting forth from the gateway to the netherworld came the three-headed beast of the darkness—Cerberus. He was the

size of a great bull elephant, and his three heads howled in synchronized rage, venom dripping from fangs the size of long swords. The
earth shook, his great paws pounding the sand as he bounded straight
for Lovely and the girls. Lovely whirled and hurled his trident, which
flew true to its mark, but it bounced off Cerberus's tough hide. The
girls scattered in panic, but Lovely stayed his ground, armed only with
a small dagger.

My sword was glowing white hot as I raced toward him, but
Cerberus got there first, crashing down with one mighty paw upon
where Lovely stood. But Lovely was not there, having spun upward off
the sand through the snapping heads of Cerberus, then jumping off the
colossal demon hound's back onto the ground. Cerberus whipped his
heads to and fro, looking in confusion for Lovely, but instead only finding me with the Blade of Truth burning a swath of pain into his right
forefoot. Garlic barked at the huge beast, but her bark only served to
make Cerberus even angrier, and he swatted Garlic away with a glancing blow. "Hey, that's my dog," I said, slicing into Cerberus's left paw.
Garlic attacked again, flying back across the sand, a white blur heading
straight for Cerberus without stopping. "Bad idea, Garlic," I yelled. "He
is too big for the likes of you!"

She did not listen and hurtled herself at Cerberus's chest, knocking the wind out of herself in the process. "Damn it, Garlic," I yelled,
jumping between Cerberus's paws and slashing furiously at his chest.
The girls had recovered and joined the fight. However, it seemed their
weapons could only annoy this demonic beast and not do any real damage. They were in more danger than anything else. Cerberus swung his
tail and took Mary Grace's feet out from under her, but she was quickly
pulled to safety by Lovely.

"Fall back, girls!" the Queen shouted. "This is your father's battle."

With each blow of the enchanted Blade of Truth, Cerberus retreated
toward the gateway to Hell. Garlic had recovered and would not leave
my side, and her barks were finally starting to have an effect on this
creature from the ultimate darkness. But Cerberus made one final rush
at me, and although I opened wound after gaping wound in the side
of the demonic beast, on it came. Garlic leaped up and sank her sharp
teeth into the tender lower lip of Cerberus's center head. The beast
whipped that head back and forth in a frenzy, trying unsuccessfully

to dislodge the vampire Maltese. But the more Cerberus swung its head, the more the cut Garlic had opened grew wider, and Cerberus's foul blood fell like hellish red rain upon the beach. Cerberus stumbled backward toward the gateway, and a slow rumble came from below.

"Let go, Garlic," I yelled. "To me!" I rushed forward only to take a huge paw to the chest, which sent me somersaulting backward on the beach. I stood up quickly, but was so dizzy from the blow of the demonic dog that I dropped to one knee for a second to catch my breath. The portal began to close in a flash of fire and brimstone. Mary Grace ran for the gateway after Garlic, screaming, "Jump, jump!" And still Garlic held tight with nary a whimper. Her plan was all too clear.

"No!" Mary Grace screamed, and I watched, helpless, as she was just two steps from entering a gateway about to close, trapping her in Hell—forever. But Lovely tackled her from behind, and they tumbled to the sand as the entrance snapped out of existence with a small pop, leaving only the sound of Mary Grace crying as she beat her small hands on Lovely's large chest.

CHAPTER 16

My heart was heavy as I examined from every possible angle the area of the beach where the gateway had disappeared. I could not really believe the Hell hole was gone just as quickly as it had appeared. Or rather, I knew all that was possible, I just couldn't fathom that Garlic was gone. And her sacrificing herself in the process—maybe that was part of the Lord of the Underworld's plan all along. If he wanted to punish me for my supposed misgivings, he had succeeded. But I vowed to make his success temporary. And I think I knew just how to get my dog back.

My thoughts were interrupted by a confrontation on the beach. "I hate you," Mary Grace said to a bewildered Lovely. "Why did you stop me? I could have—"

"Could have what?" Contessa interrupted. "Gotten your runt-ass self stuck in Hell forever?"

"Hell is listening to you prattle on and on," Mary Grace said, making a face at her sister. "I could have reached Garlic and gotten back out of the gateway before it closed. No one is faster than I am. At least I could have—if this . . . this . . ."

Lovely had turned his big green eyes upon her. "The gateway was closing," he said. "You would have been trapped. I caught you from behind, so I am even quicker than you, and I am telling you that I could not have made it out with the dog. I am *not* going to apologize for saving your life." He folded his arms across his chest and stood his ground. As much as it pained me to admit, I was beginning to like Lovely.

"Oooooo," Mary Grace howled, her inner Blackheart getting the best of her. "I don't care," she screamed. "I *still* hate you." She paused, unable to break eye contact with Lovely. "Why do you have to be so blasted beautiful anyway? Ugh!" Mary Grace ran down to the water, crying uncontrollably, and Beatrice gave me a glance and slowly followed her.

"She will be okay," Adelaide said. "Her feelings get the best of her sometimes. It is not personal, Lovely. It is just Mary Grace's nature."

"Yeah, she is such a blasted little baby," Contessa said sweetly, and then, realizing it did not sound so sweet, added. "I mean sometimes she can be a baby . . . or, uh . . . maybe just when her dog gets sucked into a Hell hole. I mean . . . never mind . . ."

The Queen sent Lovely down along the beach to ensure that there was nothing threatening left in the area, and Adelaide and Contessa joined him. "My deepest sympathies to you for the loss of that wonderful dog of yours," she said to me.

"She is not dead," I said. "I would feel it if she was. And she is not lost, because I know very well where she is! Hold your sympathies, because where she is, it is probably more accurate to say that she is not dead, yet. I have to do something to save her. She has saved my neck many a time, and now it is time for me to repay the favors."

"Sirius," she said, her face lit by the glow of the sun now lowering to the horizon, but so much more radiant. "What are you going to do? March up to the Gates of Hell, kick them down, and walk up to the Lord of the Underworld and demand your dog back from him?"

"Pretty much," I said. "I am not sure if you know this or not, but aside from the tortured souls of evil mortals, it is not exactly easy to get into Hell. In fact, I only know one way."

"What is that?"

"For starters, get married," I said. "Quickest way to Hell."

"Is that a proposal?" the Queen retorted.

"Yes, will you marry me?" I asked.

"You don't have to ask just because I am pregnant," she said. "I do not need a king who can't breathe underwater, you know."

"You are pregnant?"

"Yes, thanks to you," the Queen said.

"Now wait just a minute. It's been five years," I sputtered. "If that was the case, shouldn't we have a toddler by now?"

"No, let's just say, Justice's library isn't the only place where time behaves differently in the world," the Queen said. "And, I do really mean thanks to you. That is why I was looking for you for a hundred years. You are the only man in the entire world that could give me what I wanted most—a baby."

I was absolutely speechless. Contessa caught my eye from across the beach and waved. She was such a good girl, that one. I returned the wave. And now, I was responsible for making a baby with the mermaid queen?

"I have been the queen of my people for about two hundred years," she said. "I don't need a king to rule with me. My people are good and strong, aside from a few bad sea apples. Everything was more or less perfect for me under the sea—except one thing. Our oracle foretold that I could never, would never, have a child. I accepted the word of the oracle for one hundred years and focused on my subjects and my kingdom. Until one day a hundred years ago, I visited the oracle, and it told me of a man that had consorted with Persephone—a man that could give me what I wanted most. That man is you—Sirius Sinister."

"Why didn't you tell me?"

She looked away, ashamed. "Our meeting in the Irish Sea was not pure chance," she said. "My spies had tracked you to Peel Castle, and I was coming to see you when the Winter Witch attacked. Your exploits are legendary, Sirius. Half of immortal mankind wants to be you. All immortal womankind wants to be with you. The Blade of Truth had been in our armory for five hundred years. But the oracle told me it was now yours to possess."

"But, why me?" I asked her.

The Queen merely shrugged. "The oracle does not answer questions, it merely tells its truth. A truth that is sometimes clear and sometimes a mystery. But the blade let me wield it for the express purpose of bringing it to you. So I took it and was going to use it to free you from the chains of the Winter Witch."

"And of all the fish in the Irish Sea," I scoffed, having been lied to once or a thousand times by women so I was quite the doubter, "you find me? You expect me to believe that?"

"I was going to tell you on Lundy Island," she pleaded. "Really I was. But I was afraid you wouldn't want to be with me. What man wants children?"

I looked down the beach at my four daughters. "Actually, me," I said. "I could not love those girls any more than I do. And, honestly, if you had told me on Lundy Island about what the oracle said—or showed me a shiny shell or something—I would have lain down with you anyway. Have you seen yourself?"

"Thanks—I think," she said.

"But that does not answer the question. How did you know to come to Sardinia?"

"After I returned to my kingdom, my spies at Immortal Divorce Court brought word that the Lord of the Underworld had put a mark on your life. I found out where your daughters were and had a hunch they would be somehow involved, so I tracked them here."

"All right, you answered as to how you knew, but what I really want to know is why you came here? You got what you wanted from me," I said. "You could have just gone back to your merry undersea kingdom, never given me or my girls a second thought, and let Hades exact his revenge. So, why are you here?" One look at her face gave me the answer. "Ah, you felt guilty." I looked away, feigning hurt. I glanced over at my girls to see them all sitting with Lovely in polite conversation. He was certainly a calming figure—even to a firebrand like Mary Grace.

The Queen sighed and gently turned my face back to her. I found myself looking at her, trying to sell anger but only feeling that familiar, old lust. I wondered what exactly separated lust and love, because they couldn't coexist, could they? I stared at the Queen, and yes, she was so undeniably gorgeous, and yes, she was also carrying my child to boot. And just why did this oddly make me want her even more? The reality was that her having my baby definitely increased the naughty factor for me. Oh, what I wanted to do with her right there in the sand but for the host of youths awaiting our direction.

"Sirius," the Queen said. "I did not expect to be so attracted to you, or to enjoy it so much. You did things to me that I have never experienced. I could barely feel my face, and my tail kept twitching as I was swimming all the way back to my castle because you brought the pleasure to me so often and so strongly."

I bit my lip to keep from smiling at what the Queen said. But I couldn't speak without laughing, and I was having the hardest time not wanting to congratulate myself on a job well done. Made her tail twitch—indeed!

"I was so focused on becoming with child it did not matter what you looked like, or even what kind of person you were—you could provide what I needed," the Queen said. "What I've always needed!"

"So you used me," I said, looking away again. "And you don't even . . . love me . . ."

"I don't even know you," she said, exasperated.

"Well, that didn't stop you from being with me, now did it? You owe me."

The Queen nodded. "Yes, I do."

"Good," I said. "It is settled. You will marry me. You will divorce me. We will go to Immortal Divorce Court, and I will get myself found in contempt and get sentenced to Hell. I am going to get my dog back!"

"Are you sure that is a good idea?" the Queen asked. "Hades wants to torture you for all eternity for being with Persephone—even if they were divorced when you did it—and he knows that she really, really liked it—and I have to agree with her! Thus, he is suitably enraged. You have done what most would think impossible—you made a god look bad in the bedchambers."

"Lucky me," I said. "It's always been my goal in life to have an all-powerful deity out to exact his pound of flesh because of my skill in the bedchambers." I thought for a moment. If it weren't so dire, and my dog wasn't imprisoned in the ultimate inferno, it actually would be kind of funny in a sick, twisted way. I just knew Justice would find it hilarious. He probably hadn't been with a woman since the great landmass split.

"He is going to kill you," she said. She put a hand to her belly and then looked over to my girls. "You can't leave these girls without a father."

"What choice do I have? I have to get Garlic back," I said. "I can't just leave her there while I know she is alive."

"It's a trap."

"Maybe," I said. "But I have a plan. And I am not so entirely sure he wants to kill me." Then it hit me. "You said 'girls' just now when you were holding your belly. How do you know that?"

"The oracle," the Queen answered.

I reached out and put my hand on her stomach and felt the very faintest of kicks. "The oracle . . ." I echoed, amazed at what I had just felt.

"She knows her daddy."

Just then the girls and Lovely came up the beach, tired of waiting for the Queen and me to join them. "Girls," I said, "you are all about to have a sister."

"Oh, what blessed news!" Contessa said, clapping her hands with excitement. Adelaide and Beatrice smiled, still in awe of the Queen. Mary Grace looked from the Queen to me and back to the Queen. I thought she was going to have a snide comment, or even throw up her breakfast. Instead, she just looked at Lovely with an evil grin on her face. "You are not related to the Queen, are you, Lovely?" she asked.

"I am not of royal blood," he answered. "I am but a common soldier."

"There is nothing common about you," Mary Grace answered, to my great chagrin and her utter delight. Lovely was apparently forgiven.

The Queen had managed to have her soldiers summon two ships— one to take the girls back to Sa Dragonera and the other to take the Queen and me toward Greece and Immortal Divorce Court. We set up a camp at the tower, and Adelaide got a fire going, which was quite a shock to Lovely. The Queen merely chuckled as Mary Grace had to grab his hand to keep him from touching the fire. I gave her my best fatherly look of disapproval when she suggested taking a walk on the beach with Lovely since he wasn't fond of the fire. Lovely avoided the father-daughter confrontation that was brewing, declined the walk ever so graciously, and settled in with the rest of us by the fire. The ships were due to arrive in Sardinia in the morning, so I had a captive audience—an audience that turned out wanted to hear every word I said about their mother, how we met, and ultimately where I had been these last sixteen years.

I focused on the good of that relationship, telling them that the Howler and I had reunited the true love of Jova and Cornelia, whom the girls said now had two beautiful little boys. They laughed at my tales of Oliver and grew wide-eyed as I described the fight with the goblins, the earthquake, and our eventual escape to Harvis's farm via Garlic's crystal-enhanced collar. We all grew silent, clearly missing our valiant vampire Maltese. I saw the Queen nodding, and I think she finally understood why I was going to the very Gates of Hell and beyond for Garlic. That dog was simply family, and my lesson to these young ladies was that you never ever abandon your family.

In the end even Mary Grace grew to understand the circumstances that led me to be away from them, oh, these many years. My daughters were smart, and when I explained about Angus's plot to imprison me, I saw them all exchange glances. Clearly, though sixteen years old and maturing by the day, they already had an accurate view of the kind of man their maternal grandfather was, and for that matter, they saw who their mother was as well. They all hugged me when I finished speaking, including the Queen, leaving Lovely sitting alone by the fireside, and he just beamed happily.

"I believe every word you have said, Father," Contessa said. "For right before we were sent to train with Granddaddy, I crossed Mother by disobeying her and showing mercy to a servant, who had ruined a prized ball gown, and well, let's just say we did not part on the most pleasant of terms."

"I never saw you two have a cross word. It was the rest of us she had no use for," Mary Grace said.

"There was a lot I dealt with that you never saw," Contessa retorted.

"That still sounds so odd to me," Mary Grace pressed. "You are the favorite."

"That is a pretty low threshold, dear sister," Contessa said. "You should not tell lies to our father."

Mary Grace shrugged, not taking the bait. "I can only say what I remember, and what I have seen with my own eyes," she said.

"If I was so much the favorite, why did I get locked in that dark closet by dear Mother with all of you, and all the rats, when we were smaller, huh?" Contessa retorted.

"That was awful," Adelaide said. "I can still hear the skitter-skitter of claws on stone."

"Yeah," Beatrice agreed. "First thing I ever killed—a rat."

"Yeah, me too," Contessa nodded. "So awful—I hate Mother for what she did."

"I have no memory of you being in there with us," Mary Grace said. "I am not sure that you were . . ."

"Well, of course she was there," Adelaide said. "Where else would she have been?"

"Yeah," Beatrice agreed. "It was dark, but she was there. I definitely remember Contessa being there when Aunt Cornelia let us out, and we could finally see again!"

"Yeah, so stop your lies, Mary Grace," Contessa snarled at the sneering Mary Grace.

"Aunt Cornelia was right about so much," Adelaide interrupted, smacking her hand hard onto the sand. She was clearly used to sister on sister violence between these two. "It was all true what Aunt Cornelia told me!" she said. "I did not believe Grandfather Blackheart was involved with the goblins, because werewolves hate goblins. But he was!"

"Angus Blackheart wanted Cornelia to marry for money and his own personal gain—not love," I said, watching the collective wave of young feminine outrage travel around the fire. "But your Uncle Jova made an offer that Angus simply had no ability to refuse."

"It had to do with spiders—didn't it?" Beatrice exclaimed. "I overheard one of the soldiers talking about spiders!"

"A story for another day," I said, not sure if they knew of their Uncle Jova's true identity.

Mary Grace looked me in the eye. "Now it makes sense. Grandfather Blackheart always did say, 'Cross a Blackheart, and you are as good as dead,'" she said. "I always thought he was joking, but now I am not so sure." She caught Lovely's concerned eye. "Oh no, don't you worry, Lovely. I am not mad at you anymore."

"So what happens next, Father?" Beatrice asked. Her sisters all chimed in wanting to know what my plan was. I had considered not telling them the truth, but aside from some selective editing of my tale, I had vowed, with the full support of the Queen, to never lie to my daughters, and that included the unborn one in the Queen's belly.

"Girls, you are going back to Sa Dragonera to continue your training with your grandfather," I said. "The Queen and I have a plan to rescue Garlic."

"But, Father," Contessa pleaded. "We want to help save her. She is our dog too!"

I sighed. "You girls are not ready yet—though you are the most amazing young warriors, so far ahead of my skills when I was your age. But I cannot take you where I am going."

"You are going to the Underworld, aren't you?" Mary Grace said.

I nodded, and I expected more protests, more discussion, and more sass from Mary Grace, but instead, all I got was one big warm embrace. "I promise, girls," I said. "I will come back with Garlic." I sure hoped I could keep that promise.

"Can you tell us your plan?" Contessa said, her mental wheels turning once more.

"I cannot put you at risk, or tip my hand," I said. And the truth was that most of my plan relied on my being absolutely correct in an assumption I was making about the Lord of the Underworld. If I was wrong, instant incineration was my fate. But I knew Garlic was still alive, and I knew the reason for her still surviving was simple—bait.

The next morning the ship to Sa Dragonera was first to arrive, and I could not believe my eyes for waving to me from the deck was my father, Ernesto Sinestra. When the girls spotted him, they took off in a mad sprint. "Come meet my father," I said, grabbing the Queen by the hand and running after the girls.

Ernesto Sinestra leaped off the skiff onto the sand with the agility of the master assassin he was. He was fit and trim, his shoulders broad and strong. The girls swarmed him affectionately, and he pretended to lose his balance momentarily in their rush. Shouts of "Granddaddy" reverberated back to my happy ears as the Queen and I approached.

"My son," he said. "How crazy is this? You and I are back in Sardinia!" He reached for his sword. "Are you ready for a rematch?"

I laughed and pointed to all the death and destruction still littering the beach. "I think I already had one," I said, bringing out my blood-stained Blade of Truth. "But if you are game, then so am I . . ."

My father's eyes went wide as he took in the mystical blade I held. "And just how in heaven's name did you come to have *that* in your possession?" he said.

"It is rather a long story, but I don't think heaven has anything to do with it."

"The big boss might have need for you since, you know, you are wielding a Relic," my father said. "We really should sit down and talk about you joining the family business."

"I appreciate the offer, I really do, but his even bigger boss is not going to let that happen," I said. "And there is something I have to take care of—actually a number of things. My life is really kind of complicated right now. So unfortunately, no rematch for us, all right?"

"Of course, of course," my father said with a chortle as he again eyed the Blade of Truth. "That is a beauty, though. I will take you on any time when you aren't wielding a weapon of such caliber. Only a fool would challenge you with that in your hand."

"My dad is not a fool," I agreed, sheathing the Relic.

"You look to have been quite busy here, though you have been apparently downright prolific since you left Sa Dragonera," Ernesto continued. His dark eyes twinkled mischievously as his eyes went to the Queen. "And forget about the Blade of Truth being a beauty—this woman is beyond compare, your mother excluded, of course. So my boy, I see that you are keeping quite excellent company these days."

"Father," I said. "This is the Queen."

"Sí," he said. "That she is—and of more than just the seven seas." He took her hand and kissed it gently, with a slight bow of his head. I had not seen my father in literally hundreds of years, yet for an immortal he somehow seemed more, well . . . mature. I saw the barest hint of crow's feet around his eyes, and there were certainly more than a few strands of gray around his temples and on his sideburns. I realized I did not know how old my father really was, and perhaps he had always looked this way, even in my younger years. It just took some life experience on my part to see him for his true self.

The Queen laughed. "Now I know where Sirius gets his charm."

"Sirius? Ah, right, I forgot that my boy has changed his given name, but I like it!" my father replied. "Sirius Sinister, now that is an assassin's name!"

"Father, you always told me to find my true self, and that self is Sirius Sinister." I reached to touch his graying sideburns, which I could not take my eyes off. "What is it with this stuff—were you in some sort of disguise before you came here? Isn't this a mortal thing?"

"You know your mother asked me the very same question," he said, stroking his sideburns and looking a bit perplexed. "Perhaps the truth is that too many missions slaying souls takes a toll on your own soul."

It made sense to me. "You could tell him no," I said.

My father shook his head. "It doesn't work that way, and you know it," he answered.

"Who are you talking about?" the Queen asked.

"Oh, nobody at all," Ernesto said. "We are just musing on our family business, which is rather demanding at times."

"Father has an unusual onus," I said.

The Queen smiled. "I think we all do—no matter what our race, or if we are immortal or mortal."

"I agree with the beautiful lady," my father said. "You know, there was always something a bit unusual about my dear Sirio, I mean my dear Sirius! His mother said he would do great things. And my grandchildren are certainly a good step in that direction. But, my boy, why all these marriages? Your mother is beside herself since she did not get one invitation! Who gets married twice anyway?"

I swallowed and glanced at the Queen since marriage number three was going to happen as soon as possible. I stepped forward and embraced him tightly. "I miss you, Father," I said, walking him and the Queen up the beach away from the girls. "And as to the marriages . . . well, it's a little complicated."

"It's a lot complicated if even half of what my dear friend Hedley Edrick and your lawyer, Justice, told me is true," my father said.

"So tell me," I asked him, "how did you know the girls were mine—did Hedley Edrick tell you?"

Ernesto laughed. "No, Hedley only shares information that he feels is relevant to whatever grand scheme he has in that wonderful shiny bald head of his, and apparently telling me I was serving as the teacher for my four own granddaughters was not something he felt was important enough to tell me."

"So how did you know, Ernesto?" the Queen said.

Ernesto looked over to the girls. "Actually," he said, "when I was contacted by the Blackhearts, who I knew by reputation as bad characters, I was first inclined to say no. I kept starting to write a rejection letter to Angus, but I kept tearing it up. It was the strangest thing! I didn't even know the girls were part vampire at that point. Why would I want to train some mangy werewolves? But for some reason I had a feeling that I should teach these young ladies. I passed it off as instructing a clan with such ill manners and self-serving actions as the Blackhearts in the proper rules of combat and the honorable code of the assassin guild was an opportunity not to be missed. However, there was something else."

"What, Father? What was it?"

"Your mother, actually."

"Mother wanted you to train them?" I asked, remembering how little interest she took in the family business. "Why?"

"I don't know," Ernesto said. "I never asked. And then I got word they were traveling with a vampire Maltese. But I don't know who was more shocked when we met—me or the girls. I'd like to say it was because I was training the first vampire/werewolf half-breed assassins in history, but that was not it. The girls were stunned because Garlic, knowing you are the blood of my blood, did not so much as growl when we met. Instead, she just walked right by me into the house like she owned the place. As for me, while I was taking payment from their handlers, all I could do was stand there with my mouth wide open, staring at Contessa."

"Why? What was it about Contessa?" I asked.

Ernesto smiled and placed a hand on my shoulder. "I don't know if you know this, but I have known your mother since both of us were very young. You could say we grew up together. And Contessa is the mirror image of your mother at the same age, right down to that wondrous sparkle in her eyes. I could not believe it."

"Amazing," the Queen said. "And just like that, you knew they were your grandchildren."

"More or less, because my dear son here has not so much as dropped us a letter to let us know of his comings and goings," Ernesto said.

"I am thinking Sirius could not find a big enough piece of parchment to write about his coming things," the Queen said quickly.

My father and I exchanged a glance before bursting into tears of laughter. "She is a keeper," he said.

"You said 'more or less,' Father," I said when I recovered.

"Oh yeah, right," Ernesto added. "Of course, Hedley Edrick passed back through Sa Dragonera a week later, and confirmed the lineage of the werepires. Mere details . . ."

I realized there was something very important I needed to ask. "Father, are you the owner of that ship, and thus its de facto captain?"

"Son, you only need to see the name of that vessel to know the answer to that question," my father answered. I peered out to where the ship was moored and saw its name painted in script, *Hermosa Maria*. Of course! My mother was everything to him, and it stood to reason he would name his boat for her.

"Why did Mother not come with you?" I queried, still debating the best way to ask a small favor from the man who clearly did not approve of me being married twice, and had to live with a woman who also was not happy with what I had—or who I had—been doing.

"You know your mother," he said. "She is not one to travel, unless it is for her life's work."

"I see, right, of course," I answered. But did I understand why my mother had not come? It had been so long since I had seen her, and so much had transpired in my life. Even my talking to my father here on this beautiful beach in Sardinia was a bit surreal, and when you threw in the fact that my children—his grandchildren—were now running around the beach as near adults, it was really quite incredible. But time was growing short, and my ability to wax philosophic was ending.

"Well, I am sorry that Mother is not here," I said. "Because, Father, as the captain of the good ship *Maria*, I need you to marry me and the Queen."

My father's eyes almost bulged out of his head, and he opened his mouth, but no sound came out. The Queen stepped in. "Ernesto, we have a noble mission to embark upon," she pleaded. "One we cannot do unless we are joined in matrimony."

Ernesto recovered. "One does not get married for a mission—no matter how noble it is—one marries for love. True love! You cannot be serious!"

"Actually, he is Sirius, and he is serious," the Queen said. "And I am even more so than he is!"

"Right," I said. True love? I had been married once and not even known it. And I had been manipulated by guilt into a second go-around. At this point, a noble mission seemed to be a perfectly good reason to get married for a third time. I looked at the Queen, who flashed me that radiant smile of hers. She was absolutely gorgeous. And nice. And good with my daughters. And quite a warrior. And carrying my child. And I couldn't wait to consummate the marriage and make it official on the way to Immortal Divorce Court to get divorced.

"Father, I have to go to Hell and save Garlic," I explained, acting like what I was about to say and do made perfect sense. "She attacked Cerberus, and the portal to Hell closed, trapping her in the Underworld. She is alive. I cannot leave her there. The Queen and I will get married, go to Immortal Divorce Court, and get divorced, and in the process I will get myself found in contempt to get thrown in Hell and get Garlic back."

My father shook his head. "I will not participate in this madness. You will die." His face was red, and his eyes welled with tears, making me feel absolutely awful. "I wish I could talk to someone and see if I can put in a good word on your behalf, but the reality is that the grim one is all bones and no heart. So, I am sorry. You will have to find another way."

The Queen leaned forward and put her hand on his arm. "Ernesto, dear Ernesto," she said, "I am with Sirius's child."

Ernesto nodded, and looked at me disapprovingly, which made me stare at the sand uncomfortably. "Yes, of course you are," he said. "All right then, we go to the *Hermosa Maria*—let us hope that the third time is a charm for you, Sirius. But you are telling your daughters the truth, and, my Queen, that also goes for the child in your belly when it arrives!"

"That's a deal," the Queen said, not looking at me to see if I agreed. I didn't, but my real issue was telling my girls about the marriage they were about to witness. We weren't exactly sending the right message or showing them a great parental example. So there on the beach, I told the girls of my plan to marry the Queen, divorce her, and get sentenced to Hell to try and save Garlic.

"So you two are not marrying for love," Contessa said. "I thought as much. I thought it was because you are going to have a child together, but apparently that makes no difference, being married or not."

"No, no, no," I said. "That just happened. You should be married before you have a child."

"Why?" Mary Grace said. "You didn't do that with us or the baby sister in the Queen's belly. So what is wrong with a little 'like father like daughter?'"

It was all my father could do to not burst out laughing. He covered his mouth with one hand, remaining silent and looking to me for my answer. Any answer. I frowned—I had no answer. I felt my face growing red. They had a valid point there.

The Queen was enjoying watching me struggle, evidenced by the grin on her face. But she finally came to my rescue. "Girls," she said, "if I can have a private word with you." The Queen gathered them in a circle, and they hung on every word she said. I strained my ears to hear the conversation, but only grasped a few isolated words. At the end of the Queen's speech, they all embraced her, and I saw Contessa and the Queen each wiping away a tear as they came back to where I stood rather perplexed.

"Now, that makes sense," Adelaide said.

"Indeed," Beatrice added. "Why didn't Father just tell us that?"

The girls all hugged me, leaving my father now quite confused. He was hoping and waiting for more drama. Drama that never came. Contessa grabbed my hand. "That was so selfless and giving of you, Father," she said.

"A gift," Adelaide added.

"Destiny called and Father delivered," Beatrice said, staring up at the heavens.

"Just so romantic!" Mary Grace quipped, glancing over at Lovely with a big smile.

Romantic?

The Queen told me later that she simply explained to the girls that she had wanted a baby for centuries but was destined not to have one, until the oracle told her differently. Only one person in the entire world could give her a baby—me—their father. I sure was giving to the Queen that day, I had to admit. In fact, I gave it to her the best I could.

And now she had turned that moment of lust into a moment of, well . . . love. I was marrying one incredible woman. For a short while, yes, but she was incredible nonetheless.

So I found myself standing on the deck of the good ship *Maria* with my daughters by my side. The Queen and I were holding hands and standing in front of my father, waiting for him to pronounce the words that would make us husband and wife. The wind was blowing the Queen's golden curls ever so slightly, and the water around us was smooth as glass, marred only by the floating orcas and merfolk idling casually in the water, awaiting orders from their soon-to-be married Queen. One took out a flute carved from the jaw of a shark and began playing a delightful melody.

"What is that?" I whispered to the Queen.

"That's a flute," she said. "Surely you have those on land. Of course that one plays underwater too . . ."

"No, the song, what is that song?"

The Queen cocked an ear. "That is one of my favorites, composed by a man called Pachelbel for the wedding of a member of the famous composing Bach family. It's simply called Canon in D."

"That is the sweetest sounding cannon I have ever heard," I replied with a grin. The Queen laughed, but I wasn't kidding. If the Queen's people thought ill of her marrying what was a commoner in their mind, and a vampire to boot, there was no indication of their discontent. All of them, including Lovely, who chose to stand on the deck and not in the water with his people, gave the Queen every bit of deference she deserved. The sun caught Lovely from the side, and I admired again how chiseled his tan features were. With all the fighting, I had forgotten how he did not look at all like the mermen in the water, whose pale features were more round and full, as were the Queen's. He also was a good bit taller that his countrymen, and a whole lot more muscular. Was Lovely a true merman, or a mix of something else? The Queen caught my eye with a dazzling smile, and my thoughts of one Lovely were exchanged for that of another lovely.

My father had searched his cabin for a religious tome of any kind, but found nothing more than a few well-worn assassins' manuals. I could see by the look on his face that he was troubled by not having a script. Speaking off the cuff was never his thing. He was a man of action not words.

"Hmm, hmm," my father said. "Hear ye, hear ye, good people of this fair ship." He looked to the water at the merfolk. "And listen up good people of this beautiful sea. As the captain of this ship, I am vested with the authority to bind in holy matrimony this man and this woman." He paused, looking first to me, then the Queen, and finally to the girls for approval. Seeing nothing but happy smiles, he continued. "Who stands up for this man?" he asked.

Lovely stepped forward next to the girls. "I do, sir," he said, looking a bit uncomfortable, as Mary Grace seized the opportunity to slip her hand in his and clasp it tightly. Not as uncomfortable as I felt, however. I was powerless to admonish her at this moment, which Mary Grace certainly knew as evidenced by the giddy look on her face.

My father seemed troubled for a moment, and I soon knew why. "Who stands up for this woman?" he asked.

"I do," said Contessa, and all the other girls piped in their assent in unison.

"No, no, this won't do," my father said. "I have someone else in mind. Surprise!"

"I shall stand up for the Queen," a familiar female voice said.

I whirled to see who was walking out of the captain's quarters, and my mouth dropped open. "Mother!" I exclaimed, seeing her for the first time in centuries. Father was absolutely right. Contessa did favor her, from the heart-shaped face to the warm brown eyes and long black hair. She did not look a day over thirty and moved with the grace and deadly elegance of the master assassin she was—that is until the girls swarmed her.

"My son," she scolded. "If your father hadn't gotten word to me urgently via crystals, I would have missed yet another one of your weddings!"

"I can explain," I said sheepishly.

"Can you?"

I laughed. "Not really, but I am so glad you are here. This is my betrothed, the Queen."

The Queen and my mother assessed each other with quick glances, finally locking gazes, and I saw my father swaying back and forth from foot to foot, clearly growing more uncomfortable by the second. Then, the two women embraced to the relief of everyone on the boat and in the water. "You have amazing energy, my dear," my mother said to the Queen. "But I warn you, I can feel that the one you carry inside you will give Sirius a run for his money in terms of impetuousness! If we thought Sirius thought he knew it all, just wait for this one." She paused for a second, and reached out to touch the Queen's belly. "Hmm, she actually just might—"

"Mother," I said. "We are trying to get married over here."

"Funny you say that, Maria," the Queen said. "I can feel that too. She is Daddy's girl already."

"Hey," I said, still not sure what impetus-whatever meant, other than it was definitely not a compliment! "Can we get married some-time today?"

And we did, there on the deck of the *Maria*, with my parents and children by my side. After we kissed, there was a great cheer from the host of merfolk, and they saluted us with many great blasts of their conch shells, and we all toasted with wine from the ship's hold.

But my joy was short lived for coming into view was the ship that would take us to Immortal Divorce Court.

The Queen turned to me. "Sirius," she said. "I have been on land for so dreadfully long. I *need* to get back to the water. Can I take us to the IDC?"

I smiled. "You aren't going to make me use one of those shells, are you?"

She laughed. "We are married now, I wouldn't even think of it. Besides, we have to consummate this marriage to make it official."

"Consum-what?"

"You know," she blushed. "Like before, on Lundy Island."

"All right," I said. "Time to go!" I pretended to jump off the boat, but instead went to my girls and parents to bid them adieu for what might be the final time.

As the *Maria* sailed away, I tried without success to ignore the pain in my chest. My heart had the deepest pang in it. It was as if part of me had been torn asunder, and in a way, as the *Maria* disappeared into the horizon, it had.

The Queen put her soft lips to my cheek and kissed away a stray tear. "Are you sure you want to go through with this?"

I nodded. I wasn't, but what choice did I have? I would never forgive myself if I let Garlic languish in Hell. She had never abandoned me. Instead, when I was chained in the dungeon at Peel Castle, she did what I could not—watched over and protected my girls.

"I can swim faster than any ship," the Queen said. She handed me a satchel made from some sort of black, shiny, slippery material. "It's made from the sap of the Para tree, interlaced with some rare kelp to bind it. Put all your clothes in it and draw it closed, and everything will still be dry when we get to Greece."

I looked at the strange sack. "You aren't using this to try and get me naked, are you?"

"I don't have to try, my husband." She reached for my shirt, and pulled it over my head. I was happy to realize we were alone on a deserted beach. But something bothered me. I could not stop looking at the place where the gate to Hell had disappeared.

The Queen, her hands on the way to my breeches, followed my gaze. "Oh, Sirius," she exclaimed. "That is a bit unnerving, now that I think about it. Let's get off this godforsaken piece of earth. I know the perfect place to stop along the way."

I was naked before she stopped talking, and stuffed my clothes into the satchel, which I hung around my waist with a weapon belt from one of the mermen. I turned to see the Queen staring at my manhood.

"We had better get going before you start attracting hungry fish with that pole of yours."

"Indeed," I said, pulling her to me. "I have managed to catch you, my Queen. And I know you are quite ravenous." I kissed her long and deep, reveling in the softness of her lips and the feel of her breasts against my chest. She had changed back into a full mermaid, and curled her tail around my backside. She clasped her hands around my neck, and we shot through Sardinia's warm, crystal blue waters, heading toward Immortal Divorce Court. We swam for what seemed like two hours, surfacing briefly at the small island of Pantelleria, where I snuck ashore and liberated some grapes, and a bottle of sweet muscat wine from an unwitting seaside village. I wanted to stay and proceed with making this marriage official, but the Queen had other ideas, shushing my protests with a long kiss and many promises, and pulled me back into the sea to continue our journey.

At last, the Queen's furious swimming stopped, and if I could have broken her kiss and still breathed, I would have gasped at the incredibly clear waters we had entered. Surfacing in a white sandy cove, my eyes took in a beautiful, rocky coast. I saw a great tower, built on the highest point of the island. "What is this place?" I asked the Queen, squishing my toes into the white sand.

"It is called simply the Blue Lagoon," she said. "We are on the isle of Comino, off the coast of Malta."

"Malta?" I said. "I guess there is no more fitting a stop when trying to rescue a Maltese, even a vampire one. It looks deserted. Does anyone live in that tower?"

She shook her head and pulled me close to her in the shallows. "You may find one or two Knights of Malta. But they are more like prisoners than guards, and they never venture very far from their tower, which is why"—there was a flash of light, and those amazing shapely legs appeared—"we will be completely undisturbed in that cavern. Come on."

I didn't see a cavern, but I allowed the Queen to lead me cliffside. I presumed it was hidden by the rocks and the lay of the cliff, but as we swam closer and closer, I still saw nothing. The Queen smiled and dove down, and the crystal clear water afforded me an incredible view of her naked body as she swam. I had to remember to hold my breath since I was so distracted by her womanhood. I swam a little faster and caught up to her, reaching playfully to place a hand on one firm cheek.

The Queen spun away, kicking upward and breaking the water's surface in a hidden grotto. I surfaced right behind her, and what I saw took my breath away. The small cavern of Lundy Island where we had our first interlude was Spartan compared to this chamber. The sun shone through the crystal waters, illuminating the cavern in a warm bluish light, enhancing the light from the same sea plants as on Lundy Island. The Queen walked out of the water and shook the drops from her golden curls as she looked back at me over her shoulder. My eyes followed her fine form from head to toe, lingering on a few choice areas. My wife was simply beautiful. "Come on, husband," she said. "Do not keep your wife waiting."

I stepped onto white sand as fine and soft as sugar, and took her hand. We followed a small path, paved in gold, up to a large bedchamber hewn out of the rock, and the Queen slid under a pile of soft furs. Set in the rock were a multitude of diamonds, emeralds, and rubies that sparkled in the half-light in a rainbow of color, like little suns shining down on the furs.

The Queen's lips were upon mine, soft, warm, and ever so hungry, as her tongue darted and twisted seeking out mine. She sucked my tongue into her mouth and held it gently for a moment before releasing it, moaning slightly as she did so. I could not wait to be with her, but felt some hesitation, which she quickly sensed. "You are going to make me feel like you do not desire me, Sirius," the Queen said. "What is wrong?"

I had been with the Howler when she was with child—yes. But I did not know it, until I was right about to finish my pleasure. Now, before things had really gotten started, I had time to think. The Queen was with our child. I looked down at my manhood. Would I, could I, hurt the baby inside her? "Is it—you know—safe? I cannot hurt the baby, can I?"

The Queen laughed. "Oh, so *that* is the problem." She reached an able hand to my manhood, and stroked it to full fighting shape. "Even one as gifted as you cannot hurt the child. Nature has got it all figured out. There is no danger. Aside from what will happen to you if you do not pleasure me right now!"

As she stroked me, my worries ebbed away, and when she placed those soft lips on me, I was practically carefree. My eyes rolled back in my head, and I moaned, seeing stars, or the jewels on the wall—my pleasure so great I could not tell which nor, frankly, did I care.

"I need you inside me, husband," the Queen said, rolling onto her back and pulling me on top of her, guiding my manhood into her warmth. Now it was her time to see stars as I thrust rhythmically, bringing pleasure to the Queen again and again. She ran her hands over my chest and around to my back, pulling me down even closer to her. I kissed her neck and licked her shoulders, hearing her exhale heavily, then catch her breath once more. I sank myself as deep as I could into the wetness of her womanhood, thrusting all the while, and she moaned ever louder. "Oh, Sirius," she gasped. "I can't take any more." But she did. And she was ever so happy about it. For the briefest of time, I wondered how long her tail would be twitching this time. By the sound of her pleasure, we might have to wait awhile before we ventured out of the cavern. And that was completely all right with me. She climaxed again, as I did, and I lay inside her, our heads close together. As I drifted into blissful unconsciousness, I sensed the presence of another in the equation—the new essence of our unborn daughter reaching out to me.

When we awoke the next day, the Queen wanted to consummate our marriage again and again. As her husband, I was so very willing, and took her in the water, on the sand, and against the jeweled rocks. The cavern was well stocked with foodstuffs and wine, and we idled in the warm, crystal waters of the grotto between consummations, occasionally peering out to the Blue Lagoon. We did not speak at all of the next leg of our journey, instead pretending the cavern and lagoon were the extent of our world. Finally, a day or so later, we were swimming under the stars and looking up at the full moon and made eye contact of a different sort. I sighed, sensing our blissful *luna de miel* was over, and that night we silently agreed that the next day we would continue on to Immortal Divorce Court.

Before we started on the last leg of the trip to the coast of Greece and the IDC, the Queen proffered a breathing shell from her pouch, but I declined. I realized that it was more for her than me, as she was trying to get into the mindset of divorcing me, and traveling underwater, locked lip to lip and body to body, was certainly not going to do that. But if these were to be the last times I locked lips with this incredible creature, I wanted it to last as long as possible and insisted we travel underwater as we always had—together. And, just maybe, together was the key word here after all . . .

"Look, I have an idea," I said. "Why don't we just get remarried after I go to Hell and rescue Garlic?" I said. "Don't you want to make this work?"

"I agreed to marry you, and divorce you, and now you want me to marry you again?" the Queen said. "We didn't talk about that—it's much more complicated."

"Complicated, how?" I pressed. "Do you feel this too?"

"Yes, and that is the problem," she answered.

"Fine," I said, not feeling fine at all. "Let us see if an underwater kiss is the solution."

The Queen merely shrugged and put the shell back in the pouch, but either the water was growing colder, or her lips were not as warm and inviting as they had been. Either way, I arrived on the beach in Greece, fairly shuddering, and we both dressed quickly and apart, neither stealing a glance at the other.

The last time I had traveled to Immortal Divorce Court, I had done so hidden in a cask of wine. Maybe it was always this way, but there seemed to be an unusual amount of foot traffic leaving the IDC village as we came closer. Normally, fellow travelers would bid each other welcome and share information, or even sustenance. But it was like the Queen and I were pariahs, as all manner of different immortals shuffled by, afraid to make eye contact with us or even acknowledge we were there. Yes, this was very strange indeed.

Now, as we came ever closer to the gates of the village where the Immortal Divorce Court courthouse lay, I could see the ever-present black cloud that marked the Gates of Hell. Every step was a step closer to saving Garlic I convinced myself, in spite of the rumbles that grew louder as I approached. The Lord of the Underworld was laughing at my folly in bearding the demonic lion in his den of lies. High up on a bluff I spotted a hellhound, then another, and realized a whole pack of them was trailing behind us, slowly drawing the noose of the netherworld ever tighter. There would be no turning back. The Queen stood strong and brave—the warrior once again. "You would think those mangy curs would have had enough of you," she said. "Particularly after the last beating you gave them."

I nodded. "This close to their master, they have no fear of mortal or immortal beings." I saw the faerie guards fixated nervously on the hellhounds, wondering if they were going to attack, or what their purpose was for being outside of Hell. The faeries ignored us completely as we walked through the gate, which they slammed shut behind us, their eyes still on the hellhounds who now chose to lie down in front of the gates leading into the IDC. Hell would have quite the fury for those that now dared try to leave the village of Immortal Divorce Court. And court was about to close for business for a little while, courtesy of this demon pack of mutts from the Underworld.

The Queen looked back at the gate and saw the faeries pushing people trying to leave the IDC back into the village. One little elf got through the throng of immortal humanity and made a run for it, and was rewarded by a hellhound chomping down on his head. He ran screaming back to the village, absent his hat, the majority of his long flaxen hair, and with all the contents of his bowels now filling his breeches. "I guess we aren't going to have to wait very long to do this," she said. "Once the IDC and this village figure out that we are the reason for this siege, we will become very, very unpopular."

I felt unfriendly eyes upon us and made sure the Blade of Truth was in full view. I bared my fangs at one all too curious satyr, who backed away collapsing in a heap. "S-s-s-s-irius," he sputtered, trying to get his wobbly legs underneath him. "What did you do that for?"

"Cabernet!" I exclaimed. "I did not know it was you. So sorry! I thought you were going to attack me and my wife."

I saw the Queen taking stock of Cabernet's concave chest, spindly legs, and flea-infested fur. She picked his glasses up off the ground, brushed them off, and placed them back on his face. "Yes, my dear husband," she smirked. "He is clearly a threat."

Cabernet reached for a flask in his pack, and his shaky hands spilled half the wine down his chest, where it sopped into the fur on his flanks and sent a cloud of fleas into the air, trying to escape death by vino. "Whew," he bleated. "No one dares attack you while you carry that sacred sword," he said. "And besides, whatever business you have here they want done, so both you and those confounded hellhounds can leave. So, pray tell, other than scaring an old goat like me, may I ask why you are here?"

"My husband wants to divorce me," said the Queen, folding her arms across her chest, and playing, I think, the role of the jilted spouse.

Cabernet adjusted his glasses once, then again peered at the Queen, who looked ever like a jewel in the sun. "Now why would he want to do something like that?" Cabernet said. "Sirius, are you sure about this? She seems nice enough. And, well, after your last two, I mean this young lady is quite, and may I repeat *quite* the improvement."

"It's . . ." I started, ". . . complicated, Cabernet."

"Complicated, my left hoof," the satyr said. "You'd be an imbecile to divorce as fine a filly as this. No offense to you, my lady."

"None taken," said the Queen with a wry smile. "Cabernet," she said. "It gets worse. He is divorcing me because of a dog. Can you believe that?"

I glared at the Queen, who could barely contain her mirth at my discomfort. Her somber mood had apparently passed, at least for the moment. I turned to find Cabernet staring at me through his spectacles, his eyes as wide open as his mouth.

"So the rumors are true," he gasped. "The Lord of the Underworld called in his mark on you, and you somehow defeated his host of hellions!"

"Yes," I said, "I did, but certainly not alone. I only prevailed with the help of the Queen and her people, my daughters, and of course, the most valiant vampire Maltese, Garlic. In the final battle, Cerberus was driven back into the Underworld, but Garlic was trapped there when the gate closed."

Cabernet shook his head sadly. "So you are going to try and go get her," he said. "You really are going right at him. Oh my, you are going to get found in contempt, aren't you?"

"Yes," I said, looking around and trying to quiet his now frantic bleating. "Come on now, people are beginning to stare at us—let's move."

"You really are an imbecile, Sirius," Cabernet said.

I looked at the Queen, who returned my gaze so warmly it made my heart hurt. "I know, Cabernet, I know."

On the way to the courthouse, I considered stopping by Justice's office for advice, but I was torn about whether he would help me in this charade, and I also wondered what he could do to help me get found in contempt, since his job was to help me stay *out* of contempt. My decision was made for me when I saw his office was tightly shuttered. "Where is Justice?" I asked Cabernet.

"Been on holiday since your last case," Cabernet replied. "But you know he will come back for you for the right price."

"I know," I answered, looking at the Queen, "but I think we can get me where I need to go without his help this time." I mused that it was certainly better for the Queen not to find out I was intimately familiar with Knowledge and Wisdom. I would have to rely on my own smarts, certainly a daunting prospect when the Head Magistrate was going to be involved.

As we walked, my nose was assaulted with the stench of brimstone, the cologne of the netherworld and a personal reminder that the Lord of the Underworld was nearby and waiting for me. Behind the courthouse, the demons were not wailing but were strangely silent in anticipation, or in their preparation for what dastardly deeds they had planned for me. But Hell's flames shot ever so high in the air, crackling fiercely as they surged up from deep below. I looked to the left of the courthouse and saw the now familiar site of the Golden Rule inn. The picture of the scales of justice with gold weighing equally on both sides was especially meaningful now since I had come out on both sides of the win ledger in my visits to the court. And how much gold I had did not seem to make a bit of difference in the outcome. "He who has the gold makes the rule" was the inn's slogan, but in my experience so far, the Head Magistrate was the ruler, and losing my gold was the rule.

"The clerk's office is closed for lunch," Cabernet said, scratching his ear with one grimy finger. "That is where you will need to go to file for divorce. So come on, and I will serve you a drink. I think I have some year-old port in there somewhere." I puffed out my chest and motioned the Queen to stand behind me as I pulled the heavy oaken door open and entered the establishment. I stood ready to challenge any number of nefarious creatures that I remembered populating the inn. But to my great surprise, the inn's many tables were completely empty. There was no smoke choking the room with its stench of clove and tobacco, no challenging glares from an immortal eager to try his hand with me. There was simply silence.

"Nice place you got here," said the Queen, her voice echoing off the hardwood floor as she ran a finger across one sparkling-clean table. "Is everyone on holiday?"

Cabernet nodded knowingly. "Actually, word that Sirius Sinister was coming to challenge Hades got out, and the lucky ones fled the village before the hellhounds sealed it off."

I sat down on a barstool, and Cabernet took his familiar spot behind the bar. "Now *that* explains the great exodus we saw as we approached the village," I exclaimed. "They were leaving because of us."

"Us?" the Queen said playfully. "You mean because of you, don't you?"

I knew she was trying to keep the mood light, which I appreciated. The Queen was so thoughtful in every way, even when I was in the process of divorcing her. As Cabernet poured us a couple of drinks, I let my eyes fall upon the Queen, taking in her golden hair and soft lips, and allowing myself to drift back to the idyll of the Blue Lagoon. It seemed so long ago. Did all that amazingness really happen? She met my gaze and smiled as we raised our glasses. It did happen. "To a proper divorce," the Queen said. I drank quickly, the sweet wine somehow tasting sour on my tongue, and did not repeat her toast.

I was still transfixed by my memories of the Blue Lagoon when the door to the Golden Rule was kicked open. "Sirius Sinister," a deep voice boomed. "You need to come with us."

"What do you want of me? Am I under arrest?"

There was much confusion among the guardsmen, as clearly I was not, and they had not had any experience in asking someone to come with them nicely. "No, you are not," their gruff sergeant admitted, biting his lip and flexing his massive chest muscles up and down to quell his chagrin.

"Well, then," I said, motioning to a nearby empty table. "Have a seat, and Cabernet will pour you a drink on the house. I will go with you. But not until the Queen and I are done with our wine."

The Queen and I chatted easily with our new friends, who indeed sat as Cabernet poured them all a glass of wine. Before the soldiers drank, they looked to their sergeant for approval, and he grunted his assent. When Cabernet handed him a glass, the sergeant merely stood with his arms folded across his chest, glaring at Cabernet, like the satyr had just peed on his foot. Nonplussed, Cabernet went back behind the bar. "I'll take his," I said holding up a hand to show Cabernet my now empty glass. I studied the soldiers keenly, and I could just about hear the rapid heartbeats in their chests. Odd, for these men were trained professionals, and I had recognized a few of them from the escort that took me to Hell last time. I know they were not afraid of me. So what then?

"Are you through with your wine, Mr. Sinister, sir?" one soldier asked, a bead of sweat trickling down his temple, drawing my eye to the frantic beat throbbing ever so lightly there. "Would you be ever so kind to accompany us now, sir?"

"So now it's Mr. Sinister?" the Queen added, her interest now clearly piqued. "Why are you giving him the sudden courtesy? And you can ask nicely all you want, but you still have not stated your intentions. What do you want with my husband?" The polite soldier withered under her steely blue gaze, opening his mouth and looking like a gutted trout gasping for life, but no words came out. He looked to his sergeant, who had nixed any further attempt at conversation with an evil leer.

"Indeed," I said. "What is your hurry? We are the ones getting divorced here. Don't rush us. We might just change our minds and stay married, right, darling?"

"Quite," the Queen replied. "Perhaps we should go on honeymoon again so I may enjoy all your husbandly talents?"

"So, now you want to stay married too?" I asked.

"Going on honeymoon and enjoying your talents are not the same thing as staying married," the Queen said. "Complicated, remember?" Right.

I was beginning to think the soldier was a bit of a prude by the look of sheer terror on his face, but my attention was soon distracted by the sound of a tremendous peal of thunder in the distance. I did not remember seeing any storm clouds outside, just the dark cloud over Hell. Clearly, we were annoying the Lord of the Underworld with our idle banter so close to his lair. I really could not wait to tell him where he could go, but the reality was he was already there.

A herald came running in seeking out the sergeant. "Sergeant, the earth has split outside our gate, and a great wall of fire has sprung out of it and is headed toward the city!"

I looked to the Queen as the soldiers emptied out of the inn at a sprint. "My dear," I said, "it appears someone is sending us a message to get on with it."

"And by someone, you are referring to a deity that is big, evil, and looking for revenge, perhaps?"

I nodded. The Queen finished her wine. "Let's get this over with," she said, her gaze and countenance playful no longer. "Cabernet, take us to the clerk's office."

But Cabernet did not have to escort us. When we exited the inn, I looked back toward the gate, and indeed in the distance I saw a wall of demonic fire easily twice the height of the kraken, and hissing evilly as tendrils of flames lashed the air. The streets were deserted save for a faerie battle brigade in full riot gear, wearing the masks they had worn to escort me to Hell last time. They accompanied us up to the IDC courthouse.

I stopped for a moment and took two steps away from the building and saw the flames grow even taller and more menacing, their heat catching the top of the gate on fire, and sending the faerie guardsmen in a frantic fight to extinguish them with buckets drawn from the well and hastily thrown dirt. I realized that Hades wanted the Queen and me to get divorced, because he wanted me to suffer before I came down to his turf to really, really suffer. I was thinking that divorcing the Queen felt a whole lot worse than godly torture. But it seemed Hades was going to wreak a great conflagration upon all things Immortal Divorce Court, and us, if we did not go through with it.

"Is that how you think it is going to be?" I yelled in the direction of the wall of fire. The only thing I had ever read, or more accurately, looked at, in Justice's office was an old book on Latin insults. So it only seemed fitting, since Justice was on holiday, to extend my hand toward the fire wall and give Hades the old *digitus impudicus*. I saw the flames shoot even higher as I turned back toward the courthouse and did not hide the wide smile on my face.

When we entered, and an exasperated elf clad in gold-trimmed robes appeared in my path.

"I am Donigus Mithos, clerk of the court," he said. "Follow me, there is not much time."

I looked to the Queen, who merely shrugged. I could not help but try and read her body language. She had not seemed disturbed by the giant wall of fire threatening to immolate the village, and did not even crack a smile when I waved at Hades, using only one of my fingers. The look in her eyes was bereft of any verve, anger, or passion. The Queen simply was numb.

Donigus did not take us to the clerk's office, where I supposed we would have had to file the divorce paperwork. Instead, he led us straight into the courtroom, whose doors were wide open and absent any litigants on their now eerily smooth black surface. Head Magistrate Dough sat on the bench, absent her robe and clad in a simple gray tunic, unassisted by her deputies or any court personnel.

The Head Magistrate looked up at me and shook her head. "Sinister," she said, "only you could single-handedly threaten the very existence of something with the storied history of Immortal Divorce Court. Was it just too easy to let the Lord of the Underworld exact his painful and eternal torment upon you?"

"Let the record show that I never actually did anything to him." I puffed out my chest with pride that I almost sounded like a real attorney. "We are on the record, aren't we? I have always wanted to say that—"

"Spare me your feeble attempt at jurisprudence," the Head Magistrate snapped, looking around the courtroom warily. I saw that her eyes were red with stress, and her hair did not look like it had seen a comb in days. The hand, or more accurately, the fist of the Lord of the Underworld lay heavy upon her. "We are not even on the record, because all my reporters are either in hiding, or took a sudden vacation before you arrived and those blasted hellhounds shut down the village."

I pulled out a chair for the Queen at one of the tables, and we sat down. We looked to Donigus, and then back to the Head Magistrate, but neither one of them spoke to us. Instead they were shuffling through paperwork at the Head Magistrate's bench. The Head Magistrate peered down at the Queen. "Are you the wife of Sirius Sinister?"

"Yes," the Queen said, "I am."

The Head Magistrate nodded. "Just had to be sure, because you never know with Sinister. Are you with his child? You are, aren't you?"

The Queen flushed ever so slightly. "Yes, I am, so what of it?"

The Head Magistrate winced as a great explosion sounded from outside. "Listen," she said. "We really don't have time for the usual legal mumbo jumbo. You divorce him. You are with his child. You get gold. Simple. Got it?"

"I want nothing from Sirius," the Queen said. "Least of all his gold."

"Oh, you still must have water in your ears, sweetheart," the Head Magistrate grated. What had happened to the honor and decorum of the Head Magistrate I knew so well? Was the harpy in front of us who she really was when there was no court reporter to record her every word and action? "No matter." The Head Magistrate continued scribbling quickly. "Have you chosen a name for your little merpire?"

"I have," said the Queen. "Her name is Maria."

I whipped my head around and stared at the Queen. I could not believe my ears. "Maria?" I said. "You want to call her Maria?"

"Yes," the Queen said. "I thought we would name her after your mother, who is quite an impressive lady, and thus, I would like to honor her."

I felt a tear come to my eye and reached over and pulled the Queen to me. "Thank you," I said. "When will Maria arrive?"

The Queen held the embrace for a moment before she spoke. "Normally I would say in about a year," she said. "But I do not know what effect your seed will have on her growth. I have only known of one other woman of my race who has birthed issue with another outside our kind. It is considered the ultimate taboo."

"Well, an entire contingent of your soldiers just saw you marry me not so long ago. What did they think we were going to do when we left—pick seaweed together?"

"That is my royal guard, loyal to me to the death—which could be their fate when Maria is born. They will say nothing about our marriage and coupling, but if the high council ever sees that this child is not born of our race, they will be summarily executed for treason to our race."

"But you are the Queen, so you can stop the executions, right? Right?"

The Queen paused, taking a deep breath. "When Maria is born, and if the high council sees she is not full-blooded merfolk, I would have to abdicate my throne. I would be Queen no more."

"So that is what you meant by complicated," I replied. "That is why you can't stay married to me, or remarry me, isn't it?"

The Queen put her finger to my lips. "I knew the price of this child could be my throne, Sirius. And when I told my royal guard of the oracle's prophecy, they insisted on accompanying me, knowing the consequences would be their death if we found you, and I was able to indeed have a child with you. But it is a choice I would make again and again every single time. Maria has to be born into this world—I am sure of it!"

"And would the royal guard make that same choice with their lives in the balance?"

She grimaced. "If they breach their duty to the Queen, and thus lose their honor, they are already dead in their minds. There was no choice for them."

"If you were to lose power, who would rule your kingdom?"

The Queen grimaced. "A man named Orcinus, and that can't happen, for the lives of my people, and those on land, would surely be forfeit."

"He's that bad?"

"Yes, but I will figure out how to keep my pregnancy, and then Maria, hidden from him," she said. "Assuming you are alive after this insanity, I will also find a way for you to see her."

"What if I want to see you too?"

"Ahem!" The Head Magistrate groaned audibly. "It is very sweet and ever so touching for you two to spout such tender platitudes to one another here in Immortal Divorce Court! I would call the court artist to paint a portrait of you if he hadn't left for Rome. But instead, let me repeat those three little words that have so much power once again! Immortal Divorce Court," she said. "Do you people want to get divorced, or not?"

I did not take my eyes off the Queen. "I do not," I said. "There has to be another way."

There was a tremendous crash from outside the courtroom, followed by a host of terrified screams. "The hellhounds have breached the gate!" yelled the sergeant of the guard. "We cannot hold them off for very long. You must flee, Head Magistrate!"

"Even the Lord of the Underworld cannot interrupt Immortal Divorce Court when it is in session, so I am not fleeing," the Head Magistrate said. A blast of flame blew the doors of the courtroom open, knocking the sergeant to the ground. He bounced up with a growl, patting out a bit of flame on his shoulder, ignoring the fact that his armor was still smoldering. "But I guess he can try to destroy it altogether, come on, Sirius Sinister, lives are at stake here!" The Head Magistrate pulled a dagger with a gavel handle from beneath her tunic and placed it on the bench. "Make a blasted decision before we all die!"

The Queen had remained silent in the chaos, almost calm. "It can't work out between us, Sirius," she said. "You are land. I am water. If we stay married, my people will suffer at the hands of Orcinus. If we divorce, I can have our child and rule over my people with the protection of the royal guard. The high council will never know of Maria's true lineage."

"You are the queen. What can they do about it if they did find out?"

"Remember that one woman I told you about who had a child of mixed race?"

"Yes, what of her?"

"No one knew that she was with child. She was just what you would call a scullery maid. When she gave birth, the midwives screamed in horror at what she had birthed. I came running and saw an angelic little cherubim. The high council saw outrage and ordered her and the baby executed according to our laws. She then confessed to the council that she had been taken against her will by an evil, dark monster of the land. I was able to have her merely exiled, and convinced the high council to let me raise the child in the royal house to hide our people's shame. They agreed on one condition. If the child took on his father's pedigree and grew into a monster, I would kill him. You can imagine their collective anguish as he grew bigger and bigger. Luckily his facial features favor his mother, or he would be dead a hundred times over!"

"But, he is no monster, is he? It's Lovely," I said. "He is half troll, isn't he? His father was no evil, dark monster. His father is Oliver von Cliffingham!"

The Queen's eyes grew wide. "Yes," she exclaimed. "Yes, he is! But how could you know that?"

"Because Oliver told me he fell in love with a mermaid years ago. And we both know that Oliver did not rape her," I said. "He is anything but evil. Maybe cranky once in a while is the worst you will get with him! He does not know he has a son, does he?"

"No, she was forbidden to tell him, or to ever see him again."

"But she was exiled, how would they know?"

The Queen looked me in the eyes, and I could feel her pain. "Did I say exiled? Uh, it is probably more accurate to say she is imprisoned."

Imprisoned? That was news to pass on to my favorite wine-making troll. "But he loved her and she loved him. Doesn't that count for something with your high council and the ways of your people?"

The Queen sighed deeply. "No, I am afraid not. But scandal was avoided. The honor of our people remained intact. To this day, no one speaks of it. Well, aside from the whispers when Lovely passes. He pretends not to hear, but even though you cannot see it in his face, I know it pains him."

"His mental strength is a gift from his father."

The Queen turned away from me. "So you see, if we stay married, you, Maria, and I would be a living, air-breathing insult to our people's ways."

"Your ways are old and do not fit in the world today," I said, coming close to her again.

"Maybe that is true. Yet the high council would seek to have you killed."

"Well, at this point I guess they can stand in line after Hades. You could live on land with me," I pleaded, ignoring the howl of the oncoming hellhounds.

"No more than you could live in the water," the Queen said. "Sirius, even now I yearn for the ocean. I would wither and die."

"My Queen," I said, holding her hand and looking into those deep blue eyes for what I feared was the last time. "Is there no other way?"

The Queen did not respond, but began sobbing, shaking her head back and forth. Outside in the hallway, we could hear the faerie legion battling the hellhounds valiantly, but losing a man by the minute. In the courtroom, Hades's voice echoed, "I make the choices for you."

"No," I said, looking all around. "No, you don't. You aren't coming for me, Hades—it is I that is coming for you!"

The Immortal Divorce Court was now on fire, and smoke billowed into the courtroom. A terrified clerk who had been hiding under the Head Magistrate's bench ran screaming down the aisle and was snapped up in one crunchy bite by a hellhound as he reached the door. I put my left hand on the Queen's belly and closed my eyes, sending love to my unborn child. "Until we meet again, sweet Maria," I said. I kissed the Queen softly on the lips and wiped a tear from her cheek with my thumb. "Goodbye, my Queen. Do not cry for me for we shall meet again. Promise that you will tell Maria about me, and that you will make sure she knows her sisters."

"I promise," said the Queen. "Do it now, Sirius Sinister! Now!"

Holding the Blade of Truth high in the air with my right hand, I turned to the Head Magistrate. "Make it happen, Your Honor."

"Can you breathe water?" the Head Magistrate asked me.

"I cannot," I answered.

The Head Magistrate ducked down behind her bench as the courtroom doors buckled and collapsed, leaving just the sergeant between us and more hellhounds than I could count. "All right, all right," the Head Magistrate shouted to the Lord of the Underworld. "I am getting to it. You had better not get remarried and divorced this millennium, Hades! Now then, Sirius Sinister, I grant you this divorce on the grounds of irreconcilable differences."

"Thank you, Your Honor," I said, taking a spot next to the sergeant. "This fight is mine," I said to him. "You do not have to stand with me."

"Nonsense," the sergeant said. "I am just doing my job."

"And I'm going to do mine," the Head Magistrate said. "Sirius Sinister, for the destruction of this courtroom, courthouse, village, and immeasurable loss of life and property, I hereby find you in contempt and sentence you to one hundred years in the tenth level of Hell."

The hellhounds suddenly stopped their incessant baying and sat on their haunches quietly. The steady stream of smoke stopped billowing into the courtroom and dissipated. I nodded solemnly, and looked to the Queen for one final, torturous time. We locked eyes, and though I was headed to certain doom, I did so with my head held high.

I bared my fangs at the hellhounds. I was not afraid of their master, and buoyed with the love of my child, I had a feeling the Lord of the Underworld knew that.

As the sergeant and I walked out of the courtroom, demonic fires that a moment before had been gnawing hungrily at the floor and walls just faded away into nothingness. Indeed, by the time we exited the courthouse, even the gates to Immortal Divorce Court had somehow managed to reposition themselves on the wall. But that was not the way we were going.

The sergeant looked to the back gate and grabbed his mask, pulling it down over his face as we walked in that direction. He looked around to see if any of the other faerie guardsmen were around to join him, and saw none. "I guess it is just me," he said.

"You do not have to do this," I said, stopping so suddenly that a hellhound nearly walked into me. I bared my fangs at it and brandished the Blade of Truth, sending the beast skittering out of reach. "He knows I am coming, and it's not like I can go anywhere else, what with these demonic tail draggers following me."

The sergeant drew his own blade. "I will escort you, Sirius Sinister, because you are doing the honorable thing. That is true courage. I heard what you said to your unborn child. That is true love." He clasped my arm. "I am called Honeysuckle, and should you survive this journey, you are welcome in the faerie guardhouse any time."

"Thanks, Honeysuckle," I said. "I will do the best I can to take you up on that offer."

But as we came through the back gate of the IDC, there lay the Gates to Hell, and all the disembodied skulls that made up the gate were not screaming, crying, yelling, or anything of the sort. Every single skull was laughing at me in perfectly synchronized maniacal laughter.

But this was no joke.

CHAPTER 17

The gate creaked open, and I coughed heavily as the stink of brimstone and clouds of smoke assaulted my lungs. I gladly took the mask proffered by Honeysuckle, and instantly could breathe a whole lot easier. I wondered if he had anything that was a little more fireproof—like tenth level of Hell fireproof, ideally. Once past the gate, the smoke faded away, and I found myself on the same accursed granite spit leading deeper into Hell. Ah, Limbo, I thought. Desolate, hot, and eerily abandoned—lost souls, anybody, lost souls?

Suddenly, out from behind a rock jumped a familiar creature, but while last time all his organs dotted the outside of his skin like tattoos, this time they were all piled on top of his head, except for his nose and eyeballs, which were located where his private parts should have been hanging. Then I looked to his head and saw his private parts sticking out from its left side. "Nice look, you poor excuse for a demon!" I said, rolling my eyes.

"I am a troll," it screamed. "I will crush your bones and suck the marrow out of them for breakfast. Flee, lost souls, flee!"

Honeysuckle grimaced and swung his sword at the creature's head, and it backpedaled more quickly than his spindly legs would allow, and he collapsed in a heap of legs and bouncing organs. "Whoa, whoa," shouted the creature. "Are you trying to kill me?"

"Yes, that is the general idea," said Honeysuckle. "I most assuredly am. I am not a lost soul. I am one angry faerie guardsman."

"But I am a troll," it said. "Why are you not running, screaming in fear to pound your fists hopelessly against the Gates of Hell, and begging for mercy?"

I sighed. Not this guy again. "You are not a troll."

"I am too."

"Listen, I know trolls," I said. "They like fine wine not bones."

"I like wine."

I grimaced as he rose to his feet, his manhood smacking against the side of his cranium. "My dear phallus head," I said, "a troll has his manhood in his pants, not beating against the side of his brain. Or is your brain in your ass again?"

Honeysuckle raised his mask and laughed out loud. The creature thrust out his pelvis aiming his glassy, bloodshot eyes in Honeysuckle's direction so he could see who was laughing at him. "Oh," he said. "You are with the IDC. Where are the rest of your kind?"

"It's just me," Honeysuckle said. "The rest of us are wounded, or perhaps in the first level of Hell. It is no matter to you, so stand aside while I escort Sirius Sinister properly to the first gate of Hell."

The creature screamed and retreated, falling over awkwardly and slowly, painfully, rolling out of sight. "It is Sirius Sinister. He comes. Master, he comes!" it shrieked at the top of its lungs, wherever they were hidden.

Behind us on the spit of granite, maintaining proper following distance, was a line of hellhounds. They began howling in anticipation of my entrance to Hell. "I think he has already figured that out, my good assface," I called. "But thanks, and carry on the good work!"

Honeysuckle and I walked on without saying a word, our momentary joy quickly sapped by the heat that grew more oppressive with every step. I ignored the sweat that dropped from my brow and kept my head down as I scanned the desolate landscape, occasionally kicking an unidentified skull off the granite spit. Once, I stopped to see if I could hear one particularly large skull land below, but I heard nothing. Limbo was appropriately a bottomless pit.

Before I knew it, Honeysuckle and I came to the moving mass of black tar that was the gate to the first level of Hell. But this time there were no disembodied limbs trying to poke through, just a single word embossed on it in the King's English. "Fear," said Honeysuckle. "No doubt of the message being sent to you there, my friend."

"Never one for making you guess is the Lord of the Underworld," I said. "Your journey ends here, yes?"

"Indeed," said Honeysuckle. "Best of luck, and just remember you are a man who has known love, and fear cannot beat that."

I nodded. "Until we meet again." I clasped his hand warmly. *You don't know fear,* Hades shouted, fully inside my head now. *But you are about to.* A huge mouth formed in the center of the gate, opening wide to reveal huge fangs and a forked flickering tongue. *Come to me.*

I drew my sword, which now shone with a bright white light, and advanced on the gate. I thought of all my girls and the love I felt for them in my heart. There was nothing I had not successfully faced in my life. Oh, and I had two ex-wives that were completely evil. The Lord of the Underworld was a man, and his marriage had not worked out so well, so surely we could commiserate over some common ground, right? I shrugged my shoulders and stepped on the flickering tongue, which became solid stone. Of course, Hades would have probably been a little more receptive to me, but for that little issue with Persephone. What man wouldn't have done that? Like Hades hadn't sowed his godly oats? I had a feeling I would not be seeing unicorns and rainbows when I passed through the gate this time!

A massive blast of heat greeted me as I came through the gate and entered the first level of Hell. I stood on a narrow stone bridge that stretched out into oblivion as a molten river of fire raged and hissed far below. Ahead in the distance was the gate to the second level, and unless my eyes deceived me, it appeared to be moving closer to me. Creatures that looked to be a mad cross of vulture and bat swooped about on the currents of fire-blasted air, adding their own heat to it with blasts of flame shooting out from their toothed jaws as they shrieked, scanning all the while for prey. One bird-bat thing swooped in close to me in challenge, and I lopped off its right wing, sending a message to the others, and smiled as it careened down toward the fiery river, its left wing still flapping furiously. Its brethren dove after it, catching it in midair, and ripping it to shreds in a viciously coordinated concert of talons and teeth. But they bothered me no more, keeping their distance, content to wait for someone or something to even the odds.

They didn't have to wait long. As I neared the second gate, I heard a bloodcurdling scream of rage, and bursting through the black tar of the first gate was a golden dragon, heading straight for me. The second gate was close now, and I did not want to tangle with the dragon on the bridge, as it would assuredly send me to my doom below. I sprinted toward the second gate, which before my eyes changed from hard, cold, black iron into countless scuttling spiders each the size of a small dog—a small dog with eight sharp pinchers and glowing green venom dripping from its fangs. I skidded to a sudden halt, and for a brief moment knew the fear that Angus Blackheart had felt. I was caught on the bridge between death by dragoncide or arachnacide. *You could always jump and save us the trouble,* the voice in my head snickered.

"Not going to happen," I answered. "This little quandary is nothing to me. Did you forget about the ex-wives? Bloodsucker Number One makes that dragon look like a sweet little poodle!" I switched the Blade of Truth back and forth in my hands as the dragon and spiders rushed toward me. I positioned myself facing the spiders, who I judged would get to me a few moments before the dragon. I racked my brain for a grand plan of escape. But I had nothing.

Nothing, that is, until I saw that reflected in my enchanted blade was not a hard charging dragon. I turned so I could see the spiders approaching in the blade, and my suspicion about this level of Hell was confirmed. I whirled on my heel and raced toward the dragon, ignoring the heat of its fire building for one fatal blast. Smoke curled from its nostrils, and I swore I could smell carrion on its breath. It reared back its claws, rending the air beside me, and I dodged inside its grasp, and swung my sword in a mighty arc, ripping through wood, cloth, and paper, all of which dropped to the bridge with a clatter. I walked back to the second gate, casually stepping on the little black beans in my path, quite enjoying the crunch they made underneath my boots.

The gate to the second level was cold, hard, black iron once more, and as I approached it, the gate swung open, and out stepped a hooded figure bent forward so I could not see its face. I raised my sword cautiously and quickly took stock of my opponent. Skinny and weaponless—this surely was not the Lord of the Underworld. The cowl flipped back and staring at me with a goofy smile on his face was the Bogeyman himself.

"Well, well," I said, sheathing my sword exuberantly. "If I don't see standing before me, it is the one and only Lord Warlock Jova of Hopkinshire."

Jova laughed as we clasped hands. "I guess you are always going to be the one and only Sirius Sinister," he said. "Actually, that is a pretty fitting name, considering our venue at the moment."

"That begs the question," I said. "What are you doing in Hell? You and Cornelia didn't get divorced, did you? You weren't found in contempt?"

Jova's eyes went wide with real horror, since being divorced from Cornelia would clearly be hell for him. "No, no," he exclaimed. "It is nothing of the sort. I am here doing a study on fear. And you were the first one to pass the test—with a little help from that blade of yours."

I grabbed him by the throat and squeezed—perhaps a little harder than one should squeeze their friend's throat—snarling, "You knew it was me out there battling your little creations on the bridge, and yet you still continued your little game?"

"No, no, no . . ." Jova sputtered. "I heard the squawk of those bat-vulture things. That is the signal that someone is coming, and it is time to test their fear response. I didn't know it was you, I swear!"

"So you just hide like a little cowardly bogeyman and wait for them to fall off the bridge?"

Jova coughed, either uncomfortably from my grip, or his con-science was goading him. "I am so focused on projecting a realistic image," he said, "that I do not even think about who is on the bridge. Not all of them have fallen. Some have given in to their fear, you know."

"And that makes me feel better how?" I asked.

"I am sorry," he said.

"Apology accepted," I said, smacking him on the back of his head. I nodded and released him from my grip, my anger slowly ebbing. "You have gotten even better at being the Bogeyman since Port Royal," I said. "Even though the Blade of Truth tipped me off as to your ruse, I swear I could actually smell the stench of carrion about that dragon."

"That really was the smell of carrion," Jova said, shrugging sheep-ishly. "This is Hell, Sirius, so it is actually hard to find material that doesn't smell like carrion, or dung, if you know what I mean."

"How did you manage to get your little fear study all set up anyway?"

Jova smiled. "Good question," he answered. "Justice helped me set it up. And I have to say, the Lord of the Underworld was quite receptive. Thought it was a great idea! You know, he is really not such a bad guy."

"He tortures souls for eternity."

"I mean besides that!" Jova said. "We all have a job to do. You kill people for a living. Your dad and the Grim Reaper are on a first-name basis. Are you really being judgmental?"

He did have a point. I looked back at the bridge. "What happened to the ones that came before me?"

Jova shrugged uncomfortably. "Sirius," he said, "we are in Hell. It is not like we are talking about choirboys coming through here, you know what I'm saying?"

"None of them were from Immortal Divorce Court, were they?" I asked. "Can't say they mete out justice there so fairly all the time . . ."

"No," Jova answered. "Even the Lord of the Underworld was okay with keeping them out of my experiment. He figured they had all suffered enough at the hands of their ex-wives—present company excluded, of course."

"Of course," I said wryly. "Have you seen Garlic?"

Jova nodded and motioned me toward the gate. "And it's time you did as well," he said. "You have got to end this with the Lord of the Underworld. And I am going to arrange a meeting between you two. Does that sound good? " He saw the look of concern on my face. "Considering you are in his territory, and it's about to get a whole lot, shall we say, warmer, it is the only choice you have."

I told you I make the choices for you, the voice in my head said. I nodded grimly. This time the Lord of the Underworld was absolutely correct.

Through the gate we passed and entered the second level of Hell, and I braced for more heat, more wailing of tortured souls, and more monstrous creations from my deepest, darkest nightmares, but there was simply nothing. We were walking on a gray cloud that roiled and gyrated beneath our feet, and were it not for Jova's calming presence, I would have surely plummeted straight down to my death. "It takes a little getting used to," he said, as if we were each breaking in a new pair of boots. I relaxed and looked to each side, and glimpsed great black crystal formations. I looked a little closer, and saw trapped in them the faces of countless souls screaming soundlessly. I pulled my eyes from them with great difficulty as I could feel their desolate remorse weighing on my soul, and their dead eyes threatening to pull the very life from my own soul. "The lost ones," Jova stated. "Forgot to tell you not to look at them, sorry again."

I would have smacked him in the head again if I could have guaranteed that it would not have knocked me off my cloud. "No problem," I said, staring forward into the grayness. Up ahead a single lantern shone through the murkiness. A slab of the blackest obsidian lay across the cloud. Streaks of red ran through it, reflecting the light cast by the lantern being held by a small, cloaked figure. As we grew closer, I could see the red streaks were rivulets of blood that dripped down over the edge of the obsidian into the emptiness below. I followed Jova onto the slab, stepping carefully over the blood, as he had done. Streaming down from the black crystal cliffs that housed the lost ones was a river of blood, pulled one painful drop at a time from them and funneled through the silently screaming mouth of a great skull, which turned the river into the small stream that adorned the granite.

"What is this thing?" I hissed to Jova as we walked up to the cloaked figure.

"It is called an elevator," Jova said.

"A Hellevator?"

Jova stifled a grin. "Actually, that *is* more appropriate." He proffered a coin to the cloaked one, who reached out a definitely female hand with long fingers that ended with pointed nails, painted with wet-looking red blood on their tips.

The cloaked figure took the coin and set her lantern down on the slab. She cast off her cloak with a flourish, and before I could draw out the Blade of Truth from my waist, I found a completely naked demoness thrusting her forked tongue into my mouth for the most unpleasant kiss of my life. It felt like she was going to penetrate my skull with a tongue so cold and thick it was like a writhing snake trying to get down my throat and suffocate me. She locked her hands behind my neck and thrust her pelvis into my own, her close-cropped, coarse, black pubic hair rasping against my manhood like a hundred bits of sharp metal. She mercifully broke the kiss, thankfully leaving my tongue in my mouth still attached and working. I did not move for fear of her demonic twat causing me more harm than I feared it already had. Her dark cold eyes stared into my own for a moment, then she leaned her head back, and shook out her snaky black curls before she again coiled her sinewy arms and legs around me and squeezed so hard that I was fairly certain her hard, pointy, black iron-tipped nipples had drawn blood.

"Going down, Mr. Sinister?" she said, cocking her eyebrow suggestively, her voice several creepy octaves deeper than mine.

"Yes, yes, we are," Jova interrupted. "Tenth level, please."

The demoness looked at Jova as if seeing him for the first time. "If you were not here, fear peddler, I would stop on the way with Mr. Sinister for a little fun." She reluctantly unwrapped herself from me and put her cloak back on. I could now feel the sting of my wounded private area, and saw twin trickles of blood running down my chest where the demon's nipples had pierced my skin.

I stepped close to Jova as the demon picked up the lantern. He opened his mouth to speak, but one look from me silenced him. "Don't even think about apologizing again!" I lectured. Jova's mouth closed. I shifted my manhood to a more comfortable position under the watchful gaze of the demoness, who was literally drooling at the prospect of being with me. "Let me guess," I said. "She never tried to have a little love on the Hellevator with you, did she?"

Jova shook his head. "Well," he said. "I *am* married."

The demoness whistled at me. "Sinister," she said, bending over and lifting up her cloak to show me her womanhood, which I swear was opening and closing like a great mouth—a mouth with very sharp teeth. "Once you are with me, you will never be with another."

She was definitely right about that. I would certainly think twice before my next go-around with the fairer gender! "Sorry, sweet princess," I said. "The only bitch I am going to pick up in Hell is my dog. Take me to your lord."

"Suit yourself," she said, dropping her cloak back down over that nightmare-inducing mouth, and raising the lantern. "Going down." She cackled. "Down, down, down."

My stomach lurched as the obsidian slab soundlessly dropped. I widened my stance and drew my sword. "A word of advice, Sirius," Jova said. "You might want to stare at the elevator floor. This place is full of nightmares both imagined and unimagined."

As he spoke, we descended to a shrill concert of screaming agony that I heard coming from millions and millions of tortured souls. I drove my fingers deep into my ears to drown out this unholy harmony, and knelt with my eyes closed. I looked up at Jova when the sound faded, and as we continued our descent into the depths of Hell, I saw him shake his head and look to the Hellevator floor. "Even the Bogeyman does not need to see certain things," he said. "There is a reason only demons reside in the lower levels."

"And my poor dog is there," I added, still concentrating on looking down.

"Right," Jova said. "But she does not see and hear what you and I do in this place. That is part of the power of Hell, and for that matter, the power that allows fear to control a person's mind. Hades merely manipulates the energy put out by the dark side in all of us, mortal and immortal alike, to create what amounts to our own personal, well— hell. Garlic is pure and good, and though she has your blood, she is not tainted with things like avarice, gluttony, envy, pride, and sloth, which are so very common to mortals and immortals."

"It is usually lust that gets me in trouble," I quipped, and instantly regretted it.

"Lust is soooo good," screeched the demoness. "Having second thoughts, Sinister? We have only a little time left . . ." I could hear her flapping her cloak in my direction, and I had the awful vision of her placing her malevolent mound in my face.

"Can't this thing move any faster, Jova?" I said. "Princess over there is beginning to scare me."

"You don't need to fear me," the demoness said. "I am just a sweet little pussy. A pussy you are going to wish you had petted once my lord is done with you. I would have showed you mercy, pretty one, and given you pleasure before I brought the pain. It is a fine line that lies between pleasure and pain. I would have taught you the difference between the two, but he will only show you eternal pain."

The Hellevator slowed to a stop, and I opened my eyes carefully and rose to my feet, taking comfort in the white light the Blade of Truth was casting into the utter darkness. Jova hummed a happy song about bluebirds and did not seem remotely bothered by the overwhelming feeling of gloom permeating this dark place. He was safe in a world of his own creation.

A great marsh lay before us as we stepped off the Hellevator and bid the demoness a not so fond goodbye. She waved coyly and winked as the Hellevator rose out of sight, leaving Jova and me to our own devices. There was but a single path, composed of shiny white skulls, through the marsh. Black trees with moss hanging from their branches filled the great black bog that lay to either side of the skull path. Tendrils of smoke rose from the bog and formed the shape of faces that mocked me with their empty stares as they faded, reformed, and then faded again into nothingness. Far ahead a great black castle appeared with its many spires thrusting up violently into the ebon eternal night.

Every now and again a huge ball of fire exploded out of the bog and crashed into one of the trees, leaving yet another bit of moss hanging down. As we walked toward Hades's domicile, I realized, when one fireball struck a little too close for comfort, that it was not moss hanging from the trees of death and despair but human skin, the last remnant of a tortured soul's existence before Hades scattered its doomed essence to the cosmos.

The path was so narrow that only one person could pass at a time. I held out my hand and motioned for Jova to go ahead of me. He hesitated, and a smile crossed my face as I realized that the legendary Bogeyman was afraid. "Lead the way," I said. "I take it that you have been to big, evil, and gloomy's palace before?"

Two fireballs struck uncomfortably nearby as Hades let me know he was not amused by my comments. What was he going to do? Banish me to Hell? I was here. I took solace in the fact that if he wanted me dead, or merely tortured for an eon or two, that would have already happened. As I had surmised all along, there was something more to his vendetta against me.

"No," Jova said. "I've actually never met him. I was here once, at the entrance to the tenth level, when I got the tour, you know. I have mainly been dealing with demons, like Princess Pain and others, who actually have been nothing but hospitable."

"I think this should be a most popular holiday destination for the world's royalty, what with the friendly customer service," I said, rolling my eyes.

"They actually tend to wind up here anyway," Jova said. "But, I have never been . . . over there." He gestured to the dark palace, and I could see a bevy of wraiths playing what looked to be tag as they whipped around the turrets of Hades's castle. "You are the assassin and master tracker," Jova continued. "I am sure half the people you have killed are here anyway. So it only makes sense for you to lead the way."

"Indeed," I said. "I might meet a few old friends along the way." Sure enough, rising from the bog and forming into smoky images were the unmistakable countenances of the long-dead Trouble brothers, residing in their proper place, having found their just reward for a life of evildoing. "Well, there you go," I said. "Say hello to Big Belly Bart when you see him, boys, unless he is hanging from one of those trees out there, that is!"

One of the Trouble ghosts recoiled, and sure enough, as I continued down the path of skulls, there, hanging from a tree was saggy, white human skin with a long red scar caused by my favorite vampire Maltese where one of the legs should be. "Full circle indeed," I said to no one in particular, hoping that somehow Garlic knew that some of her finest work was displayed for eternity here in the tenth level of Hell.

The skull path was surprisingly solid underneath our feet even though they did not appear to be attached to each other with any kind of substance. Jova was picking his steps very carefully and must have been reading my mind. "Odd," he said. "I don't see anything that keeps our path held together. These skulls appear to be hovering in midair above the marsh."

"Oh, I don't know," I said, striding more confidently with every step. "These souls are bound together by the poor choices and wicked deeds that got them where they are today—under the feet of a vampire assassin and the Bogeyman. This path isn't going anywhere. And I bet it stretches down below us into eternity, what with all the evil I've seen in this world of ours!"

"How very insightful of you to say so, my learned friend," Jova said. "Life has been your university. I do recall from my studies that Saint

Bernard of Clairvaux said Hell is full of good wishes and desires," Jova said. "People mean well, but do harm."

I looked at him in confusion. "I don't see what a talking philosopher dog has to do with it. Bad is bad. Good is good. Your dog friend there knows the difference between being tripped over or kicked. The souls below our feet did not have good wishes and desires, or they wouldn't be here, now would they?"

Jova laughed loudly, his voice echoing eerily through the trees, causing a couple of spooks to poke out from the bog to see what the ruckus was all about. "Sirius," he said. "I cannot wait for you to study under Hedley Edrick after this is over!"

I kept walking, staying silent for a moment. "I will take that as a vote of confidence that there will be an after." The closer we got to Hades's castle, the larger it appeared, its five main towers poking skyward like fingers on a great black hand ready at any moment to ball into a stony fist and smash us into nothingness. The path of skulls simply ended at a massive black-bricked courtyard in front of the castle. I saw no guard towers, no sentries, no hellhounds drooling in anticipation of a vampire-and-Bogeyman snack. But then again, what did the Lord of the Underworld have to fear here on the tenth level of Hell? Absolutely nothing.

Thrusting into the air in the center of the courtyard was a spear-shaped fountain buttressed with a round shield on either side, making it appear, either intentionally or unintentionally, to be a large phallus and its accompanying gonads. And my nose told me the black substance spurting out of the top and raining down into the pool below was blood. There was nothing else in the courtyard but the fountain, making it appear even more prominent. As we entered the courtyard, the sound of the spattering blood grew into a deluge, and we stopped dead in our tracks, trying to figure out how to navigate through the curtains of misty black blood that came off the fountain. Whereas normal blood was the liquid of life, so warm, red, and sweet, this black blood was cold and smelled of bitterness and death.

"Well, that is a bit creepy," Jova chimed, staring up at the fountain in disbelief. "Not sure what the message is there!"

"It is a monument to Hades's weapon," I said. "Wants everyone in the world to know he has the biggest manhood and set of cojones around."

"But who sees this thing?" Jova said as we made our way around it with morbid fascination, dodging the curtains of mist. "Only demons and the like come down this far."

"That is an easy one," I said, noting the large streaks that looked suspiciously like pulsing veins on the side of the spear. "And I didn't even have to go to school to figure it out. He sees it. And that is all that matters to him."

I could see Jova wanted to say something as we ducked and sprinted past the black mist coming from the fountain. He paused, looking back at the fountain. "Well, he is either extremely proud of its size, or . . ."

I looked around for a fist, fireball, or other instrument of death coming my way. "No need to go there, my good Bogeyman. Men with stature issues like to be astride big horses, carry big swords, and sail as captains of big ships, no?"

"Aye," Jova replied as we both looked with relief at the empty courtyard and saw only the spurting fountain. Perhaps Hades did not hear our conversation above the noise of the fountain, or it was more likely that he had such a massive ego, that he did not think our conversation had anything to do with him! Emboldened by safely passing and insulting Hades's monument of himself to himself, Jova and I found ourselves standing in front of a series of large steps, seemingly made for a creature ten feet tall. We resorted to climbing up the huge steps, and oddly, for every step we climbed, we turned back to see that the fountain, that great monument to Hades's manhood, seemed to get closer and closer. We reached the final step and found ourselves standing next to a massive iron gate decorated with the remnants of human remains formed into English letters that I saw spelled F-E-A-R.

"Loves the symbolism, does the Lord of the Underworld," Jova said with a hint of admiration in his voice. The gate swung open like a set of iron jaws, welcoming us to the inner sanctum of its master.

I looked back out of practiced habit and nearly jumped, for the phallic fountain seemed so close that I could touch it, which was the last thing in all eternity I wanted to do. I saw details that no man ever wanted to see on another man, unless that was what he fancied. I saw

Jova start to turn and look at what had caused me to grimace, but I caught his shoulder and kept him facing forward. "You had better not," I said, remembering his relative innocence. "That would give even the Bogeyman nightmares. Trust me."

Hanging from the front door was a rather ripe-smelling corpse, stripped naked and adorned only with the business end of a cutlass protruding through his chest, and covered in streaks of dried blood from head to toe by what looked to be multiple bullet wounds from a blunderbuss. His head leaned against the door, and stringy blond hair fell to his shoulders.

"Definitely not unicorns and rainbows," I quipped, realizing the hilt of the cutlass was up against a bronze plate, and this corpse was meant to be the knocker. "Do you want to do the honors?" I asked Jova.

"That's okay, you go ahead," Jova replied, looking at the corpse with a reluctant eye. "I wonder what you have to do to wind up attached to Hades's front door."

The corpse's dead eyes snapped open, their radiant blueness causing Jova and me to nearly jump out of our skin. "I am so glad you asked," the corpse said. "No one asks. They just smash me into the door, laugh a little bit, maybe flick me in the twig and berries, and go see the lord of the house. But what do you expect from a bunch of demons, right?"

A wraith swooped down from the towers, and smacked the corpse in the face with a disembodied hand that grew solid just at the moment of impact before it faded back into the ether. "Yeah, I know," the apparently not-so-dead corpse said snidely to the wraith as it swooped back to the tower. "Teach me to show some respect. I got it. Good heavens." The corpse brought its hand to its throat to try to loosen the rope firmly affixed there, but to no avail. His eyes bulged from the effort, causing him to give up with an awkward shrug. "I mean, what else can he do to me?"

"Not so sure I would want to see him try," I said. "So what is your story, man? You are a man, right?"

"You never seen a cock and balls before, man?" the nearly dead man spouted. "I mean, I know I am not the biggest buck in the herd . . ."

"I meant you are human not an immortal," I said, stifling a grin. "You got a name, my good doorman?"

The man tipped back his head and laughed hard, and I realized I could see the back of the door through a space in his skull, caused no doubt by another run-in with a pistol—a run-in the Doorman lost. "Yes," he sputtered. "I am . . . my name is . . . damn it to Hell!" Down came the wraith for another smack, which the Doorman took without a reaction. He sighed. "Well, the Doorman works just as well as anything I have ever been called."

"What is your story, Doorman?" Jova asked, his morbid curiosity clearly piqued.

"I have not lived the most honorable life," the Doorman said.

"No!" I said. "Really? I don't believe that." I ignored Jova's look of disappointment. "Sorry, go on, Doorman. I could not help myself."

"No offense taken," said the Doorman. "Really, it was me that could not help myself. Whatever I wanted—I took. Women. Gold. Wine. Clothes. Ships. Castles. Lives. And finally, it all caught up to me."

I loved a good tale of woe. "Go on," I said.

"Ah, it was in sweet Paris that my life ended, and this existence began," the Doorman said. "I was no stranger to the brothels of that fair city. In a visit to one such place, I took it too far, and the death of one of the girls of the house was the unfortunate result. I did not return to Paris for many years, but when I did, wine and fate conspired to bring me to that very same house of ill repute, though that fact was unbeknownst to me." The Doorman paused, either for dramatic effect or because he was missing some vital gray matter.

"And?" I encouraged this scourge of humanity.

"And," the Doorman said, "I realized as I was about to reach my pleasure that the wench servicing me was the sister of the girl I killed, and she too would have to die. But there was something I did not know."

"What was that?" Jova asked.

"There were four sisters that remained alive to avenge their own," the Doorman said. "One plunged this sword into my back. One shot my brains nearly out of my skull with a blunderbuss. And the third, well, she had target practice with the rest of me."

"Indeed," I said. "A murder well avenged. But being a murderer does not get you such special treatment from the Lord of the Underworld. Murderers are here aplenty on the levels above us. So why are you hanging out as Hades's private doorknocker?"

"The one I was inside at the time of my death was a bit of a witch and banished my body straight to Hell," the Doorman said. "But as it turns out, I am not completely mortal. Somewhere up the family chain, I am part vampire, which I have to say finally explains the bad decisions I have made in my life."

"How did you find this out?" I asked, ignoring Jova covering his mouth to stifle a laugh at my expense.

"Well," the Doorman said, "my body arrived in Hell just at the exact same time as Persephone was leaving, and my eyes snapped open, not being truly dead, and well, I saw her and finished my pleasure all at the same time."

"Right in front of Hades," I said.

"Yes, and before I knew what hit me, I was hanging on this door, and staring at the Lord of the Underworld's manhood for apparently all eternity." The Doorman sighed. "Can you imagine what Hades would do to someone that actually touched Persephone?"

I swallowed with some difficulty. "I will try not to. You know they are not together anymore, right?"

"She was leaving him when I arrived," the Doorman said. "Didn't seem to help me any. So what is your business here?"

"Hades has my dog. And I came to get her back."

The Doorman's eyes widened. "You came to the tenth level of Hell for a dog? You are even crazier than I am."

"She is not just a dog. She is family."

"Wait a minute," the Doorman said. "I heard the wraiths talking about you. You are the vampire that *was* with Persephone! Sirius Smitherer!"

"Sinister."

"Whatever," the Doorman said. "He got that white dog of yours as bait! I can't wait to see what he does to you! I might even be set free! Ha ha, Mr. Smitherer, I am going to keep the door warm for you!" The Doorman started jerking his body in a frantic fashion, slamming against the door plate again and again, making booms louder than thunder. Slowly, the door opened outward, and I took a deep breath and entered Hades's castle with Jova trailing a safe distance behind.

I was not sure what to expect when I entered Hades's castle. I was betting on a legion of demon soldiers escorting me to an audience with him and certain eternal torment. Or, perhaps having the ebon fist of the Lord of the Underworld punch me full in the face or the manhood. Perhaps even having a wall of demonic fire roasting me to a fine crisp, leaving nothing but ash to be swept into the fountain and spurted skyward again and again for all time.

I heard Jova gasp in astonishment behind me. What we saw was the ultimate vision of masculine opulence with an edge of cruel insanity mixed in. Our footfalls echoed off the shiniest black marble interlaced with streaks of ruby that glowed like fire beneath our feet as we entered a vast entry hall. To either side were majestic paintings all set in the Underworld, and all featuring the Lord of said Underworld, maiming, killing, torturing, and fornicating with those unfortunate enough to be conscripted to his realm. Great weapons, some still showing the blood of recent kills, were assembled in the middle of the hall, a sculpture paying homage to death and destruction. A veritable army of naked maidens of every race, mortal and immortal, color, creed, size, and delicious shape in the world, dusted the paintings, the weapons, swept the marble floors, and carried goblet after goblet of wine and countless trays of food to the master of the house.

"Well, that does confirm what I have always known," I said to Jova, taking in the sights with a practiced eye.

"What is that?" Jova answered, clearly a bit uncomfortable with all the naked female flesh running around.

"Sure are a lot of bad girls out there."

"So it seems," Jova said, eyeing one buxom young wench, who looked him up and down and licked her lips seductively.

I was not so lucky. "Sirius Sinister," one maiden said, slapping me hard in the face. "I told you the last time I saw you that I would see you in Hell. Well, here we are! What do you have to say for yourself?"

"Uh, sorry," I stammered. That got me another slap in the face, then I watched her pert little bottom sashay away.

And on they came. "Hi, Sirius!" said one coyly. "You want to sow my garden like you did Persephone's? I want to see it grow!"

"I get off in a little while, Sirius," said another. "And then it's your turn."

Two elf twins approached, holding wine flagons. "As soon as we deliver these, we can do it like old times, Sirius," one said.

"Don't forget," said the other. "You said my ass was yours, Sirius, and I am ready to take you up on it." She bent over at the waist, giving Jova and me an eyeful of fine, tight, elf rear end.

"We'll be back," the first one said. "And we'll be ready." They walked away not taking their eyes off my crotch. I sighed and looked sheepishly to Jova.

"Guess I am not really surprised at all of that," Jova said. "And I have to say, I am sort of envious, and sort of not envious. It is hard being you. Damn, bad choice of words. But really, if you were not immortal that enchanted thing of yours would probably have fallen off by now."

I didn't have any retort for Jova. I mean, come on, what were the odds? I sighed. Apparently, the odds were pretty good. For every queen, there had been more than a few hundred, or was it thousand, harlots, strumpets, wenches, and plain old whores. But that had been in my younger days—or at least that was what I was going to tell myself. And to me, younger meant any time before my responsible, conservative present, of course. I saw two iron doors, which marked the entrance to Hades's throne room ahead. My present was possibly about to be cut very, very short.

Standing guard in front of the throne room stood two Amazonian beauties, stark naked but for the wicked phallus-shaped blades they held firmly in muscular hands. They were easily seven and a half feet tall, and their lithe, tan muscles and close-cropped hair gave them almost a masculine appearance, but for the shapely breasts the size of casaba melons that defied the pull of the earth and stuck straight out in challenge. And I had to say, the nipples pierced with little daggers were a great touch—Hades definitely knew what men liked, which was no surprise, because it seemed the Dark Lord was the ultimate alpha male. I wanted to suck on the full soft lips that the guards pursed as I awaited a challenge from these curvaceous creatures, but got only a polite nod as they stood to the side and pulled open the doors, leaving us no time and no choice but to enter the throne room.

"Damn," I muttered under my breath. I would have liked to delay matters by facing those lethal ladies in swordplay, foreplay, cosplay, going all the way, or even macramé. Maybe death at their hands was a preferable option to what Hades had in mind. The Blade of Truth felt warm on my hip, and I adjusted my scabbard. Everything felt warm in

Hell, I mused. And facing Hades's version of the truth was the epitome of being truly under fire.

"Are you ready?" Jova asked, as we entered the throne room.

I looked at him as if he were the biggest imbecile in the Underworld. "Ready?" I retorted. "Are you kidding me? How does one prepare for a showdown with the Lord of the Underworld?"

You don't, came the voice in my head. I had to agree with the Lord of the Underworld there. No amount of training and life experience was going to prepare me for this conflict. All I really could rely on was hope and faith, and the little bit of wisdom and knowledge I had gathered in the last three hundred plus years.

But what I did see was Garlic racing toward me. At least, I thought it was Garlic. Gone was her matted, bloodstained hair, replaced with a neatly cropped white coat that had seen a brush early and often. Toenails that she had nibbled to fine points for better slashing were now rounded and painted a bright shade of pink. But I knew it was Garlic all right as she put her front paws on my knee and barked excitedly. I patted her happily on the head and scratched her lovingly behind the ears. That was when I noticed the pink bows set in her ears.

"Oh, Garlic," I exclaimed. "What has he done to you? I am sorry I could not and did not come for you sooner." She ran a paw over her head to show me she had tried numerous times to get the pink bows out, but to no avail. Indeed, what sick, twisted creature would torture an innocent, little vampire Maltese like this?

"That would be me," a deep voice boomed. Hades.

The throne room was more of a massive cavern than room, with great pillars of black obsidian laced with diamonds, stretching out of sight high above. A thousand wall sconces with mini infernos of blood-red candles cast so much light that it seemed like the great sun was dying and giving its last breath to Hades here in Hell. Grotesque statues and fountains lined a wide walkway of blood-red ruby that seemed to glow brighter and brighter every step we took. The Blade of Truth was getting so hot I had to hold the scabbard away from my leg to avoid being burned. I laughed to myself—it was sheer folly to avoid a little heat in Hell. I took comfort in the vampire Maltese padding so familiarly by my side. She just knew I would get us out of this. I was not so sure. And whether he knew it or not, the closer we got to the front of the throne room, the more distance Jova was putting between us. Probably a good idea on his part, I mused.

On a throne carved from a single dragon's skull, Hades was sitting surrounded by naked nymphs, who in a well-coordinated routine, buffed his fingernails, preened his long, black hair, and offered him wine and food. He was easily more than ten feet tall, with cruel black eyes, and a seemingly permanent sneer on his bearded face. He grabbed a goblet of wine and drank heavily, his arm muscles moving and bulging like a great boa constrictor. Indeed, though Hades was clad from head to toe in black leather that I suspected was tanned from mortal hides, his freakish frame could not be hidden, as every movement and every breath he took showed he was the ultimate death dealer.

Hades shifted on his throne, reaching to spank a nymph, who giggled a little too enthusiastically. He rose slowly to his feet, and the nymphs scattered like mice, hiding behind the pillars to watch Hades deal out his revenge. He reached for his bident, whose two prongs glinted evilly in the candlelight. He pounded the bident into the floor for effect, listening for a moment with obvious pleasure at the sound it made, before pointing it straight at my heart.

"Sirius Sinister," Hades said, his fanged grin mocking me. "At last we meet. Your skills as a warrior and assassin have sent me many a permanent denizen of this fair realm."

I was not sure what to say to this incredibly powerful creature of darkness. I could smell what I thought was something burning in the direction of my feet, but was afraid to look away from Hades. Of course something was burning, I was in Hell, and if it were my boots, it was not like I could do anything about it! "You are welcome," I said, seeing Jova wince out of the corner of my eye. Wrong answer?

The grin faded from Hades's face instantly, replaced by sheer harsh cruelty. "You think a lot of yourself, Sinister," he said. "And judging by your familiarity with my palace staff, so do the females of this world—and that would include my ex-wife, Persephone, wouldn't it?" Twin fireballs flamed into existence at the points of his bident, burning so hot I could feel their heat upon my face.

"It would," I said, not taking my eyes from Hades, but ever conscious of tiny wisps of smoke coming from my boots and scabbard.

"Give me one reason why I shouldn't shove this bident up your ass and pin you outside my door for all eternity," Hades shouted, stepping down from his throne to loom above me. Garlic put her paws over her eyes, whimpered, and lay down on the floor by Jova's feet.

"Because then you would never know," I said, feeling remarkably calm in spite of the fact that my boots and scabbard were seemingly quite on fire.

Hades had cocked the bident as he spoke, in preparation of hurling it at me, but now he set it on the floor. "Know what?" he growled.

"The truth," I said, locking gazes with the Lord of Lies.

Hades laughed out loud, and several of the nymphs giggled along with him, until a cross glare from him silenced them. "I am growing tired of your game, Sinister," he said, raising the bident once again. "In this place I am the truth! What is this truth you speak of?"

I exhaled deeply. "Why a mere vampire like me could satisfy Persephone so completely, and you, a god, could not."

Hades did not laugh. Hades did not let loose the bident upon me. He merely stroked his beard thoughtfully. "Sinister," he said, "there is very little that happens in this world of ours that I do not control or comprehend. But that indeed is something I do not have the answer to. Tell me now, or I will kill you."

"Weren't you going to kill me anyway, or at least torture me for all eternity?"

Hades snorted loudly. "Uh, yes! It is what I do, vampire. Why should you be any different from the masses of the world?"

"Because I am the only creature in the world that has done to Persephone what you could not," I said. "And it is driving you insane, isn't it?"

Hades sighed. "What do you want?"

"Freedom, of course," I said. "For me and for Garlic, and you must give me your word that the mark on my life is satisfied forever."

"But forever is such a long time," Hades said. "Surely you will be in my clutches eventually."

"Maybe," I said. "But lately I have turned over a new leaf. I am a new man. I have a whole bunch of ladies to live for now. And I plan to do so honorably."

"You still have a few more whores in your future," Hades exclaimed. "You cannot help yourself."

I laughed, wondering if my burning feet were causing so much smoke, why didn't I feel any pain? "Plowing the field with a few ladies of loose morals does not make me evil," I said. "My heart is always in the right place. And that is a clue to the truth you seek!"

"Very well, Sinister," Hades said, reaching for a goblet of wine from one very brave nymph. "You and your little dog are free. That is, if, and only if, I am satisfied with your answer. Deal?"

"Deal," I said, knowing full well that making deals with the Lord of the Underworld usually only leads to eternal damnation. But I had an ace in the hole—the truth.

"All right," Hades said, returning to sit on his throne, instantly surrounded by the willing nymphs. "You do realize you are keeping the Lord of the Underworld and purveyor of pain waiting, yes?"

"I always give the woman I am with my complete heart and soul," I said. "As you know, that hasn't always worked out so well for me. But, every single time, I love hard, love all the way."

Hades scoffed. "That is your truth? Please!" He flicked a nymph on the nipple and rolled his eyes. "That cannot be it."

"But it is," I said. "I am always my true self with any woman I am with. They feel it from me. They know they are getting every bit of me. So, when we are making love, it is actually my love I am giving them."

"What a colossal heap of cow manure," Hades replied, a disappointed look on his face. "You give them real love? With your phallus? I ought to cut that thing off you and beat you to death with it! That is rich!" He arose from his throne, bident in hand, with evil, not love in his heart. And then I realized too late that was why he could never understand what I was saying.

"But, it is true, Highness," one of the elf sisters said quietly.

Hades stopped dead in his tracks. "How many of you have been with Sinister?" His eyes went to the twenty hands that were raised. "Is it true?" he commanded. A chorus of muted yeses came from the nymphs who had raised their hands. "Okay, they probably just feel sorry for the handsome man that is going to be nailed to the front door for all eternity," he said. "I have another question that will seal your fate, Sinister. How many of you ladies *want* to be with Sinister?"

One by one, all of the nymphs' hands went up, and for the first time in eons, or perhaps ever, Hades's mouth fell wide open. Jova could only shake his head in bewilderment, and Garlic yelped happily. There was a great clang as the Blade of Truth finished burning through my scabbard and clattered to the floor in front of Hades. "That explains what was burning," I said, stepping forward to retrieve the sword. "I had thought it was me."

Hades had risen off his throne and stood above me, and as I leaned down to pick up my sword, I saw Hades's image reflected back at me, and gasped in astonishment. I did not see a hulking ten-foot monster with rippling muscles, heavy black beard, and a permanent sneer. I saw something else entirely. Something I absolutely could not believe! And Hades knew it.

"What did you see, Sinister?"

"Your true self," I said. "And it explains why you have never found what you are searching for. Am I correct, you can take any form, be anything, or anyone?"

"Yes," Hades said. "I am a *god*! Of course I can. What form did you see?"

"A woman," I said, closing my eyes and waiting for the bident to pierce me, a host of demons to tear me asunder, and a great conflagration to incinerate me. But there was only stunned silence, so I opened my eyes again and continued. "I see a woman of uncommon intelligence, beauty, and one capable of love, but a woman nonetheless. That, Hades, is apparently your true self."

Before my eyes, Hades changed into the vision I had seen, shrinking down to a human-sized woman in a red leather corset, with long dark hair, gorgeous features, and a lean muscular body that was undeniably female in every way. Hades sighed happily, looking down at herself. "I feel different," she said. "I feel—free. Who knew? The devil is a woman."

"I had my suspicions," I blurted out, instantly biting my tongue. "But, you are now your true self, and that is the most important thing you can be."

Hades reached her hand out and stroked a nymph lightly on the cheek. "But, I still adore women," she said. "And that I guess explains why I like to torture hu*man*ity so much, I suppose."

"You are the Lady of the Underworld," I said. "You can adore whomever you want. I adore freedom, and we had a deal. Set me and Garlic free, Hades. The mark on my life is satisfied for I have given you a new one. A deal is a deal."

Hades reluctantly removed her hand and gaze from the nymph, who seemed to be quite all right with the attention and downright excited with her master's new appearance. "A deal is a deal," Hades said. "You are free to leave. I am a little upset that you managed to escape even a little bit of torture."

"I understand completely," I said. "And I thankfully didn't get to meet Death."

"I may be fluid, but Death and its instruments are most assuredly not, and to be honest, I do not need any party poopers in the Underworld while I explore my new self," Hades said. "But in any incarnation of the awesomeness that is me, that creature that comes for you when your time is at an end would not fit in here. Some things are sacred, you know?" Hades looked to the flood of fantastic females that were literally waiting on her hand, foot, breast, and naughty parts. "Yum," Hades said, tweaking a nearby nipple. "Grown-ass women . . ."

I nodded like I knew what in the hell Hades was talking about, but realized the Grim Reaper, with bones not boobs, would be out of place in a ménage à god. But what if, in the shock of shocks, the Grim Reaper was a girl? Would that really be a surprise to any denizen of the world that had testicles? Maybe when Hades changed appearances so did the Grim Reaper. Hades was now definitely all woman. I tried to look objectively at Hades from a man's perspective, but could not channel any feeling but wanting to get out of Hell. I did wonder, however, what Persephone's reaction would be to her ex-husband, er, now ex-wife. It might explain a lot of things to that lovely lady. I nodded in agreement, and promptly looked to collect Jova and, hopefully, get the hell out of Hell.

I turned to Jova. "Are you coming or staying?"

Jova shrugged and addressed Hades. "I was done with my work here, but since there have been some new developments, I wonder, Lady of the Underworld, if I might stay for just a little while longer and try out some new ideas."

"Suit yourself, Bogeyman," Hades replied. "Of any creature, mortal or immortal, I do find you and your work the most entertaining. Anyone can kill, maim, or murder, but it takes a real talent to scare a person to death."

I pulled Jova into a big bear hug. "Until we meet again," I said.

"Stay safe," Jova said. "And try not to keep the ladies of the world so entertained."

I laughed and became very aware of all the nymphly eyes on me. "No promises," I said. "It is after all part of my truth, apparently." I looked over to the Lady of the Underworld, busying herself with undressing a few more nymphs. "There is one more thing," I said. "Garlic was wearing a certain collar when she came here—a certain collar with some useful qualities."

"You mean this collar," Hades replied, patting a different nymph on the rear end as the nymph came forward with the collar on a silver platter.

"Yes, thank you," I replied, taking the collar and bending to place it back around Garlic's neck. Reflected in the sparkling crystals were the flames of the candles behind me, a reminder of the inferno all around me. "It's going to be good to get somewhere a little cooler than here, no offense."

"Oh, none taken," said Hades ever so sweetly. "You are one of but a few to walk out of Hell unscathed, Sirius Sinister—and you managed to accomplish that twice. What do mortals say—it is better to be lucky than good?"

I laughed. "That is said by mortals and immortals that aren't any good."

Hades laughed long and hard, and the nymphs joined in with her. "And on that note, Sirius Sinister, it is time to bid you adieu." Garlic barked loudly, and her collar shimmered with a familiar red glow of the crystals, or was that just reflected fire? But this time, I knew what to expect, and readied myself to swoop Garlic into my arms and jump into the great swirling wormhole forming in front of Hades's throne.

"Home, Garlic," I said. "Take us home to Sa Dragonera." Garlic barked again, and was in my arms, burrowing deep into my chest. She was as ready as I was to get out of Hell.

As I jumped into the wormhole, I heard Hades say out loud, or perhaps it was in my head like old times, *Enjoy the cold . . . I am sure it is to die for . . .*

But wait. Sa Dragonera isn't cold!

ACKNOWLEDGMENTS

I would like to thank my iridescent wife Susie for her unparalleled patience, understanding, and love as I created the Immortal Divorce Court universe. Writing a book is an incredibly personal experience as you are literally sharing yourself with the world. So, I want to thank Susie for allowing me to share some of the most intimate and inspirational parts of our relationship, because when you write about relationships you are not only sharing yourself, but the person you are in a relationship with. Susie is my island in the stream, my soft place to land, and she is always by my side wielding her own assassin's sword, fighting my fight. Yes, our relationship is really that damn good.

I am extremely grateful to my Maltese, Daisy for serving as the model for one of the most legendary characters ever created—Garlic, the Vampire Maltese. Sure, I may grumble as I take her outside to do her business in the snow, rain, or in the dead of night, but there is no other dog I would want barking incessantly at me because I am too slow to get her a treat. Simply put, Daisy is one of my favorite people on the planet.

Finally, I would like to express my gratitude not only to my friends and family, but also to my detractors, enemies, and haters. You all know which of these categories you fall into.

ABOUT THE AUTHOR

For the last twenty-plus years, Kirk Zurosky has practiced plaintiffs' personal injury and workers' compensation law with his firm, Tippens & Zurosky.

He started writing about the adventures of Sirius Sinister as a means of personal therapy to cope with a contentious divorce that felt endless, having no idea at first that it would turn into the seven-book Immortal Divorce Court series. Incorporating his own legal experiences into the books, Kirk puts a playful and racy spin on the worst-case scenarios that can possibly crop up in divorce court.

Kirk lives in Charlotte, North Carolina, with his wife, Susie, and their *wannabe-vampire* Maltese, Daisy.

CPSIA information can be obtained
at www.ICGtesting.com
Printed in the USA
BVHW031746100920
588568BV00001B/23